On the Precipice

Book 1 of the New Caelus Series

Brianna MacMahon

MacMahon Books

CONTENTS

PROLOGUE   1

1. RAELYNN   3

2. SILVER   9

3. RAELYNN   14

4. PUCK   18

5. RAELYNN   23

6. KOSABEUS   28

7. VISCARDIA   33

8. RAELYNN   41

9. BANNER   44

10. TAYMOR   49

11. RAELYNN   54

12. ASTROPHEL   59

13. BANNER   65

14. RAELYNN   71

15. PUCK   78

16. KOSABEUS   83

17. SILVER   89

18. RAELYNN   94

19. WHITNER   102

20. GRELL   109

21. RAELYNN   113

22. VISCARDIA   119

23. AVITUS   128

24. BANNER   138

25. TAYMOR   146

26. ASTROPHEL   150

27. RAELYNN   155

28. KOSABEUS   163

29. SILVER   169

30. GRELL   173

31. EMBRY   180

32. VISCARDIA   185

33. BANNER   187

34. RAELYNN   194

35. TAYMOR   200

36. WHITNER   203

37. AVITUS   208

38. BANNER   214

39. RAELYNN   218

40. VISCARDIA   224

41. WHITNER   231

42.	RAELYNN	233
43.	RAELYNN	237
44.	BANNER	242
45.	VISCARDIA	250
46.	TAYMOR	253
47.	GRELL	256
48.	WHITNER	260
49.	GRELL	265
50.	TAYMOR	271
51.	KOSABEUS	277
52.	RAELYNN	282
53.	BANNER	287
54.	ASTROPHEL	294
55.	KOSABEUS	298
56.	VISCARDIA	302
57.	WHITNER	307
58.	RAELYNN	311
59.	GRELL	315
60.	BANNER	319
61.	KOSABEUS	326
62.	ASTROPHEL	331
63.	RAELYNN	334
64.	BANNER	336
65.	GRELL	338

66.	ASTROPHEL	341
67.	AVITUS	345
68.	RAELYNN	348
APPENDIX 1: THE LORD REGENTS		350
APPENDIX 2: THE PROPHATES		351
APPENDIX 3: OTHER PLAYERS		352
APPENDIX 4: WORLD INFORMATION		354
ABOUT THE AUTHOR		357

PROLOGUE

Bridger's Lake was placid, quiet. Nighttime had at last descended upon the town, and the stars above twinkled in the velvet sky. It was one of those nights that was so dark all appeared soft to the touch. There was peace, interrupted only by the intermittent passage of a plane.

Tucked away in a grove of spruce trees, Bridger's Lake was the ideal place to raise a family, detached from the prying eyes of the universe. A contentious cold war raged beyond the clouds, across many worlds, but Bridger's Lake was removed from that. Everything felt safe here.

Exora was a relatively untroubled region, with an emphasis on farming. In keeping with the simple Exoran way of life, Bridger's Lake remained charmingly undeveloped. The planet Imperium boasted the capability of space travel, but Bridger's Lake eschewed such modernization, instead opting for travel by train or plane. Space, to inhabitants of Bridger's Lake, was a frontier they'd never traverse. Why would they, when they had paradise right where they were?

A couple stood on their deck, watching as their three-year-old child played on the gravel beach. Bridger's Lake was regionally famous for its exquisite turquoise waters, unblemished by pollution. Its depths and shores were home to many varieties of fish, frogs, and birds. At night, crickets chirped in the grasses, infusing the darkness with a calming hum. The air was still and warm—a picturesque solis's night.

"Is she getting too close, you think?" the woman asked, looking up at her husband.

He chuckled in return. "No. She's fine. More than fine. Look."

He motioned toward their daughter, who was transfixed on a firefly. The young girl jumped up and down, trying to catch it in her palm.

"Such a curious girl," the woman mused. "She got that from you, you know."

The man watched as the firefly escaped into the starry sky. He could see their galaxy, Mystic Arms, cascading down the horizon. He turned to his wife, taking her in. Oh, how greatly he'd loved her, for so many years. As a shooting star raced across the sky, above his wife's head, he made a wish—a wish that life would always be like this.

His wife descended the staircase, meeting up with their daughter. "Come on, you," she cooed, taking her by her small hand. "It's time for bed."

The girl grudgingly acquiesced, allowing her mother to lead her back to the house. The man beamed, ruffling his daughter's hair. They had been trying for years to have a child. This girl—their girl—was the light of their lives.

The man picked his daughter up, carrying her inside. Their house was humble but homey. Everything appeared as though it had been given to them by family members who were downsizing. None of the worn and well-loved furniture matched. The radio was on low. Toys littered the oak floor. Expertly, the man avoided them on his way to the bedroom.

Characteristically, his daughter complained as he tucked her into bed. She was a spirited child, full of life. The man could only imagine all the great things she'd do once she was older.

After she was asleep, the man kissed the top of her head. "I love you so much."

And he meant it. Every word of it.

But he didn't know it was the last time he would see her again for a long, long time.

I

RAELYNN

She wasn't going to miss the view from her apartment. That was Raelynn's main thought as she prepared her graduation robe, placing her medals in their proper positions. Despite having gone through the process a dozen times with her tutor, Raelynn still didn't have it memorized. She kept glancing at the sheet in front of her, reminding herself that once she made it through today, she wouldn't have to worry about this ever again.

At twenty-three years old, Raelynn was poised to graduate from the Satias Academy. Though she didn't yet know where she'd end up, she longed to live in New Caelus, the greatest city in Imperium. Satias was a decent city, with a lively enough nightlife, but New Caelus was where Imperium's true power players resided.

In Imperial society, becoming a Keeper was the highest honor. Although under no obligation to do so, parents could freely surrender a child to the Keeper system. There were ten Keeper academies across Imperium, located in each of the Big Ten cities. Keeper children were randomly assigned to a school, where they studied until they were at least thirteen years old. Once they became adolescents, the potential Keepers took their aptitude test to discover in which of the seven divisions they would specialize: War and Defense, Intelligence and Espionage, Diplomacy, Finance and Business, Science and Medicine, Media and Technology, or Logistics and Transportation. Many of the divisions, however, worked in close partnership, and in recent years, it'd become more commonplace for Keepers to work across two or three of the divisions over the course of their career.

Keepers served as Imperium's top politicians, in control of the seven divisions of its government. Some parents decided to sever ties with their child, contenting themselves by knowing their child would—if successful—become one of the most influential members of Imperial society. Understandably, many parents saw the cost of losing one or more of their children far too great a sacrifice to bear. Others—perhaps those less inclined toward parental affection—were keen to induct their child into the Keeper system. Keepers, however, were prohibited from yielding any of their children to the Keeper system. Imperium frowned upon family dynasties. Its founders had assumed that, over time, a handful of families would dominate Keeperdom and, by extension, Imperial government. To prevent such an occurrence, the first Cooperative—Imperium's primary legislature—passed a law forbidding Keepers' offspring from ever becoming Keepers.

Donning the black robe with a red sash worn by all Diplomacy students, Raelynn joined the rest of her peers in Darmello Field. Each of the divisions graduated individually within the academy, ensuring that the ceremony did not run for an unbearably long time. The keynote speaker for Diplomacy students this year was Lord Dynast Nisha Corinth, the second-most politically powerful Keeper in Diplomacy, inferior only to the Lord Regent, Levin Liston. She was an impressive choice but also fitting, seeing as she was an alum of the Satias Academy.

"Good morning, graduates," Nisha began. "I want to start off by congratulating you all on reaching this point. Since you were young, you've been studying within the walls of the Satias Academy. As Diplomacy students, you are gifted with the ability to negotiate, empathize, and understand. I strongly believe—and I'm not just saying this because I was a Diplomacy student myself—I strongly believe that Diplomacy students are the best Imperium has to offer."

Nisha paused, nervously adjusting her tassel. Raelynn could not help but think that public speaking did not come naturally to her.

With a smile, Nisha continued, "I have had the distinct pleasure of serving as our division's Lord Dynast for the past six years. In that time, Diplomacy has been at the front and center of major conflicts across the universe, tasked with dealing with stubborn leaders in the Civitan, the Core, and Terraria. We have never cowered from a challenge. Our Lord Regent is exceptionally bright. He is also a man of principle who refuses to allow War and Defense to force Diplomacy into a permanently submissive stance. Our Lord Regent was the keynote speaker here three years ago, even though he attended the New Caelus Academy. But we shan't hold that against him."

Friendly rivalries existed among the Keeper academies. The New Caelus Academy, which was regarded as the most prestigious, naturally bragged about its high-caliber students. And perhaps that was, to an extent, true. But the other nine academies were also impressive; each had its own specialty and strength.

"In his speech," Nisha went on, "our Lord Regent said, 'In a culture that seems to worship war as the only solution, diplomats are more crucial than ever. You all, as some of the most recent Diplomacy Keepers, will soon bear this burden and find yourselves working in an, at times, openly hostile environment. You alone are the harbingers of a new age—one that might, perhaps, see coexistence as a more cost-effective answer to the universe's most pressing concerns.'

"I am inclined to agree with our Lord Regent's vision. Diplomacy is a growing division—the fastest growing for two years straight. Of course, Satias is renowned for its strong Diplomacy program, but still, your class is larger than those of your fellow Satiates by almost one hundred. What does that mean for you? It means we are becoming a force to be reckoned with. It means we have a real shot at defining Imperium's agenda instead of being victimized by it. It means we are instating more embassies, more sanctuary cities, more human rights organizations. We are poised to usher in Imperium's greatest age. And standing here, looking out at your faces, I know that you will all make a difference. So, here's to you, graduates! And your future!"

The audience applauded. In alphabetical order, the students took to the stage to accept their diplomas. When Raelynn received her diploma, she felt a strange sense of invincibility. Now that she had her diploma in hand, anything was possible. Her life would officially begin.

It was customary that, after receiving their diplomas, graduates—now officially called Audillas—took the months of Astrum and Sidum off. Most used that time to travel and familiarize themselves with the world of Imperium, to have one last celebration before becoming part of the daily grind. Raelynn aimed to follow their lead.

As a planet, Imperium was unique. It consisted of one major landmass. Four oceans framed Imperium: Frija Ocean to the north, Desmona Ocean to the west, Auster Ocean to the south, and Taeras Ocean to the east. Imperium's vast ice shelf, Frija, dominated the planet's southern pole. Imperium was divided into five separate regions: Boreal (the northern region), Marellus (the southern region), Umbium (the central region), Exora (the eastern region), and Vesper (the western region). While most Imperials lived in urban settings, those in the lowly populated regions of Exora and Boreal, for example, favored rural, small-town life. Imperium boasted advanced train systems, which operated up and down the mainland, in and out of every major city and town. If one had a few months to spare, one could travel from New Caelus in the south to Doctro in the north by train. The scenic voyage was particularly popular among retirees.

Before Raelynn knew it, though, Sidum was over. After returning from their months of leisure, Audillas revisited their alma mater to learn which Keeper they would be shadowing for the next four to six months. It was customary for two or three Audillas to work as interns for a given Keeper. From what Raelynn understood, the academy graduates' transcripts became accessible to all

Keepers. There was, of course, a pecking order among Keepers; senior Keepers had first pick and therefore ended up with the allegedly superior students. But Raelynn—unlike most of her peers—wasn't nervous. She was ready to move on from her academy days.

Hundreds of students stood alongside her, their eyes glued to the door. Keepers started to file in. The process was mercifully quick, as the Keepers arrived knowing whom they were looking for. Yet while most of her peers left with their new mentors, Raelynn remained. She didn't think much of it ... at first. There were many possible explanations. As time wore on, however—and the room emptied—Raelynn's optimism faded.

Alarmed, the Satias Academy's overseer, Lord Trevelyan, disappeared to converse with some of the tutors. It was unusual for an Audilla to be left unchosen—highly unusual, even. There were more than enough Keepers to act as advisers to the recent graduates. After half an hour, Trevelyan returned. Raelynn knew something was wrong, just by looking at him. His eyebrows were furrowed.

"Here's the story." Raelynn already didn't like where this was going. "Lord Regent Liston wants to take you on as his Audilla."

Raelynn's heart lodged in her throat. Lord Regent Liston wanted her to be his Audilla? She could hardly believe it.

"But ..." Trevelyan sighed, and all of Raelynn's hopes dissipated. "High Justice Caine has decided to step in, claiming that Lord Regents cannot mentor Audillas."

"What?" Raelynn tried to collect herself. "But what does that ... what does that mean?"

"It means you are now in the hands of the High Court. They're going to decide what happens to you."

"What happens to me?" Raelynn instinctively tugged on her collar.

"They're not going to kill you or anything," Trevelyan assured her, chuckling. Raelynn didn't think the situation merited a chuckle; her whole future was in jeopardy. "They're going to determine whether or not Lord Regent Liston can, in fact, take you on as his Audilla." Trevelyan placed his hand on Raelynn's shoulder. "Don't worry. I don't see High Justice Caine's argument having any legal basis."

"But if it does?"

"It won't." Trevelyan smiled. "Try not to stress about it too much. I'm sure you'll love New Caelus. It's quite the place."

2

SILVER

Silver entered the Sphere at his usual time—quarter to seven in the morning. The tallest building in New Caelus, the Sphere practically touched the sky. It was an idyllic working place, with floor-to-ceiling windows in the atrium, black-and-white tile floors, exotic plants descending from the ceiling, water features, and a spiral staircase that wrapped around the dome-shaped lobby.

Silver carried two cups of coffee in his hands, though he really could have used four at least, just to power him through the morning. Lately, his work life had been packed with meetings, conferences, interviews, and galas. And, on top of everything, he was leaving early tomorrow morning for the week-long Media Summit.

As the Lord Regent of Media and Technology, Silver was responsible for organizing the summit and setting the agenda. Since he had ascended to the office some eleven or twelve years ago, Silver had been carving a name for himself. As a leader, he was involved and dynamic, acting as the chairman of at least a dozen societies and organizations. And he put his numa where his mouth was, donating regularly to his favorite charities.

Despite the frenzied nature of his life, however, Silver loved his job, in a way none of his fellow Lord Regents did. He loved attending charity balls and visiting schools and donating numa to a fabulous cause; he loved the interviews, the ceremonies, the pomp and circumstance.

"Good morning, Raze!" Iyla, one of his best employees, exclaimed.

Silver loved the camaraderie he had with his team. From the beginning, he'd implored them to address him as either Raze or Silver. He despised the demureness of being referred to as "my Lord Regent." It made him feel old. Worse still, it made him feel like Banner. He shuddered at the thought.

Silver grinned. "Good morning, Iyla! How've you been?"

"Very well. Our youngest is just heading off to university."

"No way. Already? I swear, just yesterday, he was, like, ten."

"They grow up so fast. I'm sure you're starting to learn that yourself."

That was the one drawback of Silver's job—the one regret he had. His hectic schedule prevented him from spending a lot of time with his three children. Sure, he got to see them—but not as frequently as he would have liked.

"Speaking of," Iyla went on, "do you have any plans for your birthday? It's a big one."

Silver had almost forgotten. He was turning forty in thirteen days. It was something that, quite frankly, terrified him. He knew it was silly to be scared by a number, but it seemed to signal the end of an era and the beginning of a new one. And Silver wasn't sure if he was ready for that.

"I don't know," he said, shrugging. "Probably just some quiet time with the family."

Silver and his wife, Viscardia, had the most high-profile relationship in Imperial government. Silver was a Lord Regent, and Viscardia was a Prophate. There were seven Prophates at a time, one of whom served as the Head Prophate, and each of the Prophates acted as the religious adviser of one of the Lord Regents. The Numentis Church, for its part, was composed of orphans. As with the Keeper academies, the Church had a presence in each of the Big Ten cities. After losing their guardians, the Lost Children, as they were called, were transported to the nearest Numentis school, which became their home. Deemed Numites, the children were trained in the Numentis theology, devoting their lives to serving their god, Mystis. The Prophates, who all resided in New Caelus alongside the Lord Regents, were the most prestigious members of the Church, having unrestricted access to one of the most powerful politicians in Imperium.

Silver's office was on the top floor. He opened the door with his elbow. Every time he entered, his breath left him. Three of the four walls were dominated by windows, which offered unbelievable vistas from almost every angle. Out the back, there was a private balcony, on which Silver could stand and look out at New Caelus. It was humbling to him, knowing where he'd come from and what he'd conquered to get here. By no means had it been an easy journey. But the result was worth all the blood, sweat, and tears he had shed to claim that seat as his own.

To the left of his desk was a sitting area, with a white couch and a couple of matching armchairs, all arranged around a coffee table. Silver always left his radio on so he could be greeted by the morning news. He left home so early that the day's first paper hadn't even arrived yet.

Silver sat down at his desk, taking a long sip of the first coffee. He was a man of few vices. He smoked a cigar a few times a year and hardly ever said no to a fine-looking chocolate dessert, but he cherished his morning coffee above all. It was something Viscardia teased him about.

As he prepared for the long day ahead, his door opened. He looked up and saw Grell, his temporary Prophate. Silver's former Prophate had abruptly retired, and until the Church could find a suitable replacement, Grell, one of the top Erates in the Church, would be assuming that role. Silver didn't mind having Grell as his Prophate; in fact, he much preferred her company to that of his former Prophate. No matter what time of day it was, the five-foot-one Grell always appeared sprightly. Silver was only mildly jealous.

"Hey, Raze!" she greeted.

"Hey, Grell! How was your Sidum?"

During the month of Sidum, the government and Numentis Church were in recess. Silver had spent his Sidum working on various projects, most of which were related to election season. Though it was Aestus, the start of a new quarter, Silver was already fatigued.

"It was great!" Grell cocked her head to the side. "But you're a bit hairier than usual." She motioned around his jaw. "I thought you hated having a beard."

"I do," Silver said, stroking it, now self-conscious about it. "But I haven't really had time to shave, so ... I haven't."

"What does Viscardia think about it?"

"She ... tolerates it."

"So, she hates it."

"I'd say that's a fair assessment."

"Then I guess I know what to get you for your birthday. A razor."

Silver laughed dryly. "Very funny."

Grell traced her finger along his desk, dreamily looking up at the ceiling. "At least tell me you're taking it slow for your birthday."

Silver pretended to busy himself by skimming through some papers on his desk, his eyes immediately glazing over. "I'll certainly try. But there's a lot going on."

Grell studied him carefully. "You look awful," she said frankly.

Grell was never one to pull punches. It was something Silver genuinely appreciated.

Silver sighed. "I know, you don't like the beard."

"It's not just that. You've got bags under your eyes. You look drained. Do you want me to ask Faley to ease up on your schedule?"

Silver shook his head. "It's always like this on election years. Just going, going, going."

"But you've been working around the clock. And I know you have the Media Summit soon. So, tell you what. I'll ask Faley to take the heat off you. And knock off early next week. It is your birthday, after all. Viscardia said you'll be spending it at your island house."

Silver loved their island house. He and Viscardia had visited Maswik Island, off the coast of New Caelus, right after they got engaged. They stayed at an adorable bed and breakfast along the oceanfront. They both said that once they had enough numa, they'd buy a plot of land along the coast and build their dream home. And sure enough ...

"That'd be great," said Silver with a smile.

"I thought that'd cheer you up."

"It did. Very much." Silver heaved a deep breath. "Anyway, we've got a long day ahead of us. Some sort of hearing is going on at the High Court. Caine's trying to block Lev from taking on an Audilla as his protégé."

"Can he do that? Caine, I mean. Isn't that an overreach of judicial power, trying to dictate what Keepers can and can't do?"

"That's what I'd think, but ... you never know with Caine. He's always had it out for Keepers, doing whatever he can to interfere in our affairs." Silver shrugged. "But, knowing Lev, he'll get what he wants. And Caine will just have to accept that."

3

RAELYNN

When Raelynn left the train station, the vivacity of New Caelus greeted her. The city was a predominantly walking one, but water taxis operated down the main thoroughfare, and a system of trains ran the perimeter and interior. Its architecture was attractively uniform and geometrically inspired, with skyscrapers so tall they nearly disappeared into the wispy clouds. New Caelus was strategically close to Auster Ocean, granting it peerless sunrises and sunsets across the cerulean water. Dozens of islands dotted the far-off shores, serving as retreats for the more affluent members of Imperial society.

From the station, it was only a short walk to the High Court, the top court in Imperium. The walk was scenic, weaving through one of New Caelus's most historic districts. A street band was performing, gathering quite a crowd. A farmer's market was set up, and Raelynn heard snippets of conversations as she passed. Maybe it was the salty air, but everything seemed brighter in New Caelus—and happier. It truly was the jewel of Imperium.

The High Court—now looming in the near distance—was an opulent building, with seven marble columns framing the court's front and a sweeping staircase leading up to the door. Feeling underdressed, Raelynn entered, her footsteps ringing out in the gold-and-black tile foyer. A spectacular glass chandelier hung from the ceiling, surrounded by skylights. The lobby was uncrowded, with only a few employees and visitors milling about. Raelynn stepped up to the receptionist, explaining her situation, and within an hour, she was in the High Court's chamber.

The High Court was a grand room, with hanging plants and stained-glass windows. The light shone through the windows, imbuing the room with a timeless elegance and mysticism. Raelynn sat in her chair, looking up at the seven Justices of the High Court, all seated in their oversized, crimson-cushioned chairs. In the middle of the panel sat High Justice Eliseo Caine, an officious man with graying hair.

Caine squinted at Raelynn. Something akin to bewilderment flashed across his eyes. He held Raelynn's gaze for a moment too long before looking down at his notes, clearing his throat.

"Lord ... Raelynn Mabry." He said it slowly, deliberately. "Twenty-three years old. You're a ... Diplomacy student, recently graduated from the Satias Academy. Is that right?"

Raelynn wasn't entirely sure what the protocol was for Keepers speaking to Justices, given Keepers' heightened social status, but she figured it would be suitable to address them by their proper titles.

"Yes, High Justice."

"Who was your main tutor?"

"Lord Moryn. But I also took courses with Lords Carrick, Pryor, and Knox."

"Lord Knox?" It was Justice Lubianco who spoke. "He's still teaching? Didn't we hear a case about him a couple years ago? He—"

"The claims couldn't be substantiated," Caine said. "Unfortunately." He lackadaisically returned his attention to Raelynn. "You understand why you're here, I assume? Liston, who has often shown his disregard for tradition, has claimed that he can act as your mentor. Now, precedent states that—"

The door to the High Court's chamber burst open. A man—appearing rather disheveled—hurried down the main aisle. By his dress, Raelynn guessed he was of the working class, and the High Court was most assuredly not a place he frequented. The Justices stared at him, various expressions of confusion on their faces.

"I beg your pardon, Justices," the man offered, halting when he reached Raelynn. He took a few moments to catch his breath. "But I am here on orders of my Lord Regent."

Caine furrowed his eyebrows. "Corlander, you have no right to barge in while we are deciding whether or not Liston has the right to—"

"With all due respect, there is not any legal reason why my Lord Regent—"

"You can't know that."

"My Lord Regent has done his research. And while no Lord Regent has ever assumed an Audilla as his protégé before, that doesn't mean he can't."

The Justices murmured amongst themselves. While Caine drummed his fingers on the table, the other Justices were silent, perhaps wondering who would be the first to speak. It was clear to Raelynn that Caine controlled the room—and everyone in it. However, Corlander's disruption had threatened his power.

"As you said, a Lord Regent has never mentored an Audilla before." Lubianco shattered the silence.

"My Lord Regent understands this," Corlander said.

"Does he?" exploded Caine, his eyes practically bulging out of their sockets, the veins in his neck visible. "Then why does he insist on bucking tradition, on overstepping his bounds? The Assembly must learn to stop—"

"My Lord Regent doesn't wish to overstep or—"

"But that's exactly what he's doing!"

"Eliseo," dared Justice Brare, "if Lord Regent Liston wishes to mentor Raelynn, then we don't have the authority to stand in his way. And we certainly don't have any legal basis for doing so. I know you may think that Keepers have too much leeway in our system, but the law states—"

"The Assembly cannot supersede the High Court in all matters."

"I still think we should defer to Lord Regent Liston on this."

"But the issue remains," Caine persisted. "Liston does not have the right to—"

"He's a Lord Regent," Corlander reminded him. "His authority stretches farther than yours."

"Not within my chamber."

"Do you really wish to take that up with the Assembly?"

Raelynn felt as though she were a commodity being fought over, with no say in her own fate. She didn't know why Liston wanted to be her mentor—or how he'd even learned about her. But working for Liston would be nothing short of a dream. He was, after all, the most powerful Keeper in Diplomacy—and, depending on how the upcoming election turned out, he could be the new Head of the Assembly.

Brare fretfully ran his fingers through his thinning hair. "Let Lord Regent Liston take her," he blurted, to no one in particular.

Caine shook his head. "That sets a precedent that any Keeper can simply do as he pleases."

"If Lord Regent Liston believes it is in his best interest to take Lord Mabry under his wing, then who are we to stop him?"

"We are meant to check the power of the Assembly, to prevent them from—"

"I don't see how Lord Regent Liston's decision to become Lord Mabry's patron is an abuse of his power," Brare said.

The other Justices seemed to agree with Brare, some of them nodding, others murmuring in garbled accord. Caine glanced among them, painfully realizing he had lost the battle.

"Fine," he unwillingly conceded. "Liston can take Raelynn. But understand that this is against my better judgment." To Corlander, he added, "And inform your Lord Regent I don't appreciate his interfering with the High Court."

"I will pass along your sentiments," said Corlander.

"I'm sure you will," Caine said bitingly.

Corlander's eyes fell on Raelynn. "Well, then. Shall we?"

4

PUCK

" Scuse me. 'Scuse me," Puck said as he darted in and out of the crowds.

He had to make it to Ivy Cross. It was just a couple of blocks away, in Decorus Park Square. Finally, he saw the restaurant rise before him, as welcome a sight as an oasis in the Haritum Desert. He stepped to the side of the door, fixing up his hair, adjusting his tie, and cleaning off his glasses. Glancing in the mirror, he was satisfied with his appearance.

The cutesy bell above the door pronounced Puck's arrival. A few patrons looked up, out of habit, then back down at their supposedly far-more-interesting sandwiches. Puck saw his Lord Regent, Farzah Taymor, sitting at a booth by the window, jotting down notes on a napkin. She never stopped working, that one—always thinking up something new. A cup of coffee was to her left, with steam circling its rim. Taymor absently stroked the mug's handle, as if gaining inspiration from its heat.

"Hey, Far," Puck said as he sat down across from her.

She looked up. "Oh. Hey, Puck."

Taymor glimpsed back down at her napkin, finishing up her last thoughts. She was one of those people who thought faster than she could write, as evidenced by her horrible penmanship. She was a doctor, which, to Puck, explained it. Every doctor he'd ever known wrote in scribbles that would make toddlers scratch their heads.

"You didn't eat already, did you?" Puck asked.

"I did." She motioned to her plate, which contained only crumbs. "Sorry. I couldn't wait."

"That's fine. Honestly, I didn't mean to keep you. I tried leaving early, but the Church overseers were especially chatty today."

"It's okay, Puck. I know how you are."

"But this time wasn't my fault!"

"I know," she said, touching his arm. "I'm just teasing."

There was something about Taymor that was so genuine. She was almost fifty, but she maintained a youthful spirit. Taymor was not only the Lord Regent of Science and Medicine but also the only woman on the Assembly, which was absolute lunacy. If there were more people like Taymor in government, Imperium would be a truly unstoppable force.

Puck said, "I'm just gonna order something real quick, if you don't mind."

"No, not at all. The chicken baguette is really good."

"Oooo, I'll do the same." Puck stood up, walking over to the counter. "Yeah, hi. I'll do one chicken baguette and a tall coffee, please."

"That'll be ten numa," the cashier said.

Puck fumbled in his pocket for his wallet. Shoot, he'd forgotten it. As if on cue, Taymor emerged from behind, a ten-numa note in her hand.

"Here you go," she said to the cashier, handing her the note.

Puck said, "I swear, that wasn't intentional. It's just been one of those weeks."

"Has it? I haven't seen you since Spero."

"It's been crazy." Puck retrieved his sandwich plate and cup of coffee, returning with Taymor to their booth. "Kosabeus has been trying to instate some changes in the Church. He wants more of a connection between the Church and all the local orphanages."

"And what do you think?"

Puck shrugged, taking a generous bite of his baguette. "It's ambitious, that's for sure. But that's Kosabeus." He swallowed. "Apparently, we'll be getting a new Magista soon."

In the Numentis Church, Magistas were the ones in charge of the main human resources duties. There were ten Magistas in all, and each oversaw one of the churches in the Big Ten cities. However, the New Caelus Magista was by far the most influential. All ten Magistas were responsible for hiring and firing Church personnel within their own city, but the New Caelus Magista was more monumental because they had a say in who got to be a Prophate. Indeed, the New Caelus Magista was the most crucial member of the Prophate Committee, as their vote counted more than the other members' votes. If the circumstances were right, the New Caelus Magista could also depose the current Head Prophate and call a hearing to name a new one. It was a powerful position—arguably the most powerful, besides being a Prophate.

Puck went on, "It's time for a change. Our Magista was getting a bit too crotchety. Hopefully, we get someone younger and more, you know, open to progress. But what about you?"

"This isn't a session, Puck. You don't need to pretend to be interested in my work life."

"For the record, I'm never 'pretending' to be interested in anything that concerns you."

Taymor smiled. "That's very sweet. But honestly, there's nothing new to report. Everything's been going well."

"Then how about your personal life? What's going on there?"

"Embry's coming back soon."

Embry was Taymor's spunky twenty-four-year-old daughter—almost twenty-five now. She was a reporter—and a damn good one too, as she was always off in some exotic locale.

"Where was she this time?" Puck asked.

"Sapphire Falls. It's gorgeous, by the looks of it. Up in Vesper." Taymor took a thoughtful sip of her coffee. "She should be staying put for a while now, though."

"I'm sure you have a lot of catching up to do."

"Well, you know Embry. She isn't one for phone calls. Or letter writing, apparently." She said it agreeably enough, but Puck knew how lonely Taymor was, living in her apartment by herself. "Anyway," she went on, "I just want her to be happy."

"Don't all mothers?"

"The good ones."

"The best ones."

It was strange, Puck thought, for the two of them to be talking about mothers, having grown up without them. Taymor, a Keeper, was given away by her parents, spending her formative years in the city of Doctro, the Snow Capital of Imperium. The Doctro Academy—up in Boreal, the northern region of Imperium—had the strongest Science and Medicine program, and Taymor flourished in its high stress, high stakes environment. Puck, on the other hand, was an orphan. He grew up in Animoria.

"How's the sandwich?" Taymor asked, watching as Puck scooped up some of the toppings with a chip.

"Really good. You were right. You women always know better than us men. We should know that by now."

"You'd think."

"That's what Viscardia's been saying for years." Puck took a sip of his coffee. "Ah, that's the stuff."

Taymor leaned forward conspiratorially. "I heard a rumor."

Puck's ears perked up. She had his attention. Puck was a renowned gossip hound. He lived for scandal, and Taymor knew it. She built up the suspense by folding her napkin on top of her plate, pretending it absorbed all her concentration.

Taymor cleared her throat. "I heard that—" She cut herself off, suddenly taken in with the scene outside the window. "Who's that with Corlander?" she asked, more to herself than to Puck.

Puck turned to look. Corlander, Liston's secretary, was walking past the window. A young woman—maybe in her early twenties—was a few paces behind him. Occasionally, Corlander would turn to make sure she was still there. The young woman was struggling to keep up with Corlander's long gait.

"I've never seen her before. Have you, Puck?"

No, he hadn't. And for someone like Puck—who prided himself on knowing everyone worth knowing—that was an insult.

"Maybe she's a friend?" Puck offered.

"She looks awfully young to be one of Corlander's friends. No offense to Corlander." Taymor subconsciously rested her chin on her hand. "And it looks like they're heading toward Levin's place."

"Maybe she's a new intern or something."

"Levin isn't taking on any new interns this quarter. And besides, he isn't even in town."

"Maybe it's not important."

Despite his statement, though, Puck's convictions were shaky. Looking at the young woman, Puck was convinced that things were about to change in New Caelus. But Puck differed from many Numites in one crucial respect: He worshipped change.

5

RAELYNN

"**I**'m sorry," Raelynn said, altering her stride to match Corlander's. "But where are we going?"

"Blue Circle," Corlander replied flatly. Then, sensing Raelynn's curiosity, he added, "It's a residential district. One of the best in New Caelus, actually."

"Okay," said Raelynn slowly, her interest unabated. "Why?"

"Oh. I should've led with this. It's where our Lord Regent lives."

Raelynn's pulse quickened. "Lord Regent Liston's house?"

Raelynn had never met a Lord Regent before. She'd seen them, of course—from a distance—but she'd never had a conversation with one. As a Diplomacy student, Raelynn was the priviest to Liston's accomplishments. Many of Raelynn's teachers had bragged about having seen one of Liston's presentations at a conference or perhaps assisting him with his research or attending his inauguration. He'd been built up as a legend. The thought of meeting him both exhilarated and terrified Raelynn.

They neared the row of townhouses to which Corlander had alluded. "See?" said Corlander as they crossed the grass. "Rather lovely, isn't it?"

"Very lovely," Raelynn murmured as she surveyed the neighborhood.

Blue Circle was picturesque, with lamps on every corner and rows of two townhouses together. The townhouses, Raelynn noted, were huge, especially considering their enviable city location. She figured it had to cost a fortune to afford one of them.

Corlander reached the row of townhouses on the edge. "This is our Lord Regent's," he revealed, pointing to the one on the left.

The exterior was done up in a gorgeous white slate. The black door, which was flanked by two lanterns, was absurdly ornate, with all sorts of carvings etched into the wood. Drawn curtains prevented Raelynn from seeing the interior. She could feel her heartbeat quickening.

Corlander fumbled in his pocket for his keys. He seemed like the type of man who was constantly flummoxed.

"Where are they?" he muttered, pulling out wads of crumpled paper. "Ah," he said, finally finding them. "There we are." He turned to Raelynn, as if expecting congratulatory fanfare. Not receiving it, Corlander inserted the key into the lock, opening the door. "Welcome to the home of a Lord Regent. Tread lightly now."

Corlander entered first, while Raelynn stood on the porch, as though her feet were rooted in place. The foyer illuminated, beckoning Raelynn in. She got a peek of the townhouse's interior, seeing the steel-colored carpet on the wooden staircase. The wall behind the staircase was adorned with oil paintings and sconces, the latter of which perfectly matched the foyer's neutral color scheme. The paintings alone had to be worth over ten million numa.

Corlander poked his head out the door. "Well? Are you coming?"

"Yes," Raelynn said, finding her voice. "I just—"

"He's a person. Like you and me."

"He is most definitely not like me."

"Why not? You're both Keepers, aren't you? The most beloved of our citizenry?"

There was a trace of bitterness in Corlander's tone. It disarmed Raelynn. Up until then, Corlander had been perfectly civil.

Reluctantly, Raelynn entered. As she crossed the threshold, she was instilled with a sense of reverence. This was Lord Regent Liston's home. The artwork, the plants, the tapestries ... they were all his. This was where he returned to at night, when the working day was done. He hung his coat up in the walk-in closet over there, kicked his shoes off at the door, rested his hat on the rack to the left.

Raelynn noted the crown molding on the ceiling, the gray-jasper hardwood floors, the chandelier hanging over the staircase. To her left was a door, slightly ajar, revealing what appeared to be a study. To her right was an archway that led into the drawing room, with an ebony piano in one corner and a full bar in the other. A fireplace bridged the gap between the two, surrounded by plush, inviting furniture.

As she apprehensively entered the drawing room—which smelled like wood from a long-gone fire in the hearth—Raelynn searched for photographs of family or friends. But the walls contained only more landscape paintings, and the shelves were devoid of personal effects. Curious artifacts rested on the shelves, arranged, perhaps, by location or meaning. A radio—well loved, by its faded dials—had its own pedestal, beside the magnificent phonograph. Various albums—mostly jazz, by Raelynn's reckoning—were on a small shelf.

"Does Lord Regent Liston live alone?" Raelynn asked.

Corlander was at the bar, helping himself to a glass of whiskey. "Mmmm hmmm," he answered distractedly, scanning the bottles to see which one appealed to him. Then Corlander impatiently looked up at the clock. "But where is he? He told me his last meeting would get out at three, and he was supposed to be on the train back to the city."

Raelynn suddenly felt like a trespasser. "Should we be here if he isn't—?"

"He'll be here soon." As if on cue, the phone on the wall rang. Corlander looked at Raelynn apologetically. "Sorry. I should get this." He answered the phone. "Hello? Ah, my Lord Regent. We were just talking about you." Raelynn's ears perked up. "Sorry. Me and Raelynn. Yes. That's who 'we' is." Corlander's eyebrows furrowed. "Of course. ... I understand. ... No, don't apologize. You ... what was that? Yes. Of course. ... Don't worry, I'll let her know. ... Okay, my Lord Regent. ... Bye." Corlander returned the phone to its position. "Our Lord Regent will be out of town for the remainder of the week," he told Raelynn. "I'm afraid you'll have to meet with him this weekend, if that isn't too much of an inconvenience."

Raelynn breathed a sigh of relief. "Like you said, he's busy."

"Yes. He is." Corlander took another sip of his whiskey. "But I'm sure that's not the reason. He just doesn't want to be around when the rest of the Assembly finds out what he's done. Especially Banner."

Raelynn, of course, knew about Cyno Banner. He was the Lord Regent of War and Defense, which, historically, was the most politically influential division in Imperium. He also currently served as the Head of the Assembly and the leader of the Expansionist Party. There were three main political parties in Imperium: the Expansionist Party, the Affiliate Party, and the Grounder Party. Each of these parties was further divided into factions, which made it difficult to determine what each party truly stood for. In short, the Expansionists believed in a strong military and wanted to eliminate their chief rival, the Core, primarily through military measures. The Affiliates, on the other hand, favored de-escalation and claimed the Core could be weakened through political measures alone. Finally, the Grounders championed noninterference and maintained that Imperium and the Core had to learn how to coexist with one another. Though there were three parties, the Expansionist Party and the Affiliate Party were the most electorally successful. Most Imperials had an intrinsic hatred for the Core, and thus, the Grounders' claim that the Core should, in essence, be left alone didn't sit well with the majority of voters. Raelynn admired the Grounders' sense of conviction—and even agreed with some of their domestic policies—but she, like many others, thought the Core was too dangerous to be ignored.

"Well, isn't that to be expected?" asked Raelynn. "Lord Regent Banner believes in war; Lord Regent Liston favors diplomacy. So, obviously, they—"

"There's a difference between professional disagreement and personal vehemence, Raelynn," Corlander lectured. "And let me tell you. Banner does not like our Lord Regent." He placed his glass of whiskey on top of the piano. "Don't tell our Lord Regent. I don't want to walk over to that cabinet to get a coaster."

Corlander was strikingly dissimilar from the people Raelynn had encountered at Satias. Most potential Keepers were perpetually anxious. But Corlander ... he was leaning against Liston's piano, as if it were nothing. And maybe it *was* nothing. Maybe Corlander was so familiar with Liston that it didn't matter what he did. The condensation from the glass dripped down on top of the piano, creating small pools that gradually surrounded the glass's base. Corlander didn't seem to notice—or if he did, he didn't care.

"Just curious," started Raelynn. "Why would Lord Regent Banner care about Lord Regent Liston becoming my patron?"

"He cares about anything our Lord Regent does. Banner is quite obsessed with him. Thinks every breath our Lord Regent breathes is a plot against him. Unfortunate, isn't it?" He laughed. "I count my lucky stars I don't have to deal with him. Kosabeus does, though. His Prophate. I feel sorry for the man. He must have the patience of a python."

6

KOSABEUS

The Numentis Church was at full capacity for the first sermon since the Sidum recess. At the pulpit stood Kosabeus, donning his formal white robe. Whenever he delivered a sermon, he wore the most decorated robe in his possession—which also happened to be his favorite.

"We now find ourselves in Aestus, the ultimate month of solis," Kosabeus began. "Then folium will arrive. Though the days will become shorter, Mystis's light will never diminish. Instead, it will burn ever brighter, carrying us through these final months of the year."

The chamber was quiet, enraptured by Kosabeus's sermon. People from all levels of society occupied the benches—Keepers, Numites, everyday folk. Kosabeus paced the stage, energized by the audience's interest. Delivering sermons was the best part of being the Head Prophate. He spoke the word of Mystis; he was his voice. The whole theology was at his fingertips.

"When our god, Mystis, discovered the truth, he didn't keep it to himself," Kosabeus said. "He shared it with the universe, for he understood the awesomeness of his burden. It was his divine destiny to expose the Coronian government as heretics and found his own society. Mystis stood up in front of the Coronian queen and her court and declared, 'There are not seven gods. There is but one. And I am he.'"

Kosabeus had spent his whole life studying the theology. It had brought him unparalleled comfort in the dark days of his youth. He'd had an older sister—Alia, her name was—but she died shortly after they were taken in by the Vitor Numentis School. Kosabeus was only five at the time, but he still remembered her, as clear as day. It had broken Kosabeus's heart, losing the only family he had left. The Church thus became his family and his one true home.

"We live in the greatest civilization humankind has ever known: Imperium. Look around you." Kosabeus's hands gestured outward. "Look at these stone walls, at these stained-glass windows. Look around and be utterly amazed, for we live in an extraordinary world. When Mystis defied the Coronian government, he started a movement. He lit a fire within the hearts of all those who felt disenchanted by the Coronian way of life. Seven gods and one ruler? No. Mystis stood at a pulpit, the same pulpit at which I now stand, and he said to his followers, 'The Core is backward. One ruler cannot lead us. We require seven. And we cannot divide our loyalties among seven gods. We must serve but one.'"

Kosabeus's eyes drifted upward, at the focal stained-glass window. The scene depicted the climax of Mystis's defiance. Mystis stood in front of a royal court, one foot on the steps leading up to the queen's throne. Mystis appeared as though he were lecturing the court. When the light hit it just right, what could have been a halo hovered over Mystis's head.

"Because of Mystis's boldness, I can stand in front of you, as the Head Prophate, and instill within you the values of our religion. We live to serve Mystis. He is our savior. By—"

"Kosabeus!" came a commanding voice from up the aisle. Most of the audience turned toward the entrance.

Avitus, Liston's Prophate, strode down the aisle, unconcerned with the audience's displeasure at his arrival. Black, well built, and bearded, sixty-eight-year-old Avitus was a legend in Imperium, having served in the Glass

War and been awarded dozens of accolades. The aisle—which would have taken most people twenty or so steps to descend—took the six-foot-ten Avitus seven.

"Avitus," Kosabeus said. "I'm—"

"Now."

With a heaved sigh, Kosabeus acquiesced, stepping down from his beloved pulpit. "My apologies," he told the audience. "Church matters. You understand. I will see you on Beatum for my next sermon."

The audience grumbled as they departed. Kosabeus was flattered by their devoutness. Imperials were notoriously pious people; their lives centered around Mystis. Kosabeus, a deeply pious man himself, cherished the opportunity to appeal to his congregation's souls and eternal welfare.

However, Kosabeus knew better than to keep Avitus waiting. They ducked into one of the side hallways, heading toward the Prophate offices. Once out of earshot of the churchgoers, Kosabeus grabbed Avitus by the arm. Goodness, he'd forgotten just how toned Avitus was. Grabbing him by the arm was like grabbing most people by the waist.

"Avitus," he said. "You can't just barge into my sermon and—"

"What I have to say is far more important than your theatrics."

"I worked hard on this sermon. And by forcing me off the pulpit, you have slighted Mystis."

"I'm sure he can find it in his heart to forgive a shortened sermon."

"Well, *I* am sure he *can't*."

Avitus continued down the hallway, ignoring Kosabeus, as he often did. Kosabeus hurried after him, struggling to keep up. He hated walking beside Avitus. At six-foot-one, Kosabeus was certainly not short, but Avitus simply towered above him, making him feel like a child in the company of his father. Despite his age, Avitus remained impressively fit, having never ceased the workout regime he'd employed when he was a soldier, all those years ago.

"Avitus. Please. We aren't all as giant as you."

"Learn how to set a faster pace."

"Learn how to walk like a normal person."

Mercifully, they reached Avitus's office. The cramp in Kosabeus's left side pained him. Avitus, unaffected, opened the door, leading Kosabeus in. It was, unmistakably, Avitus's office, decorated with a true patriot's tastes in mind. His walls proudly displayed the various medals of honor he'd received throughout his twenty-plus years of military service. In a case sat his prized, decommissioned gun—the one that, supposedly, had claimed over two hundred lives. Kosabeus wasn't sure if he believed it.

"Banner wants to see you," Avitus said.

Kosabeus looked up at the clock. Ten o'clock. He'd managed to make it to ten o'clock without hearing mention of Banner or Liston or their tiresome rivalry. For once, Kosabeus had felt more like a Prophate and less like a custodian, cleaning up after Banner's messes.

"Is this about Liston?" Kosabeus asked, his hands on his hips. "Because I swear—"

"Venin is dead."

Now, that was a shock. Venin was Banner's Lord Dynast. He was a young, healthy man of forty-six—only a couple of years older than Kosabeus. There had already been rumors of his promotion to the Lord Regency after fifty-seven-year-old Banner's death. His death would rattle the whole division.

"Damn." Kosabeus ran his fingers through his sandy hair. "You know, I almost wish it were about Liston. At least that, I can predict, prepare for."

Avitus smiled—or what was his tight-lipped version of one. "I'm sure my Lord Regent will come up before your week's over."

"What makes you say that?" asked Kosabeus, walking up to Avitus, who had to bend over to read the papers on his desk.

"Because he has a protégé. An Audilla from Satias."

"An Audilla? That's ... unconventional."

"You forget who my Lord Regent is. He is much more privileged than the others."

"Is he, now? Well."

Avitus laughed in that deep tone of his. Kosabeus took great pride in the fact that he was the only person who could make Avitus laugh. Though their Lord Regents were constantly at odds with one another, Avitus and Kosabeus were good friends. They met up for dinner at least twice a month, and Kosabeus was the only Prophate who knew where Avitus lived. For the most part, Avitus liked to keep his private life to himself, which he did remarkably well. Though Kosabeus had known Avitus for over two decades, there was still so much he didn't know about him. Avitus could've had a spouse, for all Kosabeus knew. Avitus never mentioned having one, but then again, there were a lot of things Avitus didn't talk about.

"Well, who would you say is the best of the lot? Banner?" asked Avitus, his eyes glinting.

"That's certainly what he thinks."

Avitus laughed again. "Fair enough." He rested a hand on his desk. "How do you think Banner will take it? Venin's death, I mean."

"Rather swimmingly. He's always hated him."

"I'm sure you have your recommendations for who could replace him."

"And I'm sure he won't heed any of them." Kosabeus sighed. "It must be nice, having a Lord Regent who actually listens to you."

Avitus was eerily silent. He absently drummed his fingers on his desk, his thoughts clearly elsewhere.

After a few moments, Avitus said, "Sometimes, I wonder if my Lord Regent would be better off with Viscardia as his Prophate."

Kosabeus cocked his head to the side. "Why, because they're both Affiliates?"

"No. Because Viscardia is the greatest Prophate."

"How charming."

"Do you disagree?"

7

VISCARDIA

Viscardia hated being the Prophate of Logistics and Transportation. Logistics and Transportation was, by far, the most pointless of the seven governmental divisions. It was ranked last in terms of prestige and political influence, and Viscardia understood why. Nearly all the lords she encountered were washed-up never-weres who couldn't do anything for themselves.

"So, we need to upgrade the train networks in New Caelus, bring them up to speed," one of the cabinet members was saying.

Viscardia didn't know which one. They all looked the same—White, male, past middle-aged, forgettable. They all talked the same too, in those dull, monotonous tones she associated with people whose lives were so dreary even their own voices were bored.

Lord Regents didn't exactly get to pick their own cabinet members. It was a process that involved several divisional higher-ups, and it was more of a favor system than anything else. The whole thing was antiquated, but so many aspects of Imperial government hadn't yet caught up to the modern era. A Lord Regent had some say in who their cabinet members were, but they would never be able to forge their dream cabinet. Indeed, most Lord Regents would have loved to stack their cabinet with party loyalists, but this could never happen. By law, all three political parties had to be represented in the cabinet. The Lord Regent's party, whatever that was, got the extra seat, so for Nix Abner, the Lord Regent of Logistics and Transportation, three of his cabinet members were Grounders, two were Expansionists, and two were Affiliates.

The idea was that this would encourage inter-party cooperation. If each Lord Regent's cabinet included officials from all three parties, then the parties would be forced to work together for the good of Imperium. However, this law failed to consider the current state of Imperial politics. Ever since the Glass War ended twenty-five years ago, politics had become extremely polarized in Imperium, and the parties had never been further removed from one another than they were now. Most notably, the Expansionist Party and the Affiliate Party had conflicting views on what kind of role Imperium should play in the universe. The Grounder Party sided with the Expansionist Party on some issues and the Affiliate Party on others, but it'd become exceedingly difficult for all three parties to agree on a single course of action. Their visions for the future were too different, too irreconcilable. Thus, this outdated belief in tripartisanship was ludicrous, and, in Viscardia's view, it prevented the Imperial government from achieving as much progress as its people deserved.

"Speed," laughed another awkwardly. "Good joke."

It wasn't a particularly funny joke—if it could even be considered a joke at all—but it garnered more awkward laughter from his look-alikes sitting around the table. Viscardia was sure that none of them had ever felt true joy before.

The clock above ticked away, ever closer to three o'clock, when she would be free from this agony. She mutely cursed Abner for forcing her to sit through this meeting while he extended his vacation. Abner, Viscardia bitterly noted, had somehow managed to do what only a man could: build a career out of nothing. And she literally meant nothing; he did *nothing*. He cowered when he was granted any sort of responsibility, immediately pushing it onto his cabinet. Cutting out as early as he could, he consistently left Viscardia in the dark, as if her whole life revolved around work. She was already occupied with Church matters, not to mention her family. She was the mother of three young children, and seeing as she was married to Silver, her life was in the public eye, on display for all the universe to see—and judge.

The media adored the Silvers. Viscardia was, of course, flattered by the attention. Who wouldn't be? She and Silver were one of the most glamorous, famous couples in Imperium. They were a staple at every social event, a favorite on every silver carpet, grace and beauty personified. And their children had stolen the press's hearts. She was a Prophate; he was a Lord Regent. Together, they conquered the press and Imperial government. They were a match for the ages. Indeed, in her personal life, Viscardia couldn't have been any happier.

But in her professional life, she felt stifled. She knew she deserved more; she knew she was capable of actually making a difference in the universe. Abner was woefully inept at politics, but he looked down on Viscardia for expressing her political views. He was one of those traditional people who believed that Numites shouldn't be openly political. Thankfully, as the Head Prophate, Kosabeus had bucked against that, setting a precedent that Numites could—and even should—be political. Even so, Viscardia still felt trapped. She wanted to work with Keepers who cared about more than trains. There were so many important issues that this division needed to address, but these Keepers seemed determined to feign ignorance for as long as they could.

"I hope we don't have any more strikes," one of the men said. "That would be a headache for Lord Regent Abner to deal with."

"Maybe if we upped their pay, like we promised, they wouldn't be so angry," Viscardia offered. "And while we're here, we should discuss why we're increasing ticket prices again. Isn't that going to be difficult for the average Imperial to afford?"

The men looked at her, similar expressions of befuddlement in their eyes, as if they had just noticed her presence. It was remarkable, Viscardia thought, how easily some men could overlook women. Had they assumed she would just sit here and listen, without contributing? They must have forgotten whom they were dealing with.

"That's not really your concern, Viscardia," one of the men ventured.

"I'm acting in Nix's place, aren't I? Therefore, if we're being technical—"

"You're a Prophate," he said, as if he were telling her something she didn't know. "And the Church doesn't mean that much in here."

"The Church doesn't even mean that much in the Church," Viscardia laughed. "But I still—"

"Viscardia. Please." One of the other men spoke up. "Can we move on?"

"May I ask what the point of this meeting is if you don't want to actually address any of the issues Imperials care about?"

"Viscardia!" roared one of the men, slamming his hand on the table. He pointed to the door. "We will meet without you. And then, we'll contact Lord Regent Abner and let him know what we've decided."

"And he'll pass it on to me. So, either way, boys, you're dealing with me."

Viscardia was no stranger to sexism's blade. It had cut her many times on her way to the top, leaving its scars. But she learned that, eventually, all scars healed, and the battles had forged her into a stronger person. She was an outspoken woman in a predominantly male hierarchy; more specifically, when she was in this room, she was a Black woman surrounded by White men. Her position scared them, made them realize that Imperium was changing. Their days in the sun would soon be nothing but a memory.

"You may leave," said their leader with a nonchalant wave of his hand.

They thought they were torturing her, the moronic bastards, by kicking her out of their boys' club. All it took was one swipe at their delicate masculinity, and they were crushed. Now she was free to leave, to be there early to pick her children up from school.

She raced out of the Axle and into the blinding light. Ah, sweet freedom. The taste of the city danced on her tongue. She could smell the metal from the train tracks, the baked goods inside the station, the various colognes and perfumes all intermingling, creating an ... unpleasant scent.

Her children attended the same school—New Caelus School, the top day school in the city for children aged four to eighteen. Its location was convenient for her and Silver, as it was between both their workplaces, making it easy to drop their kids off and pick them up.

Viscardia had made wonderful time. In just a few minutes, the school bell would ring, and her children would come running out. She found it difficult to believe that her oldest, Gray, was almost thirteen. Mystis help her, she was about to become the mother of a teenager. But she knew Gray; he wouldn't cause any trouble.

The bell chimed, and thrilled children poured out, meeting up with their parents or guardians. She inched ever closer so her kids would see her as soon as they walked out. And then, as if on cue, she saw them, with Gray in the middle, one arm around each of his siblings. She loved that about her children; they were so protective of each other.

"Gray! Sarielle! Abraxos!" she called out, waving them down, standing on tiptoe so they could see her.

"Mom!" cheered Abraxos, her six-year-old, jumping up and down. "You're here!"

"Of course, I'm here!" She pulled him in for a hug and a kiss, then did the same for Sarielle and Gray.

Eight-year-old Sarielle was almost the spitting image of Viscardia. Abraxos, meanwhile, had his father's innocent curiosity, as well as his adorably crooked nose. And Gray was a mixture of both. He had Silver's dimples but her eyes. Viscardia knew she had to treasure these moments with them while she could.

"I was thinking, since it's such a nice day, we could go get some ice cream," Viscardia offered. "How does that sound?"

"Ice cream?" asked Sarielle, her eyes agleam. "Yay!"

Viscardia took Abraxos's hand in hers, and they made their way to Three Scoops. It was a typical diner, with tiled floors, booths, and movie posters.

Forever a family of chocoholics, all four of the Silvers opted for chocolate. They sat down at a booth right by the window.

"So, how was work?" Sarielle asked, daintily licking her cone. "Those jerks weren't being jerks again, were they, Mom?"

"Don't worry about me, Sare. I can handle myself."

"Why are they so mean, Mom?" asked Abraxos, genuinely concerned about his mother being bullied.

Viscardia shrugged. "It's just the way they are."

"But why?"

Viscardia wrapped her arm around Abraxos, pulling him closer. "Not everyone is nice, Braxy. But we make do."

"They're probably just jealous," piped up Gray. "You work harder than all of them put together."

Viscardia smiled at him. She bit into her cone, the best part. "But how's school?"

"Boring!" said Abraxos. "I wish it was still Sidum vacation! I miss playing all day!" He sighed. "I miss the island house too."

"Well, don't worry. We'll be there in a couple of weeks. Your dad wants to spend his birthday there."

Viscardia watched as her kids happily finished their ice cream. She thought of Silver, a few thousand miles away, sitting in a dreary conference room. He'd told her over the phone last night just how miserable he was.

"So, how are you holding up, Raze?" she'd asked.

"As well as I can, I guess," he'd replied. "I just ... I feel like this whole summit is a waste of time. I can't believe I missed Gray's science fair for this." He heaved a deep breath. "How was he?"

"Amazing as always."

"That's what I figured. Did you take pictures?"

"I did. Lots."

"Was he upset?" Silver asked after a few moments.

"He understood."

"I wouldn't have, if I was him. I … I hate this, Viz. I hate being away from you guys like this. The kids probably hate me now."

"They could never hate you. They love you so much. They know how things are for you."

"But that doesn't make it okay." She could hear him drum his fingers on some sort of surface. "Things have to change." He sighed. "I wish I was home, Viz. I miss you and the kids so much."

"We miss you too."

Viscardia smiled, touching her necklace. It was the one Silver had given her the first time he said he loved her, all those solises ago. The necklace's chain was long and silver—naturally—with three concentric circles at its end. Every time she wore it, she remembered him draping it around her neck, his gorgeous green-gray eyes gazing into hers.

"But you'll be home soon," Viscardia went on, trying to cheer him up. "Just in time for your birthday. It's a big one too. The big four-o."

"Don't remind me," Silver laughed. Gosh, it was good to hear his laugh. "Forty is old. Like, a real grown-up."

"You'll never be a real grown-up," she teased. "You take too much time on your hair. And your outfit."

"Well, in my defense, you and the kids have given me so many great ties over the years it's hard to pick one."

"But you're always handsome, no matter what you wear."

"Even with my gray hair?"

She smiled, twirling her hair. "Especially with your gray hair." Silver's short gray hair—always impeccably tousled—was his signature feature. "Though, you could use a shave. I know you wanted to try out the beard, see if it works, but I really don't think it does."

Silver laughed. "It's so good to hear your voice, Viz. Honestly, I've been going stir-crazy here."

"Just a couple more days."

Silver had been gone for only a few days, but the apartment just wasn't the same without him. For one, Silver was a master chef. It was one of the things Viscardia loved most about him. Viscardia, on the other hand, couldn't cook to save her life, so she and the kids had been eating take-out for every meal, which was fine but certainly not sustainable. She missed fresh vegetables and fruits. Most importantly, though, she and the kids missed Silver's company. He could always lighten the mood, and there was no one better to go to for a pick-me-up.

"Can you help me with my homework when we get back, Mom?" asked Sarielle, snapping Viscardia back to the ice cream shop.

"Of course," Viscardia said. "Whatever you need. And we'll order in tonight. Whatever you kids want."

"Can we stay up late?"

Clever girl. She took after her mother.

Viscardia ruffled her hair. "Sorry, Sare. It's a school night."

"It was a good try," Abraxos chuckled, once again getting ice cream on his nose. Viscardia reached over to wipe it off. "Thanks, Mom."

"Tomorrow night, then, for *Detective Brighton*?" persisted the ever-so-resilient Sarielle. "We'll be super good, I swear!"

Detective Brighton was one of their favorite radio programs. It was family-friendly, starring a detective who solved nonviolent crimes with his trusty sidekick, Punchy Mack. Sarielle was the biggest fan. She had a poster for the radio-show-turned-successful-comic-book-franchise in her bedroom.

"Maybe," said Viscardia. "But for now, let's get home so you can do your homework. Then we can go to the park and play till dinner."

As she ate the last of her cone, Viscardia thought about how happy this moment was. The way her year had been going, she needed happy moments. And even if it was just an ice cream cone, it was enough to take her away, if only for a few minutes.

And that was a start.

8

RAELYNN

New Caelus came alive at night. The neon lights from the advertisements added a vibrancy to the city, giving it a heartbeat. String lights lined the canal that ran through the city center. There were restaurants and stores aplenty, for every conceivable taste. The bars had their doors propped open, with patrons spilling in and out. The radio blared updates from the current sports game—probably Fireball—and rowdy fans cheered or booed in response.

Back in Satias, Raelynn had loved walking the city at this hour. But New Caelus put Satias to shame. The streets were flooded with people, all laughing, having the times of their lives. Their good moods rubbed off on Raelynn, who felt indomitable as she cut through Decorus Park.

She entered the first bar she found, Terrace Cove. As she'd expected, it was overflowing with customers. Miraculously, though, Raelynn managed to claim a seat at the bar. She ordered the specialty cocktail, the New Caelus Crunch, even though she was unaware of what it was. But she figured she'd never learn whether she liked it unless she tried it.

"Are you new in town?" a woman asked her. She was roughly her age.

Raelynn chuckled. "Is it that obvious?"

"You ordered a New Caelus Crunch. That stuff is lethal."

"Oh, is it?" Raelynn made a face. She motioned to the bartender, telling him to cancel the order. To the woman, Raelynn said, "Thanks. You just saved me from a horrible decision."

"You're very welcome." She smiled. "I'm Embry, by the way."

"Nice to meet you. I'm Raelynn."

"So, what brings you to New Caelus? Work? Pleasure?"

"Work. I live here now. I just graduated from the Satias Academy, and I'll be working in the Spire."

"A Keeper. Nice."

It was refreshing, meeting someone who was so normal. Raelynn wasn't exactly sure why, but she felt comfortable with Embry. She thus told her all about her hearing in the High Court. She made sure to emphasize how intimidating Caine had been.

"Let's just say, if I never see him again, it'll be too soon," Raelynn laughed.

"I can imagine. But it sounds like you've landed on your feet okay."

"Even better than okay. I actually ... okay, this is going to sound like I'm completely making this up, but I swear it's true. I'm working for Lord Regent Liston."

Embry rested her chin between her hands. It was like a light bulb had gone off in her head. A smile slowly formed on her face.

"Wait! You're the girl my mom was wondering about."

"Who's your mom?"

"Farzah Taymor. She's—"

"—the Lord Regent of Science and Medicine. Wow." Raelynn's eyes widened. "I didn't know you were her daughter."

"It's not something I generally announce. But I guess ... yeah, she said she saw you and Corlander a couple days ago, and she was asking me if I knew who you were. Well, now I can say I do." Embry finished off her martini. "But you and Lev, huh? That should be fun."

"Lev?"

"Oh." Embry laughed. "Sorry, that's just what he goes by."

"So, you know him well, then."

"Very well." Embry smiled. "Have you met him yet?"

"No, not yet. But, uh ... to be honest, I'm kind of ... scared. I'm new to the city, see, and ... I don't really ... know what I'm doing."

"Well, hey. You're in luck. Because you just so happen to have made a new friend."

"I guess I came into the right bar."

"I guess you did."

9

BANNER

anner's day started the same as any other. He woke up in a stranger's bed, left without saying goodbye, and stopped by his apartment to change before heading to the Hall. His week had been hell thanks to Venin's sudden death. The man had been a pain in Banner's ass for twelve years. It was thus poetic for him to go out the way he came in: as an inconvenience.

Banner's cabinet was meeting next week to consider a new Lord Dynast. But that was the least of his concerns. Liston had a protégé. Bloody Liston—the bane of Banner's existence. He was constantly doing what he could to get under Banner's skin by eschewing common Keeper practices and playing by his own rules. But Banner would be damned if he allowed that curly-haired upstart to undermine his authority.

Banner called Kosabeus before going to the office, telling him he wanted to meet to discuss something urgent. Kosabeus agreed, in that smart-ass way of his, and their meeting was set for nine o'clock. But here it was, nine ten, and Kosabeus was nowhere in the vicinity. Every few minutes, Banner contacted his secretary over the intercom, asking her if Kosabeus had arrived yet. Then, finally, at nine twenty—

"Oh, will you look at that?" said Milner, the sound of her typing with her creepily long nails audible. "He just came in."

"Send him up. And tell him he's late."

"Yes, my Lord Regent."

A few moments later, Kosabeus entered, wearing his white robe. He didn't look at all embarrassed or apologetic, the bastard. He should've been begging for Banner's forgiveness.

Banner crossed his arms. "You're late."

"So I've heard," said Kosabeus, flashing Banner his characteristic grin.

"You told me you'd be here at nine."

Kosabeus shrugged. "I was optimistic."

"You wasted my time."

"I'm sure you're *very* busy."

"Venin's dead."

"Don't pretend you liked the man."

"I still have to deal with his death."

Kosabeus ran his finger along Banner's coffee table, seemingly dismayed by the amount of dust on it. "I'm sure you'll find someone who can ... better suit your needs to fill his position."

"What's that supposed to mean?"

Kosabeus gave him a look. "Please. Like you aren't going to tell your cabinet to push through Harlyn Harries?"

"Harlyn and I are friends."

"Sure. Friends. Right." Kosabeus's voice dripped with judgment.

The virtuous Kosabeus, Banner knew, frowned upon promiscuity. He was one of those monogamists, and it was likely that the only woman he'd ever bedded was his wife, Grell. But Banner didn't take his sex cues from the Church. It wasn't anyone's business what he did or whom he did it with.

Kosabeus removed his robe, throwing it on Banner's couch. "Why aren't your windows open? It's like a sauna in here."

"It's comfortable."

"Hardly." Kosabeus adjusted his collar, feigning suffocation.

"At least you amuse yourself," mumbled Banner.

"That's half the battle." Kosabeus pulled up his sleeves. "But what is it, Cyno? You sounded ... frenetic in your message."

"Liston has a protégé," Banner announced.

"Yes, I know," said Kosabeus absently, straightening the knickknacks on Banner's desk. "Avitus told me the other day."

Banner narrowed his eyes. "And you didn't think to tell me?"

"You were busy picking out flowers for Venin's funeral service."

"I was not—"

"Song arrangements, then," said Kosabeus, sitting on the arm of the couch.

"His wife did all that."

Kosabeus placed his hand over his heart. "Which left you heartbroken, I'm sure."

Banner sighed. "Do you always have to be such an ass?"

Kosabeus laughed, and Banner grimaced. Kosabeus's laugh was so jarringly different from his low, sardonic voice. There were many things Banner disliked about Kosabeus—his sarcasm, his hypercritical comments, his insertion into Banner's cabinet. But that laugh had to be the one thing Banner hated the most.

"But in all seriousness, why are you upset about this?" asked Kosabeus, promptly regaining his equanimity.

"Because it has to be illegal, right?"

"Avitus assured me it's just against precedent. And after studying the Keeper Code myself—"

"You actually read it?"

Kosabeus smirked. "Reading is a good habit, Cyno. I recommend it. It's much safer than sleeping with anyone you can get your hands on."

"You were saying?" asked Banner through gritted teeth, his patience with Kosabeus already near its end.

Kosabeus stood up. "It's unprecedented, sure, but not illegal."

"You've got to be kidding me."

"I'm not a joking man."

"Yeah, right. That's a laugh."

"I'm glad you're amused."

"I'm not!" Banner wheeled around to face Kosabeus. "This is how it starts, you know. It starts with Liston taking on an Audilla as his protégé. But the next thing you know, he's usurping me and taking control of the whole Assembly!"

"I'm sure there's a link there somewhere, but I'm not finding it."

"This is Liston's declaration of war against my leadership."

"How, exactly?"

"Well, clearly, he's going to use this kid to undermine me."

"Again, how?"

"For Mystis's sake, man!" exploded Banner, slamming his desk. "Are you blind?"

"No. But I might be hard of hearing. Because I'm not—"

"Liston's always wanted to be Head of the Assembly. If he makes a move like this, like breaking the rules and taking an Audilla under his wing, he gets attention. And with that attention, he'll turn people against me."

Kosabeus crossed his arms. "That's certainly an ... interesting thing to say."

"You're mocking me. I can see it in your baby-blue eyes."

Kosabeus widened his eyes. "My, my. Have you been gazing into my eyes again? Because although I am flattered," he went on, his own greatest admirer, "I must remind you, I am a happily married man. And my affections—"

"—are reserved for Grell," finished Banner. "Yes, I know. And I don't have affections for you. I just ... I notice your eyes. They're very noticeable."

"Thank you?"

"Don't thank me. Just help me stop Liston!"

"There's nothing we can do," said Kosabeus, scanning Banner's sparsely populated bookshelves. He then walked up to Banner. "Ah. Someone forgot to wear his lifts today, hmmm?"

Banner loved many of his physical qualities, such as his broad shoulders and strong jawline, but his height had always been an annoyance. At five-foot-eight, Banner was shorter than most of his colleagues, including Kosabeus. To compensate, Banner inserted lifts into his shoes. Hardly anyone knew. But Kosabeus, of course, knew everything.

"Shut up," snapped Banner.

"My Lord Regent?" Milner was standing at the door, appearing somehow meeker than usual. "High Justice Caine called. He says he wants to meet with you as soon as possible."

"Tell him I'll meet him for lunch tomorrow at Red Rock," said Banner. "Noon, sharp."

"Very good, my Lord Regent," she said, bowing her head before exiting.

Kosabeus looked at Banner. "What does Caine want?"

"I guess I'll find out."

IO

TAYMOR

Marellus was famous for its tremendous coffees and teas. As Marellus was the southernmost region of Imperium, it boasted the warmest climates. Hundreds of tea and coffee farms dominated the province, serving as one of Marellus's largest exports. Taymor, who'd grown up in Boreal, had been unaware that so many fabulous varieties of tea existed. She soon discovered New Caelus's tea lounges, all of which specialized in locally grown teas. Bright Leaf became one of her favorites, as it was centrally located between her apartment and the Lab.

"You met Levin's protégé?" Taymor asked Embry, who had happily accepted her mother's invitation to grab an afternoon tea.

Because Embry's career kept her living out of her suitcase, it was exceedingly difficult for Taymor and Embry to spend time together. Taymor knew she had to accept that her daughter was growing up and becoming more independent, but she still, greedily, wanted to keep her close, to see her as often as she could.

"Her name's Raelynn," said Embry.

"Raelynn what?"

"Like, her last name?" Embry placed her spoon beside her mug. "I don't know," she said with a shrug. "She just said Raelynn."

"You didn't think to ask?"

"Why would I?"

"Well, you're a reporter, Em. I thought you'd be thorough."

"So, what, I should be stalking her?"

Taymor laughed. "Finding out people's last names doesn't mean you're stalking them."

"But then, I know what you're going to do. You're going to look her up and see what you can find on her."

"Do you really think I'm so ... intrusive?" asked Taymor, her hand on her chest.

"No. But you care enough about Lev to do that." Embry smiled smugly at her, taking a bite of her cookie.

"Speaking of, Levin should be back this evening. Maybe I can learn more from him."

"About Raelynn? Why? What's the big deal?"

"I just ... I wonder why Levin's doing this. It isn't like he's made of free time."

"Well, who is?"

"Certainly not you, traveling all over, hardly seeing your mother."

"I'm only a phone call away."

"But you're hardly ever by your phone. You're always traipsing around some place, not calling your mother to let her know where or when you'll be back."

"You keep saying 'your mother,' like, talking in the third-person there," said Embry, dipping her cookie into her tea. "It's really weird."

"Then *I'm* worried. How about that? *I* miss you."

Embry gave Taymor a look she'd given her hundreds of times. "Don't worry about me," she said, channeling her father. "I can take care of myself."

"I know you can. It's the rest of the universe I'm worried about." Taymor tucked a loose strand of hair behind her ear. "Things can happen, Em. Things that aren't always in our control. I want you to be careful."

"I *am* careful."

"But would it kill you to call home every once in a while?"

"I call you when I can," said Embry with maddening levity.

"This is the first time I've seen you in over a month! I had to find out through your friends when you were coming home. You talk to them more than you do to me, I guess."

Embry's flippant nature quickly evaporated. "I'm sorry. I'll try to do a better job of letting you know where I am and all that."

Taymor smiled. "Thank you. That's all I ask."

"I just ..." Embry trailed off, her eyes scanning the artwork. "I know you don't approve of me going all these places on my own. But I'm twenty-four, Mom. Almost twenty-five."

"And I get that. But ... just ... be careful."

Embry studied her judiciously, in that reporter way of hers, expertly reading between the lines. She took Taymor's hands in hers.

"You can't let what happened to Dad scare you into staying here," Embry said. "It was a freak accident."

"But ... I'd never forgive myself if something happened to you." Taymor could feel tears stinging her eyes. She hurriedly blinked them away. "Your father had the same adventurous spirit."

"But he knew what he was getting into. He was an Intelligence officer. And I'm a reporter. Sometimes, I have to be on the front lines."

"I know. I just ... I get scared. I always get scared when you're gone. It was just another day when your father and his team ..." She couldn't even finish her sentence.

Sometimes, when Taymor looked at Embry, she could see a snapshot of her younger self. It was disconcerting, like being stuck in a time warp. Taymor absently looked at Embry's spoon, so delicate and lavish, with rose petals intricately wrapped around its handle. She wondered vaguely why anyone would work so hard on making a spoon look pretty.

Taymor continued, "I just want you to be happy, Em. I never want to be that overbearing mom who controls your life."

"You aren't. Your concern comes from love. And I love you for that." Embry sat up in her chair. "So, when is Lev getting back?"

"This evening, I thought. See, unlike someone I know, he calls me regularly when he's gone," teased Taymor.

"Wow, okay. I see who the favorite is. I get it."

"Just finish your tea. I want to get to the Corner Bookstore before three."

"All right, all right. Making me chug my tea."

"One minute, on the clock."

Embry, who never backed down from a contest, took a long gulp of her tea, which she instantly regretted. Taymor motioned toward Embry's chin.

"You got some dripping down your chin there," teased Taymor.

Embry made a face at her. "Thanks."

Afterward, they took their time perusing the Corner Bookstore. Both Taymor women were avid readers, though their tastes differed. While Taymor favored nonfiction books about great historical figures, Embry was more interested in travel books. They made their selections, then returned to Taymor's apartment to listen to the evening news and eat dinner. Only then did Embry tell Taymor what her work schedule would look like for the next few weeks.

With a hint of sadness in her eyes, Embry said, "My boss has asked if I ... if I'd be interested in going to Tarness."

"Tarness?" Taymor tried her best to retain her composure. "That's a war zone."

"I know." Embry heaved a deep breath. "But you have to understand how great it'd be for my career, Mom. This would be the most important story I've ever worked on."

Taymor knew there was no point in trying to talk Embry out of this. It was very in character of Embry to only bring it up at the end of the day, so as not to spoil the rest of their time together. Taymor was grateful for her consideration, of course, and she tried her best to appear happy for Embry, but she knew Embry could see right through her.

"I'll be safe, Mom," Embry assured her. "I'll have a great team with me."

Taymor forced a smile and reached for Embry's hand. "I'm so proud of you, you know. Me being worried doesn't mitigate that."

"I know."

Taymor drew a deep breath. "So, when do you leave?"

"In two weeks."

"That's soon."

"So, we'll just have to make the most of the time we have."

Taymor nodded distractedly. "And we will," she said with feigned cheer, wishing for the millionth time that Embry hadn't inherited her father's need for adventure. "We will."

II

RAELYNN

For the past couple of days, Raelynn had been staying in The Florus Downtown, one of the most conveniently located hotels in the city. Corlander promised Raelynn he'd take her to her new home once the workday was done. Liston hadn't returned from his business trip yet, so Raelynn spent her time shadowing Nisha, the Lord Dynast.

"Lord Regent Liston will be back in a few days," Nisha told Raelynn as she led her to her office. "In the meantime, he asked that I look after you, make sure you feel at home here."

It was odd. Not that long ago, Raelynn had been sitting in the audience at Satias, listening to Nisha's commencement address. Now here she was, standing right beside her, accompanying her to her office.

"I have to admit, I was a bit ... surprised by our Lord Regent's decision," Nisha went on. "But that's our Lord Regent for you. He does things his own way."

"I still don't know how he heard about me," Raelynn said. "I wasn't top of my class or anything."

"I'm sure he had his ways." Nisha found her key in her purse. "But here we are." She opened her door. "Come on in."

Nisha's office was smaller than Raelynn had expected, but it was airy and light, with abundant skylights and windows. Her desk was situated in the middle, and off to the side was a lounge area, complete with a couple of armchairs and a coffee table. The windows offered a stunning view of the beach. The waves spellbindingly crashed on the shore in their rhythmic pattern, captivating Raelynn's attention.

"How are you finding New Caelus?" asked Nisha as she hung up her purse.

"I love it. There's so much more going on here than in Satias."

"That's what I thought too, when I graduated."

"Did you move right from Satias to New Caelus?"

"No," Nisha said, glancing in the mirror and fixing up her hair. "I lived in Vitor for a couple years. I was working in the local government."

"Vitor?" Raelynn made a face. "Hard to get decent meat up there."

Vitor, up in Vesper, was infamous for its obsession with healthy living. The city embraced veganism and sobriety, claiming that meat, dairy, and alcohol sullied the senses—and the body. Raelynn, a lover of all meats and whiskeys, knew that she wouldn't be able to last a week in Vitor.

Nisha laughed agreeably. "It's the Vitor Diet. In Vitor, people are very into nature. All that."

"Did you like it up there?"

Nisha shrugged. "I don't think I bought into it," she admitted. "I just ... there was a man I thought ... well ..." She turned to Raelynn. "You don't want to hear about me. You want to hear about life in the Spire." Nisha motioned to the armchairs. "So, let's sit. I have an hour until my next meeting. I can answer any questions you may have."

Raelynn sat down in one of the armchairs. She didn't know how anyone could get any work done in a chair this comfortable.

"I guess I just ... I'm not sure what Lord Regent Liston has planned for me," Raelynn started. "Don't protégés usually start working in the same department as their mentor, to learn the ropes? Where would that put me?"

"Well, our Lord Regent hasn't discussed any of his plans with me. He, as you know, got his start in Public Diplomacy. Maybe you'll want to start there too. In Public Diplomacy, you work with Media and Technology, trying to encourage Terrarians and Civs to help our war effort."

"Is there really a 'war effort' to help out with, though? I mean, we aren't technically at war with the Core."

"Well, you know, we still have to keep our military prepared, just in case," Nisha said, crossing her legs. "But with elections coming up, who knows? The Cooperative may, for the first time in over three decades, no longer be dominated by the Expansionist Party. And that'd give our division a real edge. With our Lord Regent as Head of the Assembly, we'd get a bigger annual budget."

Imperials, as a people, took politics very seriously. Ever since Partura, political advertisements had been out in full force. News programs dedicated most of their airtime to the upcoming elections, profiling the Cooperative hopefuls and hosting debates between opposing candidates. Raelynn, for her part, was a political junkie. She read the news every night before she went to sleep, trying to digest everything she could.

After a day spent sitting in on Nisha's various conferences, Raelynn made her way to Corlander's office, but before she reached it, she ran into Corlander in the hallway.

"Raelynn!" said Corlander. "How fortuitous! I was just about to look for you. How was your day?"

"It was great. Lord Dynast Corinth has been really hospitable."

"Yes, our Lord Regent thinks she does a splendid job." Corlander pointed to the nearest exit. "But let's get out of here. I'm sure you want to see where you'll be living."

Corlander led Raelynn out of the Spire and down one of the cobblestone sidewalks toward the main downtown area. Raelynn hadn't given much thought as to where she'd be living, but based on where Corlander was taking her, it was somewhere very posh, indeed.

"Um. Corlander." Raelynn surveyed the nearby apartment buildings, which were all on the ritzier side, with marble exteriors and brazen animal statues at the front doors. "Where exactly are we going?"

"The Luxe."

Raelynn's eyes widened. "The Luxe?"

"Our Lord Regent spares no expense."

Corlander offered a wave to the doorman, which somehow granted him entry. The lobby had crystal chandeliers, a live jazz band, a full bar, and silver-and-gold marble floors. The furniture all appeared elegant, but Raelynn just knew they weren't the types of couches and chairs one could sink into. They were probably stiff, designed more for aesthetic purposes than comfort.

"You're near the top," said Corlander as he moseyed over to the elevators. "Apartment 815."

"The waiting list to get in here has to be a mile long," Raelynn remarked as she admired the crown molding in the elevator.

"Our Lord Regent has pull. He donated quite a bit of numa to this place to get it off the ground." The elevator doors opened onto the eighth floor. "This way."

Nothing in the world could have prepared Raelynn for the sight on the other side of Apartment 815. It was one of the sleekest apartments she'd ever seen, with cherry-wood floors and quartzite tiles on the wall. Every detail was custom designed, from the wall sconces to the built-in cabinetry to the focal mirror in the foyer.

"No way," Raelynn exhaled, taking it all in, gesturing wildly with her hands as she eagerly explored the rest of the apartment. "There's just no way."

Corlander laughed. "Good. You like it, then."

"Are you kidding? I love it! I mean, look!"

Corlander motioned to the windows, which looked out onto the heart of downtown New Caelus. "You also have your own balcony there. You look right out on Cortese Plaza."

"I could get used to this," said Raelynn, plopping down onto the scarily white couch, which—thankfully—was also comfortable. "Oh, yes," she said, placing her hands behind her head. "I could definitely get used to this."

12

ASTROPHEL

Astrophel sat at his desk, perusing his notes for Ortus. He was the guest lecturer at the New Caelus Numentis School, and it was not a responsibility he took lightly. He loved teaching young Numites about the theology, reminding them that Mystis was always there to lend a helping hand.

At thirty-two, Astrophel was the youngest Prophate. He'd been in office for less than a year. Garin, the previous Prophate of Intelligence and Espionage, had been old—far too old, in Astrophel's opinion—and his death had been expected, given his poor health and fading lucidity. Astrophel had always dreamed of becoming a Prophate, and as soon as the position opened up, he seized the opportunity and put his name forward. It was a long shot, he knew, but he ended up winning over the Prophate Committee with his zeal and piety.

His youth required him to work twice as hard to prove he was worthy of his position. Yet Astrophel was up to the challenge. Someday, he would be the Head Prophate, and he'd be able to steer the Church in whatever direction he deemed fit. He knew that day was in the far future—Kosabeus was, after all, the most popular Head Prophate in recent memory and still very young—but Astrophel dreamed big dreams. He didn't voice these thoughts aloud, of course, but he

59

couldn't help but envision himself wearing that white robe and standing at the pulpit, mesmerizing the churchgoers with his sermons. Astrophel wanted to be a Prophate who was remembered throughout history; he wanted to stand beside a powerful Lord Regent and herald in a new age for Imperium.

That was why he was so happy about being the Prophate of Intelligence and Espionage. In terms of prestige, Intelligence and Espionage was second only to War and Defense. Though these division rankings were rather arbitrary and meant little to anyone who wasn't a Keeper, Astrophel loved the idea of being the Prophate of the second-most politically powerful Lord Regent in Imperium.

Whitner, his Lord Regent, was due to arrive soon for their weekly meeting. Astrophel could hear his deliberate, heavy footsteps from down the hallway. And sure enough, thirty-four seconds later—

"Astrophel. Hi," said Whitner, pushing his graying hair out of his face.

"Good morning, Dane." Astrophel stood up, motioning to the couch. "Care to sit?"

"I'm fifty-seven," Whitner said, as if that was relevant. Seeing Astrophel's perplexed expression, Whitner added, "I long to sit." He gratefully took his seat, releasing an audible sigh of relief. "And my feet thank you too."

Astrophel sat down next to him. "So, tell me, Dane. What's on your mind?"

Whitner stretched his arms. "Well, apparently, Liston has this new protégé. And Cyno's convinced Liston's going to use her to disrupt the status quo."

"And what do you think?"

Whitner shrugged. "I think Cyno and Liston have always had their issues," he said, expertly dodging Astrophel's question.

"Well, sure. On political grounds alone, they'll always come into conflict."

"But I'm an Expansionist too," said Whitner. "And I don't have a problem with Liston. Cyno does, though. He doesn't trust him."

"Do you think there's any merit to Banner's claims?"

It was Astrophel's job, as Whitner's Prophate, to act as his therapist, helping him work through his problems, be they work-related or personal. Astrophel aspired to be as effective as Kosabeus and Viscardia, who often inserted themselves into their Lord Regents' cabinets and aided them in making crucial decisions. Astrophel wanted that sort of power too, but Whitner, it seemed, was more traditional, thinking that Prophates should be actors on the periphery of the government. Whitner kept political matters to himself and offered Astrophel only the bare minimum, telling him about petty disputes with his cabinet members or colleagues. Astrophel was patient, however. He knew that, over time, Whitner would eventually give in and grant him more leeway. They'd known each other for only a year, after all. There was plenty of time for them to deepen their bond.

Whitner's eyes roamed the room, avoiding Astrophel's. He always closed off like this when he was hiding something.

"Liston's been, uh, known to do some under the table things," Whitner said at last.

"Such as?"

"Taking on this Audilla as his protégé, for one."

Astrophel adjusted his position. "So, you agree with Banner that it's suspicious."

Whitner looked at Astrophel, his sparse eyebrows furrowed. "I don't really know what you're trying to say."

"I'm just trying to see where you and Banner differ here."

"We don't. Not really. But Cyno has a one-track mind." Whitner sought solace in the world of Astrophel's fluffy pillows. They were like his wall, his way of blocking out what he didn't want to see or hear. "All he wants to talk about is Liston."

Astrophel sometimes felt that being a Prophate was akin to being an archaeologist. He had to dig deep to find the truth, and to find it, he had to rifle through a lot of dirt.

"So, now you're saying Banner is paranoid," Astrophel said.

"About the scope of Liston's intentions? Yes. I doubt Liston is planning some sort of coup against his leadership. I guess I just"—Whitner examined his chipped nails—"I think Liston should have consulted the Assembly first."

Astrophel leaned against the arm of the couch, to better see Whitner, who had turned away from him. "But his decision to take on a protégé doesn't affect you."

"Not directly, maybe. But it's still the principle of the thing."

Astrophel propped his chin on his hand. "You seem to be going back and forth on what you think about this. On the one hand, you agree with Banner. But on the other, you seem to not care."

"I don't care. But Cyno cares. So, I have to too."

"Why?"

Whitner subconsciously tugged at his ear. "Because Liston can't just walk all over us."

"That sounds like something Banner would say."

Whitner roughly adjusted his cufflinks, which, by Astrophel's reckoning, were old and unattractive. A man of Whitner's stature could easily afford better ones.

"I don't think I like what you're implying," said Whitner.

"And what do you think I'm implying?"

"That I'm just parroting back all of Cyno's points, not forming my own opinion."

"And are you?"

Whitner's mouth was agape. "Of course not!"

"Then why don't you tell me what you think?"

Based on Whitner's squirming, Astrophel assumed he wanted the conversation to be over. His eyes continually darted to the clock and the door, as if willing time to speed up so he could be spared from the remainder of this session.

"I have," Whitner mumbled.

"No, you haven't," countered Astrophel as gently as he could. "You've told me what Banner thinks about Liston, what Banner thinks he's up to, how Banner feels about it. I want to know what *you* think."

Whitner shifted on the couch. "I agree with Cyno."

"Do you, though? Or do you just think that's what he wants you to say?"

Whitner stood up with atypical speed. "Cyno is my friend," he blurted. "I respect his opinion. Is that really such a crime?"

Astrophel stood up to meet Whitner. "There's a difference between respecting his opinion and borrowing it."

Whitner found his confidence, wheeling around to face Astrophel with an accusatory finger at the ready. "You're out of line."

"You're the Lord Regent of Intelligence and Espionage," Astrophel said, genuinely feeling as though he were reminding Whitner of something he'd forgotten. "You have more power than you think. It's time to stop cowering behind Banner."

Whitner shook his head. "You don't know what you're saying."

"This is what they trained me to do, Dane. To recognize symptoms of fear and—"

"You think I'm afraid of Cyno?" Whitner's voice cracked. "I've known him for over fifty years! I know him better than anyone! But you know what? I don't need to prove anything to you, Astrophel. You're just my Prophate."

The words fell like a rock, fast and hard. It always came back to that. Whitner didn't see Astrophel as a fellow power player, as someone who could help him achieve so much more than he had. Perhaps Astrophel's youth prevented Whitner from taking him seriously. At present, Whitner was, in Astrophel's eyes, nothing more than Banner's lackey. If he gave Astrophel a chance, though, Astrophel could help him realize his full potential. Together, they could take control of the Expansionist Party and define the political agenda instead of being merely privy to it. Astrophel didn't understand how Whitner couldn't see that; he didn't understand why Whitner didn't want to have so much more than just a seat at the table.

"I think you underestimate my position here," Astrophel said. "Prophates and Lord Regents ... we should have more open communication with each other.

You shouldn't be shutting me out."

Whitner scoffed. "You new age Prophates and your self-righteous indignation. Garin wasn't like this at all."

"I'm not Garin."

"No. You're not. You're sticking your nose where it doesn't belong, and I'm uncomfortable with it."

Astrophel took a deep breath. This wasn't going the way he'd planned. But he couldn't risk losing Whitner. Not now. He needed to swallow his pride and give in; he needed to let Whitner have this small victory. Maybe then, he'd learn to trust him more.

"You're right," Astrophel said, his hands in the air as a symbol of truce. "I apologize. It isn't my place to push you. Perhaps I overstepped."

Whitner eyed him suspiciously but said nothing. He simply nodded, and Astrophel took that as a sign of forgiveness. Whitner was often this way—difficult to read and nonverbal. But the more time Astrophel spent with him, the more he understood him. He just needed to play by Whitner's rules for a while, bide his time.

"That's a start," Whitner said, and Astrophel couldn't help but smile.

13

BANNER

Red Rock was Banner's go-to lunch venue. It was quick, casual, and always relatively empty, making it the perfect place to discuss business matters. Caine, unlike Kosabeus, was punctual, entering just before noon.

"High Justice Caine," greeted Banner, standing up.

Caine laughed. "Please, Cyno. You can call me Eliseo."

"I never thought the name fit you."

"Regardless, you've earned the right to call me it."

"Well, then. Eliseo." The name tasted strange on Banner's tongue. He signaled toward the table. "Shall we?"

Caine sat down, studying the food on the table. "Excellent, you ordered for me."

"I thought it'd save time."

"That's perfect. Thank you." Caine immediately moved his knife from the right side to the left. "How have you been, Cyno? Anything new?"

Banner knew this song and dance all too well. They'd engage in meaningless small talk for a while, pretend they had all sorts of things to catch up on, and then, rather clumsily, Caine would get to the point. Banner didn't mind;

unexpectedly, perhaps, he and Caine had quite a bit in common. For one, they were both Expansionists. But more significantly, they had both lost a child, albeit under different circumstances. While Banner's son, Bayne, had died during an Intelligence mission, Caine's child—a daughter, if Banner remembered correctly—had been abducted, and her body had never been recovered. It was the worst kind of pain imaginable, outliving one's own child, and this similarity—as tragic as it was—had bonded Caine and Banner in a strange, morbid way. Though Banner wouldn't have necessarily called Caine a friend, he had always liked him, which was why he had agreed to meet Caine for lunch.

Banner indulged Caine's questions and asked a few of his own, both out of politeness and genuine curiosity. They complained about the press, claiming the papers were far too partial in their election coverage. Then, as Banner had been anticipating, Caine's entire demeanor shifted, and he leaned forward in his seat, almost conspiratorially.

"I was wondering," Caine started, meeting Banner's eyes, "if there was anything you could do to help me block Liston's decision to take on Lord, uh, Mabry as his protégé."

That was a surprise. Banner hadn't expected Caine to care about the matter. At this point, it was practically old news, and there was nothing anyone could do to stop it.

"I wish I could," Banner admitted, adding two dollops of sugar to his coffee. "But apparently, it isn't illegal."

Caine frowned. "There has to be something we can do."

"Why, if you don't mind my asking?"

Caine heaved a deep sigh. "I can't explain it. I can't even … prove anything."

"Prove what?"

Caine drummed his fingers on the table, rattling the silverware. "I just think Raelynn would be better suited … elsewhere."

Banner added some milk to his coffee until it was beige. "And what makes you say that?"

"Call it ... intuition."

"Well, there's no law against a Keeper renouncing their Keepership once they finish their apprenticeship. Technically speaking, a Keeper doesn't have to stay in the system at all. They can leave once they turn seventeen. And Raelynn, I think, is—"

"—twenty-three," finished Caine, so quickly it disarmed Banner. "I was the one who saw her paperwork," he added perfunctorily.

Banner proceeded to drown his mashed potatoes in gravy. "So, maybe Raelynn won't like it. Maybe she won't like Liston. Or Liston won't like Raelynn. It's possible, you know."

"Regardless, Liston shouldn't have taken on an Audilla to begin with. The Court made the wrong decision, letting him do what he wanted. It sets a bad precedent."

Banner placed his knife and fork down. "Forgive me, Eliseo, but it seems you have a sort of ... personal stake in this."

"In more ways than one."

"Meaning?"

Caine sighed, sitting up in his chair. "I can't ... explain it. Because, in many ways, I can't ... well ... you see, I'm just going off a feeling, really."

Banner leaned forward. "Are you in some kind of trouble?"

"No. Nothing like that. But ... is there any way I could get my hands on Raelynn's family file?"

"What?" The request completely caught Banner off guard.

"I know they keep records of who each Keeper's family was. Keepers have to have their marriages approved, to make sure they aren't marrying their sister or something."

"Right," said Banner slowly, not making the connection. "But those files are kept under lock and key."

"But there has to be a way to get to them, right?"

"Not that I know of." Banner took a small sip of his coffee, to test its temperature. Still too hot. "It's all kept secret, you know. I'm pretty sure the people who work there are under some sort of contract."

"But you're a Lord Regent, Cyno," Caine said, acting as though the distinction meant something to him. Banner knew—everyone knew—how much Caine despised the Keeper system. "You have sway. If you started asking questions, they'd listen to you."

"I doubt that."

"Why?"

"Because they don't want us to know. They don't want us to know who our families are. It'd change everything. Because then, we'd know who gave us up, and maybe ... maybe we wouldn't be able to accept it, knowing they're off in their happy little world, happy without us."

Caine's eyes widened. "I didn't know you felt that way."

"I don't. But a lot of Keepers do."

"But not you?" Caine said it with a strange sense of sorrow.

"I couldn't care less. I've done well without them. So, why should I dwell on it? And maybe Raelynn ... maybe she doesn't want to know who her family is."

"I'm not saying she does. But ... I have to know."

"Why?"

"Do you really need to know the details?"

Banner was starting to become annoyed with Caine's refusal to tell him anything. "I need to know something if I'm going to go around asking if I can gain access to Raelynn's file. And even then, I doubt they'd understand. They'd tell me to let it go, whatever 'it' is, and move on. And maybe that's not what you want to hear, but it's the truth."

"But you have influence, Cyno," said Caine, slowly looking up at him, his eyes piercing Banner's. "You're the most powerful man in Imperium."

"I wouldn't even know where to begin."

"Correct me if I'm wrong," said Caine in a way that suggested he already knew he was right, "but aren't you Head of the Assembly?"

Banner scratched his temple. "What does that have to do with anything?"

"You can use your position to help us get some answers."

"Why is it 'us'? This seems more like your vendetta, not mine."

Caine leaned forward in his seat. "We can accomplish great things together. You and I, we have so much in common. Like you, I'd love to see Liston get taken down a peg."

Banner had to admit, it was a relief to hear that someone else didn't like Liston. These days, it seemed everyone was enraptured with that boy, caught up in his nonsense.

"Why?" Banner asked. "What'd he do to you?"

Banner could see the conflict in Caine's eyes as he rocked back and forth in his chair. "Liston has been wrongly declared 'Imperium's favorite son.' It's a lie, it's a ruse, and more than that, it's an affront to our whole government."

"I agree," said Banner, his pulse quickening in anticipation of what Caine would say next.

"And it seems to me that Liston is the only thing standing in your way. Without him in the picture, you'd have Imperium in your pocket. People would start calling *you* 'Imperium's favorite son.' It *is* your rightful title, after all, given your stature. They'd start recognizing you for the strong, patriotic leader you are. And isn't that what you want?"

Banner could already imagine it—parades thrown in his honor, songs dedicated to him and his successes, plaques announcing his connection to a given locale. He could see headlines eulogizing his virtues, exposés on his vision for Imperium's future, photographs of him on every magazine cover. Liston would be nowhere at all.

"That's all I've ever wanted," Banner exhaled.

"Then what's stopping you?"

"You already answered that. Liston."

"So, let's take him down, one step at a time. With Raelynn, we'll be taking something Liston thinks is his. And he'll learn what that feels like, to have something stolen from you."

"Does he care about Raelynn that much?"

"He must have something in store for her, if he went to all this trouble to claim her as his protégé."

Banner nodded slowly. "I'll see what I can do. No promises," he added after seeing Caine's hopeful expression.

"So, you're in?"

Banner could hear the brass band playing his anthem. He could hear the choir singing his name. Oh, he could imagine it all, so vividly.

"Yes, I'm in," he said, intoxicated by the illusion.

"Then think of this as the first day of the rest of our lives. Before you know it, Liston will be a thing of the past. And you will be the future."

14

RAELYNN

Raelynn was nervous—more nervous than she'd been in her entire life. She was about to meet Liston.

"Don't worry," Corlander had assured Raelynn over the phone. "Our Lord Regent is a pleasant man. He likes most people."

"That's a ... weird thing to say."

"But it's true. You'll see."

Liston's townhouse loomed in the distance. Raelynn cut between two lanterns, ascending the steps to Liston's front door. She knocked lightly, hearing no movement from within. She glanced at the window. The lights in the drawing room were on, but the curtains prevented her from seeing whether Liston was even home.

"Lord Regent Liston?" she called out. Again, no response.

"He usually doesn't come to the door," Corlander had informed Raelynn on their phone call. "But when he's home, you're almost guaranteed his door will be unlocked. I know, it's reckless, but that's our Lord Regent. No regard for his own safety. So, just walk in. If I know our Lord Regent, he's probably in his library. He loves that room."

Raelynn was uncomfortable with the prospect of entering a Lord Regent's home without his express permission. But after knocking a couple more times and still not receiving an answer, she tried the door handle. It was, as Corlander had suspected, unlocked. Raelynn wondered how a man as eminent as Liston could live so precariously.

To her right, she knew, was the drawing room. She poked her head in, to be sure Liston wasn't there. It was empty. Slowly, Raelynn started down the hallway, following the sounds of jazz music. To her left was a door, slightly ajar, beckoning her in.

Pushing the door farther open revealed the most stunning room Raelynn had ever seen. The library was a two-floor room, with bookshelves dominating three of the four walls on the main floor. The fourth wall was lined with windows, looking out onto Auster Ocean. In the middle of the library, there was an oversized wooden table, surrounded by plush chairs. A spiral staircase was set in the far corner, near the windows, rising to the second floor, where yet more bookshelves were perched. All the shelves—to Raelynn's endless astonishment—were full. In fact, Liston seemed to be, unfathomably, running low on space, as evidenced by the piles of books on top of the table and floor. Gazing around at the wealth of knowledge contained within the library, Raelynn was dumbstruck. She hadn't realized there were so many books.

Intuitively, Raelynn walked over to the windows. Auster Ocean appeared so close it was almost like she could touch it. She stood in front of the windows. The sun was just starting to set over the ocean. The colors were darkening, becoming a deep violet. Amidst the dreamlike scene, Raelynn forgot where she was—and why.

"You found me."

The voice came from somewhere behind her. She turned to find its owner. Looking up, Raelynn saw a figure step out from the shadows of the bookshelves and into the light. The bespectacled man was dressed in an expensive-looking three-piece black suit. His curly black fringe fell into his face, giving him the air of an eccentric academic. In his right hand, he held a book. He stood near the railing, studying Raelynn.

Raelynn had, of course, seen photographs of Liston. But seeing him up close, Raelynn was taken aback by just how young he was. Though he was only thirty-five years old—barely a decade older than she was—he was already regarded as a mythical figure in Keeper circles. Somehow, despite being a Lord Regent, Liston had managed to keep his personal life a secret. As a result, people at Satias were almost obsessed with him, desperate to find out more about the enigmatic Lord Regent of Diplomacy. Raelynn would be lying if she said she, too, wasn't curious about him.

"My apologies for the smoke and mirrors," Liston said. "But I saw an opportunity. And I rather felt I should take it." He spoke with a precision Raelynn had never known, as though every word were a piece of a poem that, if omitted, would drastically alter the work's meaning.

"Uh. Yes, my Lord Regent," Raelynn managed.

Liston descended the spiral staircase, waving his free hand glibly. "You needn't be so formal. You may address me as Liston."

"As you wish."

"'As you wish,'" repeated Liston dryly. "Is this how our relationship is going to be?"

"I'm sorry, my Lord Re—er—Liston," Raelynn hurriedly corrected herself. "I didn't mean to—"

"I was merely teasing you, Raelynn."

"Oh." Raelynn rocked from side to side. "I, uh ... I knew that."

"Yes. I can tell." Liston must have been used to beguiling people. "So. Raelynn Mabry. Twenty-three years old. You graduated from the Satias Academy, two hundred and twenty-eighth in a class of four hundred and sixteen. Your primary tutor was Lord Moryn. And—am I forgetting something?—Ah, yes. Yes, of course. You're probably wondering what you're doing here."

Raelynn's mouth was unintentionally agape. "How do you know so much about me? I didn't think Lord Regents paid attention to Audillas."

"You're right about that. But I'm of the opinion we should. After all, one day, seven of you will occupy our seats. So, is it not in our best interest to know who you are?"

"Uh. I, uh ... guess." Raelynn didn't know what was wrong with her. She prided herself on her sociability.

Liston placed his book on the table, meandering toward the windows. "Have you ever read any of Edon Rey's poetry?" He asked the question offhandedly, but Raelynn could tell by Liston's tone and body language that the answer was of crucial importance.

"Uh." Raelynn—who was usually adept at coming up with an answer her authority figures wanted to hear—floundered. "I, uh ... no. I'm sorry," she pathetically offered, her cheeks hot.

"Don't be," said Liston. "Edon Rey isn't for everyone. He's a rather ... acquired taste." Liston's eyes met Raelynn's. "Do you like any poetry?"

"No, I don't."

A flash of bored disappointment crossed Liston's face. He capably dismissed it, however, with an agreeable laugh.

"Well. It doesn't matter," Liston said in a way that hinted otherwise.

To redeem herself, Raelynn decided to change the subject. "Why did you choose me? You're a Lord Regent. And I ... just graduated."

Liston placed his hands behind his back, interlocking his fingers. "I'm currently involved in some rather ... delicate political matters. You understand? I've been trying to establish an alliance with the Civitan."

"Yes, I know." Raelynn ambled up to Liston. "If we can get the Civitan to support us, we could isolate the Core, force them into a more submissive state."

"Precisely. The Civitan has been trying to break away from the Core for years now," Liston said, watching as the sun finally slid behind the horizon. "Only recently have they achieved their autonomy."

"But unlike us, they didn't secede for religious purposes."

"No. They seceded for freedom." Liston crossed his arms, leaning against the window. "The Civitan, as you are aware, claims to be its own sovereign entity. Terraria recognizes it as an independent planet. But the Core, as you would expect, still views the Civitan as its territory. And I rather think Imperium should take advantage of the upheaval by allying itself with the Civitan. It would help us protect ourselves against the Core, if true war were to break out. With Banner at the helm of War and Defense, we can't assume we'll be safe. He may talk tough, but between you and me, he doesn't know what a real war with the Core would be like."

The casual way Liston discussed Banner—the glint in his eyes when he mocked his vision—alarmed Raelynn. She knew of Banner and Liston's rivalry; everyone did. The tension between them was practically palpable when they debated or spoke at the same events. Yet Raelynn hadn't expected the Lord Regents to talk about each other so ... disdainfully.

"Lord Regent Banner is an Expansionist," Raelynn said, purposefully using Banner's proper title. "He's merely upholding the party platform."

Liston considered this for a moment, his eyes dancing in the fading light. "Is this your way of announcing your allegiance to the Expansionist Party?"

"No. I'm an Affiliate, through and through. But I should still show Lord Regent Banner the respect he deserves, don't you think?"

"Believe me, Banner's ego is inflated enough. He doesn't need more air."

"He's still Head of the Assembly."

"A fact he reminds us all of daily. But perhaps those days are near an end."

Raelynn, of course, was engrossed by all the election coverage. She hoped, like many, that the Affiliates would take control of the Cooperative. If that happened, then Banner would be dethroned, and Liston, as the leader of the Affiliate Party, would become the new Head of the Assembly. It would be a seismic shift in Imperial government. There hadn't been an Affiliate Head of the Assembly in most Imperials' lifetimes. Still, the polls were rather close—too close for Raelynn's comfort—and anything could happen in the final lead-up to Election Day. Most pundits still seemed to favor the Expansionists holding onto the Cooperative, but each day, more people were starting to recognize the Affiliates' growing momentum.

"We can hope," Raelynn agreed.

"We can do more than that. We can win." Liston smiled. "And that would certainly send a message to Banner that Imperium wants more from its government. The Affiliates have the chance of a lifetime here, and I am going to seize it."

Raelynn was buoyed by Liston's confidence. "So, uh ... the Civitan. You think you can negotiate an alliance with them?"

"Yes. And I rather think you can help me."

"That's why you chose me? To help you with the Civitan?"

"Not entirely."

Raelynn's ears perked up. "Then why?"

Liston was eerily silent, tracing his finger along the window pane. He turned to Raelynn, his expression indiscernible as the evening's shadows crossed his face.

"What did Corlander tell you about me?" he asked.

"Not much. He just ..." Raelynn trailed off, not wanting to overstep.

"He what?"

"Well ..." There was no sense in lying. "He mentioned you live here alone."

Seeing Liston's blank expression, Raelynn was worried she'd touched a nerve. Perhaps Liston's loneliness wasn't wholly his choice. Maybe it wasn't something he'd wanted.

"And you think that must mean I'm some sort of recluse," said Liston matter-of-factly.

"No! I mean—"

"I assure you, I'm perfectly content here." Liston looked up at the bookshelves. "There are benefits to being in one's own company."

The words sounded rehearsed; the smile that came with them was equally forced. They were his defense, Raelynn figured, against people's prying questions.

"Right." Raelynn felt as though she had to say something to alleviate the tension.

"But we have the Keeper Gala in a few nights," Liston said more lightheartedly. "You and all the other recent graduates will be honored for your ... dedication and perseverance."

"Should I be nervous?"

"You'll be fine. It's one of the more enjoyable events of the New Caelus social season. Not nearly as contentious as the division galas."

"Well, then. I look forward to it."

Liston smiled. "As do I."

15

PUCK

As Puck settled upon his desired tie, he thought about this Raelynn kid. Taymor had told him who she was, and she, as it happened, had learned through Embry. Puck was, admittedly, disappointed. It was unusual for him to hear about something from other people. But this whole Raelynn business had completely slipped under his radar.

When he arrived at the Keeper Gala, Abbas Hall was still filling up. Viscardia was already there, talking with Grell. Kosabeus had to be nearby; he was never too far from Grell. And there he was, standing with Avitus off to the side. Comically, the pair looked like Life and Death, with Kosabeus dressed in white and Avitus dressed in black. Puck knew, of course, why Kosabeus was in white; he had to wear his white robe at public events, as he was the Head Prophate. But for some reason, Avitus always insisted on wearing his black Prophate robe, even when he didn't have to. Puck, for his part, couldn't wait to take off his Prophate robe when he got home. But Avitus, it seemed, never wanted to take his off.

Astrophel and Whitner were together. Puck still didn't know quite what to make of Astrophel. He was undoubtedly a capable Prophate, but there was something ... off about him. He couldn't put his finger on it, but he felt like Astrophel was hiding something.

"Like what?" Taymor had asked Puck when he broached the subject with her a few months ago.

"I dunno. But something. It's like he's putting on an act or something."

"Maybe he's just intimidated. You can remember what that was like, being a new Prophate, trying to find your footing."

That was true. Puck hadn't been the Prophate Committee's first choice to become Taymor's Prophate. Within the Church, he was generally not taken very seriously, due, perhaps, to his flamboyant sense of fashion and colorful personality. He didn't take offense to this, and he refused to change who he was to fit the mold of what a perfect Prophate was allegedly supposed to be. If the Church didn't see his merits or understand what a good Prophate he would be, then that was their problem. They didn't owe him an explanation, and he didn't need to be a Prophate to feel fulfilled.

However, when their first choice fell through due to ethical concerns, Puck was, more or less, the last man standing. The Prophate Committee had grumbled about it and dragged their feet, hoping that a more suitable candidate would make themselves known, but no one had stepped up. Thus, three years ago, Puck had become a Prophate. And, despite the Prophate Committee's reservations about his work ethic, Puck had proved them wrong by being an active, involved member of the Church.

Puck stood at the bottom of the staircase, continuing his surveillance. Bryson, the Lord Regent of Finance and Business, was staking out the snack table. Puck wondered how much longer he'd stay in his job. He was over seventy now, and he'd long since lost his love for his work. This was one of the main issues with Imperial government; people stayed in their jobs for far too long. Puck wanted the Cooperative to set term limits across the board. Garin, the former Prophate of Intelligence and Espionage, had died in his office. In what world was that acceptable? Once people were seventy, they had no business working.

Puck certainly didn't plan to be working when he was that old. No, when he was seventy, he'd be off on an island somewhere, soaking in the rays and drinking martinis.

Avitus, however, was the only exception. He was nearing seventy, but he was still as sharp as a thorn. Puck could listen to him go on about his time in the military all day. Avitus was, inarguably, one of the most fascinating figures in the Church.

Puck walked over to Kosabeus and Avitus. "Top of the evening!" he announced, tipping his hat.

"Puck," said Avitus with a small nod of his head. "Good to see you. You're looking quite ... chipper."

Gosh, Puck loved Avitus. He had an inimitable way of always seeming so apathetic. It was admirable, really. In a city where everyone always wanted something from somebody else, Avitus was uninterested in feigning pleasantries or putting on a front.

"Should be a full house tonight," said Puck. "Have you, uh, met Raelynn, by any chance?"

Avitus's eyes narrowed. "I haven't even seen my Lord Regent since he returned to the city."

That was odd. Usually, Liston and Avitus were quite communicative with each other, meeting more frequently than was, by law, required. Puck wondered if they'd had another falling-out ... and if it was anywhere near as catastrophic as the one—

"Puck," said Kosabeus bitingly, tapping his foot. "Do you mind? Avitus and I were in the middle of a conversation."

Puck stood on his tiptoes, to be on Kosabeus's eye level. "Well, so are we. See, 'cause Avitus and I are talking."

"About nothing. We, on the other hand, were discussing business."

Puck put his hands on his hips. "You're boring tonight."

Kosabeus laughed. Thankfully, unlike most of the Church higher-ups, Kosabeus had a wickedly good sense of humor. It was refreshing, having someone in a position of power who wasn't as dull as a party without music.

Kosabeus asked, "Well, why don't you go talk to someone else? Like ... Grell. She'd be more than happy to chat with you about all sorts of things."

"She's with Viscardia."

"Ah." Kosabeus smiled knowingly. "Can't say I blame you for not wanting to break that up. We all know how ... dominant Viscardia can be in conversation," he said, glancing at Avitus for a reaction.

"At least she can hold your wife's attention," said Avitus without missing a beat.

"Low blow," said Kosabeus affably.

"Everything's a low blow for Avitus, since he's at least a foot taller than everyone else," Puck piped up.

Avitus looked over Puck's head, at something in the distance. "There he is, Kosabeus," he said, motioning to the door.

Puck turned and saw Banner, wearing his white dress coat with the blue crest—the color of War and Defense. He looked like he'd just run a mile to get here. Puck didn't understand how Banner had established himself as a sex symbol. He wasn't unattractive, per se—and actually, for his age, he was in impressively good shape—but his personality left a lot to be desired. He was brusque and crass, and his arrogance was more than off-putting.

"Finally," muttered Kosabeus. "Well," he went on, a smile on his lips, "I'll see you two."

"See you, Kosabeus," said Puck, watching Kosabeus intercept Banner at the staircase. Puck turned to Avitus. "What's his problem?"

"He and Banner are at odds over the new Lord Dynast," replied Avitus. "Kosabeus thinks Banner just wants someone he can sleep with."

"So, it's true, then? He's looking at moving up Harlyn Harries?"

"Apparently." Avitus leaned against the wall, practically disappearing into it.

Puck followed suit, copying Avitus's stance. "Kosabeus can't be too happy about that."

"He isn't," said Avitus, choosing to ignore Puck's imitation of him. "He thinks Banner needs to use his head for once, think things through."

"But then, he wouldn't really be Banner, now, would he?"

16

KOSABEUS

"There are at least a dozen lords you could pick from, Cyno," Kosabeus said as they made their way to a quieter side of the hall. "Many of whom are more qualified than Harlyn."

"She's qualified."

"And what, may I ask, are you basing that off? Her prowess in the bedroom?"

"Or anywhere else we've had sex."

"This is serious, Cyno."

"You're never serious," scoffed Banner. He turned his attention to the table, which, to his dismay, had only nonalcoholic drinks. He frowned. "You're just jealous that I'm making this decision on my own, without you," he added, waving over a waitress who was carrying a tray of what appeared to be whiskeys, Banner's preferred poison.

Kosabeus helped himself to a glass of water. "I have a list of lords who would all make a wonderful Lord Dynast. I can—"

"I don't want to see it. I want Harlyn."

"You can have her anytime you want. But not in the boardroom."

"Kosabeus." Banner was trying to sound stern. It didn't suit him. "I don't care what you think. I'm doing this my way."

"Since when is there a 'my way' and 'your way'?" Kosabeus asked, cradling his glass in his left hand. "I thought we were a team."

"And we are. But I don't need you okaying everything I do." Banner nodded gratefully at the waitress who handed him his whiskey. He took a delighted gulp. "At the end of the day, you're just my Prophate, Kosabeus," he said, wiping his lips. "Not on my cabinet or anything. I don't bend to your will. You bend to mine."

"My, my." Kosabeus placed his glass on the refreshment table. "What's prompted this sudden ego trip?"

Banner shrugged, stirring his whiskey with his pinky. "Maybe nothing. Maybe everything."

"The meeting with Caine went well, then?"

Banner's clumsy attempt to be nuanced vanished. "What makes you think—?"

"You've been gruntled ever since your lunch date. So, what did he want?"

"He wants my help accessing Raelynn's family file."

Kosabeus's eyes widened. "And why does Caine want that?"

"He wouldn't say. Just that he needs it to prove something."

"Prove what?"

"He wouldn't say."

Kosabeus clenched his teeth. "Well, what *did* he say?"

"That by getting Raelynn away from Liston, we can get to Liston. Or something like that."

"Something like what? You aren't making any sense, Cyno. Why does Caine want to know who Raelynn's family was?"

"Search me," said Banner. "But I thought I'd tell you about it, see if you can take care of it."

"Me?" laughed Kosabeus. "How?"

Banner took a long sip of his whiskey. "I'm sure you'll figure it out." He helped himself to some cheese and crackers from the refreshment table, getting cracker dust stuck in his graying beard. "I don't get it. Raelynn's just a kid." Kosabeus mimed to Banner to wipe his mouth, but Banner chose not to take heed, scooping up even more cheese and crackers. "But Caine thinks a lot of Raelynn, for some reason."

"And you don't know why?" asked Kosabeus, trying not to look directly at Banner.

"Not a clue."

Kosabeus rubbed the nape of his neck. "Well, I will see what I can do. But try to get it out of Caine. He knows more than he's letting on."

Banner, Kosabeus knew, wasn't listening. Predictably, he was eyeballing various partygoers, offering them a wink or a smirk if he deemed them attractive enough. It was disgusting, Kosabeus thought, for Banner to still be so interested in these games. He was nearing sixty, for Mystis's sake. And yet there he was, still hitting up bars late at night, claiming he could bed anyone he wanted.

His superiority complex was exacerbated by his position as Head of the Assembly. It was for the best Banner hadn't attended the Batillus Academy, the premier school for War and Defense students; he would've emerged even haughtier than he was now. As it was, Banner went to the Ligva Academy, which stood out due to its emphasis on interdisciplinary learning. It was ironic, since Banner did nothing to demonstrate his interdisciplinary chops, instead heralding War and Defense as the greatest division. Kosabeus could only imagine the compliments his teachers and tutors had showered him with. Banner was the type of man who never heard no—not from his elders, his peers, or his conquests. Kosabeus was the only one in Banner's inner circle who dared to temper his inflated sense of self-worth with a much-needed dose of reality.

Banner sniffed. "Is that all? Can I go?" It was like he was a child who required his father's permission to play with the other kids.

"Yes," said Kosabeus flatly. "I didn't mean to keep you."

"Well, you did," snapped Banner. "All the singles have probably already chosen their fling for the night. But if not"—Banner signaled over to Harlyn—"I have a backup."

"You never cease to amaze me, Cyno."

Banner winked. "Glad to not disappoint you, then."

He swaggered off into the crowd of his adoring—or so he fantasized—fans. Kosabeus couldn't help but notice how many people glared at Banner as he passed or purposefully walked away. In recent years, his reputation as a philanderer had hurt his credibility. Sure, there were Imperials just like Banner who enjoyed indiscriminate sex. But Banner was the Head of the Assembly, the most powerful politician in Imperium. He should have been interested in curating a better image for himself, not haunting the Vice District.

Kosabeus looked across the hall, and his eyes fell on Grell, his darling wife. She was chatting with Viscardia. A vision in purple, Grell was, as always, the most enchanting woman in the room. Kosabeus found it difficult to fathom how he'd managed to court her. And yet she was the one who had promised to love him until her dying day.

Grell noticed him, out of the corner of her eye, and she offered a wave, beckoning him over. He shook his head; he knew better than to interrupt her and Viscardia. In response, Grell politely excused herself and started walking over to him.

As a Numite based in the Vitor Numentis School, Kosabeus didn't have the privilege of knowing Grell through classes. They were already in New Caelus by the time they met, fifteen years ago. Through various chance encounters, however, Grell eventually captured his attention—and later, his heart.

They'd flirted a bit here and there, as young people did, but they both went their separate ways. Kosabeus dated but never too seriously, and Grell ended up in a relationship with Bayne, Banner's illegitimate son. Bayne and Grell were on and off for years, never able to stay together for more than a few months at a time.

Ten years ago, Grell and Bayne had been off-again when, tragically, Bayne died on an Intelligence mission—the same mission that had killed Taymor's husband, Benton Kerrels. Compounding the tragedy, Bayne also died on his birthday; he'd just turned twenty-seven. Understandably, even though they'd been broken up for the better part of half a year, Grell was gutted by Bayne's death. He was her first love; it wasn't the sort of relationship she could just forget about and move on from.

In the aftermath, Kosabeus was there to comfort Grell, and the two ended up sleeping together. Kosabeus had always been ashamed of himself for taking things too far. He knew Grell was vulnerable, and it hadn't been his intention to sleep with her, but he'd allowed his feelings to cloud his judgment. A month or so later, Grell informed Kosabeus she was pregnant, and Kosabeus proposed, to assure her of his devotion. They had to marry swiftly, before the Church discovered they'd conceived a child out of wedlock. Though the Church was, in many ways, progressive, its stance on marriage and pregnancy remained woefully archaic.

Grell and Kosabeus's abrupt wedding surprised many—and angered a good few, including Banner. Kosabeus could still remember how Banner had screamed at him when he found out, demanding to know whether Kosabeus and Grell had been having an affair behind Bayne's back.

"I never touched Grell when she was with Bayne," Kosabeus had told him.

And that was the truth. But Banner, of course, couldn't believe it. And, to be honest, Kosabeus didn't blame him. He would've been just as angry, had he been in Banner's shoes.

"Things looked pretty heated between you and Cyno," Grell said as she neared him.

"He just doesn't want to hear reason."

"Ah. So, he's going to ask his cabinet to nominate Harlyn Harries, then? It's a done deal?"

Kosabeus discussed everything with Grell. She was his sounding board, the person he could go to for advice on anything. In many ways, he considered her to be his intellectual superior. She was remarkably perceptive, and her gut instincts were hardly ever wrong.

"It seems like it." Kosabeus smiled, reaching for her hand. "But I didn't mean to pull you away from Viscardia."

"No, it's fine. She wanted to say hi to a few other people, anyway." Even though she was wearing heels, Grell was still far shorter than he was. She looked up at him. "But I don't want Cyno spoiling the night for you. We should be having fun."

"And we will." Kosabeus kissed her. "Come on, my darling. Let's mingle."

17

SILVER

The Keeper Gala had to be Silver's favorite event of the year. Abbas Hall was one of New Caelus's largest indoor party spaces, able to house a few thousand guests. Since his graduation from the Pacalis Academy, Silver had attended the gala every year. It was a terrific way to learn who was a rising star in each division.

As was his routine, Silver made the rounds, talking to the top lords in his division, such as Elric Yale, a man who most likely resented Silver. He'd been one of the finalists for the Lord Regency a dozen years ago. But in the end, Silver had edged him out, and Yale—eight years Silver's senior—never truly got over the perceived slight. He thought he was more qualified than Silver, which he, to be fair, was. But he was too traditional in his methods, and the committee favored Silver's ingenuity and raw charisma over Yale's experience. As a peace offering, Silver had granted Yale one of the top adviser positions, to try to assuage the tension, but it wasn't enough for Yale, whose eyes were still on Silver's seat.

"Great party, huh?" Silver asked Yale.

"Sure." Yale took a swig of his whiskey.

Silver wasn't particularly fond of Yale; he was far too arrogant for Silver's liking, and he seemed dangerously aloof about the serious issues plaguing Imperium. But since Yale was an Affiliate, it was in Silver's best interest to befriend him. He didn't want any unnecessary drama in his professional life, so he continually—and unsuccessfully—tried to make Yale like him.

"So, how are things going for you, Elric?" Silver persisted. "I only ever hear good things about the Technology Department."

As with all the divisions, Media and Technology was divided into separate departments. The Lord Regent, of course, served as the leader of the entire division, making the final call on any major occurrences. But each of the departments had its own Keeper head, and those heads, alongside the Lord Dynast, Prophate, and cabinet, comprised the Lord Regent's inner circle of advisers.

Yale oversaw the Technology Department, one of the five main departments within Media and Technology—and, arguably, the most crucial. The Technology Department worked in tandem with other divisions—most commonly Science and Medicine, War and Defense, and Logistics and Transportation. Silver knew it was a good fit for Yale, as the position required someone with drive.

Yale forced a smile. "Everything's great. I wouldn't want to be anywhere else," he said, his eyes all the while on Silver's uniform.

Once he caught up with his colleagues, Silver found Liston, to chat with him before Banner's big speech. Banner's speech marked the true start of the gala, and after it was over, everyone was able to walk around more freely and talk with people they didn't otherwise get to see.

Silver and Liston caught up, telling each other about their Sidum vacations. Ever the workaholic, Liston had spent most of the month working on the details of his Civitan alliance, and he'd also spent some time doing his research on the Diplomacy Audillas. Apparently, he had big plans for Raelynn, and he was excited to see them through.

Liston took a sip of his iced tea. "But how's the family, Raze?"

"Really good, yeah. I haven't been able to see them too much, with the Media

Summit and everything."

"Oh, that's right. How was it? Did it go well?"

Silver sighed. "It was tedious. I really ... I wanted to be home."

With the word "home," his eyes found Viscardia. Damn, she was beautiful, in her crimson gown that perfectly accentuated her gorgeous curves. He'd always loved that dress. And she was wearing the necklace he got her, when he first said he loved her. Though he loved the Keeper Gala, a part of him just wanted it to be over with so he could take Viscardia home and—

"Well, I'm sure Viscardia wanted that too."

"What?" Silver was knocked out of his trance. "Oh. Right." He picked up a glass of water. "But, uh, what are your plans for the weekend? Anything special?"

"I'm meeting up with Farzah and Embry for dinner, before Embry goes off to Tarness."

"Right. Tarness. That's an interesting story. I'll bet Far's a mess about it, though."

"She's been happier," chuckled Liston.

"Ah, look," said Silver, tilting his head. "Banner on the move."

Banner weaved in and out of the crowd, gathering up the other Lord Regents, somehow appearing taller than usual. Puck swore that Banner used shoe lifts, and Silver didn't doubt it. Banner was, after all, nothing if not insecure.

Whitner ambled up to them. "Cyno wants us to get into position," he said in that downhearted way of his. It seemed to Silver that Whitner never wanted to be anywhere or do anything. It was a wonder why he'd applied to be a Lord Regent in the first place. "He wants us to look organized."

"A bit late for that," laughed Silver as Whitner walked away.

"Liston. Silver," Banner growled as he neared them. "We're going to be starting soon. Get ready."

"As you say, my Lord Regent," mocked Silver. Banner glared in response. "Wow, okay. Keep the jokes to a minimum tonight. Got it."

"This is one of the biggest events of the year," Banner said, as if he were telling them something they didn't already know. "Everyone is here. That may not mean a lot to you, but it means a lot to me. I don't need you making me look bad. Got it?" He turned his attention to Liston. "And you. We need to talk."

"I'm sure you're right," said Liston charmingly. "By the by, I don't believe I sent my condolences. Venin was a good man. He'll be missed."

Banner took a final swig of his liquid courage. "He'll be replaced, like all of us."

"That's a good eulogy," Silver piped up. "Hope that's what you said at his funeral."

Banner frowned. "Get in your positions. I shouldn't have to tell you more than once."

"Yeah, Levin. Raze," said Taymor as she made her way over. "You heard him."

Liston grinned. "So we did."

Silver laughed. "Well, I guess we should get in position," he said, his eyes on Whitner, Bryson, and Abner, who were already standing in line like the good boys they were. "We don't want to ruin Banner's moment. It might be the last one he'll ever have."

Silver, like Liston, was cautiously optimistic that the Affiliates would come out on top in the elections. Currently, the polls weren't predicting an Affiliate victory, but, of course, polls were inaccurate, and they didn't capture the whole picture. After all, it was common knowledge that Imperials had grown increasingly frustrated with Expansionist propaganda and futility, and they wanted change. The Affiliates would bring that change, if the voters gave them a chance.

"Quiet," Banner said, whipping his head back toward Silver.

"Calm down. It's not time yet. People are still coming in."

"And as they do, they want to see us acting professional."

"I guess there's a first for everything."

"Silver." It was Whitner who spoke, his eyes pleading. "Let's just all ... can we please get through this?"

Silver pitied the man more than anything, so he conceded. Whitner was

Banner's oldest friend—perhaps his only friend. That fact on its own was sad enough, but to make matters even worse, Whitner seemed to lack any sort of autonomy away from Banner. It was tragic, really. Silver wondered what had caused him to become so demure. More than that, he wondered what sort of blackmail Banner had on Whitner to keep him in line. It seemed painfully obvious that Whitner didn't truly believe in the Expansionist Party platform.

"My Lord Regents," greeted Desmond Vale, one of the most famous reporters in Imperium. "We'd like to take some photos, if you don't mind."

"Not at all," said Silver.

He was more than happy to put on a show.

18

RAELYNN

Upon entering Abbas Hall, Raelynn was awestruck by how many of Imperium's elites were in the vicinity. In the center stood the Lord Regents, all wearing their dress uniforms. Amongst the crowd, Raelynn saw people she recognized—classmates who had been both her friends and subjects of her disdain. All the patrons were dressed to the nines, catching up with old friends, making new ones. A live jazz band was off to the side, with an energetic conductor on the platform, moving with the music.

A hand fell on Raelynn's shoulder. Startled, Raelynn wheeled around and faced Brare.

"Oh! Justice Brare!" Raelynn said. "Good evening."

"And you, Lord Mabry."

From his perch at the top of the staircase, Brare looked out over Abbas Hall. Raelynn followed his gaze, taking the venue in. With its black-and-white tile floor, elegant wall murals, and indoor fountain, Abbas Hall was the pinnacle of Imperial glamour. An open bar stretched across the back wall, and the windows looked out onto a botanical garden, making Raelynn momentarily forget that Abbas Hall was in the city center.

"Abbas Hall," Brare mused. "Many a wedding has been held in here. Actually"—Brare's demeanor transformed—"High Justice Caine met his wife here. Did you know that? Many, many years ago."

"Uh. No." *Should* Raelynn have known? "I, uh … didn't know that. Will he be coming with his wife, then?"

Brare tensed up. "Um. No." He looked down at the floor. "Unfortunately, Idri … she doesn't get out much anymore. Poor thing. She still … you see, when they lost their child—"

"Aries!" came Caine's booming voice from behind them. Raelynn watched as Brare flinched, turning to address Caine. "What are you doing, terrorizing this young woman?" Caine directed his attention toward Raelynn, his manner brightening. "Hello, Seryph."

Raelynn cleared her throat. "Actually, my name's Raelynn."

Caine's face flushed. "I beg your pardon," he said, loosening his collar.

"It's okay, High Justice. I wouldn't expect you to remember me."

"Eliseo." Brare managed a smile. "We should go meet up with the others. Lord Regent Banner is about to give his speech."

"Ah, yes." Caine once more turned to Raelynn. "Have you had the privilege of hearing one of Cyno's speeches in person?"

"No," said Raelynn. "Only on the radio, which might not do him justice."

"Well, he's a marvelous orator," Caine went on, as though he were being paid to exalt Banner's virtues. "Just marvelous. You can tell, he really cares about his work."

"He's no Kosabeus, though," laughed Brare.

"Well, no," conceded Caine. "But he's probably the best orator on the Assembly."

"Eliseo, we really must go."

Caine looked down at the crowd below, sighing. "Yes, of course." He smiled at Raelynn. "Nice to see you again."

"Yes, you too," said Raelynn absently.

As Caine and Brare vanished into the crowd, Raelynn saw Silver motion for the band to quiet down, which most likely meant that Banner was about to give his speech. Raelynn hurried down the stairs, joining the semi-circle that had formed in the room's center.

"Excuse me. May I have your attention?" Banner's voice came over the loudspeaker. Slowly, the din in the room quieted. "Thank you." A warm smile graced his lips. "Good evening, everyone. We are gathered here this evening to honor all recent graduates from the ten Keeper academies. For those of you who may be unfamiliar with me, I am Cyno Banner, the Lord Regent of War and Defense, current Head of the Assembly, and an alum of the Ligva Academy. And these are my colleagues." Banner motioned to his left, where the other six members of the Assembly stood, in descending order of political influence. "Dane Whitner, the Lord Regent of Intelligence and Espionage and a fellow alum of the Ligva Academy. Levin Liston, the Lord Regent of Diplomacy and an alum of the New Caelus Academy. Pinn Bryson, the Lord Regent of Finance and Business and an alum of the Vitor Academy. Farzah Taymor, the Lord Regent of Science and Medicine and an alum of the Doctro Academy. Raze Silver, the Lord Regent of Media and Technology and an alum of the Pacalis Academy. And lastly, Nix Abner, the Lord Regent of Logistics and Transportation and an alum of the Carito Academy."

After Banner announced Abner's name, the room broke into applause. The Lord Regents—some more naturally than others—waved at the room. Whitner and Abner, Raelynn noticed, appeared extremely uncomfortable, offering no more than a meek wave and tight-lipped smile. Silver, on the other hand, exuded self-assurance. Photographers rapidly snapped pictures.

Banner cleared his throat. "Thank you," he said as the hall once again fell silent. "Now, as Head of the Assembly, it is my duty to address the new Audillas and offer them my sincere congratulations. I know I speak for the whole Assembly when I say that we value your sacrifice, courage, and dedication to Imperium. It wasn't too long ago that we were Audillas, ourselves—bright-eyed, ready to serve Imperium in any way we could. We all share a common love for Imperium, regardless of our party alliance or division. You know"—Banner started to chuckle prematurely—"I always like to say we will not allow our divisions to divide us."

Raelynn couldn't help but snicker, despite her dislike for Banner. Caine had been right; Banner was a lively orator. At the very least, he had the ability to control the room.

"The road to becoming a Keeper will not be easy," Banner continued, once the laughter seceded. "But you have all been chosen by wise Keepers who will see to it that you are prepared for what comes. There may be times when you feel that too much has been expected of you. You may sometimes feel that you have failed. But know this. All must overcome adversity. Those of you who are truly dedicated will rise to the occasion and do the job you have been trained to do. It is a great honor to serve as a Keeper. And seeing your faces, knowing that someday, seven of you may occupy our seats on the Assembly, fills my heart with pride.

"Imperium is best suited when all her Keepers work toward the common goal of ensuring Imperium's safety. We in War and Defense know the importance of strength, and each of you has attributes that will benefit Imperium. We may not all see the universe in the same way, and we may all hail from different cities. But Expansionists, Affiliates, and Grounders all have at least one thing in common." Banner paused momentarily, a smug smile forming on his lips. "We are all under one banner. The *Banner* of Imperium."

The room erupted in laughter. Banner looked out across Abbas Hall, absorbing the energy, feeding off it. A man standing to the side, wearing white, raised an eyebrow. Raelynn knew who he was—Kosabeus, the Head Prophate. Raelynn had attended many of Kosabeus's sermons over the years. Beside Kosabeus was someone no one could miss—an astoundingly tall man, taller than anyone Raelynn had ever seen.

"To conclude, I would like to offer my congratulations to all the new Audillas!" Banner's speech winded down. "And here's to the road ahead!" The audience clapped as Banner stepped away from the podium, and the band once again resumed playing.

"Some speech, isn't it?" asked Corlander, emerging from behind Raelynn.

"I didn't think it was too bad," said Raelynn.

"I didn't either. The first time I heard it."

"The first time?"

Corlander chuckled. "He alternates between two or three different speeches. But I'm pretty sure this is the exact same one he used last year."

"Come, now, Corlander. That isn't fair." Liston walked up, a smile on his lips. "This time, I believe he said 'road' at the end instead of 'path.'"

Out of protocol, Corlander bowed his head. "My Lord Regent."

"Please," said Liston, resting his hand on Corlander's shoulder. "You needn't do that. In fact, starting right now, every time you try to follow that blasted Keeper protocol, I will deduct one of your vacation days."

Corlander laughed. "As you wish, my Lord Regent."

Up close, Raelynn could see that Liston's dress coat was adorned with all sorts of medals and badges. Raelynn wasn't sure what they all signified, but she knew the red crest above the right breast pocket indicated that Liston was in Diplomacy. And the crown on top of that crest meant he was the Lord Regent. Raelynn had to study the badges and crests in school, so as not to offend a Keeper by calling them by the incorrect title. Unfortunately, like so many of the minutiae she'd been subjected to learn by heart, Raelynn had forgotten most of it. All she remembered was the Lord Regents all wore white dress coats with black slacks, while the Lord Dynasts all wore black dress coats with white slacks. All other Keepers wore gray.

Liston turned to Raelynn. "There is someone I'd like you to meet. If you want, of course."

"Sure," said Raelynn distractedly, still focused on Liston's impressive collection of badges. "I mean, yes."

Liston led Raelynn through the crowd. "It can get a bit stuffy in here with so many people up and about," Liston said, nodding at partygoers they passed. "So, if you ever feel overwhelmed, just step outside for a few minutes. I know I will."

"I've never seen so many important people in the same place."

"Concerning, isn't it? Raze always jokes that if a bomb were detonated in Abbas Hall on the night of the Keeper Gala, Imperium would be crippled." Seeing Raelynn's horrified expression, Liston added, "It's just a joke, Raelynn."

"That stems from a place of truth."

"If there's one thing you can count on Banner for, it's heightened security. No one is getting into this place who isn't on the guest list. I've lived in this city all my life. It's remarkable how much has changed. Now, thankfully, they have a magnificent jazz band playing the event."

"You like jazz?" asked Raelynn.

"Oh, yes." Liston's eyes lit up as his gaze drifted to the jazz band. "I absolutely adore it." He looked at Raelynn, somewhat nervously. "Why, what about you?"

"I'm more into blues myself," Raelynn admitted. "Though," she quickly clarified, sensing Liston's disappointment, "I like jazz too."

"Jazz isn't something to be 'liked,' Raelynn," Liston said, jokingly solemn. "It's something to be adored."

"Well, maybe it'll grow on me. You know. As I get older."

Liston laughed. "Very well." He scanned the nearby attendees. "Ah! There she is."

They cut through a large group of Audillas—some of whom glared at Raelynn—and made it to the edge of the dance floor, where Taymor stood. When compared to other women, such as Nisha, Taymor was decidedly understated, but there was something innately striking about her. Perhaps it was her poise. She clearly could, and did, take care of herself. Having met Embry, Raelynn could see the family resemblance. Besides their physical similarities, they emanated the same confident air.

Liston smiled as he neared Taymor, and she smiled back. "Farzah," Liston started. "I want you to meet Raelynn. And Raelynn, this, of course, is Farzah Taymor, our brilliant, irreplaceable Lord Regent of Science and Medicine."

Taymor shook Raelynn's hand. "It's nice to meet you, Raelynn. I hope you won't allow Levin's ... exaggerated description to color your view of me." Raelynn was impressed by her firm handshake and steady eye contact.

"Exaggerated?" asked Liston, feigning insult.

"The whole 'brilliant, irreplaceable' spiel? Lies. Inflated lies."

Liston beamed, his eyes drifting to her lips. "They were perfectly accurate." The band finished playing its current song, and the attendees clapped. "Wonderful stuff, isn't it?"

Taymor nodded dreamily. "You know how much I love jazz."

"Raelynn here just 'likes' it. Can you imagine?" Liston glanced at his watch. "Well, how about I leave you two to chat a bit?"

"Wait. Liston," began Raelynn, but Liston was already gone, yet another face in the crowd.

Taymor laughed. "That's Levin for you. Always quick on his feet."

"That's a habit of his? Disappearing like that?"

"Almost always."

Raelynn felt inextricably at ease around her, though she shouldn't have. Taymor was a Lord Regent, for Mystis's sake. She should have been treating Raelynn like a child or mud on her shoes.

"I, uh ... met your daughter," Raelynn said, hoping to find some common ground. "She's lovely."

"Oh, thank you. I certainly think so." She tugged on her necklace. "She'll be heading off to Tarness soon, which ..." Taymor trailed off. "But, you know, she loves traveling. It's such a young person's game. Old people like me prefer to just stay home."

"You're hardly old."

"Just for that, I'll buy you a drink. What do you fancy?"

"Whiskey."

"Ah." Taymor nodded slowly. "Levin was the same way."

Raelynn learned a lot about Taymor as they sat at the bar. She had grown up in Doctro, the smallest of the Big Ten cities—and the coldest. She loved ice sports. Apparently, she never missed the Tally Hall Ice Auctamens.

"If I can't be there in person, I listen over the radio," Taymor told her. "It's not the same, but it's still nice. I just love ice dancing. It's so regal."

She'd demonstrated a proclivity for a career in science and math from early adolescence, sailing through her entrance exams. Impressively enough, Taymor had been admitted into an accelerated medical program, and after graduating from Doctro, she was not only an Audilla but also a doctor. Usually, after graduating, Audillas had to enter medical school separately, if they wished to pursue that facet of Science and Medicine.

"I loved it," Taymor said. "The rigor, the intensity, the difficulty."

"Well, I hate math, science, all that stuff," said Raelynn. "And I'm terrible at it. But I'm glad there are people out there who love it."

"And I'm glad there are people like you and Levin, with the ability to fend off conflict," said Taymor. "We need that, with the Expansionists running things. But elections are coming up, so who knows what'll happen?"

If Raelynn had known a few months ago that this was where she'd be, she would have been floored. She could feel some of her former classmates' covetous eyes on her as she and Taymor chatted away.

Raelynn, the nobody from Satias, was Big Time.

19

WHITNER

He had seven minutes of peace at the bar before Banner found him and slipped into his speech on how much he loathed Liston. It was a spiel Whitner knew all too well, and it always made a reappearance at parties, usually after a couple of drinks. By this point, Whitner could practically quote it alongside Banner.

"He's an arrogant bastard," Banner was saying as he nursed his whiskey and soda.

Whitner took a sip of his Ligvan Liqueur. "I think you'd be a lot happier if you stopped worrying about Liston."

"I'll never be happy, Dane."

He didn't say it dejectedly, but Whitner knew that beneath Banner's gruff exterior lay a broken heart. Banner hadn't been the same since his son's death. Bayne was only twenty-seven when he died, with his whole life before him. It was a tragedy on all accounts. Thousands of Imperials had lost a loved one that day.

"Admit it, Dane," Banner said, slamming his empty glass on the bar. It was already his third drink of the evening. "Our lives would be a lot easier without

Liston."

"That is hardly—"

"He's been a pain in my ass ever since he made it onto the Assembly." Banner waved over the bartender for a refill. "And we all know he only made it because of Avitus, spewing his crap about Liston being 'Imperium's favorite son.' Whatever the hell that means."

Whitner pulled on his tie. "Jealousy isn't a good look for you."

"I'm not—"

"Give it up, Cyno. You may as well be green."

Banner laughed, despite himself. "I may as well be green?"

"Yes. You know. With jealousy."

"I thought it was 'green with envy.'"

"Envy is jealousy."

"I thought envy was about wanting what you don't have, that sort of thing," said Banner with a bored shrug.

"Which is what jealousy is. You want to be Liston."

"I wouldn't want to be Liston in a million years. If I was, I wouldn't be drinking this, would I?" Banner took a great gulp of his replenished whiskey and soda, to make a point.

Whitner sighed. "You're still on that?"

"On what? What do you mean?"

"You know what I'm talking about."

Banner shrugged. "I'll stop thinking it's true when I see him drink a whiskey and soda with my own two eyes."

"I thought whiskey and sodas went out of style."

Banner glanced over at Whitner's choice of drink. "Coming from the man drinking Ligvan Liqueur."

"I love Ligvan Liqueur," said Whitner, pulling it closer.

"You're the only one." Banner rolled his shoulders. "But that's what I like about you, Dane. You're not like the others. You never have been. Not even back in Ligva."

Whitner smiled at him. "Those were some good years."

"The best. You and I, at the top of our game."

"I don't think I ever had a 'game.' But even if I did, I was not at the top of it."

"Sure, you were. I mean, Ligva wasn't the most … exciting city, but … we made do."

Ligva, located in Exora, was surrounded by farms. It wasn't as developed as some of the other Big Ten cities, and the sources for entertainment were … questionable, to say the least. Most Ligvans spent their leisure time gambling, attending horse races, or watching Chessy Ball, a game that pitted two teams against each other, where the goal was to "capture" the other team's members by hitting them with balls until one player remained. Banner—someone who longed for more exhilarating thrills—spent most of his free time in what few nightclubs Ligva had.

That was how he'd ended up becoming a father at twenty—by knocking up an eighteen-year-old girl. Banner hadn't wanted to claim responsibility for the child at first, but the girl's mother threatened to ruin Banner unless he paid all the major bills her daughter would face. Reluctantly, Banner agreed, and he, against all odds, became involved in his son's life. They named their son Bayne, which always struck Whitner as odd. Why would anyone name their child after a word that meant scourge? Sure, they spelled it differently, but it still seemed like a strange choice. But it wasn't any of Whitner's business. All that mattered to him was Banner enjoying fatherhood and learning to view Bayne as a gift, not baggage.

And Whitner was pleasantly surprised. After Bayne's mother proved herself to be uninterested in parental duties, Banner had stepped in and decided to raise Bayne on his own, changing Bayne's surname and enlisting him in the best boarding school in New Caelus. Despite Banner's flaws, he'd truly loved Bayne, and his death had sent Banner into a long depression.

"You were always the one with everything, Cyno," said Whitner, placing an extra napkin on his lap. "I was just your friend."

"You've never just been my friend. You're my best friend."

It was moments like these—when they talked about the past—that Banner was most like his old self. For a moment, the light would return to his eyes, and he would lose himself in anecdotes about their academy days. He'd been one of the big men at Ligva, popular among everyone. Whitner and Banner had shared many classes, and they had developed a close, albeit unexpected, friendship.

"And you're mine," Whitner said with a smile, taking another—very careful—sip of his Ligvan Liqueur.

Banner looked out across Abbas Hall, sighing. "Kosabeus is mad at me," he announced suddenly.

"Why?"

"Because I want Harlyn to be my new Lord Dynast."

"Ah." Whitner nodded knowingly. "One of your ... lovers."

"One of my best," Banner added, as if that contributed any substance. "She's the best candidate for the job. But Kosabeus can't see that. Know why? 'Cause he's a hypocrite. I mean, he's married to Grell. So, he can't lecture me about mixing work and pleasure."

"But they were married well before she became Silver's temp Prophate. By the way, what's the news with that? When will the committee name Silver's new Prophate?"

"Not sure. But I assume it won't be Grell. They'll want to choose someone who isn't, you know, sleeping with their Head Prophate."

Whitner furrowed his eyebrows. He hated how Banner always made everything sound so salacious. He was preoccupied with sex; apparently, it was all he could ever think about. He hadn't used to be this way. Or maybe he had, and Whitner had just elected not to see it.

"I think Grell would make a fine Prophate," Whitner said. "She deserves to be judged on her own merits, not just as Kosabeus's wife."

Banner scrunched his nose. "So, you're on Kosabeus's side? You think I shouldn't make Harlyn my new Lord Dynast?"

Whitner scooted closer to Banner, their shoulders brushing. "Aren't you tired of all this sleeping around? Why not … settle down?"

"Because I don't want to." Banner half-heartedly flicked his wrist. "Oh, look. There he is. The shining star of Imperium," he mumbled, more to himself than to Whitner.

Whitner turned and saw Liston, dancing with one of his cabinet members. Banner was watching Liston—a bit too intently. In recent years, this had become Banner's obsession: studying Liston and waiting for him to make a wrong move in a public place.

Whitner raised an eyebrow. "You're staring."

"What?" scoffed Banner. "No, I'm not."

"Whatever you say." Whitner shook his head, taking another sip of his Ligvan Liqueur.

Banner glared at him. He stood up, too quickly, reaching out and using his stool to steady himself.

"Harlyn's here somewhere," he slurred. "I'm going to find her."

Banner stormed off in a huff, leaving Whitner alone at the bar. Whitner didn't mind; he liked being by himself. It gave him time to think. People were always on his case, asking for his opinion on this or that. There was hardly ever a moment to breathe.

Astrophel had monopolized all his attention when he first arrived in Abbas Hall. Luckily, Astrophel seemed to have digested Whitner's message, and he was less intrusive than he'd been in previous sessions. They discussed nonpolitical matters, and Whitner was surprised to find that he was actually interested in hearing about Astrophel's views on religion and charity. He'd had his doubts, when the Prophate Committee named Astrophel as his new Prophate, but maybe he'd been too hasty in his judgments.

"Hey, Dane."

Whitner looked up and saw Taymor. "Hey, Far!" There was always time to talk to Taymor. "How are you liking the party?"

Taymor shrugged, claiming Banner's vacant stool as her own. "It's nice enough."

"But you'd rather be home?"

"You know me too well." She motioned to his glass of Ligvan Liqueur. "What's that?"

"Ligvan Liqueur."

She made a face. "I don't know how you can drink that. It's way too sweet."

"It's an acquired taste."

"For people who have no taste," she teased. "But what more would I expect from someone who grew up in the hick town of Ligva?"

"'Cause Doctro is so much better."

"I love it up there. If I had it my way, I would've stayed in Doctro. Up there, everyone knows everyone. Here ... there are too many people. And they're nowhere near as nice."

"People in Ligva are nice too."

Taymor laughed. "Banner's from Ligva. So, that line won't work on me."

Whitner smiled. "I've missed you, Far. I feel like we haven't spoken in ages."

"Well, things have been so crazy." She leaned forward conspiratorially. "Banner left looking pretty upset. So, what, pray tell, did Levin do this time?"

"Who knows? Cyno's just in one of his moods."

Taymor rested her chin on her hand. "I'm sorry."

"No, don't be. I'm used to it. After fifty years, you learn to just nod your head and let him go at it."

"Fifty years." Taymor whistled through her teeth. "That's quite the feat, Dane. Half a century with Banner."

Whitner laughed. "It hasn't been that bad."

"Whatever you say."

Whitner watched as Taymor's attention averted to Liston. Taymor smiled, dreamily caressing her now-faded marriage tattoo. In Imperium, couples out-wardly denoted their love for one another by getting matching tattoos on their middle fingers. Each partner placed the tattoo on opposite hands so that when they stood side by side, their tattoos were touching; this was supposed to sym-bolize their unwavering bond. The tattoo designs differed slightly depending on the region and artist, but they all had underlying similarities. Engaged couples' tattoos were a singular band with any sorts of embellishments the couple desired. Married couples then added another band on top of the first one, with matching embellishments. If a couple were to break up or divorce—or if one of the partners were to die—the tattoos were to be removed. Taymor had bucked against this for the longest time, refusing to adhere to the custom, but within the last year or so, she had acquiesced. Whitner wasn't exactly sure what had changed her mind, but it seemed that perhaps she was finally ready to move on with her life.

"Why don't you get a dance or two out of him?" Whitner asked.

Taymor looked at Whitner, wide-eyed. Clearly, she'd thought she was being subtle.

"Because he's with someone else right now," she answered.

"The song's almost over."

"Hmmm." Taymor drummed her fingers on the counter. "You know what?" She stood up and straightened her coat. "I will."

Taymor weaved through the dance floor to meet up with Liston. When Liston saw her, he beamed, reaching out his hand. Whitner was rather envious. Oh, it'd been years since someone had asked him to dance. He wondered if he'd ever have that chance again—if the man he loved would ever be able to cross the room, look him in his eyes, and ask him to dance.

20

GRELL

Grell enjoyed fluttering about, talking to all sorts of interesting people. She didn't particularly think of herself as political, but she was curious about all the divisions and who their up-and-coming Keepers were. Things had changed a lot in Imperium, especially in the last few years. Bit by bit, their government was becoming more inclusive, and the all-boys' club that had previously dominated the Cooperative was, mercifully, nearing its end.

Unfortunately, the Assembly, many of the Lord Regents' cabinets, and the Church hierarchy were still controlled by men. Though there was talk of who would replace the aging Bryson—and whispers about Abner wanting an easy way out—there was no guarantee their successors would be women. This infuriated Grell. She wondered how Imperium could be so progressive in some ways but so regressive in others. It was almost like women were second-class citizens.

She and Viscardia spent a lot of their time championing women's issues, mostly within the Church. That was where they could truly make their mark. As a Prophate, Viscardia had real power and pull, while Grell was just an acting Prophate—for the moment, anyway. She hoped the Prophate Committee would allow her to apply for the position full-time, but she also knew they had their reservations about her, seeing how she and Kosabeus were married.

It wasn't illegal for two Prophates to be romantically involved, but the optics of it weren't great. Grell understood this, but she also believed she was qualified for the position. She'd served on multiple Church committees and spent thousands of hours working on Church projects. Kosabeus seemed convinced she would get the Prophateship, which she appreciated, but he didn't have a say in the matter. It all depended on who the new Magista was.

"It should go to you," Puck was saying as they found a quiet corner to chat in. "You know that, I know that, the Prophate Committee knows that."

Grell smiled. "Thanks, Puck. I really hope so, but ... I have to say, I'm worried. And whoever the new Magista is ... I just want them to give me a chance."

"Me too. We need good Prophates."

"What do you mean by that?"

Puck leaned forward conspiratorially. "What do you make of Astrophel?"

Grell shrugged. "Nothing, really. He's quiet, sort of keeps to himself, but that's it."

"You don't get a ... feeling off him?"

Grell's eyes widened. "You think he's bad news?"

"I dunno. It's too early to tell. But there's something about him that's just ... not right."

"I haven't spent much time with him, but I'll try to grab lunch with him sometime soon, see what I think for myself."

Grell and Puck had spent a lot of time together back on the Charity Outreach Committee. They spearheaded local projects for children, visited schools, donated toys, and built playgrounds. Though they enjoyed the work, they'd both complained about the other Numites on the committee. Their mutual dislike for their colleagues had, in turn, cemented their friendship.

"But what else is new, Grell? We haven't talked much."

"I'm doing well. Can't complain."

Grell smiled when she saw Kosabeus, standing off to the side with Avitus and

Viscardia. Before she fell in love with Kosabeus, Grell had been with her fair share of men. Most famously, she'd dated Bayne, Banner's son. Their relationship had been unhealthy—toxic, even—full of trust issues and infidelity. Well, the infidelity had been on his end; Grell never cheated on Bayne. He got that from his father, she assumed—his inability to commit to a single person. She'd spent years hoping he would change, but he never did. Though his premature death had devastated her, it had also opened the door for better things.

"Don't look now, but here comes Banner," said Puck, signaling with a nod of his head.

Sometimes, Grell found it difficult to comprehend that, had she married Bayne, Banner would have been her father-in-law. They would have been family. In another life, she might have called him "Dad" and spent holidays at his home.

Grell had tried to reach out to Banner in the aftermath of Bayne's death, but he hadn't been amenable. Grell had, after all, been the one who ended things with Bayne for the final time. And though Bayne had wanted to reconcile in the weeks before his death, Grell had told him it was over, that they both needed to move on. No doubt, Banner knew this, and he'd probably held it against her all this time. His son had died brokenhearted.

Still, Grell regretted all the things she hadn't said to Banner. After the funeral, she'd stopped trying to call or talk to him. She didn't know what to say. Really, what was there to say? Nothing would help. And nothing would ever bring Bayne back.

Bayne's birthday—and the tenth anniversary of his death—was coming up soon. He would've been thirty-seven. She wondered what Banner would do to commemorate it.

Maybe this would be the perfect time for her to reach out again. She could try to make things right between her and Banner, even if it was ten years too late. She'd always wondered what he thought of her. Did he hate her for moving on so quickly? Did he think she'd been cheating on Bayne the entire time?

She wanted to clear the air. No, more than that, she had to clear the air. Even if he wasn't willing to accept her apology, she needed to say it. For the past few years, Grell had been trying to be a better person. She'd been selfish in the past, and she'd hurt people who didn't deserve it, all in the name of self-preservation. Most likely, Banner was one of those people, and Bayne may have been too. Maybe Banner had expected her to be there for him, to mourn Bayne together, but she'd let him down. Maybe she was partly responsible for the person he'd become.

"I feel bad for him," Grell said, unintentionally aloud. Then, after seeing Puck's expression, she added, "I just think there's a lot of ... unresolved sadness there."

Puck smiled. "You're a far better person than I, Grell."

Oh, no, she wasn't. Not in the slightest. No, Grell would wager that she was one of the worst people in this room. She'd done some heinous things in her past, some truly cruel things. And the worst part was, she had done it all willingly. Mystis, she couldn't believe all the lies she'd spun, all the secrets she'd buried. Sometimes, she wanted to come clean, but she knew she couldn't. It would destroy everything. Worse than that, it would—

"I mean, giving Banner the benefit of the doubt? That's something I could never do," Puck went on. "But I guess you're right. We're all human. We all make mistakes."

"That's true," Grell said, forcing a smile, hoping he didn't notice how fake it was.

He didn't. They never did.

She took a deep breath, to calm herself. She was just getting in her head. Puck didn't know. Everything was fine. As long as no one ever found out what she'd done, everything would be completely fine.

21

RAELYNN

Raelynn and Embry met up for breakfast at Primrose. It was in downtown New Caelus, in the Arts District, surrounded by museums and eccentric shops. The café itself was unconventional, with unique food combinations and drink flavors. Younger people flocked to it—perhaps due to its relatively low prices.

Raelynn, for her part, was supposed to meet with Liston later to plan the next four months under his employ, and she figured Embry was the perfect person to ask for advice, given her familiarity with Liston.

"Just be yourself," Embry said, sipping her coffee. It was some weird, fruity flavor that sounded disgusting to Raelynn, but clearly, Embry loved it.

Raelynn stirred her—according to Embry—boringly plain coffee. Embry claimed someone couldn't come to Primrose and order something basic. But Raelynn wasn't sure how adventurous she could be with coffee.

"So, where are you heading off to again?" asked Raelynn.

"Tarness."

"Whoa." Raelynn's eyes widened. "That's ... intense, reporting on a war."

"I know. But apparently, Banner's hoping to take advantage of the civil war

113

by conquering Tarness and making it another Imperial colony. Lev, on the other hand, wants to topple the current government and install a regime that's more friendly toward Imperium."

"And what do you think?"

Embry cut her muffin in half. "I'm a Grounder, you know. I don't think we should be involving ourselves in everyone else's business. But Lev ... he's very idealistic. Some may say a bit zealous. He sees things his way, and he'll never change his mind."

"And yet you're still close."

"Well, yeah." Embry gave her a strange look. "Politics isn't everything, Raelynn."

"In a perfect world, maybe. But in New Caelus? It controls everything."

"So, you don't have any Expansionist friends?"

"Why would I? They're all warmongers."

"Really?" Embry crossed her arms. "All of them?"

"Well. No. But you know what I mean! Most Expansionists are idiots."

Embry laughed. "So, you're excited about the upcoming elections, I assume?"

"Of course. Well ... and anxious."

"What news sources do you follow?"

"*The Imperial Gazette*, all day, every day."

Embry raised an eyebrow. "Is that all you read?"

"No. I read a couple others too. Like *New Caelus Now* and *Affiliate Rising*."

"Those are all, like, pro-Affiliate newspapers. They're totally biased!"

"Oh, come on," said Raelynn, placing down her silverware. "You're really going to tell me to put stock in papers like *The Agenda* and *The War Front*? Those are garbage."

Embry laughed, shaking her head. "You're an interesting person, Raelynn. You're like the uncensored version of Lev."

"Is that supposed to be an insult?"

"No. Not at all. He's one of those Affiliate diehards too. He bleeds blue and black. But, you know, since he's supposed to be diplomatic and all that, he can't really say what he thinks. When he's asked about Banner, he'll just say vague things—you know, stuff that won't get him in trouble."

Raelynn finished off her coffee. "Want another?"

"I can't. I have to go meet with my team to discuss the logistics of our trip."

"Good luck."

"Thanks." Embry stood up. "And good luck with Lev. When are you meeting him?"

"Four to four thirty. It's the only free time he has."

Embry nodded knowingly. "The life of a Lord Regent. But hey, you never know. That could be you someday."

"Maybe," said Raelynn, though she sincerely doubted it.

Raelynn spent the first part of her day getting more acquainted with downtown New Caelus. She saw a few interesting restaurants and shops and decided she'd check them out on a weekend. Before Raelynn knew it, it was twenty to four, so she wandered over to the Spire to meet with Liston. She wasn't sure what to expect. Usually, after graduating, Audillas began working in the department of their given Keeper mentor. But since Liston was the Lord Regent, he didn't work in one department; he oversaw them all. Raelynn couldn't help but think she was in a dream—that one of these days, she'd wake up, and she'd be back in Satias, waiting for her real mentor to walk through the doors.

"Raelynn!" Corlander caught her in the lobby, waving her down. "You're here to see our Lord Regent, correct?"

"Yes. Is he in his office?"

"No. And he wanted me to catch you. He was wondering if you'd like to grab a cup of coffee in Aquarial. It's the restaurant here." Corlander motioned to his left. "It's right upstairs. He'll join you shortly."

In keeping with the rest of the Spire, Aquarial embraced its oceanic location, with blues, purples, greens, and oranges dominating the restaurant. Beautiful glass sculptures—fashioned by local artists, according to the plaques—were displayed along the curved walls. The walls added a strange motion to the room. Windows, of course, lined the back walls, peering out onto Auster Ocean. Goodness, Raelynn would never get sick of that view. The room appeared more like a museum than a restaurant, but Raelynn didn't mind.

"Is this table acceptable, my lord?" asked the host as he led Raelynn over to a table right by the windows.

Was the man crazy?

"Yes," answered Raelynn. "It's perfect."

Raelynn's gaze immediately drifted to the windows. A few New Caelites sat on the beach, taking in the dimming sun. Raelynn remembered the first time she'd visited New Caelus and seen Auster Ocean rise before her. She'd jumped out of her shoes faster than anything, running across the shore to feel the salty water between her toes.

"Spectacular place, isn't it?" Liston claimed the seat across from Raelynn. "Aquarial has some of the best dark-roast coffees I've ever had. Really, if you like coffee, you must try the house blend."

Liston made eye contact with one of the waitresses, who somehow—perhaps through telepathy—knew what he required. She promptly darted into the kitchen.

"Embry informed me that you two had breakfast this morning," Liston said.

"Yes. We did."

"She also mentioned you seemed nervous."

Raelynn mentally cursed Embry for being so chummy with her new boss. "A little."

"Well, don't be. I pride myself on being approachable."

"I'm sure you do," said Raelynn, fidgeting with her sleeve. "But you're a Lord Regent. And whether you can see it or not, that's intimidating."

Liston adjusted his glasses. "Well, we must remedy that. I don't want you to fear me."

"I don't fear you. I just ... I don't really know how this will work. What do you want me to do?"

"It's like a normal office job. Nine to five, five days a week, Spero through Ortus. As I told you, I'm pursuing an alliance with the Civitan. It would be a great help to me if you could act as sort of the liaison between me and the Civitan. Ambassador Barringer—she's the one we'll be working most closely with—is a lovely woman. Very personable. She and her team have many questions about Imperium—what we are like, how we see the rest of the universe. And I thought you'd be an interesting person for them to talk to about that."

"Me?" Raelynn cocked her head to the side. "I'm hardly the resident expert on all things Imperial."

"Well, no one is. But you're young, from a different generation. And every generation, they say, becomes more open-minded. You and your peers are the future, Raelynn. You're the ones who'll be at the forefront before you know it. And, correct me if I'm wrong, but didn't you write your thesis on Imperium's connection to the Civitan and how our parallel origins could allow us to grow together?"

Raelynn's jaw dropped. "You know about my thesis?"

"It was one of the main reasons I chose you. Not enough Diplomacy students care about the Civitan. All the theses are about the Core or Terraria or Imperium itself. The Civitan, for some reason, is a footnote, a sidebar. But you see it the way I do."

The waitress returned with a tray holding two cups and a coffee pot. "Here you are, my lords," she said. "The Aquarial House Blend."

"Thank you so much, Glenda," said Liston with a smile.

Raelynn watched as Liston poured each of them a cup of coffee. "Did you, uh, by any chance ... read my thesis?"

"I did." Liston was focused on not spilling a single drop of the precious elixir. "Every solis, I skim through the Diplomacy graduates' theses. Across all the academies, you were one of three students who focused on the Civitan. But the other two ... they assumed rather archaic views of the Civitan. They claimed that because the Civitan was a part of the Core for so long, it's almost inseparable from it. Which is just—forgive my saying so—ludicrous."

"Were those two students Expansionists, do you know?" joked Raelynn.

Liston laughed, nearly spitting out his coffee. "Raelynn. Please," he said, dabbing his mouth with his napkin, trying to maintain some semblance of his dignity. "Don't make me laugh when I'm drinking."

"I'm sorry," Raelynn chuckled, taking a sip of her coffee.

Liston indicated toward the coffee. "How do you like it?"

"It's excellent."

"Good." Liston leaned back in his chair. "By the by, I picked out an office for you. It's on the fourth floor, and it has a view much like this one," he added, gesturing toward the windows. "You aren't too far away from Corlander, so if you have any pressing concerns, you can always contact him, and he'll find me. I would have preferred, of course, for you to be closer to me, but my office is all by itself on the ground floor, with nothing but storage space next to it."

"No, that's great. I can't wait to get started."

"Spero, then. Nine o'clock. It shall begin."

22

VISCARDIA

Silver and Viscardia lay side by side, catching their breath. During Silver's birthday weekend, he and Viscardia had talked a lot about making their relationship more of a priority. The conversation had been long overdue, but it'd been more than worth it. Ever since, they'd been meeting up at their apartment once a week for their lunch hour, taking turns as to who brought the food and drinks. And they'd enjoy a wonderful lunch together, chatting about their days. Alone time with Silver was increasingly rare, so Viscardia made sure to treasure it.

Silver turned to her, a euphoric smile on his lips. "I think we're doing really well at this whole 'not losing the spark' thing," he said.

"Oh, yes," Viscardia agreed.

Silver glanced over at the clock on the end table, sighing. "I should get going, Viz. It's almost one o'clock."

"Already?" Viscardia leaned over to see for herself.

"I know. And I hate to run out of here like this was a one-night stand, but I've got a meeting at one fifteen with Yale. And if I'm even a minute late, I'll never hear the end of it."

"Okay, gorgeous," laughed Viscardia.

Silver slid out of bed, putting on his clothes more quickly than Viscardia could rip them off. She was impressed. In less than thirty seconds, he was fully clothed, including his tie, and he turned to her for inspection.

"How do I look?" he asked. "Does everything look good, in place, professional?"

"You're perfect," she said, a smile on her lips. She was relieved he'd finally shaved that hideous beard.

"And you're a gem." Silver leaned over the bed to kiss her. "And remember, I'm picking the kids up from school today."

"And I've got a meeting that will hopefully be done by five thirty. But I'll call you if I think I'll be late so you and the kids can have dinner without waiting around for me."

"We can wait." Silver kissed her one last time. "Sorry," he said with a sheepish smile. "Couldn't resist."

"Do you hear me complaining?"

Silver laughed. "I love you."

"I love you too."

Viscardia watched as Silver darted out the door. Alone in the bed, she stretched out, sinking back into the pillows. Oh, how badly she wanted to take a nap. She didn't have anything on tap until three o'clock, so she could sneak in some shut-eye. She leaned over and set the alarm for two fifteen, just in case she ended up falling asleep. And sure enough—

BEEP! BEEP! BEEP! BEEP! BEEP!

Viscardia sprung awake. Had it already been an hour and fifteen minutes? Time could certainly play its cruel tricks. Groaning, Viscardia forced herself out of bed, and she jumped into a quick shower before she exited the apartment.

At three o'clock on the dot, she strolled into Abner's office. He was meeting with Garibaldi Kessler and Cason Owusu, two Cooperative hopefuls. Viscardia hadn't met them before, but all her hopes for them being the types of candidates

Abner should support washed away when she learned their party affiliation. She waited until they left before she turned on Abner.

"Nix. They're Expansionists."

"I know, I know," he said, bobbing his head. "But Titus and Maxton think they're great."

"Titus and Maxton are Expansionists too. Of course, they want you to back all the Expansionist candidates."

"Well, what do you expect me to do?"

Viscardia could hardly fathom what Abner was saying. He was a Grounder. He should've been throwing his numa behind every Grounder candidate he could. It was his job, as a politician, to secure his power base, not to cater to a minority faction of his cabinet.

"Why are you listening to Titus and Maxton on this?" Viscardia asked. "There are other members of your cabinet who are—gee, I don't know—Grounders. You know. Your people."

"Titus and Maxton have served my division well."

They hadn't. In fact, Viscardia would've been hard pressed to name any two Keepers who were more destructive to their given divisions than Titus and Maxton. With their dated stance against social modernism and refusal to vote on any bill that wasn't beneficial to the patriarchy, Titus and Maxton were the problem personified in contemporary Imperial politics. They hung on to the old ways, railing against progress, shunning diversity, and embracing stagnancy.

"You shouldn't be standing by Titus and Maxton," Viscardia said. "Not only have they never helped you personally, but they sully you politically. When they run off to reporters, spewing their—"

"I know you don't like them, Viscardia. But they have served me—and this division—for years. Don't underestimate loyalty."

"They don't give a damn about you, Nix. They care about their party. Which isn't yours."

"I like the fact that my cabinet has people with all sorts of political views. Isn't that the point?"

"It's an outmoded system." Viscardia neared him. "Don't you see that by listening to them, you're undermining your own ability to get things done? You're letting Titus and Maxton run this division for you."

"It doesn't matter who you listen to—Expansionists, Grounders, Affiliates. The universe will always be a shit show. So, I may as well just do whatever makes the most sense in the moment. And I trust Titus and Maxton."

Viscardia was a woman of many pet peeves. She hated it when people breathed heavily while eating and chewed with their mouths open. She hated it when people referred to their child as twenty-four months old when they could more easily say two years old. She hated it when strangers felt the need to comment on her clothes or tell her that her makeup scheme didn't suit her skin tone. But most of all, she hated it when people in positions of power didn't use their celebrity to enact meaningful change.

"That is bullshit," she spat. "And worse than that, it's lazy bullshit. It's you trying to justify the fact that you do nothing, day in, day out, and yet you still get paid more than I do."

Abner put his hands on his hips. "Look," he drawled. "Just because I see things a little differently from you doesn't mean I'm wrong. This is the way Imperium's always been run, and it's done well by us so far. Why fix what isn't broken?"

"But it *is* broken. It's stymying progress and—"

"I don't want to hear about this anymore."

"You're the one who called me here. I assumed you wanted to hear—"

"I knew you'd be angrier if I didn't tell you myself." Abner looked at her wearily. "I just wish you'd give me a little more credit, that's all."

"Credit for what?"

"I may not be the most ... outspoken Lord Regent, but I don't think I should be. I keep my head down, mind my own business, and everything seems to work out."

Viscardia took a deep breath. "Those days are nearing their end. People want transparency from their Lord Regents. They want to hear from you, see you, know you. They don't get to vote for you, so the least you could do for them is—"

"We're never going to see eye to eye on this. I accept that. But I need you to accept that too. I ... I need you to understand that I want my own autonomy, and I don't want you to make me feel guilty about that."

Viscardia could hardly believe what he was saying. Abner was one of the most bungling politicians she'd ever met. It was rich of him to say he wanted autonomy when he spent most of his days pawning off his responsibilities onto her, his cabinet, and his Lord Dynast, Tinsley Iaconetti, one of the only competent Keepers in Logistics and Transportation. No, what he really wanted was a Prophate who wouldn't question him, a Prophate who wouldn't speak unless spoken to. He, like most men who benefitted from the Imperial system, didn't want to be held accountable for his own actions—or lack thereof.

"All the other Lord Regents have autonomy," Abner went on, pacing his floor desultorily. "They can make decisions without their Prophate trying to make them do things their way."

"Have you met Avitus or Kosabeus?" laughed Viscardia.

"But it's more acceptable for them to do that."

"Why? Because they're men?"

"No," said Abner slowly. Clearly, that was what he thought, but he couldn't admit to that—not in front of Viscardia. "Because they have more experience. Avitus was a soldier. He knows what he's talking about when he tells Liston about war. And Kosabeus—"

"And Kosabeus what?" asked Viscardia, her patience wearing thin. "He and I have held all the same positions. We were both Erates and members of various internal Church committees. There is nothing he's done that I haven't."

"But he's the Head Prophate."

"It's a title without much distinction."

Abner shook his head. "And you think *I* have the ego."

"Do you want me to apologize for defending my qualifications? Because I'm not going to do that. And if you really want to know—"

"I've made up my mind, Viscardia. I'm going to trust Titus and Maxton on this and support the candidates they're backing. You won't get your way. Not this time."

Viscardia left the Axle feeling tense all over. She absently made her way back to her office, her mind racing. She knew she was a great Prophate; she knew she deserved more respect than Abner was willing to give her. He took advantage of her competence but refused to ever acknowledge all the work she did behind the scenes to make sure that Logistics and Transportation was a somewhat functioning division. It wasn't easy. It seemed to Viscardia that all the least ambitious and motivated Keepers—from all three parties—had decided to specialize in Logistics and Transportation. They were unable to do even the simplest of tasks. Happily, they just settled into their lives of mediocrity and obscurity, never daring to challenge the status quo. It was truly mind-boggling just how disastrously run the whole division was.

"You appear ... deep in thought."

Kosabeus was standing in the doorway of her office. He'd just finished a sermon, as evidenced by the ostentatious white robe he was wearing.

"Oh, it was just ... one of those days," Viscardia said, forcing a smile.

"Anything you want to talk about?"

Viscardia shrugged. "It's much of the same, really."

"Abner doesn't deserve you, you know."

"And yet here I am."

Kosabeus met her eyes. It was always alarming to Viscardia just how piercing his eyes were. There was an underlying intensity to Kosabeus, but somehow, he was still approachable. Indeed, he could masterfully compel people to open up and bare their souls to him. That was probably why he was such a natural Head Prophate.

"I know we've had this conversation before," he started, "but I can try talking to the Prophate Committee, see if you can—"

"And where would I go? It's not like any of the other Lord Regents would be willing to switch. And besides, you know it's not that simple. When it comes down to it, it's all in the Magista's hands, and at the moment, we don't even have one."

"Well, that should be remedied soon. I've heard rumblings that they'll announce the new Magista after the upcoming fundraising party."

"Any idea who it will be?"

"Not a clue. They don't let me know those sorts of things."

"They should."

"I know."

Viscardia eyed him carefully, trying to gauge his mood. "Do you ever think the Church is …?" She trailed off, shaking her head.

"No, finish your thought. I want to hear it."

"You may think it's blasphemous."

"I may agree with you."

"It's just … the way things are run … it's like there's no transparency. All these decisions they make without even consulting us … it's insulting."

"See, I told you I may agree with you."

"So, what can we do about it?"

Kosabeus smiled. "I'm optimistic that with a new Magista, one who is younger and more, well … shall we say … in touch with modern-day Imperium, the Church will be in a better position to address and solve these issues."

"I hope you're right. Because I don't know how much longer I can take this."

"Do you ever think about leaving?" There was a hint of nervousness in his voice.

"Do you?" she countered.

"No. Never. The Church is my home. This is where I belong."

"But do you ever wish you had another Lord Regent?"

Kosabeus laughed. "You mean, do I ever get sick of cleaning up Cyno's messes?"

"Well, do you?"

"Yes. But I'm afraid I've made myself rather indispensable to him. I don't think he can live without me."

There was usually a sarcastic edge to everything Kosabeus said, a jab, a poke. People who didn't know him that well sometimes wrote him off as arrogant. And maybe he was, to some extent. But Viscardia appreciated his candor. She knew that he, like her, was often frustrated by his Lord Regent. Abner was woefully incompetent, sure, but he was nowhere near as trying to deal with as Banner, whose tantrums, tirades, and escapades were all well documented. Kosabeus had to walk a fine line by publicly distancing himself from Banner while also being a loyal Prophate. It was a difficult balance, but Kosabeus seemed to do it adroitly.

"But in all seriousness, Viscardia, I might be able to help," he went on. "Hopefully, whoever the new Magista is is more ... receptive to these sorts of requests."

"But what do you think will happen? It's not like Avitus would ever leave Lev. And I can't be Raze's Prophate, even if I wanted to."

By law, a Lord Regent was prohibited from being romantically involved with their Prophate. Viscardia wasn't sure how many times that law had been broken over the centuries, but she figured a fair few Lord Regents and Prophates had found some sort of prurient delight engaging in a forbidden love affair.

"No, I know. But maybe ... Whitner?"

Viscardia made a face. "Is working for him any better than working for Abner?"

"Fair point." Kosabeus smirked. "Well, you and I, we'll meet with the new Magista, whenever they make themselves known, and we'll see what we can do."

Viscardia didn't want to get her hopes up, but she was cautiously optimistic. Their former Magista had been a stickler for Church protocol, to both her and Kosabeus's chagrin. It had been nearly impossible for any of the Prophates to make their voices heard, and healthy debate within the Church hierarchy had been all but abolished.

Hopefully, their new Magista would be more approachable and interested in what the Prophates had to say. That was the way things should have been done, anyway. Viscardia wanted honest communication with the Church higher-ups. No more of those closed-door hearings or backroom deals. She wanted everything to be out in the open, for everyone to see.

"Then let's make it happen," she said, a smile on her lips.

23

AVITUS

It was the same nightmare Avitus always had. He was back on Lalek, during the Glass War, cutting through the Coronian and Civ forces. He was thirty-three years old but already jaded. Gunshots rang through the air, bodies fell, screams echoed. Avitus hadn't slept in two days. His last meal had been leftover gruel. But somehow, he summoned his strength. He was fighting for freedom, to protect the Imperial way of life.

He had left the Batillus Numentis School at sixteen to pursue a military career. The Glass War had been raging since Avitus was eight years old, and he was determined to fight in it. According to the laws of the Church, Avitus was supposed to wait until he was seventeen to leave, but he worked out a deal with the overseers. They were sad to see him go, but they assured him there would be a place for him in the Church after his contract expired. Avitus didn't think he would take them up on it. He wasn't sure if he'd come back alive. To be even more honest, he wasn't sure he wanted to.

In his youth, he was religiously skeptical. He didn't believe in any of it—in the theology, the faith, the tomes. It all seemed so unbearably arrogant to him, saying that Mystis was their only savior and that the Imperial way of life was far superior to all others. How could they know? They hadn't lived anywhere else; they hadn't ever ventured outside their comfort zones. Were they not the least bit curious as to whether the stories they'd been fed were even remotely true? Where was their intellectual curiosity? Where was their doubt?

When he left the Church, Avitus felt relieved. He hated the way the Church corrupted and deluded people. Imperials were so damn scared of death, of what Mystis would make of them, of how they'd be judged for their failures. But Avitus wasn't. He didn't believe Mystis existed.

But on Lalek, everything changed.

Avitus and his regiment were on a reconnaissance mission, to discover where the Coronians and Civs were based. They hadn't expected to find them. The battle was brutal and bloody, the worst Avitus had ever witnessed. But his men fought like lions. At the end, just he and Sergeant Kaso were left. Avitus ordered Kaso to return to the base. He was going to see what he could scavenge, to see if the Coronians and Civs had left behind any plans or ammunition. As Avitus ransacked their abandoned tents, he couldn't shake the feeling he was being watched. Still, he decided he was only being paranoid.

But then—

BANG.

The bullet struck him in the side. He blacked out and fell to the ground. When he awoke, he saw a blinding light in the sky, shining down on him.

Was it Mystis? No. It couldn't be. Mystis wasn't real.

Sluggishly, Avitus stood up, wincing in pain. He took off his jacket, wrapping it around the wound. He followed the light, unsure where it was taking him or if it was all just a dream. Maybe he was already dead, and this was his afterlife. This wasn't Obasus Garden, and Mystis was nowhere to be seen. He'd been right; the theology was a lie, a blatant lie.

The light, as it turned out, led Avitus back to the base. When he arrived, he passed out from exhaustion, and he was attended to by the medical personnel, who had, until that moment, assumed he was dead. The next time he opened his eyes, he was on a cot, having just been in surgery. They told him he was lucky the bullet hadn't pierced any vital organs or that he hadn't bled to death. It was a miracle. By all accounts, he should have died out there.

But the light saved him.

That was thirty-five years ago, but the memories still gave Avitus goosebumps. His near-death experience had ignited his religiosity. He served another four years, and when his contract expired, he returned to the Church—having been relocated to New Caelus—older, wiser, and colder. Quickly, he ascended through the ranks until he became a Prophate. And nothing had rewarded Avitus so much as being Liston's Prophate.

Avitus had known Liston since he was a boy. He'd met him through Nicolai Carbury, the former Lord Regent of Diplomacy. Avitus had the dubious honor of serving as Carbury's Prophate. Carbury was a strange case—in more ways than one. He'd trained in War and Defense, but when the position of Lord Regent of Diplomacy became available, he applied. Avitus knew why; Carbury was ruthlessly ambitious, and he wanted to get onto the Assembly as swiftly as possible. He didn't care which division he had to work for, as long as he got a seat at the table. And he did.

What Avitus still couldn't rightly understand, all these years later, was how Carbury, a proud Expansionist, had managed to convince the divisional board for Diplomacy to name him as the new Lord Regent. There were very few Expansionists in Diplomacy, just as there were very few Affiliates in War and Defense. Those two divisions were more politically polarized than the others. However, Carbury had masterfully positioned himself as a pragmatist, claiming the Diplomacy division needed to assert itself much more aggressively. He said the previous Lord Regent of Diplomacy had been far too meek, giving up ground and appeasing the Core. Carbury, on the other hand, would be a force to be reckoned with, a forthright leader. Evidently, he charmed the divisional board with this sales pitch, as he became the new Lord Regent of Diplomacy.

Carbury, like most Lord Regents, ascended to the office when he was young.

He was only twenty-seven at the time. Imperium revered youth, in a way, and preferred its officials—including Lord Regents, Prophates, and Cooperative representatives—to start young. While this was admirable, as it helped breathe fresh life into the government, it also meant that some officials stayed in office for fifty or sixty years. That sort of tenure made people apathetic at best or corrupt at worst.

The latter happened to Carbury. Though his tenure was, mercifully, cut short by his death sixteen years ago, he accomplished a lot in his seventeen years on the Assembly. For twelve of those years, he'd served as the Head of the Assembly and the leader of the Expansionist Party, which had permeated him with an even greater sense of self-importance. Carbury was a neurotic person. He was always fixated on his mortality, his place in history, the legacy he was leaving behind. Avitus couldn't help but wonder if somewhere deep inside, Carbury had always known that he would die young, just days before his forty-fifth birthday.

Because of his obsession with his ultimate demise, Carbury had taken an interest in Liston. He'd heard rumblings in the New Caelus Academy about an exceptionally bright young student, and Carbury, who'd never felt inclined to marry or have children of his own—despite his all-consuming fears about his mortality—decided to mentor the boy. That, to Avitus, was one of the strangest things about Carbury. If he was so afraid of dying without an heir, then why did he never marry?

But Carbury, it seemed, was optimistic that Liston would follow in his footsteps and carry on his work long after he was dead. For his part, Avitus was never comfortable with this relationship; he couldn't believe that the New Caelus Academy had allowed Carbury to spend so much time with the young, impressionable Liston. Avitus had more than his fair share of reservations about Carbury's intentions, and though Avitus made his stance abundantly clear to anyone who would listen, it didn't matter. Carbury continued to get his way, as men like him always did, and Avitus was forced to stand back and watch.

Over time, Avitus got to know Liston, and he grew to care for him. He knew that Liston wanted to break away from Carbury, and Avitus did what he could to help Liston establish his independence. Though Carbury hated Avitus's interference, he also feared Avitus, and thus, Carbury never confronted him. Though Avitus had done everything in his power to protect Liston from Carbury, he still, all these years later, felt like it hadn't been enough. After Carbury's death, Avitus had made a promise that as long as he was alive, no one would ever hurt Liston again.

Liston was bound to arrive soon for a last-minute session. Avitus stood by the window, looking out at the garden. Butterflies fluttered about, adding even more vitality to the colorful scene. Avitus worshipped nature, deeming it Mystis's greatest gift for humanity. He had blessed them with a truly magnificent planet. To be an Imperial was to know you were one of his Chosen. Avitus couldn't believe he'd been such a cynic when he was younger. How hadn't he seen all these little marvels? How hadn't he felt Mystis's presence beside him, guiding him home?

"Avitus."

"My son." Avitus turned to face Liston. "Welcome." He signaled toward the couch. "Shall we sit?"

There was a light in Liston's eyes that Avitus hadn't seen in weeks. It was both refreshing and distressing. Refreshing, of course, because Avitus wanted Liston to be happy. Distressing, however, because Avitus knew that look all too well; it meant that Liston was doing something he shouldn't have been doing, something that would, in the end, cause more harm than good.

"Is everything well?" Avitus carefully ventured.

"Yes. Very well." Liston folded his hands on top of his lap. "I was just meeting with Raelynn, explaining the situation with the Civitan, all that."

And there it was—the reason to be alarmed. The Civitan, like Imperium, had been a part of the Core. But unlike Imperium, which had broken away from the Core due to religious persecution, the Civitan mainly disagreed with the Core over economic policies. Ever since the Glass War ended, the Civitan's leadership had been openly speaking out against the Core, claiming they wanted the complete autonomy the Core had promised them. And in recent years, the Civitan had succeeded in establishing its independence, with a seventy-thirty referendum allowing them to break free. No doubt, the Civitan could help Imperium take down the Core, once and for all. The enemy of an enemy was, after all, a friend. But Avitus was wary of the Civitan's motives. They'd fought against Imperium in the Glass War with a gory vengeance. Avitus had lost many a friend to a Civ bullet. And besides, the Civitan and the Core were still trading partners, and from the outside at least, their relationship seemed alarmingly chummy.

"I thought I told you to give it up," Avitus said.

"I know you did," said Liston, sitting up to match Avitus's posture. "But the Civitan hates the Core, Avitus. Almost as much as Imperium does. It'd be foolish to ignore this opportunity. With the Civitan's backing, we can force the Core to stand down, make them end this standoff."

"The war won't end. Not in your lifetime."

"We aren't even at war with the Core," said Liston with that maddening sanguinity. Avitus had a bad feeling that Liston's childlike idealism was going to get him in the end.

"Yes, we are." The soldier within Avitus resurfaced. "I don't want you negotiating with the Civs. They're monsters. Terrorists. You weren't there. You didn't see what I saw. One of my lieutenants was massacred by them. He had surrendered. They should have just taken him prisoner. But they didn't."

"The times have changed. The Civitan is now—"

"Thirty years isn't that long, in the scheme of things."

"It's practically my whole lifetime."

"And you are still but a child." Avitus's eyes were imploring. "Please, my son. Give it up. No good can come of it."

"I disagree."

Avitus could feel his temper flaring. He did his best to control it, but it was rising within him, threatening to explode. He hadn't been this way when he was younger, but the war had changed him, hardened him, made him into someone his civilian friends hadn't been able to recognize.

"The Civs aren't going to play by your rules," Avitus reasoned. "They're opportunistic bastards. That's what they've always been. Back during the Glass War, they were more violent than the Coronians. They slaughtered us."

"Again, you fail to see that that was then, not now," Liston said, trying to illustrate the time continuum to Avitus by pointing to the left as *then* and the right as *now*. He went on, "The political stage has changed drastically in three decades. Commander Heston is more willing to work with Imperium than his predecessor was."

Avitus clenched his fist. "Commander Heston? He was a general during the war."

"He was just doing his job." Avitus had never heard something so foolish come out of Liston's mouth. "But he isn't fighting against us anymore. He's fighting against the Core—politically, anyway. Like us."

"No."

"Well," said Liston, slapping his thigh, "it's a good thing I don't need your permission."

"Don't fight me on this, my Lord Regent. It won't end well."

"Are you threatening me?"

Avitus stood up, towering above the sitting Liston. "Perhaps."

Liston stood up to meet him, though he remained significantly lower to the floor than Avitus. "I've already made up my mind. And I've been in close contact with Ambassador Barringer during this entire process. She has assured me that the Civitan is working to reform its image."

Avitus walked over to his display case, gazing at the various artifacts from his service. One was a Civ flag, its edges tattered and torn, its colors fading. He'd taken that flag from the son of a bitch who'd killed his greatest friend, Jaxton Moore. The flag was a constant reminder of the Civitan's cold-blooded methods.

Jaxton was going to be a father. He was only twenty-two. He was near the end of his contract. He had his whole life before him.

"Tell her it's fruitless," Avitus said, his eyes still on the flag, "that you're pulling out."

"No."

Avitus wheeled around to face Liston. "Why not?"

"Because I don't share your view. I think the Civs, like us, have drifted apart from the Core, and they want our backing, our assurance, that they will be looked after as they fully transition into a sovereign power."

Avitus rested his hand on the display case, hearing Jaxton's final words—"Tell her I love her"—drift through his mind like a haunting lullaby.

"Give it up," he said.

"No."

Avitus had to hand it to Liston: He wasn't going to back down. His mistake.

"Fine," Avitus snapped, his blood boiling. He pulled away from the display case. "Then do it. Make a fool out of yourself again. Just make sure to stay away from whiskey this time. Unless, of course, you really do want to end it. In that case, I'd recommend a razor or a bullet to the head. Quick and efficient."

Avitus sometimes surprised himself with how callous he could be. But he knew Liston's weaknesses and vulnerabilities. If he couldn't get Liston to see the light through reason, he'd bully him into submission.

Liston didn't even flinch. "I'm not going to—"

"That's what you said last time. And yet—"

"I wasn't trying to—"

"Is that what you're telling yourself these days?"

"I wasn't."

"Then what *were* you trying to do?"

"I wanted to escape."

"From what?"

"From everything! Work. The pressure." He slowly looked up at Avitus.

"You."

"Well." Avitus returned to his full height. "If it hadn't been for me, we wouldn't be having this conversation right now. And after everything I've done for you, you could at least be grateful."

"I *am* grateful, Avitus. You're the closest thing I have to a father. But—"

"Then why don't you show it?"

"I do. I—"

Avitus paced the floor like a caged animal. "Five years ago, after the Zenith fiasco, when you locked yourself in your office and drank every whiskey bottle you could get your hands on, you wanted to make sure I'd see it. You wanted me to feel responsible for it."

"No. I didn't."

"But I got there too soon. And you weren't expecting that. When I saw you there, I had two choices. I could've saved you, or I could've left you. And you never thanked me—"

"I'm sure I did."

"No." Avitus halted, now very close to Liston. "You *resented* me for it. Because you wanted to take the coward's way out." Avitus narrowed his eyes. "Never forget the choice I made that day. I could've easily left you there."

Liston looked back at him steadily. "Maybe if you had, you'd finally have a Lord Regent you could be proud of." He then turned away from Avitus and left the office.

Whenever Avitus and Liston quarreled, it was never petty. Avitus knew he'd pushed him too far, mentioning the Zenith incident. It was ancient history. But damnit, Avitus was so angry. Liston was leaving him out of all his decisions lately—the Civitan, of course, but also Raelynn. It was like Avitus didn't exist. And finally, he'd reached his limit.

Yet it was needless, reopening old wounds. The Civitan wasn't worth losing Liston over. Liston hadn't touched a drop of alcohol since that night, and though it took a long time, he and Avitus had started to mend their relationship. The last thing Avitus wanted was to push Liston even further away, back into his wasteful ways. For as long as Avitus had known Liston, he'd used alcohol—particularly whiskey—as a crutch. He was at his worst in his teenage years—belligerent, morose, withdrawn. There'd been such a darkness to him then, the sort of darkness Avitus had seen only in his fellow soldiers. Impressively, though, Liston's alcoholism never impacted his schoolwork; he was the top of his class.

At only nineteen, Liston graduated from the New Caelus Academy—a remarkable feat. After, Avitus encouraged Liston to admit himself into a Vitor-based alcohol treatment center. In no uncertain terms, Avitus told Liston he couldn't hope to build a successful career for himself if he was so dependent on alcohol. Liston may have been able to keep his alcoholism under wraps while at school, but he wouldn't be able to do so once he started working at the high-pressure environment of the Spire. Liston, thankfully, agreed. His admittance into the treatment center was kept confidential, and that was where he spent his summer as an Audilla. When he left the center, there was a lightness to him again, a sense of hope and purpose. He thanked Avitus profusely for his intervention. And, as far as Avitus knew, for the next eleven years, Liston stayed away from alcohol. At the very least, he didn't overindulge. Maybe he had a glass of whiskey every once in a while, but he'd learned how to cut himself off.

Until Zenith. Until Avitus pushed him over the edge.

Avitus shook his head, trying to dispel these thoughts. It was the weekend. Maybe that was what he and Liston needed—a couple days to cool off. Come Spero, they'd both be fresh, and they'd put this whole incident behind them.

After all, they'd been here before. It was just another argument. But they'd get through it.

They always did.

24

BANNER

Banner hated the suburbs. It took him almost two hours to get from his apartment to Kosabeus's house. And that was if everything went smoothly. But Kosabeus had invited him to dinner, and it would've been rude to decline.

Grell was a decent chef, though she cooked only vegan-friendly meals, since Kosabeus had corrupted her into living on the Vitor Diet of rice, beans, and fresh produce. Kosabeus and Grell's two kids, Eddard and Magdalena, went to the most prestigious boarding school in New Caelus. It was a popular choice among Numites and Keepers. Eddard and Magdalena came home for a weekend every month and all major holidays. They were a happy enough family; Kosabeus and Grell clearly loved their children, though they were perhaps not as family-oriented as the Silvers—hence the decision to send their children to boarding school.

Both of their children looked more like Grell than Kosabeus, with their dark hair, brown eyes, and brown skin. There was something about Eddard, however, that puzzled Banner. Sometimes, he'd see something in him that was familiar, but he couldn't quite place it. Eddard was just as sharp as Kosabeus and possessed that same dry wit. The two seemed to enjoy bantering back and forth, as if it was their love language. Banner didn't know how Grell or Magdalena could live with it, though they both seemed amused by it, from what he could tell.

Afterward, Banner and Kosabeus headed to the living room, and Grell bid her goodbyes. Apparently, she was heading back to New Caelus for a girls' night out. Banner thought it was odd, but Kosabeus didn't seem bothered by it.

"You really believe that's why she's going out?" asked Banner.

"Why wouldn't I?"

"Because it sounds like a lie."

"It's the weekend. She has lots of friends. I'd told her to go earlier, but she wanted to eat dinner with the kids." Kosabeus opened the sliding door to the living room. "Go on in."

Kosabeus's whole house reminded Banner of a grandmother's. The furniture was old and upholstered in floral fabrics. Grell's odd collection of creepy dolls and glass jars decorated the shelves and fireplace mantel. It was funny, really, how distinctly un-Kosabeus the house was.

"So, apparently, Avitus and Liston got into a huge row yesterday," Kosabeus said, assuming the persona of a schoolgirl gossiping about someone they mutually hated. "Avitus doesn't support Liston's decision to strike a deal between Imperium and the Civitan."

"So? It's not like Liston needs his permission."

"No, I know. But Avitus, if you recall, hates the Civitan." Kosabeus adjusted one of the lampshades. "Even more than he hates the Core. He feels betrayed by Liston, and I think ... well, Liston might think twice before he tries to continue along that path."

Banner sauntered over to Kosabeus. "How do you know all this?"

"Because I have ears, Cyno. I listen. I do what I can to gauge the current mood around the office."

"No, really. How do you know? Were you talking with Avitus?"

Kosabeus sighed. "Yes, fine," he conceded, brushing his hands against his shirt, pleased with the lampshade's position. "We met up for dinner last night. He was upset—more upset than I've seen him in a while."

"And this concerns me why?"

"Because the alliance may fall through if Liston doesn't have Avitus's backing. Yes, of course, he doesn't need Avitus's support, but Liston craves his approval. I don't see him making such a big decision on his own."

"Again, why should I care?"

"For Mystis's sake, Cyno! How daft are you?"

"What do you mean, how—?"

"If this alliance implodes, Liston would suffer a PR disaster, just like he did with Zenith. It'd destroy his credibility, and if you play your cards right, you could paint him as a complete incompetent. Maybe even get him out of office. Then who knows? Maybe Nisha would take over as Lord Regent."

"Nisha?" Banner scrunched his nose. "Why her?"

"She'd be more ... open to working with you."

"Is she an Expansionist?"

"No."

Banner raised an eyebrow. "Then why would she be any different?"

Kosabeus sighed. "Nisha and I knew each other back in Vitor. Let's just say, she ... fancied me."

Banner grinned. "Did she, now?"

"Yes. I didn't reciprocate, but ... we've remained friendly."

"And Grell's okay with that?"

"Why wouldn't she be?"

To Banner, Grell seemed like the type of woman who thrived on jealousy. She certainly had when she was with Bayne. She'd hated the fact that Bayne had female friends. Granted, Bayne was, in fact, sleeping with most of them, but that didn't mean Grell had the right to try and control Bayne.

"I don't buy it," said Banner. "There's no way you and Nisha are on good terms. If she loved you, and you didn't love her back, why would she ever—?"

"Because nothing bad ever happened between us. It just ... I didn't look at her like that."

"Why not? Nisha's hot."

"How ... chivalrous of you."

"She is!"

"She's not my type."

Banner looked at him, his eyes narrowed. "It was always Grell for you, wasn't it?"

Kosabeus rubbed the nape of his neck. "I don't ... not 'always.' Once we got to know each other and—"

"But you always wanted Grell. You wanted Grell when you couldn't have her. When she was with my son."

There was an uncomfortable silence between the two of them. Bayne was a topic they knew to avoid, for obvious reasons. Kosabeus had swooped in and claimed Grell as his own barely a week after Bayne's death. Banner knew that Bayne and Grell had been broken up for months at that point, but in his final days, Bayne had seemed adamant that he and Grell would get back together. Banner hadn't exactly approved of Bayne and Grell's relationship, but he wanted his son to be happy. What Kosabeus did was nothing short of betrayal in Banner's eyes, and he'd made sure that Kosabeus knew how livid he was about the whole situation.

Slowly, Banner and Kosabeus reconciled, and Kosabeus promised Banner he and Grell were not involved while she was with Bayne. And though Banner was still hurt, he did trust Kosabeus. Besides, Banner had to admit, Kosabeus treated Grell far better than Bayne had. To Bayne, Grell was maybe just a temporary amusement, someone he would've eventually outgrown. But to Kosabeus, Grell was the whole universe.

"I never touched Grell when she was with Bayne," Kosabeus said for the millionth time. "I've told you that."

"I know." Banner looked at his feet. He hated thinking about Bayne. "I'm just saying. You wanted Grell for a long time."

"Is that a crime?"

Banner shrugged. "I guess not."

Banner could, after all, see the appeal. Most obviously, of course, Grell was beautiful. Indeed, if she hadn't been with Bayne—and now Kosabeus—Banner would have absolutely pursued her. There was something utterly mystifying about her. All too easily, Grell could pull people in and charm them—especially men. Men, she could wrap like ribbon around her finger. She was an asset to the Church, able to wring numa from even the stingiest congregants.

Kosabeus walked over to the curtains, fine-tuning them. Banner sometimes wondered how Kosabeus could live a good life, with his incessant need to fix things that were out of place. If it wasn't curtains, it was a lampshade or a pillow or a rug.

"Well, the elections are coming up," Kosabeus said, tugging on the curtains, no doubt desperate to change the subject. "How do you think they're going?"

"We'll get a majority, no problem."

Currently, thirty-four of the seventy seats in the Cooperative were dominated by Expansionists, while the Affiliates claimed twenty-four and the Grounders twelve. All the seats were up for reelection in three months' time. Cooperative elections were held every five years, while smaller local elections were held every two years. This just so happened to be one of those years when both the Cooperative elections and local elections were taking place. Banner was positive the Expansionists would maintain control of the Cooperative and pick up seats in various local contests. He hoped that would put the Affiliates back in their place. They'd been rather gutsy lately, making all sorts of outlandish, unfounded claims about the Expansionists.

"That would solidify your position," said Kosabeus, still unsatisfied with the curtains.

"My position is already solidified. I've been Head of the Assembly ever since Carbury died. You know that."

"Ah, Carbury." Kosabeus drew the curtains more to the left. "He was a wing nut."

"He was a great Expansionist leader. One of the best." Banner walked over to the bar, scanning the various liquors. "Don't you have any whiskey?" he growled.

"Grell doesn't drink whiskey," laughed Kosabeus.

"So, what, you drink these fruity concoctions with her?"

"You know I don't drink."

Banner groaned. "You and your Vitor 'purity of the body' crap."

"I'll have you know, I am in optimal health."

"Don't feed me that bullshit. You had cancer."

Kosabeus's cancer diagnosis was a well-kept secret. Only the higher-ups at the Church and Banner knew about it. The news had been shocking. Kosabeus was young—only thirty-seven at the time—so the thought of him dying like that was unfathomable. The Church, for its part, didn't want their Head Prophate to appear weak, so they had considered forcing Kosabeus to resign, despite his immense popularity. After all, Kosabeus's prognosis had been beyond dreadful; the doctors had all but written his obituary.

Kosabeus, however, had refused to step down, saying he would continue to serve as Head Prophate until his dying breath. He did so with mesmerizing grace and strength. When Kosabeus told Banner about it, he was his usual sarcastic self, making all these little quips about how Mystis gave his hardest challenges to his best warriors. But Banner had seen something in Kosabeus's eyes that night that he had never seen before or since: fear.

When Kosabeus entered remission, it was nothing short of a miracle. He just had his six-month checkup last week, and he was, by all accounts, doing very well. Imperium had made stunning advancements in medical technology over the past few decades, and the possibility of curing cancer was no longer a pipe dream. In fact, it seemed like something they would witness in their lifetime.

Kosabeus chuckled. "Well, I feel wonderful, truly wonderful. Grell has been such a blessing, standing by me through all of it. And, for what's it worth, the cancer had nothing to do with my diet."

"Well, you know, just to be safe, when I get back to the city, I'm going to the nearest food vendor and getting some cheap, greasy meat."

"Mmmm." Kosabeus met Banner by the bar. "Sounds ... fatty."

"It's food. Real food. Not that vegan garbage."

"I thought you liked Grell's cooking."

"I'd like it better if it had meat. And I'd like coming here more if you had whiskey."

Kosabeus glimpsed at the liquor bottles. "I've never seen the appeal of getting drunk. Because of my abstinence, my mind is clear."

"You and Grell aren't having sex?"

Kosabeus gave him a weary look. "Abstinence from *drinking*, Cyno."

"Oh. Gotcha." Banner winked, leaning against the bar. "By the way, have you gotten anywhere with Caine's request?"

"You mean the request he asked you to complete?"

"And the one I pawned off on you. Yes, exactly."

"No."

"Why not?"

"Because I've been busy. I've made some inquiries, but they've all led to a brick wall."

"Where's the wall?"

Kosabeus stared at him, long and hard. "I was being metaphoric. A brick wall. You know. Nowhere. They all led me nowhere."

"Don't act like that was obvious."

"You thought there was a literal brick wall I kept finding?"

"Yeah, sure. Why not?"

"You seriously need help," laughed Kosabeus, straightening the liquors Banner had just touched—and wiping them off, for good measure.

Banner crossed his arms. "You afraid I have cooties?"

"Yes," replied Kosabeus flatly. His eyes found the clock. "But it's getting late,

Cyno. You should go. I have to check on the kids, make sure they're getting ready for bed."

"How fun."

"I've rather missed them, so I'm looking forward to it."

"When are you expecting Grell back?"

"Late. Why?"

"It's just weird, that's all, her going out this time of night." Banner raised an eyebrow. "You really don't think she's hiding something from you?"

"Why would she?"

"Because she's a liar."

"Grell doesn't lie."

"She did to Bayne."

Banner said it before he could stop himself. He knew it was a low blow, that he couldn't keep bringing up Bayne, but he couldn't help it. Deep down, there was a part of him that still hated Kosabeus for what he'd done.

"Well, she doesn't lie to me," said Kosabeus, no trace of frustration in his voice. He gestured toward the door, as if Banner didn't know where it was. "Now, have a pleasant trip back, Cyno. And please, don't call me. I don't want to hear your voice until Spero."

25

TAYMOR

Taymor always hated saying goodbye to Embry, but she knew she'd have to get used to it. Embry was all grown up, and she was doing something she genuinely loved. Taymor didn't want to hold her back.

She met up with Liston at his townhouse. She needed a distraction, she'd told him, something to get her mind off Embry and Tarness. As always, Liston obliged, and they'd spent the next couple of hours chatting about all sorts of nonsense—books, radio shows, places they'd love to go. It had always been like that with Liston—easy and comfortable. They had the same intellectual curiosity, and they loved playfully sparring with each other.

After a particularly spirited debate about term limits—something Taymor and Puck had been discussing a lot in their meetings—Liston sat down at his piano, tracing his fingers across the keys, refamiliarizing himself with them. He started playing a beautiful ballad. Liston had a brilliant memory. He had to look at something only once, and he'd remember it forever. He never needed any sheet music.

"I haven't played in a while," Liston said distractedly, deeply focused on the music, his eyes glazing over in concentration.

Taymor touched her necklace, swaying to the sounds. "You sound perfect to me."

Liston looked up at her. "That's kind of you to say."

"Well, it's true. You always look so happy when you're playing."

Liston disappeared, then, into a haze of melodies and rhythms. He was still in the room, of course, but his mind was elsewhere, floating around in some other world. Taymor let him wander. She knew he'd find his way home eventually. And sure enough, after a few minutes, he snapped back to reality, surprised to see her still standing there.

"Sorry, Farzah," he said, slowing down. "I spaced out there."

"You always get like that when there's something on your mind you're trying to forget."

Liston shrugged, stroking the keys. "Just a lot of tedious things."

Taymor walked over to him, placing her hand on top of the piano. "Call me crazy, but I think it's healthier to talk it out rather than just bottling it up and hoping it goes away."

Liston heaved a deep sigh, turning away from the keys. "It's Avitus."

"Ah." Taymor sat down next to him on the bench.

"He has this ... idea of what I should be. But that's not who I am. And I don't understand"—he clasped his hands together—"I don't understand why that isn't enough for him."

"Levin. You're more than enough for him. For all of us."

Liston furrowed his eyebrows, looking down at the keys. "You should have seen the look in his eyes, Farzah. It was like ... like it was Zenith all over again. And I just ... I needed to get away. There's too much history in his eyes, sometimes."

Taymor touched his arm. "You can't keep blaming yourself for that. You did everything you could. It isn't your fault the ceasefire on Zenith fell through. Avitus just ... expects too much."

Liston toyed with his sleeve. "Well, that's why I ..." He trailed off, his gaze lingering on the whiskey bottles for a beat too long.

Taymor was proud of Liston for getting sober, and he'd been doing so well, but she was always scared that in times of extreme stress, Liston would fall back into it. She'd asked him a thousand times to get rid of all his bottles, but he promised her he wasn't tempted. They were there to test his willpower, he'd told her, nothing more; he was never going to drink again. And she believed him. But with these renewed tensions with Avitus—not to mention all the election nonsense—Taymor was frightened that Liston would be pushed over the edge.

"Anyway," Liston said, turning away, starting to play again.

Taymor listened to him for a few moments, giving him time to cool off. "May I ask why Avitus brought up Zenith again?"

"He's upset about my proposed alliance with the Civitan."

"Because of their association with the Core?"

"And because the Civs killed a lot of Imperials during the Glass War. And, you know—"

"—that was when Avitus served."

Liston nodded, his fingers still dancing up and down the keys. He shook his head, unhappy with his chosen chord. He adjusted his position.

"I've been keeping him out of the loop on everything," Liston went on. "Because ... well ... I don't know." He abruptly stopped playing. "Ever since that night ... he thinks we're fine, you know. He thinks we've ... moved past it. But I haven't."

Taymor scooted closer to him. "Have you brought it up with the Church? Maybe they can get you a new Prophate."

Liston laughed, despite himself. "Not a chance. They love Avitus. He's a war hero."

"But if you don't feel comfortable talking to him—"

"Avitus would never let me replace him. I just have to ... get over it."

"And how do you plan on doing that?"

"The same way I always do. I'll just tell him it's okay, I know he didn't mean anything, that we're fine. That always does the trick."

"That's insane! You can't let Avitus think it's okay to—"

"Avitus doesn't do 'feelings.' All he cares about is whether I'm doing my job well. And in his view, since I'm trying to negotiate an alliance with someone who was our enemy three decades ago, I'm failing him. It's always black and white with him. He doesn't understand we aren't at war with the Civitan anymore. And he seems to think this ... standoff with the Core is a legitimate war, that our soldiers are facing each other on the battlefield."

"It's not his choice what you do or don't do." Her fingers interlaced with Liston's. Something akin to an electric shock pulsed through her, but she ignored it, like she always did.

"But Avitus doesn't see it the way I do."

"It's not about what he thinks. It's about what *you* think. Your people put you in charge, not Avitus. It's you they believe in. You can't let Avitus shake your convictions. Seeing you work on this ... it's made me so happy for you. It's something you really care about. The Civitan today isn't the same as it was thirty years ago. And if Avitus can't see that, tough. The fact of that matter is *you* see that. And if the elections go your way ... there's a high likelihood of the alliance moving forward."

Taymor could sense that Liston's mood had alleviated. There was a warmth to him again, a buoyancy.

"You're right, Farzah," he said, a reignited flame of passion in his eyes. "I can't give it up. And not just because of Avitus but ... because it's what's right." Liston glimpsed down at the piano. "Well, how about I play some more for you?"

"I'd love that."

And then, once again, Liston's music filled the room, and Taymor felt at home.

26

ASTROPHEL

Even though Whitner was a Lord Regent, swimming in numa, he lived a humble life, residing in an astonishingly simple one-bedroom apartment with minimal amenities and a rather unattractive view of a back alley. It was the kind of apartment that was meant to be a first-time home for some twenty-something just out of university, not a grown man with a legitimate job. Whitner's neighbors were decades younger than he was.

"The rent's cheap," Whitner had said once, offhand. "And it's just me. I don't need anything more."

True enough, Astrophel thought, though he couldn't help but wonder what Whitner *did* spend his numa on. It certainly wasn't his wardrobe; that was also astonishingly simple. He had been wearing the same brown and tan suits for decades, with the same boring, ugly ties. When his suits ripped, he'd take them to be mended.

Whitner's way of life baffled Astrophel. Though a man of the Church, Astrophel enjoyed the finer things in life. Whitner teased him about it, telling him he was too into his looks. And maybe he was. But Astrophel couldn't imagine living the way Whitner did, refusing to throw out even moldy bread because "I paid for it, didn't I?"

He and Whitner had just had dinner—a steak that was more like a slab of concrete than something edible. But apparently, that was how Whitner liked his steak—cooked to the point of being charred. Astrophel wondered how Whitner had any teeth left.

"I know I'm an awful cook," Whitner started, his couch squeaking as he leaned back into it. "But, in my defense, I didn't think you were coming over tonight."

"Well, I wanted to see how you've been holding up with all that Banner, Kosabeus, and Harlyn drama."

Whitner took a sip of his port. "They keep me out of it."

"And you're okay with that?"

Whitner laughed. "When you get to be my age, Astrophel," he said with a languid wave, "you'll realize it isn't half as exciting being in the middle of things as you think."

Whitner spoke of his age as though he were ninety. He wasn't even sixty; statistically speaking, he still had plenty of life left. Astrophel wasn't sure why he was so adamant that his best days were behind him.

Astrophel rested his glass of port on the coffee table, turning to face Whitner, his movements causing the couch to squeak some more. He winced.

"I'm curious ... what's your stance on Liston's proposed alliance with the Civitan?" asked Astrophel.

"Why do you ask?"

"Because people are talking about it. I heard Avitus going off about it the other day. It's important. And it'll probably end up affecting you."

"If it goes anywhere. Which is still unlikely. Liston would need the Cooperative's backing."

"Which he might get, if the elections go his way."

"And they very well may."

"Doesn't that bother you? You're an Expansionist. You should be standing up against this alliance, doing something. For all we know, the Civitan is still allied with the Core."

"What? No. They're trying to break away from the Core."

"So they say. But what if they're not? What if it's all a ruse, a way to trick us into a conflict we're not ready for? That's what Avitus says, anyway. And he would know."

Whitner crossed his legs, studying Astrophel carefully. "You don't think highly of them, do you? The Civs."

"Of course not. You know our history with them."

"Our *ancient* history with them," corrected Whitner.

"That still affects our present." Astrophel reached for his glass of port. "We can't just forget what the Core did."

"But we can forgive."

"It's too late for that. After everything they did to us? We can't just forgive them."

"But maybe we should."

"I don't know how you can say that. Weren't you close with Bayne?"

Whitner heaved a deep breath. "Don't bring Bayne into this," he snapped. "It isn't fair."

"But the Core—"

"It was never proven that the Core was behind that attack."

"Are you kidding me? There was no other—"

"It could've been an accident."

"It was on purpose. And we just let the Core get away with it."

"That's not—"

"That's the way I've always seen it."

"So, what, the only solution is total annihilation—us or them?"

"It'll have to be them."

Whitner shook his head. "I've never believed that. And, for the record, if Bayne were still alive, he wouldn't want that either."

"He'd still be alive if it weren't for the Core." Astrophel took a sip of his port, eyeing Whitner. "I don't know why you're acting like what I'm saying is crazy. You should be agreeing with me. You're supposed to be an Expansionist too, Dane."

"And I am," said Whitner hastily, running his fingers through his hair. "But I'm also rational." He sighed. "And we can debate politics all you want, but please, I ... don't use Bayne against me." Whitner paused. "You know, it's bad enough, knowing that he worked in my division, that he only died because I—"

"Surely, you don't—?"

"I think about it every day. I wonder why we didn't double check our intel, why—"

"It wasn't your fault." Astrophel met his eyes. "Nobody blames you."

"Cyno did, for a bit."

"He was just angry."

"And he had a right to be. I would've hated me too, if I were him, if he'd killed my son."

"You didn't kill Bayne."

"Mmmm." Whitner looked up at his ceiling. "I will always have those two hundred and thirty-three deaths on my conscience. That's just something I have to live with."

"You shouldn't have to."

"But that's what comes with a position like this, Astrophel. You make the calls, you make the decisions, and sometimes ..." Whitner trailed off. "Anyway." He reached across and touched Astrophel's arm. "But I'm sorry. I didn't mean to bring the mood down or—"

"Don't apologize for missing Bayne. It just means you loved him."

"I did." Whitner's eyes glistened with tears. "So much." He cleared his throat. "But I don't really ... you were talking about the Core, yes?"

"We don't—"

"No, no. It's quite fun, hearing your take on these things." Whitner readjusted his position. "So, you have strong feelings on Liston's proposed alliance with the

Civitan?"

"I do. And I think you and Banner should stand up against this alliance, make it clear that what Liston is trying to do goes against the very foundations of our government."

"That's not really our place, Astrophel."

"Of course, it is! Who else's place would it be? Only you two can stand up to Liston."

Whitner stared at Astrophel, his eyebrows furrowed in wonderment. "I don't know what to make of you," he said at last.

"How do you mean?"

"You're so ... different from Garin."

"And you think that's a bad thing."

"I don't know. You're certainly more ... dynamic than he was."

"I have political views. Is it so wrong for me to share them with you? We're both Expansionists, are we not?"

"No, I know. It just ... it surprises me. That's all."

"Because I'm a Numite?"

"No. A lot of you young Numites are politically outspoken. We have Kosabeus to thank for that, I guess."

"I vote. I should be allowed to express my views in whichever way I deem fit."

"Fair enough." Whitner raised his glass to him. "Can't argue with that."

Things had improved between them over the past few weeks. Whitner seemed to be more at ease with Astrophel, which was good. This meant Astrophel was getting somewhere with him. With a little more prodding, he might be able to encourage Whitner to make his presence known this election season, to announce to all of Imperium that he was a force to be reckoned with.

"Then here's to the Expansionists and their bright future," said Astrophel, clinking glasses with Whitner.

"I'll drink to that."

RAELYNN

Corlander had taken the initiative and excused Raelynn from work for the next couple of days. Apparently, she wasn't needed in the office, so she could take some time off and rest up. Work would resume on Spero, at the start of a new week. Raelynn was incredibly grateful, and she took the opportunity to explore the city.

She visited the Glass War Museum, which commemorated the service of all the men and women who had defended Imperium from the Core's encroachments. The revered Imperial General Gorman Whitlock had famously said, "This war is shattering us, like we are nothing but glass." The name stuck, and the conflict raged on for thirty-five long, bloody years. It was chilling, reading the names of all the fallen soldiers. Tens of millions of people had died, on both sides. Raelynn couldn't envision what it'd been like on the front lines, with gunshots echoing all around like an amphitheater. She was a self-admitted coward. She couldn't imagine what it must feel like, staring down the barrel of a gun.

Since her birth, Imperium and the Core had been engaged in a staring contest of sorts, building up their arsenals, improving their technology, energizing their people with patriotic sermons. The Glass War had ended inconclusively twenty-five years ago. Though Imperium came out as the alleged victor, as it gained more planets than it lost, both sides had lost an unfathomable number of soldiers, and nothing had substantially changed. Somehow, the Head of the Assembly at the time, Nicolai Carbury, had managed to put a spin on it, saying that the Glass War had successfully stopped the Core's incursion into Imperial territory. This was, for the most part, true. In the aftermath, the Core floundered, unable to recoup its economic or military losses. But the shame of defeat still lingered, and the Core desperately wanted revenge.

Indeed, despite the Glass War's cessation, the Core had never truly given up, and ever since, it'd been refining itself, trying to match Imperium's technological prowess. Those enlisted in the military didn't see conflict. Their purpose was to defend Imperial outposts, to demonstrate Imperial superiority, to send a clear message to the Core that Imperium did not cower in the face of danger.

The closest the Core and Imperium had come to combat in recent memory was ten years ago, when the Core allegedly shot an Imperial Intelligence ship to smithereens, unprovoked. The Core's guilt was never proven, and the Core had steadfastly denied any responsibility, but Banner and many others in the government had tried to use that as a way of finally declaring war on the Core. The Cooperative, however, had narrowly—and controversially—killed that motion, saying there wasn't enough evidence, that they couldn't be sure whether the Core had been behind it. Apparently, the Intelligence ship had been experiencing engine trouble in the days leading up to the tragedy, so it was possible that the explosion had actually been more of an implosion—and thus nothing more than a catastrophic accident. To this day, many Imperials still grumbled about it, wondering why the Cooperative had allowed the Core to get off so easily. Some muttered about cover-ups and bribes, but Raelynn was grateful. War wouldn't have solved anything.

Banner, Raelynn knew, was beyond frustrated with the lack of progress. In his view, Imperium couldn't rest until the Core was soundly beaten in war. He continually argued for more funds, more soldiers, more weapons ... but to no avail. The Glass War had defined multiple generations, but younger people—having grown up hearing and learning about the horrors of the Glass War—were war-weary. They didn't want to vote for a war that too many of them would be forced to die in.

Currently, the Cooperative was Expansionist-dominated, but because the Expansionists didn't command a majority, they couldn't pass their military-oriented measures on their own. Consequently, the military remained significantly smaller than Banner would've preferred—though the Imperial military was still the largest military in the universe, with millions of active personnel spread across several worlds.

Raelynn slowly explored the museum, wanting to take it all in. There were all sorts of artifacts from the Glass War, such as uniforms, weapons, and letters. There was artwork too. During and after the Glass War, Imperials had struggled to make sense of all the death and destruction, so they turned to art for answers. Oftentimes, visual mediums could convey emotions that words could never adequately capture.

"Lord Mabry?"

Raelynn wheeled around and saw Caine. "High Justice Caine. Uh. Good afternoon."

Caine stepped closer to her. "What brings you to this place?"

"I wanted to take in some history."

"Always a good thing to do." Caine smiled. "I come every so often, you know. I had a friend who served in the Glass War. He ... didn't make it. I guess coming here ... it's my way of keeping him alive."

"I'm so sorry."

"Don't be." Caine smiled wryly. "He lives on every time someone says his name. Damascus Ravel. There. I have just given him life once more. But I didn't mean to startle you. I just ... I saw you, and I recognized you, and ... I thought I would be polite and say hello."

"No apologies necessary. I was just kind of ... spaced out."

"This is as good a place as any to do that." Caine stared straight ahead at the painting in front of them. It depicted soldiers on a battlefield. "Remarkable, isn't it, what humans are capable of when they're put under pressure?"

"They were far braver than I'll ever be."

"You'll never know unless you're tested. But, of course, I hope for your sake that you're not. My generation suffered enough during the Glass War. We don't want the same for you." Caine turned to Raelynn. "But how's everything with you? Liston's not working you too hard, is he?"

"No. Everything's been great."

"Well, that's good. He certainly went to a lot of trouble to get you on his team, so I'm glad he's treating you well."

Raelynn didn't really know what to say. Caine wasn't doing anything wrong, per se, but it made Raelynn uncomfortable, engaging in small talk like this. What was Caine's end goal? Did he want to become friends with Raelynn? That seemed odd. Caine and Raelynn had next to nothing in common. What sort of friendship could they ever hope to have?

"You know, I'd like to talk more about this in a less ... inappropriate venue," Caine said after a few moments. "Cyno and I were going to have dinner next Domus. I was wondering if you'd care to join us."

"Cyno ... Banner?"

"Is that a problem?"

Of course, it was a problem. Everyone knew how much Banner and Liston disliked one another. Their rivalry wasn't news. Why did Caine think that Raelynn would want to sit across the table from her boss's political nemesis? This was far too strange. She felt like she'd entered an alternate reality.

"I really ... I don't think that's a good idea," Raelynn said at last.

"Oh, come, now. It'll be harmless. What, Liston doesn't allow you to enjoy the company of Expansionists?"

"No, it's not that. I just ... he and Lord Regent Banner aren't really ... close."

Caine smiled. "I think you'll find that Cyno is not at all as Liston describes."

Raelynn knew this wasn't the case. Even before she'd met Liston, she'd heard all sorts of stories about Banner—and most of them were unflattering. She wasn't sure why Caine was trying to convince her of Banner's virtues. Was he under the impression that she was an Expansionist sympathizer, that she didn't view their party as morally bankrupt and extreme? Raelynn didn't want to be rude—particularly not to the High Justice—but she couldn't understand why he had put her in this position. Why were he and Banner so eager to have dinner with her? And what were they hoping to accomplish by doing so? Did they think they'd be able to cause some sort of schism between Raelynn and Liston? Or were they simply fishing for information?

"I'm sorry. I ... I don't want to, um ... intrude," said Raelynn.

"I'm inviting you."

"I know. But ... it might be ... there might be something going on."

"You'll be missing out. We have reservations at Starlight. It has some of the best views of the New Caelus skyline. Truly breathtaking. And the food ... well, the food is sublime."

The way he was talking, Raelynn could tell that Caine wasn't going to take no for an answer. His eye contact was far too direct, and Raelynn didn't know how much longer she could hold out. Her best course of action was to delay.

"I, um ... well, I don't know," Raelynn sputtered. "I'll have to, um, check my schedule, make sure that nothing else is going on. How about I call you later, let you know then?"

Caine and Raelynn exchanged numbers. Afterward, Raelynn made her way to Liston's office. She needed to talk to Liston about all of this. She knew that Liston wouldn't approve. But hopefully, he'd give Raelynn a good excuse so she could politely decline Caine's offer and go on with her life.

When Raelynn reached Liston's office, she saw the door was already ajar. Her eyes widened as soon as she stepped inside. Liston's office was nothing short of an engineering feat. Somehow, they'd managed to build an underwater office. Three of the four walls were dominated by windows. There was also a full bar, which was stocked with nothing but whiskey. Through the windows, Raelynn could see various fish, turtles, and stingrays swimming about. The ocean's waves played along the wall, making it seem as though the room were swaying. Raelynn hoped that the windows were strong enough to hold all that water back.

"Raelynn." Liston stood to meet her, adjusting his glasses with his forefinger. "I wasn't expecting you. What do you need?"

"Well, I just ..." Raelynn's eyes lingered on the bar. She furrowed her eyebrows. "I've never seen you drink," she said matter-of-factly.

"Pardon?"

"You've taken me out to dinner a few times, and I've been to your home, but I've never ... I've never seen you drink. And yet—"

"—and yet I surround myself with whiskey."

"Exactly. Why?" Seeing Liston's shoulders tense, Raelynn added, "No, you know what? Never mind. I don't need to know. It's none of my business."

"No, it's fine. You ... should know." Liston heaved a deep breath. "I used to drink. More than I care to admit. But I ... stopped because I ..." He trailed off, running his fingers through his hair. "I don't know why this is so difficult to tell you," he admitted.

"You don't have to—"

"No, I do. It's time." He met Raelynn's eyes. "I'm an alcoholic," he said at last. "That's why I stopped."

Raelynn swallowed hard. "I ... I'm so sorry. I didn't know."

Liston smiled wryly. "Yes, that was rather by design. Avitus did everything he could to make sure that'd never get out."

"Well, if it helps, he did a good job. Because I never ..." Raelynn cocked her head to the side. "It's just ... you don't ... look like an alcoholic."

"And what, in your view, does an alcoholic look like?"

"I dunno. Not ... this. Not a Lord Regent."

Liston laughed, despite himself. "I'm sure that's meant to be a compliment, but—"

"I'm sorry. I just … I didn't …" Raelynn's eyes again settled on the bar. "Then why do you still keep it around? Isn't that … dangerous?"

"Because I need to be tempted. That's the only way I … yes, sure, I could try to live in a world where I never have to see whiskey again, but that's not real. This …" He motioned toward the bar. "… this is real. And it's something I have to choose to avoid. You understand?"

"Sure," said Raelynn, though she didn't.

It seemed like a bad idea to her, but what did she know? She wasn't Liston. Maybe this was what worked for him. At the very least, his admission helped her understand him more. Previously, she'd been under the impression there were no skeletons in his closet. Like all politicians, of course, Liston had his fair share of public blunders and missteps, but his personal life had always been a well-kept secret. Everyone knew about Banner's dalliances; everyone knew about the Silver family; everyone knew that Abner was currently going through his third divorce. No one knew a thing about Liston's home life. Now Raelynn knew why: Avitus. He'd clearly gone to great lengths to protect Liston's image. Raelynn was impressed he'd managed to keep something as volatile as Liston's alcoholism from the Imperial media—and the Expansionists.

Liston leaned against his desk, eyeing her carefully. "Was that why you came to see me?"

"What? Oh. No. I wanted to tell you about High Justice Caine."

"What about him?"

As succinctly as possible, Raelynn explained the conversation she'd had with Caine to Liston, and to her absolute shock—

"Oh, you're going," Liston said.

"What? Why?"

"Because it's an adventure, Raelynn. It's exciting. Aren't you curious about what they want?"

"No."

"Well, *I* am. So, you're going to go, enjoy a free meal, and then come back and tell me everything.”

“But ... it’s Banner.”

“And I’m sure it’ll be a dinner to remember. Make sure you dress well. Starlight is quite fancy, you know.”

Raelynn looked down at her outfit. “What’s wrong with what I’m wearing?”

Liston laughed. “It’s fine for work, but ... you don’t want to give Banner and Caine any more ammunition than they already have.”

“You really think what I’m wearing is that hideous? That it isn’t good enough for some restaurant?”

Liston pretended to busy himself by looking over some paperwork. He skillfully avoided Raelynn’s eyes, acting as if she had already left.

“Wow, okay,” said Raelynn, shaking her head. “So, this whole time, you’ve just been judging my wardrobe?”

“Go to Ludo’s,” Liston said, not even looking up. “They sell the best suits and dresses in New Caelus. They’ll tailor them right there for you.”

“Can I afford that?”

“Just put it on my tab.” Sensing Raelynn’s discomfort, Liston added, “Consider it an investment. And a gift. For the work we’ll be doing together, you’ll need to, you know, look the part. So, go. Have fun. But not *too* much fun. I don’t want you becoming an Expansionist on me.”

28

KOSABEUS

Kosabeus had spent the last hour and a half in the Fiscus Room with the Treasury Committee, discussing the dismal state of the Church's finances. The Fiscus Room was one of his favorite rooms in the Church; it was adorned with glass images of Mystis's rise, fall, and redemption. The mahogany table was situated under the skylight, which illuminated the Crest of Mystis etched into the table.

As Head Prophate, Kosabeus shouldered dozens of responsibilities, such as giving at least five sermons a week, leading the inauguration of new Erates into the Church, delivering the eulogy at the funerals of high-ranking Numites, and bimonthly hosting a soiree for all New Caelus–based Numites at his house. But by far, the worst of his duties was dealing with the inept Treasury Committee.

"We haven't met our fundraising goal?" Kosabeus asked, his arms crossed.

"No," one of the Treasury Committee members admitted, adjusting his glasses with his chubby thumb. "Not yet."

"Why not?"

"Because there isn't as much interest," he clumsily explained. "People want something to go to, some kind of event. They aren't going to give us numa just because we ask them nicely. They want something in return."

Kosabeus couldn't believe how useless this committee was, lecturing him because they couldn't do their jobs. This was why the Church was accused of being irrelevant. This was why he had done everything in his power to revitalize the Church, to help it catch up with the times. For years, the Church had dragged behind the rest of Imperium. It'd been bogged down by its incompetent hierarchy and socially unaware officials. The Treasury Committee, it seemed, was the embodiment of all these vices, somehow managing to waste money on doing nothing.

Kosabeus didn't even try to cover his yawn. This meeting was supposed to last only twenty minutes, but here they were, an hour later, and practically nothing had been accomplished. Next time, he would try and pawn this off on someone else—someone gullible.

"Fine," said Kosabeus exasperatedly. "Well, we have that Numite party coming up soon. What if we open it up to the general public, turn it into a fundraiser for the Church? We make sure we invite a lot of Keepers—especially the Lord Regents and the Lord Dynasts—and we appeal to their innate sense of charity, their love for the Church."

They liked that idea. By attending the party, Imperials from all walks of life would be able to see for themselves all the good the Church did—and just how pervasive the Church was in their daily lives. Truly, most Imperials weren't aware that Numites didn't just work in the Church; many worked as therapists, caretakers, and tutors, and they were active, involved members of their community. At this party, the Numites would request—not demand—donations, and they could use that numa to fill up their dismal coffers.

"Good work, Kosabeus," one of the men said. "We'll get right on that."

As Kosabeus left, he cursed them out. What the hell did they do all day? They were supposed to be on top of this, not him. It was their job to drum up support for the Church. He'd served his time on the Treasury Committee; he had the empty ibuprofen bottles to prove it.

He entered his office and took off his robe. He'd been running on too little sleep for far too long. Though Kosabeus had always been politically inclined, even he had to admit, election season was far too long. Unofficially, election season ran for seven months—from Partura to Ciemo. The first three months, from Partura to Sidum, the parties prepared their lists of candidates and determined how much numa they would invest in each race. Three people ran for each Cooperative seat—one from each party. One of those people was defending the seat, either as the incumbent or as the candidate the party named to take a retiring or deceased representative's place. The other two were the challengers, attempting to steal the seat for their party.

Historically, incumbents had a high chance of reelection in Imperium. But in recent years, political novices had been securing more contests, altering the makeup of the Cooperative. More Numites were running for office. Kosabeus welcomed this change, as Imperial politics seemed, as of late, to be severely lacking in piety. Too many politicians—especially Expansionist politicians—emulated Banner, engaging in sexually promiscuous activities and making headlines for all the wrong reasons. Consequently, the public wasn't as hospitable to the Expansionist Party as it'd been in previous cycles.

Banner, for his part, was not doing all he could to mobilize Expansionists across Imperium. Even more strangely, he wasn't doing much to repair his tainted image. He didn't seem at all concerned about the elections; on the contrary, he seemed to think the Expansionists were in a comfortable position. Most recently, his cabinet's rash decision to push through Harlyn Harries as his Lord Dynast had raised more than a few eyebrows. It was widely known in political circles that Banner and Harlyn were involved, and the idea of a Lord Regent and their Lord Dynast being romantically linked concerned a lot of people, including Kosabeus. He'd told Banner how it'd look to the outside world, but Banner was determined. He wanted Harlyn, and he was going to get her.

Expertly, Kosabeus was able to distance himself from Banner; he'd been doing that for years. After all, though he and Banner were both Expansionists, Kosabeus was a Mystic Expansionist. Mystic Expansionists wanted to liberate other planets from the Core's tyranny and annex them as Imperial territories, but they believed in doing so by encouraging those planets to leave the Core by holding referendums. In Kosabeus's opinion, the main wing of the Expansionist Party had become sullied; they were so war-hungry that they had completely lost sight of their morality. The universe didn't need more war; it needed to stand up to repression, wherever it was, and root it out. The Core could be broken up, piece by piece, without ever having to pull a trigger.

"Kosabeus?"

Kosabeus looked up. It was Avitus, not wearing his black robe. That was unusual. Kosabeus had assumed the Prophate robe was surgically attached to Avitus.

"What is it?"

"My Lord Regent," said Avitus, an unnerving humanity in his eyes. "I haven't met with him in ... a while. I've tried calling him, but he never picks up." Avitus shifted on his feet. "I don't know what to do."

It was unsettling, seeing Avitus so vulnerable. He, as a former soldier, was highly disciplined, able to conceal his emotions effortlessly. In all his years of knowing and admiring Avitus, Kosabeus had never once seen him cry. No one in the Church had. There were conflicting theories as to why. Some simply chose to believe it was because Avitus was a true man, and true men didn't cry. Others—those less corrupted by stifling gender roles—purported that Avitus had cried all his tears during the Glass War, for his fallen comrades, and he had no more to shed.

"Have you gone to his office?" offered Kosabeus, standing up.

"I don't want to confront him. I want him to come to me, on his own terms." He fidgeted with his sleeve. "He needs me."

"Clearly, he doesn't think so."

Right away, Kosabeus knew he shouldn't have gone for the joke. On a good day, Avitus wasn't in the mood for jokes. But on a bad day ... on a bad day, Avitus most definitely didn't like jokes.

"You don't know anything about our relationship," Avitus said heatedly.

"Maybe not. But Liston, I'm sure, has his reasons for not wanting to see you."

It was risky to aggravate Avitus—for a plethora of reasons. Avitus was, after all, the one the Prophate Committee had originally wanted to serve as Head Prophate, some fifteen years ago. But Avitus—for reasons unknown to everyone but Kosabeus—had deferred. It had been an unprecedented move—and one Avitus never adequately explained to anyone in the Church. But Kosabeus knew that Avitus was waiting for the perfect moment to play that card, to remind Kosabeus that he owed him.

"And you'd know all about that with Banner, right?" chided Avitus. "No wonder he didn't take your advice and nominate someone other than Harlyn Harries."

Avitus meant it like a knife, to cut through Kosabeus. But Kosabeus wasn't so easily wounded.

"Cyno has never gone out of his way to avoid me."

Avitus retorted, "My Lord Regent ... when he's upset, he needs some space, some time to think. But he hasn't frozen me out like this in ... years."

"Not since Zenith?"

Avitus was eerily quiet. He stepped deeper into the office, closing the door behind him. Kosabeus subtly backed up toward his desk, to be in reach of his phone in case he needed to call security.

"You have no right to bring up Zenith like that," Avitus snapped.

Kosabeus held up his hands in a symbol of truce. "I'm sorry. I didn't ... what do you want me to do?"

Avitus heaved a deep sigh. "I don't think there's anything I can do other than just wait. He'll come to me when he's ready. He always does." He looked at Kosabeus. "I just ... I wish he'd listen and ... it won't work, you know."

"What won't?"

"His alliance. It'll fail."

"What makes you think that?"

"Because I know the Civitan. They aren't ... they haven't changed."

Kosabeus neared Avitus. "At some point, you'll have to accept that our Lord Regents don't ... they don't have to listen to us."

"They should. They'd be better off."

"I don't disagree. But sometimes, we just have to ... let them make their own choices."

"Or their own mistakes."

"Those too."

Avitus's eyes were on the window. "I can't lose him."

"Then don't. Tell him you support him, that this isn't something worth fighting over. Unless, of course, you think it is."

Avitus faced Kosabeus. "Nothing is more important to me than my Lord Regent."

"Then tell him that."

29

SILVER

"Really?" asked Silver. "Caine and Banner want to talk to Raelynn? What do you think they're planning?"

Silver and Liston were out at Keys, one of the premier jazz lounges in New Caelus. There were always different acts coming through, and almost all of them were sensational. Liston was the one who had introduced Silver to this place—and jazz. Before, Silver had liked jazz, sure, but it was a completely unique experience hearing it in person and watching the musicians. Coming here, he finally understood what all the fuss was about.

Keys, like most jazz lounges, smelled like cigars and leather. It could get a bit stifling after a while, as there were no windows to the outside world, but Silver enjoyed the atmosphere. This was a place where people went to listen to music, have a good time, and escape their troubles.

"No clue," Liston said, cradling a tonic water. "But that's why I told Raelynn to go. Keep your enemies close and all that."

Silver took a drag on his cigar. "I didn't realize Caine and Banner were friends."

"It seems to be a recent development."

"Hmmm." Silver leaned back in his chair. "Anything we should be worried about?"

Liston shrugged. "Caine's always been rather ... distrustful of Keepers. I guess that's why I find this to be so intriguing."

"Do you think they'll try and get anything out of Raelynn about the Civs, all that?"

"Oh, I have no doubt. But they won't learn anything. Raelynn doesn't know the specifics."

Silver nodded distractedly. "I guess I'm just concerned how this all relates to the elections."

"I don't think it does."

"No?"

"I mean, it's not like Caine can do anything publicly to help the Expansionists. He has to remain politically neutral. So, I don't see how he could help Banner hold on to the Cooperative."

"Maybe Banner will try to shove some sort of lawsuit through the High Court, say the election was rigged, that there were all these inconsistencies. And by getting Caine on his side, he's, you know, hedging his bets."

"You really think he'd do something like that?"

"If he loses? Absolutely. Banner's whole identity is wrapped around being Head of the Assembly. If he loses that, he'll try to take the whole system down with him."

Liston was quiet, his eyes on the saxophone player. "We have to hope the system is stronger than that." He turned to Silver. "What do you think it will be like? If we win?"

"Everything will be different. We'll be able to change Imperium's priorities, scale back our military presence in Neutral Space. We won't have this threat of war constantly hanging over our heads."

"But you don't think Banner will go down without a fight."

Silver shrugged. "I don't trust him. Never have."

"Me neither. But I don't think he'd do anything ... treasonous. Besides, he has people around him who can ... ground him. I don't think his advisers would let him attack our electoral system."

"They might not be able to hold him back." Silver adjusted his position. "But he seems rather comfortable, doesn't he? He isn't doing as many interviews or rallies as I thought he'd be doing, which is odd. The polls seem split. It's not like there's a consensus on who will take the Cooperative, so ... I don't know if he's being told he has this in the bag or what."

"I don't think Banner's ever cared about the polls."

"But you'd think he'd be doing more, right? I mean, if I were in his position, I'd be doing whatever I could to help my party, to get a majority in the Cooperative. But he's just been ... coasting." Silver took another drag on his cigar. "Maybe he's been Head of the Assembly for so long that he just can't imagine losing it. He's become complacent." Silver looked over at Liston, to gauge what he was thinking. "Do you disagree?"

"No. I think you're right. Banner can't envision a world where he doesn't control our government. But ... I can't see him doing anything to jeopardize Imperium's position. If he tries to make a move against us, to claim the election was rigged, that'd give the Coronians an opening. And Banner would never do something to give them any sort of power over us."

"Fair enough. I guess I just ... there's nothing more dangerous than an erratic man with a wounded ego."

"It won't come to that." Liston ran his fingers through his hair. "What do you think about the Civs?"

"I don't know as much about the Civitan as you do, but ... it seems like things are changing there, just like they're changing here."

"That's what I think too. But Avitus seems to think the Civs are still aligned with the Core, that they're ... playing along with this idea of an alliance so they can catch us unawares."

Silver let out a low whistle. "I have to hand it to him; he gives the Civitan a lot of credit, thinking they could come up with that sort of strategy."

"You don't think that's possible?"

"If they didn't want an alliance with us, why wouldn't they have just joined forces with the Core and attacked us already? Why wait?"

"That's what I want to know." Liston took a sip of his drink. "I think Avitus is letting the past cloud his judgment."

"He never struck me as the type to just … let something go."

"No. He isn't." Liston's eyes darkened for a moment. "But he's wrong about the Civitan. I know it. And if we get the Cooperative, it'd change everything."

"And only for the better. We just have to hope that the Imperial people see it the same way we do."

Liston smiled at him. "Why didn't you want to be the head of the party? You're much more … magnanimous than I could ever be."

Silver laughed. "I'm perfectly fine where I am, letting you take the reins."

"You don't think you'd be any good at it?"

"Oh, I'd be magnificent." Silver grinned. "But I'd hate every second of it. All that bureaucracy? No, thanks. I deal with enough of that already. I'm pretty sure that's why I went prematurely silver."

"Not that it hurt you or anything. It's your trademark now."

"Well, with a name like 'Silver,' you just have to capitalize on it."

Liston laughed. "I guess we'll have to wait and see how this all goes, then."

"Raelynn's having dinner with them, what, next week?"

"Yes. Next Domus."

"You'll have to tell me how that goes."

"Was there ever any doubt?"

30

GRELL

Grell wasn't sure how to best go about this, but she needed to unburden her conscience. She thought about writing a letter, but that seemed too formal—and strange. Maybe she'd swing by Banner's apartment and try to catch him there. No. That was too informal. It wasn't like they were friends. Besides, knowing Banner, she'd probably stumble upon him and one of his lovers. And that was something she didn't want to see.

Thus, she decided to visit his office. She'd never been in the Hall before. It was about as bleak as she'd thought it would be. Everything about it was overkill. She knew this was the home for the War and Defense division, but it didn't need to be so ... violent. There were weapons and war memorabilia everywhere. It was far too macabre for Grell's tastes. She knew about the horrors of war, of course, but she didn't need to be confronted with them so viscerally. She didn't understand how anyone could work here and feel at ease.

Milner, Banner's secretary, told her that he was free for the rest of the afternoon. She'd hoped he would be. It was, after all, the end of the week, and things were usually quiet. It wasn't like Banner was the type to burn the midnight oil. From what Kosabeus had told her, he was usually the first one out

173

the door every night.

"You may go in now," Milner said after a few minutes.

"Thank you," said Grell, offering her a smile.

She entered Banner's office. It was smaller than she'd expected. She had to say, out of all the Lord Regents, it seemed like Silver got the best deal. His office had stunning views, while Banner's was just a typical, boring office. Grell had heard rumors that Liston's office was underwater, but she hadn't seen it for herself, so she couldn't properly judge it.

Banner was sitting at his desk, fidgeting with a pen. He saw her come in but didn't say a word. He just continued to watch her, his eyes roaming up and down her body. Grell pretended not to notice, more for his own sake than anything else. Maybe he didn't know he was leering. Maybe that was just how he looked at everyone.

"Hi, Cyno," Grell said, offering a smile.

Banner bit the end of his pen, deep in thought. "When Milner told me you wanted to see me, I have to admit, I was ... confused."

"I figured you would be. But ..." She looked at the seat across from him. "May I sit?"

"Sure."

Grell sat down, crossing her legs. "I just ... I guess ... I wanted to apologize."

Banner furrowed his eyebrows but again didn't say anything. He seemed cold to her, detached. She wondered if he knew why she was here, if he knew she was going to mention Bayne. Maybe he was mentally preparing himself for that. She knew Bayne wasn't an easy subject for him to talk about, for obvious reasons.

"I know I ... I wasn't there for you. After Bayne. And I know it's been a while—"

"Ten years."

"Ten years. But I wanted to reach out and see if we could ... well, I guess I wanted to just, you know, make up for that. It was wrong of me to not make you a priority."

Banner put down his pen. He leaned forward, his elbows on his desk. "You were busy keeping Kosabeus's bed warm," he said bitingly.

Grell knew that he was going to make some sort of crass comment—that was just how he was—but she hadn't expected him to be so angry. He was glaring at her as though she were the one who had shot Bayne out of the sky.

"I know you have ... resentment toward me and Kosabeus—"

"I've made my peace with Kosabeus. He apologized to me. You never did."

"Bayne and I broke up long before he died."

"That makes it okay to sleep with my Prophate?"

Grell was surprised. She had always thought that Banner disapproved of her and Kosabeus because it had been, in his mind, disrespectful to Bayne. But it seemed like Banner was more upset that she'd specifically slept with Kosabeus, someone whom he considered to be a friend. It was sad, really, how Banner could twist anything to make it all about him.

"I didn't sleep with Kosabeus to hurt you."

"No? Then why did you do it? I've always wondered about that." Banner met her eyes. "Who instigated it? I always assumed it was Kosabeus, but—"

"It wasn't."

Her answer disarmed him. Grell couldn't tell what he was thinking, but she seemed to have captured his attention.

"Why?" Banner asked after a few moments.

"Because I wanted to."

It wasn't a lie—Grell had been attracted to Kosabeus—but it certainly wasn't the whole truth. Banner, however, didn't need to know all the details. Nobody did. It was in the past now, and everything had worked out for the best.

"Hmmm." Banner smirked. "You're more beguiling than I'd given you credit for."

It made Grell uncomfortable, the way he was looking at her. He'd never made a pass at her before, out of respect for Bayne, but perhaps he'd always wanted to.

Grell cleared her throat. "Regardless of what happened with me and Kosabeus, you know that I loved Bayne." She took a deep breath. "Tomorrow is his birthday. And the anniversary of his death. And I was wondering if you'd come to Table Rock with me."

"What?"

"I thought that maybe you'd want to go to Table Rock with me, share some of our favorite memories of him. I was going to go in the evening, around six. After work is done."

Banner vehemently shook his head. "No. That's not where ... they never ... recovered their bodies, so ... there's nothing there of him."

In Imperium, when people died, they were cremated, and their ashes were either scattered by their loved ones or turned into bricks, which would then be used for a public works project. Banner had wanted to cremate Bayne and sprinkle his ashes on top of Table Rock, Bayne's favorite hiking trail in New Caelus, but his body had never been recovered. The ship Bayne was on had been blown into smithereens, and there were no survivors. The lack of closure had haunted so many of the victims' families, made them hold out hope that their loved ones were still alive out there. They all knew better, of course; deep down, they all knew the truth. But some things were just too horrible to fathom.

"I just thought—"

"Shut up!" Banner's entire demeanor changed. His face was red. "I ... I want you to leave. Right now!"

Grell did as he asked. She took the first train home and was greeted by Kosabeus. Grell told him all about her afternoon and how she'd gone to see Banner.

"... but he didn't want to come," she concluded.

She'd been afraid that Banner would react poorly, but she hadn't expected such fury. She'd clearly underestimated just how much Banner disliked her. He'd always been civil enough when he came over for dinner, and he was kind to her kids—especially Eddard. Sometimes, Grell caught Banner looking at Eddard, and she wondered if maybe—

"I'm sorry, my darling." Kosabeus's voice returned her to reality. "Cyno can be a bit erratic. Especially when it comes to Bayne. And with this being the ten-year anniversary, it hurts a lot more."

"I know. I just thought it'd help."

He smiled at her, taking her hands in his. "It was a wonderful thought. And if you want me to be there with you, then I will."

She looked up into his eyes and wondered for the millionth time what she'd done to deserve him. A part of her wished he wasn't so perfect. That would have made everything a lot simpler. It would have allayed a lot of her guilt, made her feel like less of a horrible person.

"I mean, I don't want to intrude," he went on, "but I know how much this means to you, and I will support you in whatever way you want me to."

She kissed him. The next evening, she and Kosabeus made their way to Table Rock. It was a beautiful, well-kept trail. She liked to think this was where Bayne was. She didn't like to think about him being in pieces, floating through space. That was far too cruel a fate for someone who'd been as vivacious as Bayne.

"Here we are."

Grell stopped in front of the Seat, the trail's most famous rock formation. From here, Grell could see all of New Caelus, shining down below. This had been Bayne's favorite spot. This was where he'd gone to get away from the world.

Kosabeus stood beside her. He hadn't said a word since they'd started hiking the trail. She knew he was uncomfortable, but he'd insisted on being here with her. She loved him for that. She loved him for a lot of things, but his selflessness was one of his most endearing qualities.

"I, um ..." Grell looked at Kosabeus. "I'm going to talk to him for a bit."

"I'll give you some space." He kissed her forehead, turned around, and stepped out of earshot.

Grell began talking to Bayne, catching him up on everything. She wondered what he'd think about her being a temporary Prophate. She was so different now than she'd been back then. In her youth, she'd never dreamed of having a real job or staying in one place. She and Bayne had had all these dreams of traveling the universe. She wondered if he'd even be able to recognize her. So many things about her had changed.

After Grell finished talking to Bayne, she turned back to Kosabeus. He walked over to her and gently pushed a stray hair behind her ear.

"Are you okay?" he asked.

Grell nodded. "I'm ready to go home."

They made their way back down the trail. As they did so, they saw Banner, his hands shoved deep in his pockets. He looked between them, a wistful, knowing look in his eyes. To Grell, it felt like the first time he'd truly realized that she and Kosabeus were a couple. He'd known it, obviously, but as he saw them together, holding hands, it was like he'd finally reached acceptance. Perhaps that wound had been healed for him, once and for all.

Banner cleared his throat. "I didn't ... I didn't know if you'd ... I remember you said six. But I, uh ... hope I'm not too late."

Grell stepped closer to him. "I'm glad you came."

Together, Grell and Banner walked up to the Seat. Kosabeus stayed near the trail's entrance, to give them privacy. Neither Grell nor Banner said a word as they approached. When Banner saw the view, however, his eyes teared up.

"I haven't been here since ... that day," he said, his voice little more than a whisper. He glanced around. "It's so ... peaceful here."

"He's happy here."

"You think so?" Banner looked at her, his eyes glossy. "You think he'd like it?"

"I do."

He laughed, despite himself. "It's hard to know for sure. He wanted to be so many places, do so many things. Who knows where he would've ended up?"

They spent the better part of an hour reminiscing, sharing stories about Bayne. It was cathartic, talking about him to someone who'd known him so well.

Grell had never thought of Banner as emotional, but there were several moments when he nearly cried. She wished he had; maybe that would have released some of his pent-up helplessness. But this was a good first step. Maybe this would help him heal.

"Thank you, Grell," Banner said as they returned to the trail's entrance. "I'm glad I came too."

31

EMBRY

Embry loved Liston's library. It was, hands down, the best library she'd ever seen. When she thought of Liston on rainy days, she always pictured him there, sitting at the table, listening to the rain pitter-patter outside while he read a book.

As an adolescent, she'd spent countless hours in his library, playfully messing up his books. In hindsight, she couldn't believe she'd done that. How angry Liston must have been, walking in and seeing his precious books and rare manuscripts all over the floor. But he never lost his temper with her.

Embry had an aunt on her father's side but no uncles. Liston, however, filled the vacancy and became her pseudo uncle. But because of her father's unbelievably busy work schedule, Liston also became a sort of father figure. He and her mother had been friends for as long as Embry could remember—even before Liston was a Lord Regent. They'd met at one of the Keeper Galas, many moons ago, and they'd been friends ever since. Liston had thus been a staple in Embry's life from an early age. In fact, some of her best memories were with him.

Embry was always so impressed by Liston's mind. He had to see something only once, and he'd have it committed to memory forever. Embry loved testing him by picking up random books, calling out a page number, and asking him to recite it for her.

"'... and I knew that I'd never meet another like her,'" Liston said. He looked up at Embry. "How was that?"

"Incredible. I don't know how you do it."

"It's a good parlor trick."

"It's a lot more than that. I've never met anyone else who can do that."

Liston smiled. "Well, I'd be more than happy to keep you entertained by quoting all these books for you, but I really—"

"I know. You need to reorganize your shelves for the millionth time. Don't worry. I know the drill."

Liston had always been this way. He was never quite satisfied with how his bookshelves were laid out. Embry didn't mind watching, though. She simply enjoyed being in Liston's company, chatting with him about everything from her career to their shared love of reading to their hopes for the future. He was remarkably easy to talk to. It was strange, perhaps, for her and Liston to get on so well, but he'd always been there for her, for as long as she could remember.

The radio, which was perched along the wall by the door, was on some channel Embry had never heard of. The sound was staticky, sometimes cutting in and out, but it all sounded rather repetitive. She wondered if Liston even noticed; he often became engrossed by his books and tuned out the world around him.

Radio was one of the primary sources of entertainment for Imperials. There were dozens of radio shows—some that played music, others that relayed the news, and those that did neither. One of her and Liston's traditions during the colder months was listening to mystery shows in his drawing room, a fire roaring in the hearth, and playing an intense game of Regency or Stampede—two of Embry's favorite card games.

"Have you talked to your mother yet?" Liston held his book up to the light, to better inspect it.

"She was my first stop."

"She must have been happy to see you."

"Well, of course! I'm the light of her life."

Liston laughed. He placed the book on a shelf. "But how does it feel, being back?"

"Great. I'm happy to be home." Embry propped her feet up on the table. "It means I get to spend time with you."

Liston brushed some of the dust off his hands and turned toward the radio. "Is it just me, or has this song been playing for the last hour?"

So, he *had* noticed. Embry had to admit, she was surprised.

"Must be one of those experimental pieces."

Liston furrowed his eyebrows. "You can change it if you want," he said, returning his attention to his beloved books. "It's eleven o'clock. Lena Hannigan should be on."

Embry groaned. "I hate that channel. They're so biased! They act like everything an Affiliate says is fact."

"Well, that's because it is, Em," teased Liston, a playful glint in his eyes. Embry made a face, and Liston laughed. "Then what would you like to listen to?"

"Jazz works."

After Embry changed the channel, Liston once again became absorbed in his books, while Embry wandered over to the windows. She'd missed New Caelus. Though she enjoyed traveling for work, this was her home. This was the place she felt happiest.

"But I'll be staying put for a while now," Embry told him.

"Good. New Caelus isn't the same without you. But I know you have that same adventurous spirit your father had. You can't stay in one place for long."

Embry didn't like talking about her father. Sure, she'd loved him, but she didn't have as many fond memories of him as she wanted. He'd died when she was fourteen, but she hadn't felt particularly close to him. A lot of her colleagues at work had known her father and thought the absolute world of him. Still, Embry couldn't help but think of him as a no-show. He was always away for work, more frequently than was reasonable. He could've asked for a transfer or a less active job, but he didn't. He spent months away from them at a time. And when he returned, he acted like everything was the way it'd been when he left.

"I guess," Embry said, shrugging. "I just"—she kicked her legs—"It was the tenth anniversary of his death last week." She looked up at the absurdly ornate ceiling. "Mom didn't take it as hard as she usually does."

Liston placed books back on the shelf with adorable love and affection, as if they could feel pain. Embry, meanwhile, wondered how many hours it had taken the painter to finish the vibrant portraits on the library's ceiling. Liston had always had expensive taste, and he'd no doubt spent millions of numa on this room alone. It was, after all, the perfect sanctuary, the place he went to escape the world.

Liston moved on to the next shelf. "But that's good, right? That's what you've wanted—for your mother to not take it so hard."

"No, I know. It's a really good thing. And I'm proud of her." Embry smiled wryly. "Maybe this means she's ready to, you know, move on."

"Maybe."

Embry watched as Liston skimmed his piles of books, trying to figure out which one to pick up next. "Has she ... said anything to you about that?" she asked at last.

"About what?"

"About ... moving on."

Liston shook his head. "Not particularly."

Embry knew she was entering potentially dangerous territory. She had to tread cautiously, so as not to disarm or even upset Liston.

Clearing her throat, Embry said, "Because I just ... I know Dad would want her to be happy, to live her life."

"Sure." Liston gave her a strange look.

Embry moved closer to him. "I mean, maybe I'll bridge the topic with her, see how she'd feel about going on a blind date or something."

Liston laughed, stepping away from his bookshelves. "I can think of a million things your mother would do before she'd agree to that."

"You never know. I might set her up with the man of her dreams."

"Sounds like you have someone in mind."

"Maybe I do. Would that ... bother you?"

"I want your mother to be as happy as you do."

Embry rolled her eyes. It was such a politician answer. But what more should she have expected from the future Head of the Assembly? Liston was never one to show his hand—especially where her mother was concerned. Sometimes, Embry wished that her mother and Liston would just—

"How would you feel about lunch?" Liston asked suddenly.

Embry smiled. "As long as you're paying."

32

VISCARDIA

To Viscardia's surprise, Abner had called her to arrange an extra meeting, apart from their usual weekly one. She wasn't sure what he wanted. Maybe he'd thought about what she'd said regarding Cooperative hopefuls and realized it wasn't in his best interest to be supporting Expansionist candidates. This would be a welcome change—and a step in the right direction.

When Viscardia entered Abner's office, she saw his Lord Dynast, Tinsley Iaconetti, standing beside him. That was odd. She'd never had a meeting with both Abner and Iaconetti before.

"Viscardia." Abner smiled. "I'm glad you could make it."

Viscardia's eyes darted between the two. "What's going on?"

"Well." Abner turned to Iaconetti. "After Election Day, I'll be stepping down as Lord Regent, and Tinsley here will be taking my place."

Viscardia didn't know what to say. Abner had always seemed like a hesitant leader, to put it mildly, but he was still young—only fifty-four years old—so his sudden retirement was unexpected. However, Viscardia would have been lying if she said she wasn't excited about being Iaconetti's Prophate. Iaconetti's promotion to the Lord Regency would breathe some much-needed life into the division.

"Well, I ..." Viscardia didn't want to sound too excited, as she didn't want to wound Abner's fragile ego. "I have to say, Nix, you didn't give me any indication of this during our last meeting."

"It's been in the works for a while. I just ... the division wanted to pick my successor before everything went public. That's why I didn't tell you sooner. I wanted to make sure everything was all settled. And, um ... well, I figured you'd approve of Tinsley."

Viscardia smiled at Iaconetti. "Congratulations."

"Thank you." Iaconetti smiled back. "It was a shock when Nix told me, but I have a few months to get everything lined up."

Abner explained, "I thought it'd be a good idea for you two to get to know each other so you can, you know, make sure this will work. From now on, Viscardia, Tinsley will be meeting with you every week, as I'll be taking on more of an ... observatory role. I'll still be available, of course, if you need me, but ... I assume you won't."

How fitting, Viscardia thought, for Abner to spend his last couple of months as a Lord Regent completely checked out. It made sense for him to step aside so that Iaconetti could learn the ropes before her official inauguration as Lord Regent, but it wasn't like Abner was being pushed aside against his will. No doubt, he was the one who had suggested that he should take on more of a supervisory role so that Iaconetti could get used to her new position.

"That works for me," Viscardia said, struggling to contain her palpable excitement.

Finally, after all these years, she would be working for a real Lord Regent.

33

BANNER

The Hall was both a place of work and a museum, exhibiting various artifacts from Imperium's war history. Banner was always deathly quiet as he walked the corridors, overcome with reverence for the noble men and women who had put their lives on the line for Imperium. He wished he could have had the honor of serving in the military, but his Keeper upbringing prevented him from being able to enlist. It humiliated him, in some regards, but he compensated by doing everything he could to support his military families.

When Banner opened the door to his office, he was dismayed to see Kosabeus standing in front of the window—dressed, of course, in his white robe. Banner hadn't known Kosabeus had a key to his office. He surely hadn't given him one.

"What are you doing here?" Banner demanded.

Kosabeus turned around. "Haven't you ever heard of knocking?"

"This is *my* office."

"You should have been here half an hour ago."

"Oh, really? You're going to give me that shit?" Banner carelessly tossed his briefcase onto the armchair. "I don't remember scheduling a meeting with you."

Banner hoped he wasn't here to talk about that night at Table Rock. It wasn't the sort of thing Banner ever planned on talking about again—and he certainly didn't want to talk about it with Kosabeus. He'd been at his most vulnerable, and he didn't need Kosabeus making any jokes about it.

"We're meeting with your Expansionist cabinet members in, oh, fifteen minutes ago," Kosabeus said, glancing at his watch for humorous emphasis.

"What?"

"We're—"

"I heard what you said. I just ... you've been scheduling meetings with my cabinet behind my back?"

"Well, you're coming. So, it isn't like I'm—"

"They're on *my* cabinet, Kosabeus. Not yours."

"I'm fully aware of that."

"Then why are you—?"

"Please," said Kosabeus, raising his hand. "Keep your temper. They merely wish to discuss the upcoming election with you, away from your other cabinet members, and since you weren't reaching out to them, they reached out to me."

Banner glared at Kosabeus. "You just wanted to show me up," he said, throwing his suit jacket on top of his briefcase.

"I assure you, that wasn't my intention."

"Bullshit."

"Look, it won't be that painful. We're just touching base with them, that's all."

"We?"

"Well, I was planning on being there."

Banner stared Kosabeus down. "Is this about the other night?"

"What? No." Kosabeus's tone softened; his sardonic edge was gone. "You know I'd never ... I didn't think you'd want to talk about it. Especially not with me."

Well, he was right about that. No surprise there. Kosabeus was right about everything.

"I don't," Banner said. "I just ... I know you saw me when I was ... it wasn't my best moment."

"I don't know what you're talking about."

He said it so earnestly that Banner almost believed him. Of course, he knew Kosabeus had seen the tears in his eyes, heard his shaky voice as he and Grell returned from the Seat. He could hold that over Banner's head all he wanted, but it didn't seem like he was going to. Not at the moment, anyway.

Banner patted Kosabeus's shoulder. "Thank you."

"Of course."

Banner cleared his throat. "So, um ... back to other matters."

"Like the cabinet meeting."

Banner turned away from him, walking over to his desk. "Go without me. Because clearly, if you think you can schedule meetings without my—"

"This wasn't a personal slight, Cyno. They reached out to me."

"You expect me to believe that?"

"It's the truth. You can ask them yourself."

"That won't be necessary. Because I'm not going."

Kosabeus crossed his arms. "If you don't come with me to this meeting, then you are, in essence, turning your back on your party—and, if you wish me to be histrionic, Mystis."

Banner scoffed. "You can't threaten me, Kosabeus. No one takes a man in a pretty white robe seriously."

"Is that a no?"

Banner huddled over his desk. He knew Kosabeus was right, but damnit, he hated it when Kosabeus was right. He lingered for a few moments, to make it seem as though he were debating his options.

"Fine," Banner said grudgingly. "But I'm not happy about it."

Five minutes later, they were in the Cabinet Room, where the three Expansionist members of Banner's cabinet were already seated. There was an empty seat at the head of the table, which Banner claimed. Kosabeus could have sat in one of the other empty chairs, but he instead elected to stand against the wall, where he could pass his judgments in relative privacy.

"Sorry we're late," Banner addressed them. "We were, uh, held up."

"No apologies necessary, my Lord Regent," said Hiram Randolph, the oldest and longest-serving member of Banner's cabinet. He bled red and white, the colors of the Expansionist Party. "We wanted to ask if you think we should do anything more to help drum up support for the Expansionists."

"Well, I know you've been giving interviews on the radio, things like that. So, that should do the trick."

"As you say, my Lord Regent," said Devlin Crew. "Things are looking great. The latest poll from *The Agenda* has us leading the Grounders by six points and the Affiliates by four. Needless to say, they don't stand a chance against our party."

"But you're not arrogant," quipped Kosabeus from the corner. Banner glimpsed over his shoulder, shooting him a warning glare.

"Really, my Lord Regent, you don't need to worry," added Hugh Gibson. "We just need one more seat to have a majority in the Cooperative. Then you'll be able to get your bills and motions passed, no problem."

"He needs more than a simple majority to get anything crucial passed," Kosabeus reminded him. "Our system requires a sixty-percent agreement on any key piece of legislation, which, by my reckoning, is the equivalent of forty-two votes."

"Well, yes," stammered Gibson, loosening his collar. "So, we can hope to gain eight seats on Election Day, to get us forty-two."

Kosabeus laughed out loud. "In this political climate? Keep dreaming."

"Kosabeus," growled Banner. He returned his attention to Gibson. "Do you think it's possible for us to unseat that many Grounders and Affiliates?"

"Oh, yes," said Gibson. "The people have supported the Expansionist Party for years. We're the party that keeps them safe."

"Then just keep the pressure up. We have a history of being there for the

Imperial people when they need us. They'll show us their love on Election Day."

"They certainly will, my Lord Regent," piped up Crew.

"What are you doing to combat the Affiliate rally?" asked Kosabeus. "They're going to dominate the press for days unless you fire back with something just as big, if not bigger."

"Well, their 'rally,' as you call it, is only being headlined by Viscardia," snickered Gibson. "I don't think she has that much traction."

"Right. Because she isn't married to the most popular politician in Imperium, who is, coincidentally, an Affiliate and best friends with the leader of the Affiliate Party."

Gibson's mouth was agape. "But Silver and Liston aren't on the program."

"What, you think they're just going to sit in their offices and not do anything to help their party? How stupid are you?"

"Kosabeus," snapped Banner, clearing his throat. He smiled at Gibson. "What Kosabeus means to say is, we should probably host our own rally."

"You think so?" asked Gibson, and in his peripheral vision, Banner saw Kosabeus facepalm.

"I think it'd be a good idea," said Banner, nodding.

"Okay," said Crew. "We'll get right on it, my Lord Regent." He looked up at Banner. "We can count on you to speak at the rally, right?"

"Of course."

"And Kosabeus?" asked Crew gently, perhaps afraid of being humiliated like Gibson. "What about you?"

"I may be busy that day. And besides, public speaking isn't really my forte," Kosabeus said.

"Um. Aren't you the Head Prophate? You give sermons all the time."

Kosabeus widened his eyes. "Yes, very good. I'm glad you know that. Perhaps you're smarter than I gave you credit for."

Crew, Gibson, and Randolph exchanged confused looks. Banner couldn't believe that after all these years, they still didn't understand Kosabeus's sense of humor. They took everything he said so damn literally. Maybe Kosabeus had been right all along; these were the three dumbest Expansionists in War and Defense.

"Well, um ..." Randolph dared to speak. "Will you be there?"

Kosabeus melodramatically sighed. "I'll see if I can fit it in."

"Do you think you could convince Avitus to speak on our behalf as well?"

"He'd never stump for you."

"Not even if you ask nicely?"

"Not even if I offer to sleep with him."

"He's kidding," said Banner hastily, laughing awkwardly, for good measure. "He's just, uh ... had a long day. Would you all, uh, mind giving me and Kosabeus some time to talk?" Once Randolph, Gibson, and Crew exited, Banner turned on Kosabeus. "What the hell are you smoking? You can't talk to them like that."

"In my defense, they're all idiots."

Banner couldn't argue with him there. Though there had been a time when he'd counted on Randolph, Gibson, and Crew for advice, for several years now, Banner had treated Kosabeus as his primary adviser, and his cabinet had become, for all intents and purposes, defunct. They met only when they were required to, and their meetings were often brief and superficial. Banner let his cabinet members work without too much supervision. He didn't want them bothering him, and they didn't want him bothering them. It was a mutually beneficial relationship.

Kosabeus peeled away from the wall. "I don't know why they're acting as though this election has already been decided, that the Expansionists will win."

"Because we will."

"Have you been following the news? The Affiliates are picking up steam, mobilizing voters across Imperium. Vitor, my hometown, which has always been a hub for Mystic Expansionists, is wavering. The Affiliates are gaining ground there for the first time in a generation."

"Mystic Expansionists," spat Banner, shaking his head. "Your lot. The Fundamentalists."

"Don't you dare loop me in with the Fundamentalists," said Kosabeus hotly. "They are a corrupted wing of the party. There is no religion in them."

Banner raised an eyebrow. "Because you have the final say on what religion is."

Kosabeus adjusted his collar. "I don't like to boast—"

"Sure."

"—but I like to think I'm somewhat of an expert on the topic. I am, as you might recall, the Head Prophate."

"Are you really? I had no idea."

"How strange. Even Crew knew that. And I at least thought you were smarter than him."

Banner laughed. He rested his hands behind his head, rocking back and forth in his chair. "Well, I'm not worried."

"You should be. Because if things go sour these next few months, you can say goodbye to being Head of the Assembly and say hello to the reign of Liston."

Banner scowled. "Don't threaten me."

"It isn't a threat. It's a possibility." Kosabeus leaned over the table. "You need to take this election seriously. You don't have it in the bag, despite what your ... sad excuse for Expansionist advisers may be telling you."

"You're wrong. For once in your damn life, Kosabeus, you're wrong. And I'm going to prove it."

34

RAELYNN

When Raelynn arrived at Starlight, she felt like she'd entered a different world. She was grateful Liston had told her to buy a new outfit; she would have been hopelessly out of place if she were wearing one of her work pantsuits. Starlight was on the top floor of one of the tallest buildings in New Caelus, with an outdoor terrace that had panoramic views of the entire city. It was magical, looking down on the city from this height. Raelynn still couldn't believe this was her life.

"Raelynn." Caine found her. "I'm glad you made it."

Raelynn gestured toward the skyline. "This is incredible."

"Isn't it? Makes you feel proud to be an Imperial."

"Is, um ... Lord Regent Banner here yet?"

"Not yet. But we're still a few minutes early. I've never known him to be late. Ah, and there he is now." Caine's smile, however, quickly vanished, and his eyebrows furrowed. "What the hell is *he* doing here?"

Raelynn turned to see. Banner had just entered ... but not alone. Kosabeus was standing beside him. Judging by Caine's reaction, Raelynn surmised that Kosabeus was not someone he had expected—or wanted—to see.

As Banner and Kosabeus neared them, Banner preemptively held up his hands in a symbol of truce. "I know, I know. This was supposed to just be the three of us."

"Then why is *he* here?"

"Because Cyno couldn't bear being away from me," said Kosabeus, a smirk on his lips.

Banner rolled his eyes. "Look, Eliseo, it was a last-minute thing. I didn't think it'd be a problem."

Caine glared at Kosabeus. "If I wanted you here, I would've asked."

"Touchy, touchy." Kosabeus shook his head. "Look, you'll hardly even know I'm here. I don't drink. I don't eat meat. I'm merely here to ... observe. Oh, and I'll want a salad. But I can pay for that."

"And he will," Banner piped up. "He won't cost you a thing, Eliseo."

"Fine," Caine acquiesced. To Raelynn, he said, "Apologies for the change in plans."

"No, no problem," Raelynn said, forcing a smile.

Honestly, she was grateful for the extra company. This would hopefully make the dinner less awkward. With more people there, Raelynn wouldn't be expected to speak as much.

"Well, introductions are in order. Raelynn, this, of course, is Lord Regent Cyno Banner." Caine signaled toward Banner, who simply nodded at Raelynn. "And this, um ..." Caine heaved a deep breath, as if he were preparing himself for what came next. "This is Kosabeus. He's ... Cyno's lapdog."

"Charming," said Kosabeus dryly.

"Come on," said Caine, stepping forward. "Our table is ready. Of course, I'll have to ask them to bring over another chair." He again glared at Kosabeus, who didn't seem to notice.

The dinner was about as strange as Raelynn had expected. Caine and Banner kept asking her all these questions about Liston and what was going on with the Civitan. They didn't seem to understand that Raelynn didn't know too much about it, but even if she did, she wasn't going to divulge everything to Liston's primary political rival and the High Justice.

"It's just … the Civitan … the idea of an alliance with them concerns a lot of people, including us. We're just worried about the public reaction," Banner claimed.

That sounded like a clumsy excuse to Raelynn. Clearly, Banner didn't care about the public reaction; he was more concerned with his slipping political power. If Liston became the next Head of the Assembly, then an alliance with the Civitan would practically be guaranteed. That, in turn, would give Liston, and the Affiliates, a major political victory—something Banner obviously couldn't stand. Like most Expansionists, Banner didn't want the Civitan to be its own entity; he wanted Imperium to annex it by force. As such, he vehemently opposed Liston's alliance, which would recognize the Civitan's sovereignty and essentially prevent Imperium from ever being able to claim the Civitan as its own.

"Lord Regent Liston doesn't discuss all the details with me," Raelynn said for what felt like the hundredth time. "I really don't know a lot about it."

"But he must have you working on some kind of deal or something."

"We're still in the early stages."

"But that can't be true. Liston's been working on this for years. I know it."

"I really … I don't know what else to tell you."

Banner turned to Kosabeus, who hadn't spoken for the better part of two hours. Kosabeus was just watching them, his facial expression annoyingly indiscernible. He must have been masterful at Regency, one of the most popular card games in Imperium. Raelynn couldn't help but wonder why he'd insisted on coming to dinner. He'd said he was here to observe … but what did that even mean?

Banner looked at Kosabeus imploringly. It was evident he wanted Kosabeus's help with something, but Raelynn didn't know what Banner expected her to say. Raelynn truly didn't know a lot about the Civitan alliance. She wasn't trying to be obstructive on purpose.

Banner cleared his throat and said, "Did you know, Raelynn, that Kosabeus here is one of the Church's leading experts on the Civitan?" While he asked this question, he reached over and touched Kosabeus's arm. Kosabeus glanced at Banner's hand but didn't seem put off by it.

"No." Raelynn turned to Kosabeus. "We'd have a lot to talk about, then."

Kosabeus met her eyes. "I'm sure we would," he said at last.

Caine, unwilling to be left out of the conversation, cleared his throat. "Well, I can see we're, um ... maybe we should talk about something else. Like ... Satias. How did you find it there?"

"Fine," said Raelynn. "A little boring, to be honest, but it was a good school."

"Nisha went there," Banner said, side-eyeing Kosabeus.

"Yes, she did," Raelynn said slowly, her eyes darting between Banner and Kosabeus.

There was a strange power dynamic between the two of them. Raelynn had thought that Banner, as the Lord Regent, would be the one in control. That was what she'd been taught, anyway—that the Prophates were there to serve their Lord Regents. But it seemed as though Kosabeus held all the power. Throughout the night, Banner had continually looked over at Kosabeus, trying to gauge his reaction to something Raelynn had said.

"What do you think of her?" pressed Banner.

"Of Lord Dynast Corinth?"

"Yes. Have you spent much time with her?"

"A little. Not a lot."

"Well, I'm sure you'll learn a lot from her. She's been in the division longer than Liston. She can be a real asset to you."

Caine nodded, taking a sip of his wine. "She's one of the more pragmatic Affiliates in government."

Raelynn wasn't sure what they wanted her to say. Did they not know she was an Affiliate as well? But if they did know she was an Affiliate, then why were they going out of their way to criticize her party? None of this made any sense. She wondered for the dozenth time why Liston had encouraged her to attend this dinner.

"She seems great so far," Raelynn offered. "She was really hospitable to me when I first came to New Caelus. She let me shadow her, all that."

Caine leaned forward. "You must realize how remarkable that is, someone your age being given that sort of opportunity. Why do you think Liston chose you?"

"Um ... I don't know."

"You haven't thought about it?"

"I've thought about it, sure, but ... he told me it was because of my thesis."

"What was your thesis on?" piped up Banner.

"I—"

"That can't be the only reason." Caine swiftly interrupted her. "There must be something else, some other reason why Liston went out of his way to get you."

Raelynn squirmed in her seat. "I guess you'd have to ask him that."

Caine grimaced. "Maybe I will."

Finally—and mercifully—the dinner winded down. Raelynn glanced at her watch. Mystis, she'd been with them for over three hours. She couldn't believe she'd made it that long. Hastily, she made her way through the lobby. At long last, she'd be able to go home and—

"Raelynn." It was Kosabeus who spoke. He had caught up to Raelynn in the lobby. "I just wanted to say, I ... well, I hope you didn't find that dinner to be too intrusive."

"Oh. Um. No. It was fine." Raelynn wasn't sure what else to say. She was too tired to think.

Kosabeus moved closer. "You must know how rare it is for students to write their theses on the Civitan."

Raelynn looked up at him, confused. "I didn't ... I don't think I told you my thesis was on the Civitan ... did I?"

Kosabeus smirked. "Would you care for a drink?"

Kosabeus led Raelynn toward the bar. He waved over the bartender and ordered two Pratem Herbs. Raelynn had never heard of the drink before, but it looked repulsive. It was green and came with some sort of yellow garnish. Even worse, it didn't have any alcohol. According to Kosabeus, it was a Vitor specialty.

"Now, there's a bit of a ... well, there's a certain way to drink this," Kosabeus explained. "Just follow my lead."

Kosabeus picked up the garnish and bit off the tip. He then rubbed the tip of the garnish around the rim of the glass, swallowed the garnish whole, and started slowly sipping the Pratem Herb.

Kosabeus, no doubt noticing Raelynn's uneasiness, laughed. "It's sort of an initiation ceremony in Vitor. Go ahead. Try it."

Raelynn did as Kosabeus instructed. To her surprise, the drink wasn't nearly as bad as it looked, but the whole garnish thing was beyond strange. Raelynn had always known that Vitor was off its rocker, but this proved it.

"So, how did you ... know about my thesis?" asked Raelynn after a few moments.

"Curiosity." Kosabeus smiled. "But I only know the basics, you see, so why don't you tell me more about it?"

35

TAYMOR

"Tinsley Iaconetti? Wow." Taymor nodded in approval. "I must say, I didn't ever think the division would consider her for the Lord Regency, given Logistics and Transportation's track record of, you know, nominating men to the position."

"I know," Viscardia said. "But I'm so glad they did. This will be a seismic change, Far. Logistics and Transportation might actually become a serious division."

Viscardia had told Taymor the great news over the phone, and the two of them met up to walk through Viren Park and enjoy the lovely evening. Taymor was a bit taken aback, as Abner hadn't announced his intentions to the rest of the Assembly yet, but it wasn't exactly a surprise, given his distaste for his job. Besides, it would be wonderful having another woman on the Assembly. Iaconetti was young and keen, and she would be a force to be reckoned with.

"And Tinsley is an ... Affiliate, yes?"

"Yes." Viscardia's eyes sparkled. "Finally, someone on the right side. No offense, Far."

"None taken," laughed Taymor. "Well, I'm happy for you, Viscardia. I know that you've been miserable for a while now, so ... hopefully, Tinsley will be a better fit for you."

"Oh, I know she will. We've met up for coffee a couple of times, and I can already tell, we'll get along just fine."

Viren Park was starting to fill up, as the workday was coming to an end for most people. Even though it was the end of Braytus, New Caelus was still mild, as it usually was. New Caelites were, by and large, lovers of the outdoors, and they hated being cooped up. Though Taymor loved New Caelus, she had to admit, she missed the change of seasons she'd experienced in Doctro. There was something intrinsically delightful about colorful foliage and the first snowfall. But in New Caelus, everything stayed green, and snow scarcely graced the landscape.

"So, that would mean ... there would be two Expansionists, two Grounders, and three Affiliates on the Assembly," Taymor said.

"Have you heard anything about Bryson? Is he retiring?"

"I think so. It makes sense. But I don't see his Lord Dynast taking over as Lord Regent, seeing as he's in his sixties, so I think the division will have to do a bit of searching for a good candidate."

"Another woman, perhaps?"

"We can hope." Taymor smiled. "Wouldn't that be nice? Then I wouldn't feel so singled out."

They were near Auster Ocean, and the salty air filled Taymor's nostrils. She loved this part of the city and resented the fact that the Lab was in downtown New Caelus, far away from the ocean. It'd been far too long since she'd allowed herself to enjoy all the wonderful amenities that New Caelus boasted.

"And it looks like the Prophates are starting to head in that direction too," Viscardia said, stepping onto the sand. She looked like a model, with her hair blowing in the wind. "I think Grell will officially get the Prophateship, and once Lisbeth retires, it's more than likely another woman will take her place."

"Do you know who?"

"I'd wager it's between Halliwell or Adelphi. We'll have to see what the Prophate Committee decides."

Taymor stood beside her. "It's beautiful, isn't it?" she asked, looking out across the ocean.

The sun was just starting to set. It had been a clear day, so the colors were particularly vivid. Reds, oranges, pinks, and purples streaked across the sky, reminding Taymor of those gorgeous Marsden Drow landscape paintings she'd seen in art galleries. Other onlookers stopped to take in the scene, whispering amongst themselves, trying to memorize it as best they could.

"Stunning," Viscardia exhaled. "I didn't get views like this growing up in Pacalis."

"Doctro was its own sort of beautiful. But New Caelus has its charms."

Viscardia laughed, skipping a stone on the ocean. "Do you see yourself moving back up to Doctro, once you've had your fill of life as a Lord Regent?"

"I do," Taymor admitted. "Everything's much ... quieter up there. More peaceful. It's a world away from all this hustle and bustle."

Viscardia made a face. "Sounds horrible."

"It's not for everyone. I give you that." Taymor crossed her arms to brace herself against the wind. "This is your forever home, then?"

"I can't see myself anywhere else. Not anymore. Maybe I used to have ideas about what it'd be like to live in another city, but ... once you've made it here, it's hard to picture yourself in another place." Viscardia placed her hands in her pockets, her eyes still on the ocean. "This is where I belong. And for the first time in a long time, I feel ... excited about my future here. And it seems like Imperium is starting to move in the right direction."

Taymor and Viscardia watched as the sun slipped beneath the horizon. They'd both seen their share of New Caelus sunsets, but this one felt different. It was like they were saying goodbye to the lives they'd known before. A shiver of anticipation ran down Taymor's spine. She wondered if Viscardia felt it too.

WHITNER

"There's been a lot going on, Dane," Banner said, crumbling some crackers into his soup. "A lot going on. Elections are coming up, obviously. But that's hardly the most interesting thing. Eliseo, Kosabeus, and I had dinner with Raelynn the other night."

"Who's Eliseo?"

"Caine. Eliseo Caine." Banner snickered. "You didn't know his first name?"

"Why would I? He and I aren't friends."

Whitner wanted to add that he hadn't been aware Banner and Caine were friends, but he let that slide. He took a bite of his soggy, saturated salad and grimaced. He'd specifically asked for the dressing on the side, *on the side.*

"But why did you go to dinner with Raelynn?" pressed Whitner.

"Eliseo wanted my opinion, to see what I think of her."

"And?"

"And nothing. She's just a kid. I don't get what's so special about her."

Whitner picked up one of his slices of chicken, saving it from the soup that was his salad. "So, you don't think Liston has some grand, devious plan for Raelynn?"

"I don't know. It's still too early to tell." Banner took a sip of his drink. "But Kosabeus was really ... quiet at dinner."

"Really? Huh. I didn't think he knew how to shut up."

"Well, there's a first for everything."

Whitner pushed his salad aside, disgusted by the mere sight of it. "Like maybe letting me pick where we go for lunch?"

"What's wrong with this place?"

"Do you see my salad?"

"It looks fine to me."

"It's more like a soup than a salad."

Banner laughed, shaking his head. "You're so dramatic." He proceeded to drown his soup in pepper. "But what do you think of the current political climate, Dane?"

"The Affiliates have a lot of weapons at their disposal," said Whitner. "I mean, Silver and Liston ..." Whitner grabbed one of the rolls from the bread basket. "The public adores them."

"The public adores Silver. They ... tolerate Liston." Banner slurped up more of his soup. "But I think the Expansionists are going to run away with it."

"That's presumptuous."

"Don't you mean optimistic?"

"No. I mean presumptuous. No one's predicting an Expansionist blowout."

"What, I assume you're talking about some of those Affiliate-run polls?" Banner scoffed. "They never get it right. And besides, you know how things are. The Affiliates always look good at a glance, but they don't have any actual, solid policies. Unless, of course, they think holding hands and becoming friends with everyone is a policy."

"They're not as naive as you make them out to be. A lot of their proposals make sense." Seeing Banner's expression, Whitner added, "If you're into that, I mean."

Banner leaned forward, shooting daggers at Whitner. "You're not jumping ship on me, are you, Dane?" he asked, his hand far too close to his knife for Whitner's comfort.

"No. I would never."

"Because it sounds like you're giving them a second thought."

"I just ... whether you like it or not, things are changing."

"I'm still Head of the Assembly," Banner reminded him. "The press may not be on my side right now, with the whole Harlyn thing, but the press is, and always has been, biased."

As Whitner listened to Banner, he tried to remember what Banner used to be like. Sure, Banner had always been confident, bordering on conceited, but his intentions, at least, had been good. He'd written his dissertation on creating fast tracks to Imperial citizenship for foreign soldiers who fought on Imperium's behalf. Back in Ligva, supporting the military had been Banner's top concern. Whitner could remember late-night conversations they'd had, when Banner relayed to him his views on Imperial military policies ...

"We do a good job of taking care of them when they're deployed, but once they come home ... a lot of them need help reacclimating to civilian life," Banner had once told Whitner. "And yes, I know, we have programs that do that, but we need more—and better ones. These people put their lives on the line for Imperium. The least we can do is show them we were worth it."

That Banner was nowhere to be seen in the man sitting across from Whitner. He'd barely said a word about citizenship or veteran support all election season. Instead, he was focused on Liston, the supposedly partial press, and the Affiliates' empty promises. Whitner was almost positive that Banner's unrelenting obsession with Liston would be his undoing.

Whitner sighed. "You know there are dozens of pro-Expansionist newspapers and radio shows that love and support you."

"But it's not enough," said Banner, adding so much salt to his soup that Whitner felt as though he were going to have a heart attack by proximity. "No one's demonized the way I am."

"I hardly think that's true."

"Oh, come on. You know it is."

"Well, have you ever stopped to consider that maybe there's something you're doing that is ... making people dislike you?"

"I just want fair treatment, that's all. We all make mistakes. Why am I the only one who's ever criticized for them?"

"You're not."

"You know, in some people's eyes, it's like—"

"For Mystis's sake, Cyno! Enough!"

Whitner's outburst surprised Banner; the latter put down his spoon and gawked at him. Banner then scanned the restaurant, making sure no one was staring. A few people were, naturally, but when they saw the look in Banner's eyes, they immediately turned away.

"Dane," muttered Banner. "Don't make a scene."

"Why did you invite me out to lunch? Just so I could sit here and listen to you gripe for the millionth time about your sinking approval ratings?"

"No, I ... I wanted to see you, talk to you, catch up."

"Oh, you did, hmmm? Well, have you asked me one question about what's going on in my life?"

Banner sat there in silence for a few moments, then said, "Well, I was getting to that, wasn't I? But I had some things I needed to get off my chest first."

"It's always you first."

"That's never bothered you before."

"Well, maybe it should."

"Oh, come on, Dane. Don't be like that."

"Be like what?"

"All angry at me. Let's just ... look, we'll have a nice lunch, and then—"

"I'm leaving." And with that, Whitner stood up and left in a huff.

As he walked down the street, he wanted to feel proud of what he'd done. He'd finally stood up for himself, said what was on his mind. For the past few months, Banner had been exasperating, going on and on about the same things, never taking a second to reflect or look inward. Though Whitner was no admirer of Kosabeus's, he couldn't help but grudgingly respect him for putting up with Banner as much as he did.

Indeed, Whitner wanted to feel like he'd done the right thing, leaving Banner. Maybe Banner would stop and wonder what he'd done to make his best friend walk away from him like that. Maybe this would all be for the best. Maybe this was the sort of fight they needed to have to make Banner realize just how much he'd taken Whitner for granted.

But as it was, all Whitner felt was shame. He felt badly about leaving Banner there, all alone, with no one to talk to—or split the check with.

And he knew, deep down, that whenever Banner came by with his inevitable, shallow apology, he'd forgive him, just like he always did.

37

AVITUS

Avitus stood by the window. The garden's tranquility taunted him, reminded him of better times. He'd been so lonely since his and Liston's falling-out. He hardly said a word to anyone, save Kosabeus. But even Kosabeus was starting to annoy him.

Avitus played it over and over again in his head, trying to determine whether it was worse than the argument they'd had after the news about Zenith broke out. The Zenith fiasco, Avitus decided, was definitively worse.

Avitus closed his eyes, shuddering as the memories returned to him. He could still so clearly see Liston's shock and betrayal. But Avitus hadn't stopped; he'd persisted, verbally attacking Liston with everything he had. He hadn't noticed Liston turning more and more inward, his fighting spirit dissipating, his voice barely a whisper.

That night, as Avitus drifted to sleep, he had a nagging feeling that something was wrong. He ignored it, but the next morning, the feeling was stronger. Avitus tried to get in touch with Liston; he swung by his home, but he wasn't there. Avitus thus made his way to Liston's office, all the while wondering why he would still be there.

When Avitus entered Liston's office, his heart leapt to his throat, lodging itself there. Avitus would never forget what he saw when he opened Liston's door. There was Liston, face down on the floor, whiskey bottles littered around him. Avitus had dropped to his knees, turning Liston over. He could smell the whiskey, the reeking whiskey. How much had he drunk?

Thank Mystis, Liston was breathing. His eyes flickered open, and he mumbled something incoherent. Avitus dialed the nearest hospital, demanding a medical team at the Spire. Avitus stayed with him, holding his hand so tightly he was worried he might break it. The whole time, Avitus had only one thought running through his head: *Don't die.*

Not only did Avitus have to contend with the possibility that he had pushed Liston over the edge, but he also had to defend himself from the impressive rage of Silver, who was, according to Viscardia, prepared to pummel Avitus right there in the waiting room. Taymor and Embry, for their part, wouldn't even look at him. It was its own kind of punishment, sitting there surrounded by people who hated him. Feverishly, Avitus prayed. He prayed that Liston would make it.

And he did.

In the aftermath, Avitus and Corlander worked alongside Liston's PR team to mitigate the damage. They couldn't fully protect Liston; news had already gotten out about the ceasefire on Zenith falling apart, and that was a major hit to Liston's political agenda. The Expansionists, and especially Banner, would use that misstep to drag Liston through the mud for weeks. Still, Avitus, Corlander, and Liston's PR team hid the truth from the Imperial people, simply stating Liston had been hospitalized due to excessive overwhelm, and he would undergo further examination at an undisclosed location. They said nothing about the whiskey or his mental state; instead, they discreetly sent Liston back to the treatment center he'd attended all those years ago, where he stayed for only two weeks.

Avitus wished Liston had remained at the treatment center longer, but he also recognized that a longer stay would have been politically risky. Indeed, if Liston had been there for more than two weeks, the press would have figured out that Liston's problems were much more serious than they'd been told, and this very likely would have destroyed Liston's credibility—and possibly his career. For those two weeks, Nisha stepped in as the temporary Lord Regent of Diplomacy, though she was also unaware of what had actually happened. Avitus had assumed—perhaps unfairly—that if Nisha knew the truth, then she would use it to claim she should be the new Lord Regent. Consequently, he decided to keep her, and the rest of the division, in the dark.

There were whispers about Liston's alcoholism—mostly from Banner's camp—but they couldn't be substantiated. When Liston returned to office, he did so to great fanfare. The Imperial people, by and large, were relieved he was okay. And Liston put on a marvelous public performance—one for the ages. He made himself accessible to the press and sat down for interviews, explaining what had happened. Though Liston didn't acknowledge his alcoholism, he did admit to suffering from severe depression and anxiety. His candor appealed to the Imperial people, and shockingly, his approval ratings skyrocketed. From all outward appearances, everything was completely fine. The worst of the scandal had been avoided, and Liston had emerged mostly unscathed.

Behind the scenes, however, Liston and Avitus quarreled incessantly. Liston, now wary of Avitus, wanted to keep him at arm's length, while Avitus, fearful that Liston would fall back into his inebriated ways, wanted to keep a close eye on him. For almost four months, their relationship was riddled with trust issues and resentment. It was beyond excruciating. Desperate for help, Avitus reached out to Kosabeus and told him what had really happened after Zenith. Though Avitus trusted Kosabeus implicitly, he had been concerned that Kosabeus would let it slip to Banner, and Banner, in turn, would run to the press and try to discredit Liston. Kosabeus promised Avitus he wouldn't say a word to anyone, least of all to Banner. And that seemed to be true. No more rumors about Liston's possible alcoholism ever materialized—not in mainstream circles, anyway.

For about a month, Kosabeus spoke with Liston one-on-one, trying to persuade Liston to let Avitus back in. Whatever he said ended up working, for eventually—and mercifully—Liston and Avitus mended their bridges. Liston came out on the other side, and he never touched alcohol again. Avitus couldn't go back to those dark days, when Liston would sit on his couch and stare blankly at the wall, refusing to engage Avitus in conversation.

A knock on the door jolted Avitus out of his trance. He turned, expecting to see one of the other Prophates, but instead, he saw Liston. Avitus almost felt as though he were seeing a ghost.

"May I come in?" Liston asked finally.

"Yes," Avitus managed, clearing his throat.

Liston didn't sit down on the couch, as was his usual custom. Instead, he gravitated to the bookshelf, his safety net, examining the texts, pretending he hadn't seen them before and that they were absolutely fascinating to him. Avitus knew this routine all too well. They were both experts at avoiding talking about what was on their minds.

"It's been a while," Liston offered. "And I ... thought it was time."

Avitus watched as Liston adjusted his glasses with his forefinger. It was one of his tells, a sign that he was uncomfortable. Avitus decided, in the moment, that he would allow Liston to lead the conversation. Indeed, he didn't want to say anything to change Liston's mind or deepen the divide between them.

Liston looked up at Avitus. "I never wanted our political differences to tear us apart. And I'm sorry I made you feel like your hands are tied. But ... I just needed some time to clear my head, think about what I want."

"And what do you want? Because whatever you want, my Lord Regent, I will grant it. Even if that means you want me to step aside."

"No, I don't want that. I want us to ... communicate better. Even when we disagree, I want us to talk about it in ways that don't seem so ... divisive." Liston met Avitus's eyes. "I know I haven't been as open with you as I should. And I'm sorry for that."

Avitus knew it wasn't easy for Liston to admit his wrongdoings, just like it wasn't easy for Avitus to admit his. They had more in common than they cared to see, which was perhaps why Avitus became so exasperated with Liston; Liston was just as stubborn as he was, and whenever people saw their worst qualities reflected in others, their primal instinct was to admonish them. Avitus knew that Liston meant well, that he always did what he believed to be right, but that didn't excuse his actions.

Yes, he should have told Avitus about Raelynn, just like he should have listened to Avitus when he had said the ceasefire on Zenith wouldn't hold up. And Liston should have listened to Avitus when he'd first told him that an alliance with the Civitan would end only in disaster. Avitus didn't approve of this alliance, and Liston would never be able to convince him otherwise. But perhaps it was too late to right the ship. Perhaps all he could do now was stand back and hope that Liston would prove him wrong. Maybe the Civs had changed. But Avitus sincerely doubted it.

"I assume your mind hasn't changed on ... other things," Avitus said cautiously, not wanting to upset Liston.

"If all goes well on Election Day, then an alliance with the Civs will truly be on the table," said Liston. "But even if the Expansionists keep the Cooperative, there's still a chance we can lobby them, get them to see that an alliance with the Civs is in our best interests. And then, we can finally end this standoff with the Core and focus on issues that matter."

Avitus decided he would keep his thoughts to himself. He had tried to get Liston to see that the Civs were no better than the Coronians, but clearly, Liston was too invested in his alliance to back out now. Maybe it was Liston's deep-seated pride that prevented him from acknowledging he'd made an error in judgment. Or maybe he genuinely believed this alliance would be the first step toward de-escalation.

Liston studied Avitus. "I know you don't agree."

"That doesn't matter. You're the Lord Regent, not I. You must do what you think is right."

That seemed to assuage some of Liston's concerns. The tension in the room alleviated, and all was as it'd been before. Avitus knew that to maintain an open line of communication with Liston, he could never bring up the Civitan again. It would be difficult, of course, but his love for Liston ran deeper than his hatred for the Civitan.

He couldn't risk losing Liston. Not again.

He'd make sure of that.

38

BANNER

Banner hadn't expected to spend his evening at the Ostend Theater, but when Caine called him and asked if he wanted to go, he didn't feel like he could say no. His friendship with Caine was still new, and he didn't want to risk doing anything to offend or upset him. Consequently, Banner donned one of his best suits and took the train to the Theater District.

"I heard Janelle Morrisey was reprising her role as Henna Rodgers just for this weekend, and I couldn't let that opportunity pass me by," Caine explained as they stood in line for the bar.

Banner had no idea who Janelle Morrisey was or what this play was about or why it mattered so much to Caine, but he didn't care. The drinks were free, and as far as Banner was concerned, that was a good enough reason to come.

"By the by," Caine went on, his voice a whisper, "have you gotten anywhere with Raelynn's family file?"

"Uh ... no," Banner answered. Sensing Caine's disappointment, he hastily added, "But that doesn't mean Kosabeus isn't working on it."

"Kosabeus?" Caine furrowed his eyebrows. "Why did you have to get him involved?"

"Because he's the most resourceful person I know."

Caine crossed his arms. "I'm still ... I don't know why you brought him to dinner."

"I wanted to see what he thought of Raelynn."

"And?"

"And he didn't tell me what he thinks. Not yet, anyway. But—"

"I don't trust Kosabeus," Caine said bluntly. "And I'd appreciate it if in the future, you kept him out of this. If I wanted his help, I would've asked for it myself."

"I didn't know you two had a history."

"We don't," Caine snapped, his composure slipping. "I just don't trust him, that's all." He heaved a deep breath. "Look," he drawled, "if you don't think you can deliver—"

"I can. And I will. Promise."

"I'm trusting you, Cyno," Caine said, waving a finger. "Don't make me regret it."

Banner didn't want to press the issue anymore, so he nodded mutely, collected his whiskey, and headed into the theater with Caine. The play was fine, but Banner wasn't really paying attention to it. His mind was on other things—such as Whitner.

Banner hated it when Whitner was angry with him. It ate him up inside. A few days had passed since their awkward lunch, but Banner knew he couldn't put this off forever. At the end of the day, Whitner's friendship meant more to Banner than his ego—which was what ultimately led him to Whitner's door at one in the morning.

"Go away," Whitner said from within.

"Come on, Dane. I came to apologize. I mean, the way I acted at lunch the other day ... you had every right to leave."

Banner could hear movement from inside the apartment. Sluggishly, the door unlocked, and Whitner was standing on the other side.

"You're really sorry?" Whitner asked, hands on his hips.

"I'm really sorry."

Whitner smiled. "Then I forgive you."

Whitner was the most forgiving person Banner knew. Holding a grudge just wasn't in his nature.

Banner hadn't been inside Whitner's apartment in a while. It was still the same boring place it'd always been. Whitner wasn't one for wall decorations, personal touches, or anything that could have made his apartment seem even remotely homey. But Banner didn't mind; his place was rather barren too.

"Would you like some coffee or something?" asked Whitner.

Banner laughed. "I didn't come here for coffee, Dane."

"No, I know. You came to apologize."

"That's not all I came here for."

"Oh?" Whitner cleared his throat. "But it, uh ... it's been a while."

"Shouldn't that help?"

Whitner's hands were shaking. "I wasn't prepared for this, Cyno. I mean, where were you tonight? Were you with Harlyn or—?"

"No."

"And how can I believe that?"

"Because it's the truth."

Whitner eyed him. "Where were you, then?"

"If you must know, I was at the theater with Eliseo."

"So, if I asked him, he'd back that up?"

"Yes." Banner took off his suit jacket. "But you're stalling."

"No. I'm just trying to get all the facts."

"Well, does that ease your mind, knowing where I was?"

Whitner nodded. "It ... helps."

Banner stepped closer to him. "I figured it would." He had Whitner cornered against the wall. "But I don't want to do this if you're not—"

"No, I am." Whitner met his eyes. "But you already know that."

A few hours later, as Whitner lay in bed, Banner collected his clothes from the floor. He freed his tie from the bedpost, slinging it around his neck.

"That was fun," he said, all the while looking in the mirror. "We shouldn't let so much time go by next time."

"Whatever you want, Cyno."

39

RAELYNN

Raelynn was about to meet Liston to discuss the next step of the Civitan alliance. Raelynn had been in close communication with Ambassador Barringer's team for weeks, relaying to them her thoughts on how Imperium could help the Civitan secure its autonomy. She had won them over enough, it seemed, to warrant a trip to New Caelus to meet with Liston and Raelynn on Imperial soil. It was a move that, frankly, shocked Raelynn, but Liston seemed unfazed by it. Ambassador Barringer would arrive in Imperium during Aperysis, when all Imperial government offices were closed. Consequently, they had a lot of work to do to make sure that everything was ready.

When Raelynn neared Liston's office, the door was already open. Raelynn had known Liston for quite a while now, so she knew how flippant Liston was about his own security. He didn't lock his townhouse or his office, it seemed. It didn't make sense to Raelynn, but then again, it also didn't make sense why Liston, as an alcoholic, surrounded himself with so many whiskey bottles. Raelynn just had to accept that Liston was an enigma she would never fully understand.

Liston stood by his desk, absently looking over some documents, his glasses on the ridge of his nose. Instead of his usual three-piece suit, he was wearing suspenders.

Hearing Raelynn, Liston looked up, a smile on his lips. "Ah. Raelynn. Come in," he said, waving her in.

Raelynn meandered over to the windows, looking out at the schools of fish passing by. "So, Ambassador Barringer has agreed to come to New Caelus to meet with us?"

"Yes. Aperysis will be here before you know it, so we don't have a lot of time."

Aperysis was a religious holiday that lasted for the whole month of Brumus. During Aperysis, Imperials celebrated the past, present, and future of Imperium, all while paying their respects to Mystis. For the most part, all government and Church offices were closed, though there was still some activity. Aperysis was high time for travel. Kosabeus, as the Head Prophate, was the leader of Aperysis. He spent the month traveling all over Imperium, delivering sermons in every major city and town, instilling Imperials with hope and charity. Raelynn had attended several of Kosabeus's sermons when she was in Satias. She remembered thinking how gifted Kosabeus was. In a three-hour-long sermon, he could pull people into his world, make them believe every word he uttered. It was a talent that could, very easily, be abused.

Liston retrieved his suit jacket from the back of his chair. "But let's get out of here, shall we? I thought we could get out in the city, go to Taeras Stadium."

"Taeras Stadium?" Raelynn cocked her head to the side. "The Fireball arena?"

Fireball was one of Imperium's most popular and beloved one-player sports. The purpose was to skillfully guide the ball—always colored as red as fire—through a series of uniquely sized ground rings as quickly as possible, taking care to not lose control of the ball or trip. The course involved various obstacles that impeded the dribbler's journey, such as hills, sand and water traps, wires, and blocks. There were one hundred rings in all, spread out across the entire field, and the dribbler had to lead their ball through all the rings, in any order they wished. The course differed slightly each time, although the number of obstacles remained the same. It was a sport that required precision, speed, strategy, and agility.

"I've been told you're quite the Fireball fan, and apparently, Declan Jericho is going to be challenging Kendall Myers today." Liston picked up his hat, dusting it off. "Why, do you not want to go?"

"Are you crazy? I love Fireball! And Declan Jericho ... well, he's one of the best. I just thought you wanted to discuss business."

"And I do," said Liston. "But we can discuss it there, in our box. It's much more entertaining than sitting in here, don't you think?"

Because it was Spero, Taeras Stadium wasn't as crowded as it usually was, and Liston and Raelynn easily made it through security and up to their box on the top level of the stadium. Raelynn had never been inside a Fireball box before. All types of food were attractively displayed on the table, along with a wide assortment of nonalcoholic drinks. The windows offered them a perfect view of the entire arena. Raelynn could see Declan on the green, practicing before his run.

"So, do you know exactly when Ambassador Barringer is coming?" asked Raelynn. "I know you said Aperysis, but ... that's a whole month."

"You want to get right to business, then?"

"Isn't that what you said?"

"Well, yes. But I thought you'd want to relax for a bit, take it all in." Liston rested his glass on the table. "But regarding Ambassador Barringer ... I don't know yet. I assume she'll be here in the middle of Aperysis. They don't have the time off, you know, as they don't share the same religion, but ... she'll be able to visit for a few days. It's a good time for her to come to Imperium, when everything is quiet. It'll make the news, I'm sure, and people will have their opinions, whatever they are. But this will be a monumental moment for Imperial history."

"So, obviously, if the Affiliates win control of the Cooperative, it'll be much easier for you to get this alliance through. But what about the Directorate? Do you think they'll approve of the alliance?"

The Directorate was the Civitan's main governmental body. Like the Cooperative, it was in charge of drafting treaties and laws, which meant that for an alliance between Imperium and the Civitan to be secured, both the Cooperative and the Directorate needed to support it.

"The terms we've laid out are favorable to the Civitan—more favorable than they could have hoped for. Imperium will recognize their political independence and sovereignty. We will also guarantee Imperial military support against possible Coronian aggression for the next fifty years. And for us, we request to be the Civitan's premier trading partner."

"Do you think that's enough for Imperium?"

"The Civitan is a top exporter of fine silks, jewelry, spices, you name it," said Liston, propping his feet up on the table. "But their planet lacks more ... biotic resources and has to rely heavily on Coronian imports to survive. I reckon that Imperium could step in and replace the Core. We could become the Civitan's primary trade partner. If we cut out the Core from any possible dealings with the Civitan now and in the future, we stand to make billions in profits, if not trillions. Imagine what we could do with that extra numa."

Raelynn tried to ignore the rowdy fans outside the box, all cheering Declan on. "Just curious. How long have you been working on this alliance?"

"The better part of three years."

Raelynn's eyes widened. "That's a long time."

"Diplomacy is tedious, Raelynn. You soon learn that everyone has an angle, and they don't always make sense. But you must work with what you have. There have been a few missteps here and there. I've had to change some elements, make some addendums, all that. But I believe our final product is quite remarkable. But for now." He reached over the arm of the couch and retrieved his briefcase. He opened it up, removing a book. "I have some reading to catch up on."

Raelynn raised an eyebrow. "You brought a book to Fireball?"

"Well, you know how these things go. They will both run the course a few times, and there will be all these starts and stops. It can be rather ... monotonous."

"So, you hate Fireball, is what you're saying."

"I don't hate it. But ... I certainly don't ... love it. I just thought it'd be a nice change in pace."

"Well, I really appreciate you bringing me here." Raelynn pointed at Liston's book. "But don't you ever get sick of reading?"

"Sorry?" Liston asked, leaning closer to Raelynn, perhaps hoping he'd misheard.

"Don't you ever get sick of reading?" repeated Raelynn. "I mean, your townhouse has that library with a couple thousand books."

"You can never have too many books, Raelynn."

"I disagree. Back at Satias, I was drowning in textbooks. Lord Knox assigned ten books for his course. Ten. It was only twelve weeks."

"Ah. Lord Knox." Liston chuckled, not even glancing up from his book. "He's still teaching, then?"

"If you can call it that," scoffed Raelynn, the terrible memories of Knox's class returning to her. "He basically just yelled at us and thought that was enough."

"He's an unorthodox educator."

"He's crazy."

"That too."

Raelynn turned toward the arena, watching as the ground crew prepared the green for Kendall's run. She stood up, walked over to the windows, and looked down on the stadium. She could see diehard Fireball fans, decked out in the uniform of their favorite player.

"Look at all these people, skipping out on work to be here," she mused.

Liston finally looked up from his book. "Is that some sort of remark?"

"If you want it to be."

Liston jokingly dropped his jaw, placing his book beside him. "I did this for you," he said with feigned incredulity, pointing his index finger at Raelynn.

"Right, sure. 'Cause it's so torturous to skip out of the office for the rest of the afternoon and watch Fireball."

"Well, yes. It is."

Raelynn laughed, her hands in the air in mock surrender. "Fine. I take it back."

"Then I forgive you." Liston smiled. "Now, would you mind moving a bit to your right? You're blocking my view."

40

VISCARDIA

Viscardia loved all her colleagues in their own, special ways, but she felt the closest affinity with Avitus. At first glance, perhaps, Viscardia and Avitus had nothing in common. Whereas Viscardia was a wife and a mother, Avitus was a bachelor. Avitus was an Expansionist, and Viscardia was an Affiliate. Avitus had served in the military, and Viscardia hadn't.

And yet Viscardia and Avitus were also strikingly similar. They both saw the universe for what it was: flawed. They hadn't allowed the Church to delude them into thinking that Imperium was the most perfect, tolerant power the universe had ever seen. They knew there was much work to be done to make things right. Though they disagreed on what that work would entail, they weren't idle visionaries; they had the ability—and desire—to act on their convictions.

Avitus, Viscardia knew, was a guarded person. He kept much of himself to himself, and what little warmth he had he reserved, it seemed, for Liston. But unlike most of her colleagues, Viscardia had never been intimidated by Avitus. She was just as blunt with him as she was with anyone else. If she disagreed with him, then she said something.

Over time, Avitus came to like and even trust Viscardia. He became more open with her, inviting her to lunch and requesting her opinion on various matters. She knew that Kosabeus and Avitus were good friends—far better friends than she and Avitus were—but they spent most of their time discussing their Lord Regents and Church matters. Viscardia and Avitus talked about philosophy, mortality, and religion, and neither ever held back. They knew that with each other, they were in a safe space, and nothing they said would ever be relayed to anyone else.

Avitus and Viscardia both had Fidem morning off, so they agreed to rendezvous at the indoor shooting range to brush up on their skills.

"I think I beat you last time," said Viscardia, removing her revolver from her bag. She loaded the ammunition, and Avitus did the same.

"No, no, no," said Avitus agreeably. "Though you did come close." He turned to her. "I remember when I first started taking you here. Even back then, you were a good shot. But now you're almost as good as me."

"That's certainly high praise, Mr. Former Colonel."

Avitus cracked his knuckles. "I did well for myself in the military. Could've made a real career out of it."

"Tell me honestly. If you could go back and change it, would you still leave the military and rejoin the Church?"

"Being in the military was an honor. But when you're on the ground, you can't see the use of what you're doing. All you see is the slaughter. And you start to wonder if what you're doing is making a difference. As a Prophate, I get to see the fruits of my labor."

"And it's worth it?"

"Most assuredly." Avitus smirked. "But you're stalling. Five rounds, into the target."

Viscardia assumed her stance, securing her earmuffs. In her peripheral vision, she saw Avitus do the same. Because her left eye was slightly better, she closed her right one, aiming her revolver at the target. Steadily, she moved the revolver up a little higher, then—

BANG! BANG! BANG! BANG! BANG!

Avitus applauded from a few yards behind her. "Very nice," he praised, removing his earmuffs. "You kept your form the whole time. Let's see it up close." Viscardia reeled the target in, and Avitus leaned forward, studying it. He nodded, impressed. "Four of the five were fatal shots."

Viscardia draped her earmuffs around her neck. "So, I'm rusty."

"You're a great shot," he said, patting her on the back. "You would've made a fine soldier. They need more people like you—people who are uncowering in the line of duty."

"Well, I don't know how I'd be on the actual battlefield," Viscardia admitted. "I've never been in a life-or-death situation before."

"But you're smart, quick on your feet. You'd be magnificent."

Viscardia took down her target and replaced it with another. "All right, you go. Five shots, on the clock."

They both put their earmuffs back over their ears. Avitus stood artfully, as if it were a rehearsed dance. She figured it was, in a way. Avitus must have been a glorious sight on the battlefield, coming in at almost seven feet tall. She'd seen the accolades on his dress uniform; she knew how valiantly he'd served Imperium. Sometimes, Viscardia wondered how many people had faced death when staring down the barrel of his gun.

Effortlessly, he fired his rounds straight into the target. Without even seeing the target up close, Viscardia knew they were all headshots.

She again removed her earmuffs. "And ... yup, all headshots," she said as Avitus reeled the target in. "You're a beast."

"I was in the military for twenty-one years," Avitus reminded her, taking off his earmuffs. "This was my life. You had to shoot to survive."

Viscardia unhooked his target for him, putting up a new one. "Still. I have hope that one of these days, I'll get the better of you."

"I'm an old man, with fading vision. Believe me, you will." Avitus rested his revolver on the table. "You know," he said, eyeing Viscardia carefully, "when I first met you, you were quite young. Do you remember? It was in Pacalis. I had to visit your school to give a lecture. And even then, I knew you were going to be a Prophate. You were one of the most brilliant Numites I'd ever met. If I recall correctly, you were the only student in the class who could recite the opening lines of *Imperium for the Ages: Book I* from memory. Am I remembering that right?"

"Maybe," laughed Viscardia, her face reddening.

"I wonder if you still can." Avitus drummed his fingers on the table. "Go on."

Viscardia cleared her throat. "'There comes a time in a man's life when the decision to stay is more dangerous than the decision to leave. The Core no longer serves our interests. It has attempted to destroy us by conducting a genocide against our people, the Keepers of the True Faith. Mystis is our god. A cleansing of the Keepers will not cleanse the truth. The light will break through, and the Coronians will be revealed as heretics. We thus move to found our own society, away from the carnage and prejudice. Our society is built upon the True Faith, with one god and seven rulers. We will call it Imperium. And we will serve Mystis.'" Viscardia looked up at Avitus. "Want me to keep going?"

"No. That's fine."

Viscardia prepared to shoot again, moving toward her revolver. She wiped her hands to ensure she would have the best possible grip.

"Do you believe it?" Avitus asked suddenly.

Viscardia's hand froze in midair. "No one's ever asked me that before."

"That's because they feared the answer."

Avitus stepped closer to her. Although Viscardia knew Avitus would never hurt her, he could sometimes frighten her with his sheer physicality. His hand appeared as though it could grip her entire neck.

"I know you, Viscardia," he murmured. "I know you as well as a man should know his greatest colleague. But there's something in you that isn't in the rest of us. Doubt. All of us Prophates, we're so sure the Numite faith is right, that Mystis is our true god, that we will reunite with him in Obasus Garden. But you aren't."

Viscardia looked down at her revolver. "Some things are more certain in life."

"Does it scare you, then? The afterlife?"

"No."

"Do you believe in Mystis?"

"I believe in what I can see."

"And do you see Mystis?"

"Every day," said Viscardia dryly, her hand to her chest. "He's in my heart."

"I didn't mean to question your faith. It's just ... when you quote from the theology, you don't have the same ... vigor the rest of us do. But maybe you show your faith in different ways."

"Or maybe faith only gets you so far." Viscardia focused her attention on the target. "You can't live your life through faith alone."

"They certainly didn't teach you that in the Church."

"I taught it to myself. Growing up an orphan, you learn to take care of yourself."

"We're all orphans, Viscardia. The Church saved us from a life on the streets. Our faith gave us hope."

"Faith didn't put food in my mouth or clothes on my back. It just gave me something to pray to at night to make me feel less alone. But in the morning, when the sun broke through, it was always just me. Mystis wasn't anywhere to be seen."

Avitus put his hands behind his back, his posture as straight as an arrow. "So, you don't believe it."

Viscardia laughed, tracing her revolver's handle with her finger. "They say you aren't doing any public events for the Expansionists this election season. Is that true?"

"It is," said Avitus with a humorously solemn nod. "Prophates, like the Justices, shouldn't be openly political. Especially when their political beliefs differ from their Lord Regent's. Banner and Whitner are the ones who will speak for the Expansionists."

"And Kosabeus, probably."

"Kosabeus isn't a politician."

"He seems to think he is."

Avitus scoffed. His eyes roamed, seeing something Viscardia's couldn't. It was remarkable, Viscardia thought, how enigmatic Avitus was. She couldn't help but feel like she'd never truly know him, like a part of him would always be concealed.

"There are many things I admire about Kosabeus," he started judiciously. "Even at his lowest times ... even when he was sick and should've stayed home ... he was always at the Church, delivering his sermons, chatting with his constituents. I remember a few times, after he'd given a sermon, when he'd go to his office and just ... collapse. He's always worked himself too hard. But he said, repeatedly, that he had to be on that stage every day. He wanted the Imperial people to know he was with them." Avitus smiled. "He is, undoubtedly, a great Head Prophate. He's breathed life into the Church. And he's shepherded in many changes that have put the Church back on the map. He really ... he's a good friend. But Kosabeus ... he wants the Church to be something it isn't."

"You mean politically engaged?"

Avitus sighed. "Numites shouldn't be running for office or otherwise acting like politicians. It upsets the entire ecosystem, blurs the boundaries, makes our different spheres all too linked."

"But you could argue that the Church is already political. Prophates work with the Lord Regents. We're intrinsically connected to Imperial government."

"But we're there to serve our Lord Regent, to offer guidance, not to give our political opinion."

Viscardia couldn't help but laugh. "Are you trying to say you've never tried to push Lev into doing a certain thing? Because I know you don't approve of his alliance with the Civitan."

"That's different."

"How?"

"It's in private. The conversations I have with my Lord Regent about politics are not aired out in public for all of Imperium to hear."

"So, do you think less of me and Kosabeus for letting our views be known?"

"No." Avitus met her eyes. "But I do think it makes you both dangerous."

"In what way?"

Avitus was silent. He distractedly traced his revolver's handle, a pensive expression on his face. Then he slowly turned back to Viscardia.

"I've had this same discussion with Kosabeus numerous times," he said. "And I know that with you, it'll end in the exact same way it does with him."

"And how is that?"

Avitus smiled wryly. "I'll keep my opinions to myself."

"Oh, come on, Avitus. You can't just say something like that but refuse to back it up."

"I think you'll find that I can."

"Fine." Viscardia smiled, despite herself. "Well, how about four more rounds?"

"Why not? You could use the practice."

41

WHITNER

It wasn't something he was proud of. It wasn't even something he could explain or defend. He knew all about Banner's past—and present—but that didn't matter. It didn't change anything.

Whitner had been in love with Banner for practically his entire life. He wasn't sure if Banner had always known, but he assumed he must have; it wasn't like Whitner was particularly subtle about his affections. Back in Ligva, he'd followed Banner around like a puppy, waiting for him to see him in a different light. The idea of Banner someday reciprocating his feelings wasn't far-fetched. After all, it wasn't like Banner was uninterested in men. He was interested in everybody. It didn't matter how someone identified; Banner slept with them all. Thus, Whitner had allowed himself to hold out hope that one day, Banner would start to look at him as more than a friend.

And finally, after decades, he did.

They first started sleeping together a few years ago. It happened randomly, and neither of them had expected it, but it was even better than Whitner could have dreamed. It was like Whitner's teenage fantasy had finally been realized, forty years later. Afterward, Whitner had deluded himself into thinking that this was it, that Banner was going to choose him. At last, all Whitner's years of pining would pay off, and he and Banner would be together.

But here they were, years later, and nothing had changed. Banner continued to sleep with anyone he could get his hands on, and Whitner continued to wait for Banner to change. Whitner knew that Banner cared for him, but he wasn't sure if he loved him. He wasn't sure if Banner loved anything, least of all himself. He'd never been one to talk about his emotions, and Whitner never pushed him, worried that his answer would be something he couldn't unhear ...

And so, Whitner kept his thoughts and fears to himself. He didn't date or pursue anyone else. His mind had been made up years ago, and nothing would ever change it.

Banner was it for him. And that was perhaps Whitner's greatest flaw.

42

RAELYNN

Raelynn sat in her office, compiling details of the upcoming summit with Ambassador Barringer and her team. Raelynn was, expectedly, excited about the whole ordeal. She found the Civs to be a fascinating group of people. Civs were renowned for their intelligence and practicality; their education system promoted curiosity, encouraging students to dabble in a litany of different subjects. Raelynn, like all students in the Keeper system, had been awarded the chance to minor in one of the six other fields, but she'd chosen not to. In retrospect, Raelynn didn't know why; she wished she'd spread her wings and developed a better understanding of Media and Technology. Instead, partly due to laziness, she'd decided to focus solely on Diplomacy.

"Raelynn."

Raelynn looked up and saw Corlander standing at the door, a wry smile on his lips. "Hi, Corlander." Raelynn pushed away from her desk. "What do you need?"

"It's not me. It's Avitus, our Lord Regent's Prophate. He ... wishes to speak with you."

Raelynn stiffened. "He, uh ... does?"

"Yes. Shall I send him in?"

"Uh." Raelynn quickly loosened her collar. "Sure. Um. Yes."

After Corlander left, Raelynn stood up, hastily spiffing up her office by filing away some of her papers and shoving her knickknacks into her desk. She didn't know Avitus at all, but she assumed he was the type of man who preferred a clear working space.

"Lord Mabry." Avitus had to bend down to make it through Raelynn's door. "Thank you for agreeing to see me."

Raelynn hadn't really agreed to this meeting, but she didn't think it was appropriate to tell Avitus that. She simply gestured to the two armchairs off to the side.

"Do you care to sit?" asked Raelynn as calmly as she could muster.

Avitus didn't answer. Instead, he strolled the perimeter of Raelynn's office, taking it all in. He was an infuriatingly difficult man to read. It was impossible to tell whether he approved or disapproved of something; his facial expression remained unchanged as he surveyed all of Raelynn's belongings.

"Our Lord Regent didn't put you in one of the shoe boxes, then," he said at last, looking at the windows. "You must know how unusual that is, for someone your age to be in an office like this."

"Yes. I am very grateful for Lord Regent Liston's, uh, help."

Avitus peeled his eyes away from the ocean. "I didn't know about you, you know. Our Lord Regent didn't tell me he was assuming a protégé. He doesn't usually leave me out of such decisions. But when I found out you'll be helping him with his Civitan alliance ... it all made sense."

At five-foot-six, Raelynn was taller than most of her female peers. But she felt positively dwarfed next to Avitus, who appeared almost as though he were going to burst through the roof.

"I specialized in Civ history and culture back in Satias," Raelynn said, feeling as though she had to justify herself. "Liston—er, our Lord Regent—seems to think I can help him with the ins and outs of this alliance."

"You agree with him, then? That the Civitan can be trusted?"

"Yes." Making eye contact with Avitus was one of the most difficult things Raelynn had ever done. She wondered if her neck would ever recover. "They are a fast-evolving society. They are hardly the same people they were during the Glass War."

"So I've been told." Avitus rested his hand on the back of one of the armchairs. "But I can't help but think our Lord Regent is making a mistake."

"He's been working on this alliance for years."

"But, you see, our Lord Regent is a man of tireless idealism. And idealism ... it isn't the best tool to bring to such negotiations. Especially when Commander Heston will be sitting across from him at the table." Avitus traced his finger along the armchair. "But I have relayed my sentiments to our Lord Regent, time and time again, and he has decided to not heed them."

"He's very passionate about this alliance."

"And why do you think that is?"

Raelynn pulled on her sleeve, to occupy her hands. "I don't think that's any of my business, knowing why he wants this alliance. I'm just helping with communications. I know about the Civitan's history, see, and as an Imperial, I—"

"I know about the Civitan's history too. They spent decades killing our people on the battlefield. They killed my brothers in arms. What makes your textbook knowledge more valuable than my real-world experience?"

Raelynn fought the urge to vomit. She'd never been made to feel so woefully insignificant in such a short period of time. There had been times back in Satias when one of her teachers had embarrassed her in front of her peers, but that happened to every student at one time or another; it was more of a rite of passage than anything else. This was completely different. A Prophate was openly questioning Raelynn's competence. Her face blanched; her hands shook. To Avitus, she must have appeared as nothing more than a little girl masquerading as an adult.

Avitus stepped away from the armchair, nearing Raelynn. "I will say this only once," he said, a malignant edge to his voice. "I will not stand aside and let you become my Lord Regent's chief confidant. I know our Lord Regent far too well to be eclipsed by some upstart with a penchant for being in the right place at the right time. Do we understand each other?"

Raelynn's heart thumped in her chest. "Yes. We do."

Something akin to a smile formed on Avitus's lips. "Good."

43

RAELYNN

When Liston told Raelynn about the fundraising party the Church was hosting, Raelynn had tried to come up with some sort of excuse to explain why she couldn't go. She was still rattled by her confrontation with Avitus, and she didn't know what she'd say or do if she had to make small talk with Avitus next to the drinks table.

"Avitus doesn't drink, so you don't have to worry about that," Liston had said brightly.

"But ... I don't think you're understanding just how traumatic it was, him coming into my office and ... and just ... laying into me."

"Avitus can be a tad territorial. Don't take what he said to heart. He just ... he finds it hard to trust new people. And besides, if you don't want to talk to Avitus, you don't have to. There will be plenty of other people there. You'll have fun."

"Sure. Because standing around listening to sermons and feeling compelled to donate numa sounds like a really fun Ortus night."

"Oh, come on, Raelynn. Don't be so morose."

Thus, against her will, Raelynn found herself spending her Ortus night in

Mystis Concert Hall. It was a nice enough venue, though certainly not as grand as Abbas Hall. Expectedly, there was a lot of religious art on the walls, and the place was filled with Numites. Raelynn knew that all the Prophates had to wear specific robes—black robes for everyone but the Head Prophate, who wore white—but she hadn't been aware that regular Numites also wore robes. Theirs seemed to come in three main colors: blue, red, and gold. Raelynn, for her part, didn't know what the colors represented.

Embry, of course, had the answer.

"Well, you see, the Numites wearing blue all work in the Numentis schools. The Numites wearing red work outside the Church. They're more … community activists, that sort of thing. And the Numites wearing gold work within the Church. They're also called Erates. They're the ones on all the various committees and stuff like that."

"Where'd you learn all of that?" asked Raelynn.

"In school." Embry raised an eyebrow. "What, they didn't teach you Keepers all about the Numites?"

"Maybe they did. But I certainly didn't remember any of that."

"You should've paid more attention."

"Why? I seem to have done all right for myself."

Embry laughed. "Fair enough. Well, hey, let's make sure we're in a good spot. Looks like Kosabeus is about to give his 'Give me all your numa' speech."

"Excuse me." Kosabeus was standing at the podium. "Excuse me, everyone. May I have your attention?" Slowly, the din in the room quieted. Kosabeus smiled warmly. "Thank you very much. I am Kosabeus, the Head Prophate of the Numentis Church. I have had the honor of serving as a Prophate for twenty years and as Head Prophate for the past fifteen. I truly cannot express how humbled I am to hold this position. When I was a child, I could only fantasize about how my life would turn out. I was always ambitious. You can ask any of my teachers, some of whom, actually, are here with us tonight—and who are, I am hoping, kind enough to share only the flattering stories."

There were a few laughs in the audience. Thanks to the information that Embry had shared, Raelynn now knew that the Numites in blue were the ones who worked in the Numentis schools, so she scanned the crowd, wondering if she could tell who Kosabeus's primary teachers had been.

Kosabeus continued, "But my ambition was always closely matched by my faith. I see Mystis as so much more than a god. He is, in many ways, the symbol of Imperium itself, for if he hadn't stood up to the Coronian monarchy, we wouldn't be here today. Mystis gave the ultimate sacrifice—his life—to ensure that Imperium would prosper for thousands of years to come. And here we are.

"It is with immense pride I introduce my esteemed colleagues." Kosabeus indicated to his left, where the other Prophates stood. "I may be biased, but I believe our current lineup of Prophates is nothing short of the finest in Imperial history. We have Astrophel, the Prophate of Intelligence and Espionage. Avitus, the Prophate of Diplomacy. Lisbeth, the Prophate of Finance and Business. Puck, the Prophate of Science and Medicine. Grell, the acting Prophate of Media and Technology. And Viscardia, the Prophate of Logistics and Transportation." As he introduced each one, he gestured toward them. "Please, if you will, give a round of applause for my wonderful colleagues."

The room erupted with applause. Raelynn was somewhat taken aback. She knew that the Prophates were esteemed, but she hadn't expected them to be celebrated like this. Then again, she'd never been to a Church-run party before, so perhaps this was how they all were.

"Now, I'm sure you know that the Church is responsible for so much more than daily sermons and religious services. We have Numites who work in every city, town, and hamlet in Imperium, and the work they do is not always directly connected to the Church. They organize drives to help underprivileged families afford books, clothes, food, and other necessities. They offer counseling services for those dealing with grief, loss, depression, or any other type of crisis. They offer scholarships to students who show immense potential but lack the resources to go to their dream school. They arrange free childcare for working parents. You see, the Church permeates every facet of our lives, and it is so much more than a single institution.

"We hope that tonight, you will consider giving whatever you can to aid us in all our future pursuits. Without your generous donations, we wouldn't be able to offer a quarter of all the services we do. We have some representatives from each of the ten orphanages and Numentis schools here tonight. They will be more than happy to answer any questions you may have about the Church or how you can become involved in, say, tutoring or assisting with childcare. And, of course, my fellow Prophates and I are available too, if you wish to learn more about who is giving a sermon on which day. For any queries you may have regarding Aperysis, please come see me. I would be delighted to discuss it. We also have many of our Erates here. Please, engage them in conversation about what the Church means to them. But again, I thank you all. Enjoy your night!"

Raelynn turned to Embry. "What do you do for Aperysis?"

"Mom and I usually go see Dad's family for a bit, or they come down and see us."

"Oooo, did I hear you talking about Aperysis over here?" asked Taymor, coming up behind Embry, resting her hands on her shoulders. "It can't come soon enough, if you ask me. I could use the time off."

"I know you could. I was just telling Raelynn how we usually spend it," Embry said. "Do you know what we're doing this year?"

"Well, it's been a couple years since we went up to see your father's family, so we could do that. If you want."

"No problem. I will make sure to pack my warmest winter jacket."

Taymor smiled, then turned her attention to Raelynn. "It's good to see you again, Raelynn. Levin tells me you've been busy."

"Yes," said Raelynn, nodding. "There's a lot of work to do to prepare for Ambassador Barringer's arrival in Brumus. And the elections are coming up, of course."

"Yes, of course. And how does Levin feel about the elections? What does he say?"

"He seems confident."

"Does he, now? Well, I hope you'll at least get some of Aperysis off."

"We'll see."

"If you need me to talk to Levin and get him to ease up on you, I will."

Raelynn laughed. "I don't mind. It's been the most exciting stuff I've ever done, helping him work on this alliance."

"I can imagine." Taymor absently clutched her necklace. "Well, I'll let you two chat. I have to go mingle, pretend to be social."

"Sorry, Mom," Embry said, offering her mother a sympathetic look. "But just think ... in a couple hours, you'll be back home, all tucked up with a book."

"Mmmm." Taymor put her hand to her heart. "Something to look forward to."

Raelynn watched as Taymor made her way through the crowd. A few Numites stopped her, no doubt trying their best to get some numa out of her. Taymor seemed to take it in stride, though, and she politely chatted with them. It had to be exhausting, putting on this sort of front at every public event, having to pretend to be interested in everything everyone was saying.

"Maybe we should take our cue from Mom and, you know, mingle a bit, make some new friends." Embry turned to Raelynn. "What do you think?"

"That sounds like hell."

"You're so dramatic! Come on!"

Raelynn winced as Embry darted away. Not wanting to be left alone, she followed her, hoping this night wouldn't be as painful as she thought.

44

BANNER

Everyone's footsteps rang out on the tile floor, giving Banner a migraine. He hated Mystis Concert Hall. The acoustics were jarring, and the place was not nearly big enough to house the number of partygoers currently within its walls. People kept bumping into him, stepping on his toes, brushing against his back. Yet somehow, in the crowd, he found Kosabeus.

"Kosabeus," growled Banner. Kosabeus didn't look up. His arms were wrapped around Grell's waist, and he was whispering something into her ear. "Kosabeus."

Annoyed, Kosabeus glowered at him. "What?"

"We need to talk." Before Kosabeus could object, Banner grabbed him by the arm, pulling him away, over near the bar. "Here," he said, stopping underneath one of the faux lemon trees. "Here's good."

Kosabeus crossed his arms. "This had better be worth my time."

"Eliseo and I went to the theater the other night."

"And you didn't invite me?"

Banner glared at him. "This is serious."

"I know. You know how much I love the theater. I'm absolutely gutted you didn't—"

"Will you just stop with the jokes for one minute?" Banner glanced around conspiratorially, even though Caine wasn't in the vicinity. He never attended Church events. "Eliseo's starting to lose faith in us. He thinks we're hiding something from him."

Kosabeus furrowed his eyebrows. "What are you talking about?"

"You know. About the whole Raelynn thing. Eliseo's ... turning on us. Well, really, he's turning on you. He doesn't seem to like you that much. And ... to be honest, I don't think I want to work with a man who doesn't trust you."

"I must say, Cyno, I'm deeply moved."

"Yeah, yeah, yeah," grumbled Banner with a dismissive wave of his free hand. "Don't get too high a head about it."

"'Too high a head'?" laughed Kosabeus.

"That's a saying, isn't it?"

"Not even a little bit."

"Well, you know what I mean. Don't get all high and mighty."

"I'll make sure my head stays low to the ground." He leaned against one of the pillars. "But you needn't worry about Caine, Cyno. I've taken care of it."

"Taken care of what?"

"Let's just say, Caine will have his answer."

"What do you mean by that?"

"I know why he's so interested in Raelynn."

"You do? Why?"

Kosabeus smirked. "I'll let him tell you that."

"Tell me what? Come on, Kosabeus. You never hold out on me."

"I know. But I'm feeling rather ... evasive tonight." Kosabeus laughed. "Well, if you'll excuse me, Cyno, I should continue milling about, wringing as much numa out of these people as possible."

"How much do you need?"

"The Church was aiming for at least twenty million."

Banner whistled through his teeth. "Steep."

"I know," said Kosabeus, distractedly examining his nail beds. "They had months to raise it, but they were sitting around, doing nothing. So, this party's our only shot. Apparently, we're not doing so badly. They think we've raised about three million. But once Grell makes her way through the crowd, we'll hit that target, no problem. She's the best closer we have."

"Well, this place is full of Keepers who don't know what to do with their numa. So, you should do pretty well."

"How much can I put you down for?" asked Kosabeus charmingly, smiling at Banner.

"Really?" laughed Banner. "You're trying to get numa out of me?"

"Think of it as helping out a friend." Kosabeus cleared his throat. "Liston and Silver donated, you know," he added purposefully.

"So?" asked Banner, though he knew Kosabeus could tell his sales pitch was getting to him.

"You don't want them to show you up, do you?"

Banner scowled. "Put me down for half a million."

"That's it?"

"You want more?"

"Between Liston and Silver alone, we made almost two million."

"They're over half your profits?"

"As of now. You can change that, if you donate, say, two million. I mean, two million is nothing to you. It's not even what you make in a week. Now, if it were me, it'd take me over fifty years to make that sort of numa."

Banner's nose scrunched. "Glad I'm not you, then."

"I make do." Kosabeus sized Banner up, his eyes radiating judgment. "But you could do with being a bit more ... philanthropic."

"I don't like giving away numa. I know a noble cause when I see one, and no offense, but this isn't one of them."

Kosabeus crossed his arms. "Are you really saying you don't want to help poor little orphans get a roof over their heads, food on their tables, and clothes on their backs?"

Banner rolled his eyes. "You would've been a terrible salesman."

"So, does that mean you'll donate?"

"Fine. But you owe me."

"What do you have in mind?"

"I want you to convince Avitus and Astrophel to speak at the Expansionist rally next week."

Kosabeus laughed. "Fat chance Avitus will do it. He doesn't want to upset Liston. They've just started talking again. And besides, even if he and Liston weren't in such a precarious place, Avitus would never do it. He doesn't do political events. You know that."

"Then Astrophel. Get Astrophel to speak."

"You really think that will detract from the Affiliates' rally?"

"It could."

"I'll see what I can do," Kosabeus said, running his fingers through his hair. "But I'm not a miracle worker."

"I disagree."

"You think too highly of me."

"Don't get a high head over it," joked Banner.

Kosabeus grinned. "I think I'm having a beneficial effect on you."

"And why's that?"

"You're getting funnier."

"You think I'm funny?"

"I said *funnier*. You're *funnier* than you were. But you still have a long way to go."

"I'm done with you," Banner said, waving Kosabeus away.

"Right, right," said Kosabeus, backing away. "Three million, that's what you said?"

"Two million," corrected Banner.

"Four?" Kosabeus had his hand to his ear.

"Fine. Four." It was never worth arguing with Kosabeus; he always got his way in the end. "You better name that new wing after me!" Banner yelled after Kosabeus, who pretended not to hear him.

Banner's eyes fell on Whitner, who was standing off to the side with Astrophel. They'd been rather close lately, and Banner wasn't sure what to make of it. Astrophel was an ... interesting young man. He hadn't been a Prophate for long, but that hadn't diminished his confidence. In fact, he seemed quite comfortable cozying up to one of the most powerful men in Imperium. In the few interactions Banner had had with Astrophel, he'd gotten the impression that Astrophel was biding his time. Banner wasn't certain what exactly Astrophel was waiting for, but he had the feeling Astrophel wanted something more.

Banner took a swig of his whiskey and rolled his shoulders. He wanted to get Whitner alone and ask him if he was interested in going back to his apartment. Knowing Whitner, he wouldn't refuse; he never did. Banner started to walk toward Whitner, but along the way, he accidentally bumped into a cocktail waiter.

"Oh. Sorry," the waiter said.

"No, it was me. I'm sorry."

When Banner met the waiter's eyes, he forgot what he'd been doing or where he'd been going. Immediately, Banner was struck with the thought that this man was wasting his potential. With a face like that, chiseled to angelic precision, he could carve a real career for himself in show business. But instead, here he was, handing out drinks to Imperium's elites.

"Well, would you like another drink, my Lord Regent?" the waiter asked.

"Yes, please," Banner said absently, his mind wandering, picturing all sorts of depraved things. He met the waiter's eyes, which were framed by gloriously dark lashes. "So, what do I owe you?"

"Oh, the drinks are free."

"Well, do you take tips?"

"I don't."

"Really? Young man like you? You could make a killing here tonight. There are all sorts of rich people who don't know what proper tipping etiquette is. You could probably get five hundred numa a pop out of us if you wanted."

The waiter laughed. "I'm forbidden from accepting tips."

"So, you don't get anything out of this?"

"Well, I get paid."

"But you don't get tipped." Banner shook his head. "How are you supposed to make a living?"

"I get by." He flipped a loose hair out of his tanned face. "I must say, I didn't think someone of your ... stature would much care about the working class—people like me."

"When I was at the Ligva Academy, I used to volunteer at snooty events like these. All the older Keepers would be milling about, drinking more alcohol than I'd ever seen in my life, and I'd be a waiter. So, believe me, I know what it's like to feel unappreciated."

The waiter looked at Banner, his lips slowly curving into a smile. "You waited tables?"

"I did."

"Were you any good at it?"

"Absolute rubbish."

"Well, maybe that's why they didn't tip you." The waiter simpered. "I'm Ledger, by the way. Ledger Surrett."

"Cyno Banner."

"I know. Everyone knows."

"And is that a ... good thing or—?"

"It is for me." Ledger bit his lip. "I've always wanted to meet you."

Banner smiled, shifting on his feet. "So, do you have any other talents I should know about, besides your skills as a waiter?"

"What do you have in mind?"

"Oh, you know ..." Banner's eyes shamelessly roamed down Ledger's body, taking it all in. "... anything, really."

Ledger laughed. "Nothing I can show you right here, among all these people."

Banner stepped closer to him. "Well, when are you off shift?"

"Fifteen minutes."

"Then meet me in the hallway."

The hallway was practically empty, except for the scattered people going to and from the bathroom or slipping out to grab a smoke. Banner jealously watched as two men outside lit up their cigarettes. He wished he'd remembered to store a pack in his suit pocket.

"Well, aren't you punctual?" Ledger asked as he sauntered up to Banner. "Where are we going, then?"

Banner had spent far too many nights at Mystis Concert Hall. He knew that to the left of the main hall, down one of the long side hallways, was a bathroom hardly anyone knew about. It was, he had discovered one Fidem night, an ideal place for hookups. Before they made it all the way down to the bathroom, however, Ledger shoved Banner against the wall, kissing him with a zeal that Banner all too happily reciprocated.

Banner hadn't made out with someone like this in ... years. It was liberating, running his fingers through the thick, beautiful hair of someone who didn't have a single wrinkle on his face. Finally, here was someone with a sex drive, a real sex drive.

"The bathroom," Banner sputtered within the brief few seconds their lips were apart. "Let's take this to the bathroom."

He and Ledger stumbled in, not even checking to make sure it was empty before they started devouring each other. Ledger was every bit as carnal as Banner had hoped. With the limited tools at his disposal, he managed to make Banner beg like he'd never begged before.

Ledger stood back up, pulling Banner in for a wet, sloppy kiss. "Turn around."

Banner did as Ledger commanded. In the throes of passion, he forgot all about the elections and Liston and his sinking approval ratings. He forgot all about Caine and his strange obsession with Raelynn. He forgot all about Whitner. In this moment, he was happy—happier than he'd been in a long, long time.

All of a sudden, he didn't want this night to end.

45

VISCARDIA

Viscardia couldn't wait to take off her stupid Prophate robe. She wished it was optional, that she could have just left it in her office. But no. For Church events, all Numites had to wear their robes. It was pretentious, but worse than that, it was cumbersome. She had a stunning gold dress on underneath, but no one could tell.

"Well, *I* know," said Silver, smiling at her, a coy glint in his eyes. "And, for what it's worth, you make that robe look really sexy."

Viscardia laughed. "Well, I appreciate that."

They were standing at one of the food tables. Viscardia was wholly unimpressed by the selection. All they had were rolls, vegetable trays, and various sliced cheeses. If she'd known the food was going to be so scant, she would've eaten dinner before she got here. How could this food possibly fill her up?

"This is pathetic," Viscardia muttered, shaking her head. She turned to Silver. "We're stopping somewhere for food on our way out."

"You got it." Silver helped himself to a roll and some cheese. "Hey, weren't you guys supposed to announce your new Magista tonight?"

"We were. But apparently, the Church hasn't made its final decision yet."

"What's taking them so long?"

"I have no idea. This was supposed to be done weeks ago, but they've been dragging their feet for whatever reason."

"Maybe they have too many good candidates, so it's hard to pick just one."

"Knowing the Church, it's more likely they have too many bad candidates, so it's hard to pick the best of the worst." Viscardia sighed. "But, on the bright side, my days working for Abner are numbered, so that's great."

"Lev and I can't wait to work with Tinsley. She'll be a real powerhouse." Silver took a bite of his roll and scowled. "Stale."

"No surprise there." Viscardia didn't even pick up a plate. "In what world would this horrible party make anyone want to donate to the Church? The food's lousy, there's no live band, and the place is far too small to fit this many people."

"See, all of that is what makes me want to donate. Because I look at this, I see how low your budget clearly is, and I can't help but feel sorry for you. I mean, this roll ..." Silver hit it against the table, and the roll was unaffected. "... this is beyond tragic."

Viscardia laughed. "Then I guess the committee did its job, making us look as impecunious as possible."

"Speaking of committees ... any word yet from the Prophate Committee? Is Grell going to be my permanent Prophate or what? 'Cause if I can speed things along by just going to them and saying that I'd love to have Grell as my Prophate—"

"They can't make the decision without the Magista. And right now—"

"—there is no Magista."

"Right. So, it's a complete mess." Viscardia cupped Silver's face in her hands. "I know it's been frustrating for you, and I'm sorry for that."

"Eh, I'm fine. It's Grell I'm worried about. She's in this weird place where she's sort of a Prophate but not really. But she's been acting as my Prophate for so long that they should just make her one already. I don't get it."

"I don't either. I think the Church is concerned about the optics of, you know, two Prophates being married. Not like that should matter. But they'll justify their inaction in whatever way they can."

Silver rolled his eyes. "So, this bureaucracy bullshit exists everywhere, huh?"

"Afraid so."

"Well." Silver reached out his hand, an adorable smile on his lips. "You wanna dance?"

"Absolutely."

46

TAYMOR

Parties had never been Taymor's strong suit. As soon as she could, she politely excused herself and stepped outside. Mystis Concert Hall boasted an expansive outdoor patio that overlooked a pond. In the middle of the pond, there was a fountain modeled after Desmona, one of the premier figures of the Numentis theology. The fountain was supposed to represent Desmona watering Obasus Garden, giving it life and vitality. All sorts of exotic flowers grew along the pond's edges, granting credence to this interpretation.

Out on the patio, Taymor saw Liston, his hands behind his back, his eyes on the pond. A smile formed on Taymor's lips. She had a feeling he'd be out here. After all, she hadn't seen him in Mystis Concert Hall for the better part of an hour.

"Getting some air?" she asked as she neared him.

In response, Liston turned around. "It can get a bit ... stuffy in there."

Taymor chuckled. "We've never been good at these events, have we?"

"No. We haven't." Liston exhaled. "Sometimes, I wonder if ... if I chose the right path for myself."

"How do you mean?"

"Just ... well, maybe I would've been happier doing something else, something less public."

Taymor stood beside him. It was a brisk evening, unnaturally so for New Caelus. She loved this kind of weather, but she knew that Liston, who had never lived outside of this city, wasn't built for cooler weather. He crossed his arms, shielding himself from the breeze.

"Maybe Raze should've been the head of the party," Liston went on. "He said he never wanted it, that it would've driven him crazy, but ... he's more ... natural in these sorts of settings."

"Ah." Taymor nodded knowingly. "It's becoming real to you, isn't it? The prospect of being the next Head of the Assembly."

Liston was silent but slightly bobbed his head. He looked down at the ground, pretending to be riveted by the intricate patterns of the stones.

"It's one thing to think about what it'd be like," Liston explained, "but it's another to ..." He shook his head. "It's all happening too fast. I mean, don't get me wrong, I've been dreaming of an Affiliate-dominated Cooperative for years, but—"

"—you're scared you won't be able to live up to people's expectations."

Liston laughed. "Am I that easy to read?"

"You are to me." Taymor smiled. "I'm sure every Head of the Assembly has felt the same way, at one time or another."

"You really think Banner cares what people think?"

"Are you kidding? He's obsessed with his image, with what people make of him." Taymor met Liston's eyes. "It won't be easy. I know that; you know that. But things will be better on the other side." Taymor cleared her throat. "You know, I was talking to Raelynn tonight. And she said you're confident about an Affiliate victory."

"Did she, now?"

"She did. So, who are you lying to? Her or me?"

"I don't think I'm lying to either of you. It's just ... well, my thoughts ... they're so scattered right now, Farzah. One minute, I think I'm ready, that I'll be able to do exactly what needs to be done, but the next … it's all so … up in the air. The uncertainty is maddening. Some of the polls predict an Affiliate blowout, while others suggest it'll be a close race, with the Expansionists still maintaining power. If I could be assured of what will happen—"

"But you can't. You can't know that. No one can. Not now."

"No, I know." Liston ran his fingers through his hair. "I just wish it were Election Day already, that everything was decided."

"It will be soon enough. There's no sense in worrying about things you can't control. Or change."

Liston smiled at her. "You always know just what to say."

"I may not be an Affiliate, but that doesn't mean I wouldn't love to see you as Head of the Assembly. And, for what it's worth, I think you'll be great at it."

"Thank you."

Taymor reached out and touched Liston's arm. There it was again—that familiar sensation. At the same time, they looked at one another, holding each other's gaze for a beat too long. Taymor felt the need to say something, but just as she was about to—

"My Lord Regent?" It was Avitus, standing in the doorway. "There are some people I would like you to meet."

"Of course." Liston cleared his throat. To Taymor, he said, "We'll talk later, okay?"

"Okay," Taymor said, pushing a loose strand of hair behind her ear.

She watched as Liston walked away, a strange sadness washing over her. In just a few months' time, his world was either about to change completely or stay painfully the same. She wanted him to know that whether he was the next Head of the Assembly or not, he still had so much to be proud of. But Taymor knew Liston all too well; he always felt like he had something to prove.

For better or worse.

47

GRELL

Grell knew very well what her primary job for the evening was. She had to work her way through the crowd and charm all the partygoers she could out of their hard-earned numa. It wasn't a difficult task; in fact, it was one she rather enjoyed. The key was to not be too pushy. Some of the Numites were a bit aggressive, demanding an insane amount of numa or trying to guilt people into donating. Grell assumed a more personable approach, chatting people up and thanking them for attending. More often than not, people wanted to be acknowledged, and that was when they decided to part with their numa.

She'd been working the crowd for the better part of an hour, and she was parched. Some of these Keepers could really talk her ear off. It'd been worth it, though; apparently, she'd helped the Church raise a few million, which put them closer to their goal.

Grell made her way up to the refreshment stand to help herself to a glass of water. As she scooped up some ice and placed it in her glass, she could sense someone in her peripheral vision staring at her.

"Hello, Grell."

She froze. She knew that voice. Oh, she knew that voice all too well. Stunned,

Grell looked up and saw someone she'd never expected to see again. Images flashed through her mind, all at once, and a pit formed in her stomach. What was he doing here? Hadn't he moved up to Doctro, never to be seen in New Caelus again?

"Weylon," Grell exhaled. "What … are you doing here?"

"Oh, you haven't heard?" He looked so smug. Grell had almost forgotten just how smug he could be. "If all goes according to plan, I'll be the new Magista for the New Caelus Church."

"What?" Grell's face blanched. "How? Who decided that?"

"Kind of a strange way to congratulate me for my promotion, but I'll take it."

"You went to Doctro. That was part of the deal, that you'd stay away."

"But now I'm here. Isn't it funny how life works out?"

Grell pushed a strand of hair behind her ear, glancing around. "What do you want?"

"What do you think?" he countered, his hand subtly brushing against her thigh.

"Don't do that."

"Why not? You used to like it." He smirked. "And … other things." She shook her head, turning away from him. "What? Are you worried Kosabeus will see us? He's not even in here right now. I made sure of that before I approached you."

"How considerate."

"I thought so." He reached for a glass of water. "You know, the offer's still on the table."

"No deal."

"But you were so sure of us."

"That was a long time ago."

"So, you can honestly say you don't love me anymore?"

Grell looked up at him, meeting his eyes for the first time in seven years. He'd been one of those artsy types who drank and smoked too much. He was almost fifty now, but he'd never matured past the mental age of twenty-four. That should have been a turn-off, but infuriatingly, it'd only further endeared him to Grell. The words "bad news" may as well have been tattooed across his forehead. Women were just another one of his vices, but he sure knew how to charm them. He'd certainly charmed Grell, all those years ago—to her endless shame.

"It's over," Grell said pointedly.

"It doesn't have to be. We can pick up where we left off."

"I'm with Kosabeus."

Weylon sniggered. "That didn't stop you before. In fact, if I recall correctly, you were—"

"It's ancient history," Grell said, reddening. "It was a mistake."

"You don't believe that."

"Yes. I do. I shouldn't have ... we shouldn't have ..." Grell cut herself off when she saw Kosabeus reenter the room. She moved away from Weylon. "We can't talk."

"Not here, maybe, but—"

"Not ever."

Weylon looked her up and down, not even trying to mask his intentions. "If I were you, I wouldn't be so hasty. After all, now that I'm here in New Caelus—and, more likely than not, the new Magista—it'd be all too easy to just go into Kosabeus's office and chat with him about ... oh, I don't know ... all sorts of things. We have something very important in common, after all—besides the Church, of course."

"You wouldn't."

"Do you really want to take that chance?"

Grell looked down at her feet. "What do you want?"

"To meet up, just the two of us. And we can ... talk. I live downtown, above the Rowdy Wrangler. Apartment 2B. I'm home after nine on most days. If I'm not there, I'm probably at the bar downstairs."

Grell didn't say anything; she just kept her head down, hoping that her guilt wasn't too evident. When she at last looked up, Weylon was already gone. She could feel her heartbeat returning to normal. She glimpsed around, trying to find Kosabeus, to make sure he hadn't seen anything. Oh, good, he was talking with Avitus. She breathed a sigh of relief. She was safe.

"What was that about?"

It was Puck. Grell inwardly panicked. How much had he seen? No, more than that, how much had he heard?

Grell turned to face him, hoping her cheeks weren't as red as they felt. "Oh, that's Weylon. He'll probably be our new Magista, once everything's finalized."

"You know him?"

"We've run into each other a few times. We were just catching up."

That answer seemed to satisfy Puck. Grell was grateful he didn't ask any more questions; she wasn't sure what sorts of lies she'd be able to concoct on the spot.

48

WHITNER

"Do you know what you'll say at the Expansionist rally, Dane?" asked Astrophel.

Whitner and Astrophel were strolling through the gardens outside the Church. It was Astrophel's idea. He'd said it'd be a good change in scenery, getting out of his office and basking in the sunshine. Whitner was inclined to agree. He'd forgotten how nice it was spending time outside.

"I do." Whitner watched a few butterflies flutter about. "I don't know if it will change anything, but ... it should suffice."

"Do you want me to look over your speech?"

"I'm sure you're too busy for that."

"Not at all. I'll be speaking at the rally too, you know."

"What?" Whitner stopped. "Since when?"

"I've always planned on speaking. I believe in my party. And I'll do whatever I can to help our chances."

It was ironic, perhaps, that Astrophel believed in the Expansionist Party platform far more than Whitner did. Sometimes, Whitner wondered whether he was even an Expansionist at all. Initially, he'd declared his allegiance to the

Expansionist Party to spend more time with Banner. Over time, he'd managed to convince himself that he really did agree with the Expansionist Party on several issues, but he didn't know how honest that was.

"You seem ... distracted," Astrophel said, knocking Whitner out of his trance.

"Sorry. I was just ... thinking."

"Anything you want to share?"

"It's just the typical election nonsense. The Expansionists in my cabinet have been on my case, trying to get me to donate more numa to Expansionist candidates, but—"

"You should be doing everything you can for the Expansionists, Dane."

"I know. And I have donated. But ... it's never enough for them, it seems. They always want more."

Astrophel appeared rather stoic, his posture alarmingly perfect. Whitner knew that he was itching to say something; he always had that look in his eyes when he disagreed with whatever Whitner had just said. Dreamily, Astrophel ran his fingers along an elm tree's trunk.

"If I were in your position, I'd do more interviews, really get my voice out there. Banner has been doing a lot to drum up Expansionist support. I just ..." Astrophel trailed off, shaking his head.

"No, go on. Say what you want to say. I won't get upset."

Astrophel met his eyes. "I just wish you'd do a little more too. That's all."

After his meeting with Astrophel, Whitner returned to his office in the Center. The building was a bit too showy for his tastes; there were too many winding hallways, and it'd taken him a good month or so to learn his way around. His office was on the top floor, but his views were nowhere near as stunning as one would have assumed. The Hall, the headquarters for War and Defense, was directly across from him, blocking any downtown views he might have had. Sometimes, he could see Banner walking through the hallways, making his way to his office.

So, maybe the view wasn't that bad, after all.

"Lord Regent Whitner?" His secretary poked her head in. "Lord Regent Banner is here to see you."

"He is?" Whitner couldn't hide his surprise. "Well, um ... send him in, then."

Banner entered, with more of a swagger than usual. He looked particularly chuffed. That could mean only one thing: He'd spent the weekend having incredible sex with some new conquest. That would explain why Whitner hadn't seen him since the Church party on Ortus.

"Cyno." Whitner offered a smile. "I didn't know you'd be coming."

"I figured I'd drop by, see if you were in."

"You got lucky. I just got back half an hour ago."

"Oh? Where were you?"

"Meeting with Astrophel."

Banner walked over to the windows. "And what were you two talking about?"

"The usual nonsense. The elections. The upcoming Expansionist rally." Whitner eyed Banner carefully. "I'm assuming that's what you want to talk about too?"

"Not really." Banner turned to him. "I was hoping I could convince you to go on Darius Madden's show with me."

Darius Madden was one of the most famous—or infamous, depending on one's political persuasion—Expansionist radio hosts. He always repeated the party line, word for word, never straying. Whitner didn't know if his loyalty was admirable or insane. Over the years, Darius had practically bent over backward trying to justify some of the horrendous things various Expansionists had done. He hated the Affiliates—and particularly Liston—with a burning, insidious passion. No doubt, that was why Banner wanted to go on his show: for validation.

"I don't know, Cyno. Darius's show is a bit ... sleazy."

"Sleazy?" laughed Banner.

"Well, you know, it isn't a good look for a couple Lord Regents to go on it."

"Darius has a huge fanbase. By going on his show, we'll reach millions of Expansionists. We need to excite our base here, Dane. Get them to the polls."

"I just ... I don't think it's a good idea."

"Well." Banner neared him, a spirited sparkle in his eyes. "Is there anything I could do to maybe ... convince you?"

"Cyno." Whitner tried to sound firm. He didn't think he did a very good job. "Maybe we can go on another show, one that's less—"

"—sleazy?"

"Yes, exactly."

"But they won't have the same pull that Darius does. Come on, Dane. You know this makes sense."

Whitner sighed, running his fingers through his hair. "Will you let me think about it?"

"He needs to know by tonight."

"Tonight?" Whitner scoffed. "Well, thanks for the warning."

"I just found out about it this afternoon."

Whitner knew there was no use in pretending he wouldn't go on the show. He'd never been one to say no to Banner, and he surely wasn't going to start now.

"Okay," Whitner said nonchalantly. "I'll do it."

Banner smiled. "That's what I wanted to hear."

He started to leave, but Whitner stopped him by asking, "Do you want to come over tonight?"

"I can't. I have plans."

"With who?"

Banner crossed his arms. "What makes you think there's another person?"

"Because it's you. There's always another person."

"Well, have you ever thought that just maybe, I'd like to have a night by myself?"

"You're never alone, Cyno. You always have someone with you." Whitner stood up. "So, who is it?"

"A friend."

"So, someone you're sleeping with."

"Does it matter? We're not in a relationship. We can see whoever we want."

And there it was: the words that always stung, no matter how many times Banner had uttered them over the years. Whitner knew it was hopeless, that Banner would never give him what he wanted—or needed—but he couldn't seem to help himself. He couldn't bring himself to let Banner go—not after all they'd been through.

"Fine." Whitner didn't want to dwell on it any longer. "Then I guess I'll see you tomorrow for Darius's show."

"Dane."

"Don't worry about it, Cyno. It's fine. I know how you are."

"So, why do you try and make me feel bad about it? I've never once told you that I—"

"I know." Whitner could feel his cheeks burning up. "I said it's fine, didn't I?"

"But you clearly don't mean it."

"It's. Fine."

"Okay." Banner put his hands up. "I guess that, uh ... that that's it, then."

Whitner didn't say anything. He simply watched as Banner left, wondering for the billionth time who Banner would be with and why it wasn't him.

49

GRELL

Grell didn't feel good about what she'd done. No, instead, she felt horribly about it. She knew it'd been wrong, cheating on Kosabeus, but at the time, she'd managed to justify it to herself.

After all, she hadn't married Kosabeus out of love; she'd married him out of necessity. They were not only Numites but also high-profile members of the Church. She was pregnant, so she had to marry him. She felt guilty about it, as she knew that Kosabeus truly loved her, but she told herself it was for the best, that she could learn to love Kosabeus.

And she did.

But it wasn't like it'd been with Bayne.

Grell knew that her and Bayne's relationship had been toxic. She knew that they weren't good for each other. She knew that they exacerbated each other's worst tendencies. He cheated on her all the time, then they got into arguments, broke up, and made up. It was a vicious cycle, but it was so ... electrifying. And Grell missed that; she missed that adrenaline rush.

Everything with Kosabeus was safe. He didn't get jealous, he didn't raise his voice, and he didn't ask too many questions about where she was going or whom she was hanging out with. She knew these were great qualities—enviable ones, even—and Kosabeus was such a loving, doting husband.

But he wasn't Bayne.

And so, in Bayne's absence, Grell searched for other things that could make her feel that rush again. At first, she just flirted a bit when she was out and about. It was harmless, as it never went anywhere, and it was enough to satisfy her urges. For a while. But eventually, she wanted to do more, to take things further, to have a wild and passionate night with someone.

She'd tried to be happy, to focus on Eddard and Kosabeus, but after some time, she started to feel ... empty. She found herself fantasizing about other men, wondering what it'd be like to jump into bed with someone new. She longed for that excitement, that thrill, that feeling that she was doing something that was wrong but felt so right.

And that was when she met Weylon.

Grell looked out the train window, watching as the neon lights of New Caelus flashed by in the dark. She didn't know what she'd say to Weylon. She didn't want to fall back in with him; she couldn't. She'd dedicated herself to her marriage, and she didn't want to hurt Kosabeus any more than she already had.

Weylon was a Numite, so Grell had known about him beforehand. She'd heard all sorts of stories, and she knew more than a few women who'd had their hearts broken by him. She'd wondered if she could be the exception—if she could be the first woman to tame him.

They started sleeping together a couple years after Eddard was born. It was tantalizing, sneaking around, keeping it a secret from everyone. She and Weylon met up in hotel rooms under fake names, completely engrossed in their charade. It was supposed to be just sex, but somewhere along the way, they fell in love with each other. Grell couldn't believe she'd done it; she'd gotten Weylon to fall in love with her. A part of her wondered if she'd lose interest in him. Above all, it was the chase she craved, and she hadn't been looking for something real.

Instead, the opposite happened. They started planning a life together. They started talking—very seriously—about how they'd approach the whole situation. She'd leave Kosabeus, but she didn't want it to seem like she'd left him for another man, so she'd wait for a while before she settled down with Weylon. They had it all planned out.

But everything changed when Kosabeus became sick.

Seven or so years ago, Kosabeus gave his usual three-hour-long sermon to commemorate Mystis's birthday. Afterward, he stepped down from the pulpit and ducked into the side door, heading toward his office. On the way, however, he suddenly fainted. Avitus was the one who found him, and he promptly called a doctor.

Later, Kosabeus was diagnosed with a rare, aggressive form of cancer. His prognosis was grim; his doctors didn't want to give him any false hope, and they let him know that, most likely, he would be dead before the end of the year. Such an abysmal outlook would have crushed most people, caused them to spiral into self-destructive behaviors, but Kosabeus was different. He refused to let his illness change him. He continued working, and he insisted that his sickness be kept a secret from the public.

At that time, Grell was with Weylon in a Ligva hotel room, talking dreamily about what their lives would be like. They'd both gone there for a Numite convention, and it'd been the perfect opportunity to spend some time together, away from New Caelus. The hotel receptionist told Grell that Kosabeus had tried to call her and that she needed to get back to New Caelus immediately. Grell's anxieties got the best of her; she convinced herself that Kosabeus had found out about her and Weylon, and the whole way home, she thought about what she'd say.

But when she got home, Kosabeus told her what had happened, and Grell was racked with guilt. She hated herself for what she'd done. There she'd been, locked away in a hotel room with Weylon, while Kosabeus had been receiving the worst news of his life.

What made Grell feel even worse was that for the briefest moment, when

Kosabeus told her about his prognosis, she was … relieved. Mystis, it made her ill, how callous she'd been. She thought, for a moment, that maybe it'd be for the best if Kosabeus just died. Then she'd be able to be with Weylon without ever having to tell Kosabeus about it.

But as soon as the thought crossed her mind, Grell pushed it aside. She couldn't believe she'd disregarded her marriage vows and gone behind Kosabeus's back for so long. He was the perfect husband. How could she have treated him this way?

"I'm going to need you, Grell—more than ever," Kosabeus had said, looking at her with those gorgeous eyes of his.

She wondered why she wasn't in love with him, why she couldn't just be happy with a good, decent man. He was so handsome—far handsomer than either Bayne or Weylon—and they got on remarkably well. Kosabeus was also far more romantic and attentive than any of her former lovers. He respected her, asked for her opinion on his sermons, told her about his problems, asked her all about hers. She didn't know what was missing.

But she resolved, in that moment, to be there for him, to love him, to help him through his sickness. She owed him that much. In truth, she owed him so much more, but this was a start. She promised that from then on, she'd be faithful to him. She'd be the wife he deserved.

"Of course," Grell had said, forcing a smile. "I'll be here."

Grell ended things with Weylon the next day. He was shocked, of course, and he demanded an answer. Fair enough, Grell thought. After all, they'd just been talking about where they would live, once all the dust had settled. But all Grell could say was that she'd had a change of heart. In response, Weylon moved to Doctro, never to be seen again.

Until that night at Mystis Concert Hall.

When Grell got off the train, she headed to his apartment. She checked the bar first, and just as she'd expected, Weylon was down there, nursing a gin and tonic.

"Grell." He smiled. "I thought for a second you weren't coming."

Grell sat down beside him. It was a quiet bar, far away from the main drag. They wouldn't be recognized here. At the very least, this wasn't the sort of place Numites or government officials patronized. They'd be safe from prying eyes.

Weylon eyed her suggestively. "I'm surprised Kosabeus let you leave the house looking like that."

"He isn't the jealous type."

"He should be." Weylon chuckled. "If only he knew the things I was thinking about right now ..." His hand grazed her leg. "Oh, he'd be absolutely beside himself."

Grell had always wondered about Weylon and Kosabeus's past. There was some tension there, predominantly from Weylon's side. She could remember a few times when Weylon had made some offhanded remark about what Kosabeus would say or do if he ever found out about them. She didn't think much of it at the time, as she was caught up in the allure of it all, but now ... a part of her wondered whether that was the reason he'd bedded her in the first place: to one-up Kosabeus. And perhaps, deep down, she already knew the answer to that.

"What do you plan on doing as the Magista?" asked Grell.

"Make my mark on the Church. Change the very course of history."

"Oh, if that's all."

Weylon laughed. "Why so serious, Grell? Look, yes, I came for you, but I've also been working my ass off for this. So, can you really hold that against me?"

"I just want to know what your intentions are."

"You mean, am I going to tell Kosabeus that I had you in almost every conceivable position for the better part of a year?"

In that moment, seeing his self-satisfied sneer, Grell couldn't fathom what she'd ever loved about him. He was a pig, and he actively repulsed her. How had she ever considered leaving Kosabeus and running off into the sunset with this man-child?

Grell shook her head. "That's all it ever was to you, wasn't it? Just a game. Just another conquest."

"Come on, Grell. You know I'm just teasing. Look, we can—" When Grell stood up, Weylon stared at her, his brows knitted together. "Wait, where are you going?"

"Home. Whatever you thought would happen ... it won't."

"You bitch." He practically spat the words, and his entire demeanor shifted. "You really think you can turn me down?"

"I just did."

"Oh, you'll regret that."

"Are you threatening me?"

He glared up at her. "Yes. I am. Mark my words, Grell. You'll regret this."

Grell took the next train out to the suburbs. When she got home, it was past one o'clock in the morning. She quietly tiptoed upstairs, and she saw Kosabeus, tucked up in bed. Her heart ached. She knew she had to tell him. Oh, how she'd been dreading this moment. She'd hoped to avoid it forever, but now, with Weylon in New Caelus, it had all come to a head.

"Grell?" Kosabeus stirred, having heard her.

She froze in place. She wanted to speak but couldn't.

"Ssshhh. Go back to bed, hon," she said, offering him a warm smile.

She took a shower, to rid herself of Weylon's stench, then climbed into bed. She felt like an imposter, lying next to Kosabeus. Guilt was eating her up alive. She wanted to admit everything, but she needed time to think of what to say. She didn't want to hurt him.

But perhaps it was too late for that.

50

TAYMOR

Taymor was making her way to the Church to meet with Puck. Along the way, she ran into Liston, who was going to the Church to see Avitus. They stopped by a beachside café to grab a cup of coffee, then continued walking toward the Church.

"Viscardia told me about Tinsley," Taymor said, taking a careful sip of her coffee. "You and Raze must be thrilled."

"Well, of course. Tinsley will be an asset. It's just odd, isn't it, that Abner waited so long to make his retirement public knowledge?"

"I don't think he and Bryson wanted to take any attention away from the elections."

"Bryson's retiring too?"

"Well, that's what I've heard."

"From whom?"

"Puck." Taymor smiled. "It's quite advantageous, you know, having a Prophate who has eyes and ears everywhere."

"Clearly." Liston appeared deep in thought. "Any idea who'll replace him?"

"Apparently, they're conducting interviews with all sorts of Keepers. I just …

271

I hope they'll be a Grounder. It'd be too depressing, being the only Grounder on the Assembly."

"You can always come on over to our side," said Liston brightly.

Taymor laughed. "Nice try."

"I'm just saying, we might have the numbers ... if things go our way, that is."

"But regardless of what happens, you won't have a majority on the Assembly. And you'll have to work just as hard as Banner does to persuade me to vote in your favor."

"I look forward to that."

Over the past few weeks, the Affiliates had been making impressive gains in the polls. Recently, Silver had been stumping for Affiliate candidates, shedding a spotlight on contests that hadn't been getting attention in the press. Though Taymor wasn't an Affiliate, she was impressed by their strategy. Silver's charisma and popularity were tools that the Affiliates didn't let go to waste. She wished the Grounders could be more like that, but she, Abner, and Bryson were hardly as magnetic as Silver.

Liston took a sip of his coffee. "Raze is rather nervous about how Banner will react—if things don't go the way he wants, that is."

"In what way?"

"He seems to think that if the Expansionists lose, Banner will try to claim that the election was rigged."

"I don't think Banner's stupid enough to do that. Especially without any evidence."

"No, I know. I don't think so either. But Raze is worried that if Banner is backed into enough of a corner, he'll ... lash out."

"His advisers will hold him back." Taymor threw her empty coffee cup into the trash. "I don't think we need to worry about Banner doing anything like that. He'll be angry, sure, and he'll give a slew of interviews bashing you Affiliates, but he won't attack the system."

Though Taymor had entered the Church thousands of times over the years, whenever she walked through the double doors, she was struck by just how beautiful it was. The stained-glass windows, vaulted ceiling, teak wood, and ornate pulpit all exemplified the power and influence that the Church possessed. The building was meticulously cared for. Everything was polished daily, and there were never any noticeable cobwebs or dust. None of the Prophates were currently giving a sermon, but a few Numites were bustling about.

Taymor ducked into one of the side hallways and made her way toward Puck's office. His door was open, as it always was. His black Prophate robe hung on the coat rack near the door. Taymor wondered vaguely how much the Prophates hated their robes. They looked rather heavy, and they must have been unpleasant to wear in warmer weather.

"Hey, Far!" greeted Puck, standing up from his desk. "Great to see you! What's new?"

"Well." Taymor plopped down on the couch. "To be honest, I'm a bit … irritated."

"About?"

"The Cooperative has approved the budgets for each division for next year, and let's just say, it's … not what I was hoping for."

"They're still underfunding you?"

"It's worse than that. They've slashed my budget by almost twenty percent. And, adding insult to injury, they increased War and Defense's and Intelligence and Espionage's budgets."

Puck shook his head. "Leave it to the Expansionists to go out with a bang."

"It's absurd. I never understood why we decide on budgets before the elections. Especially since we all know that the Expansionists will most likely be losing seats. So, here they are, passing budgets that won't reflect the new Cooperative's priorities."

"Can you contest it at all?"

"Well, the Assembly will have to approve of the budgets, and we'll make some adjustments, but … it just seems like my division is always being overlooked."

Puck sat down on the arm of the couch. "And why do you think that is?"

"Because Imperium is obsessed with involving itself in affairs that it shouldn't be involved in. We spend far too much numa on our military and sanctions and regime changes. It isn't our place to make the rest of the universe how we want. We should start focusing on ourselves. We should be investing more time and resources into improving our infrastructure, expanding healthcare access, eliminating poverty, all of that. But how can we when we spend billions upon billions establishing military bases all over the universe?"

Puck wiped his glasses. "See, this is why we need more Grounders in government. You're the most sensible of the lot."

Taymor sighed. "It's just frustrating, that's all. If we were given the same amount of love and attention as the other divisions, maybe we would've cured cancer by now. Sometimes, I feel like the Expansionists and the Affiliates ... they're so concentrated on Imperium's universal reputation that they don't stop and wonder how our own people view our government. I've talked to a lot of people this election cycle, and so many of them have said how let down they feel, by everyone. It's like Imperium's lost sight of what really matters."

"And that's why you should be Head of the Assembly."

"Please." Taymor laughed. "Do you know how many public events the Head of the Assembly has to attend? I'd hate every second of it."

"But you're the exact kind of leader Imperium needs. The problem is, the Grounders have never gotten the amount of airtime the Expansionists and Affiliates get. People often act like those are the only two parties that matter, that the Grounders are just there. But if people hear more from you, if they start to see that the Grounders are the ones who have real policy ideas, then maybe they'll change their minds ... and their vote."

"Maybe." Taymor shrugged. "That won't happen this time around, though. The Affiliates are in a good position."

"And that's great for them. But who knows what'll happen next time? Maybe the Grounders will gain some ... ground." Puck snickered. "I didn't even mean to make that joke."

Taymor laughed. "Well, we'll see how the rest of the Assembly views the budget. Hopefully, I'll be able to secure some more numa for Science and Medicine, but ... I'm not optimistic."

"They're idiots if they don't see your point of view."

"Oh, I'm sure they'll see what I'm talking about. But ... it's not like any of them will want to see their budgets get cut. So, it's just a matter of how we divide up the numa."

"Well, keep me in the loop. Tell me how it goes."

Taymor was grateful she had Puck as her Prophate. He was nothing if not empathetic, and he acutely understood her frustrations with Imperial government. Imperium had always prioritized War and Defense and Intelligence and Espionage over the other divisions. This was nothing new, but that didn't make it any less exasperating. She couldn't help but wonder what Imperium would look like if more numa were allocated to the other divisions. For one, they wouldn't be lagging behind the Core in terms of medical advancements, and they'd be able to build a more equitable healthcare system across all Imperial worlds.

"I know it sometimes feels like you're fighting alone," Embry comforted her mother as they strolled through the gardens that surrounded Taymor's apartment. "But things are starting to change in Imperium."

"Not quickly enough." Taymor heaved a sigh. "The kinds of changes I want won't happen overnight."

"But they will happen."

"Maybe not in my lifetime."

"Don't talk like that! You have to believe!"

Taymor couldn't help but smile. Embry hadn't yet been jaded by the system, the way Taymor had. She hoped Embry could retain her idealism for as long as possible—maybe even forever—but Imperial society had an inimitable way of beating people—especially women—down. Stifling beliefs and systemic sexism prevented Imperium from being the great power it could have—and should have—been.

The Core, though flawed in other aspects, had always been more matriarchal; its leader, Queen Quintella, came from a long line of strong female rulers, and the Coronian Royal Court was almost entirely composed of women. Taymor had long been the only woman on the Assembly. Though Iaconetti would soon join her, the Assembly would still be tilted toward men. In Taymor's opinion, many of Imperium's root problems, including its lopsided divisional budgets, would be solved if more women were granted positions of power.

She hoped Embry's generation would help bring about that much-needed change. She could already see the tide was changing. More women were running for office now than ever before. They were standing up to the system, demanding meaningful reforms. Maybe this election season would be the one they looked back on years from now as a defining moment in Imperial politics.

Taymor put her arm around Embry, pulling her close. Imperium wouldn't—and couldn't—change overnight, but as long as she had Embry, everything would be all right.

51

KOSABEUS

Kosabeus knew that Caine didn't like him—that much was obvious—but he also knew that Caine would be interested in what he had to say. It'd been a long time since he'd entered the High Court, and when he walked through the doors, he was instilled with a strange sense of patriotism. This was, in many ways, the heart of Imperial government, the place where justice was either served or denied.

"Hello," Kosabeus said as he stopped at the receptionist's desk.

"Hello, Kosabeus," she said. "What can I do for you?"

Kosabeus was flattered she knew him. "I was wondering if High Justice Caine is in his office?"

"He is." She motioned to her left. "He's down that hallway, fifth door on the right. You can't miss it. It's got his name on it."

"Thank you so much."

Kosabeus wandered down the hallway, mentally counting the doors as he went along. And there it was, Caine's office, fifth door on the right, just as the receptionist had said. His name was carved in ostentatiously bold lettering. Out of politeness, Kosabeus knocked on the door, but he didn't receive an answer,

277

despite hearing noise from within. He knocked again—still no answer. Annoyed, he opened the door, and Caine glared at him from behind his desk.

"What the hell are you doing here?" Caine growled. "I didn't answer because I don't want to be disturbed. And I certainly don't want to talk to you."

"I know you don't trust me," Kosabeus said, not in the mood for elusiveness. "Which is why I assume you went to Cyno for help instead of me."

Caine crossed his arms, staring Kosabeus down, trying to force him to cower in submission. Perhaps it worked on others, but Kosabeus wasn't so easily frightened. He'd looked fear in its eyes many times without flinching.

"You can't just barge into my office and expect me to treat you civilly," Caine said.

Kosabeus stepped deeper into the room, familiarizing himself with its contents. He saw photographs of Caine and a woman, along with a baby girl. Kosabeus knew the story; everyone did. Twenty years ago, Caine's daughter—only three years old at the time—was kidnapped. Her captors never relayed a ransom note. The police were useless, finding no evidence as to where their child might have gone. The years went by, and Caine and his wife descended into a sort of mad desperation, futilely taking the search for their daughter upon themselves. Finally, tired of living in the same house, being haunted by the ghost of his daughter, Caine moved, while his wife was hospitalized in a nobody town in the boondocks. According to reliable sources, she'd never been the same since her child's abduction.

Kosabeus faced Caine. "I know why you're so interested in Raelynn."

"You don't know shit."

"Look, we can stand here and waste time, or we can work together and get the answers you want. Your choice."

Caine moved closer to Kosabeus, his eyes narrowed. "You're an arrogant son of a bitch, aren't you?"

"You wouldn't be the first to think so. But I think you'll find I—"

"I asked Cyno to access Raelynn's family file. So, why are you the one—?"

"Sooner or later, you'll realize that Cyno can't do anything for himself. He told me about it, like he always does, so like it or not, you're stuck dealing with me."

Caine shook his head. "I don't ... I didn't want to involve too many people. Cyno, I can trust. But you?"

"I can help you. And I assure you, I can be quite discreet."

Years of having his hopes up, only to watch them deflate and die, had greatly jaded Caine. But still, there was a twinkle of something akin to faith in his eyes. Kosabeus pitied Caine more than anything; he could scarcely imagine what it'd feel like, losing a child so suddenly.

"How can I trust you?" asked Caine warily.

"Believe me, I make a far better ally than enemy."

"Well, um ..." Caine fiddled with his sleeve. "I assume you think I'm interested in knowing more about Raelynn because of what Liston did. You know I dislike Liston, so you think this is some sort of ... revenge trip."

"No."

"Then what do you think?"

"I know you think Raelynn is your daughter."

Caine nearly choked. He gawked at Kosabeus, unable to process what he had just heard.

"How ... how did you ... how could you possibly know that?" asked Caine, a strange dread in his voice, as if he knew but didn't want to know.

"Don't insult my intelligence. I was at that dinner. I knew the moment I saw you and Raelynn together."

"You ...?" Caine trailed off, his latent grief resurfacing. He shook his head. "You don't understand."

"You want to be in your daughter's life. Of course, I understand that."

"But you don't know what it's like." Caine looked out the window, his eyes tired. "I can't let her go. Not again." He hung his head. "You must think I'm crazy."

"I don't think that."

"Everyone told me she was dead, that I should stop looking for her, but ..." Caine closed his eyes. "Well, you know what happened."

Kosabeus remembered that night vividly. Every frame of it had been etched into his memory. He'd been in Exora, giving a lecture at the local Numentis school, and Avitus had reached out to him, saying there was an emergency, that Caine and Nicolai Carbury, the then Head of the Assembly, had gotten into a heated argument. When Kosabeus arrived on the scene, he'd seen the bloody mess for himself, and there was Caine, holding the—

"I ... I know Nicolai took Seryph," Caine went on. "I know he did. He practically admitted it, the smug bastard. And that's why I—"

"I know."

"And when I saw Raelynn ... it all fit. Her age, the way she looks so much like Idri ... she has to be Seryph."

"Do you have definitive proof?"

"Not yet. I ... that's why I asked Cyno for her family file."

"There are other ways for you to find out. Ways that are far less involved. Ways that don't require you to find out where they keep those files."

Caine stared at him. "Like what?"

Kosabeus handed him a folder. "Like this."

Caine blanched. "What ... what is this?"

"Your answer. If you want it."

"I don't understand. How did you—?"

"Never mind that. Just ... that should help you figure it out."

Caine held the folder, his hands shaking. "I ... I don't know what to say."

"You don't have to say anything." Kosabeus turned to leave, but Caine reached out and grabbed his arm.

"Kosabeus, I ..." Caine trailed off, tears in his eyes. "I ... I don't know how to thank you."

"You won't be thanking me if it isn't what you want to hear."

"No, I will because ... because this is the closest I've felt to my daughter in twenty years. And maybe ... maybe getting her back ... maybe Idri could ... maybe I could help her." A light flashed across Caine's eyes. "But no matter what happens ... I'll have my answer. And that's all I want. I want that closure. I ... I need it."

52

RAELYNN

Raelynn had front-row seats for the Affiliate rally, which was in Templeton Stadium, one of New Caelus's outdoor music venues. It could seat fifteen thousand people. During the solis, Templeton Stadium was a revolving door of musical acts. Every night, for the entire month of Sidum, a different band performed, and half of the proceeds went to Reading Learners, a Church-sponsored nonprofit that provided books to families below the poverty line.

The rally was to commence at one o'clock. Thousands of people were pouring in. Raelynn didn't think there would be enough room for everyone. The poor souls who arrived last would be forced to stand at the back for the hours-long ordeal. Raelynn was grateful she'd heeded Liston's advice and secured her seat early.

At one o'clock, Nisha stepped out from behind the curtain. "Good afternoon," she greeted the noisy stadium, adjusting the microphone. "Thank you for joining us. Today, we gather to voice our support for the Affiliate candidates aiming to unseat an Expansionist or a Grounder this election season. Usually, an incumbent's reelection is all but guaranteed in Imperium. But the Expansionist Party has revealed itself to be negligent, refusing to live up to the promises it has made to its constituents over the years, and the Imperial people are not having it. For too long, the Expansionists have controlled the Cooperative, and for too long, they have failed us.

"As of now, a dozen major news sources, from all over the political spectrum, have claimed that the fate of the Cooperative is still very much up in the air. For obvious reasons, this excites us. We cannot endure any more Expansionist inaction. We cannot allow their dangerous, aggressive rhetoric to continue to define who the Imperial people are and what we believe. And I know you're all ready for a change!"

Boisterous cheers and claps emanated from the audience. The energy in the arena was almost tangible. Raelynn felt an inexplicable urge to jump up and start screaming. She'd never been so overcome with patriotism before.

Nisha continued to speak for a while, then she handed the podium over to Viscardia. Viscardia, notably, was much more natural than Nisha; she possessed raw charisma, and it was clear that the audience had especially been looking forward to seeing her.

"Thank you, thank you," Viscardia said, a smile on her lips. Raelynn could hardly hear her over all the noise. "Thank you. I'm overwhelmed by how many of you decided to spend your day with us. We'd estimated that maybe fifteen thousand of you would attend, and that was astounding. But based on how many people I'm seeing standing at the back ... I think we've surpassed that number."

Raelynn glanced over her shoulder. She was right; there was a sea of people standing at the back, but none of them appeared agitated. Instead, they were some of the loudest attendees in the arena. It was unlike anything Raelynn had ever experienced.

"I may not be a politician," Viscardia went on, "but I've always had an interest in politics, in bringing about change. I know some Imperials believe the Church should be removed from politics, but I am not one of them. As an Imperial citizen, I believe it's my duty to be informed, to vote, to stand up for my beliefs.

This year, the Affiliates have a once-in-a-lifetime opportunity of ushering in the sort of government we've been dreaming about for years. We don't have to live in the shadow of failed Expansionist policies or leaders. We can vote for a better, more just society!"

After Viscardia finished speaking, the stadium broke out into applause. Then, to everyone's delight, Silver and Liston stepped out onto the stage. The arena went wild. Raelynn was aware, of course, of Silver's immense popularity; his approval rating was shockingly high, and even some Expansionists liked him. But still, Raelynn was overwhelmed by how loud Templeton Stadium was. She wished she'd brought earplugs.

Silver gave a good speech, explaining how the Affiliate Party would tackle the issues that mattered most to Imperials. Raelynn thought that Silver excelled at highlighting some of the Affiliate Party's domestic policies, such as its emphasis on inter-divisional cooperation.

"In school, we were all taught that the divisions have their own rankings, that we're not all equal," Silver said. "I disagree. I think we're strongest when we work together, when we bridge the gaps between our divisions and come together to serve the Imperial people. We all have so much to offer, and we must fund more inter-divisional projects. By doing so, we can improve our infrastructure, healthcare, public safety, and carbon footprint."

The crowd seemed enraptured by Silver. He commanded the stage, and he seemed at home up there, talking about a topic that clearly meant a lot to him. Vaguely, Raelynn wondered why Silver wasn't the leader of the Affiliate Party. He had seniority over Liston, after all, and it was clear that Silver was a major asset for the party. But perhaps he preferred being second-in-command.

"Now I'd like to hand the microphone over to Lev Liston, the current leader of the Affiliate Party ... and, if we all vote on Election Day, the future Head of the Assembly!" said Silver, stepping aside and allowing Liston to take center stage.

"Thank you, Raze," Liston said, smiling at him. He looked out at the audience. "It's truly humbling to stand here before you, seeing nothing but a sea of enthusiastic faces. When I was sixteen, I attended my first political rally. Even back then, I remember how impressed I was by the contenders. There was something about the Affiliate Party's message that stuck with me. Even now, almost twenty years later, I can still remember the feeling that washed over me as I sat in the audience, listening to the candidates speak about the Affiliate Party—what it stood for, what it could accomplish.

"I remember staying behind, to meet some of the candidates. One of them saw me, and he invited me backstage to meet the other candidates. They made me, a sixteen-year-old boy, feel like one of them. Afterward, they told me how I could get involved and expressed their hope that maybe someday, I, too, could be like them, on a stage, talking to a crowd of people.

"Over the years, of course, the Affiliate Party has experienced its difficulties. We have lost our share of elections, earned our share of negative press, and had our share of ineffectual politicians. But despite the setbacks the Affiliate Party has faced, and will continue to face, we have never lost sight of our goals. We're united by our belief that our future doesn't have to be defined by our past. War is not the only solution. We can weaken the Core's influence through nonviolent measures. If we succumb to the Expansionist agenda, we run the risk of starting a war we can't finish. Hate will breed hate; violence will breed violence. But we can choose a different path, one that will not end in the same, inconclusive way that the Glass War did.

"When we were born, we were told that we must hate the Core because that is the way it's always been. But that doesn't mean that is the way it should always be. We don't have to be defined by war, by the victory of one way of life over another. We don't have to commit our precious resources and people to wars that will never resolve the quarrel they were intended to. I believe there is a way for Imperium and the Core to end this blood feud. I hope that one day, our governments will agree on this, and we can sit down across from each other and negotiate an end to this standoff. That day will not come tomorrow ... or in the next year. But I am confident it will come ... as long as we elect leaders who prioritize our future over our past."

When Liston spoke, a mystical air surrounded him. Everyone in the stadium went quiet, deathly quiet, their eyes glued to him. Afterward, all the Affiliate speakers took photographs for the press and went off to do separate interviews. Raelynn, for her part, left the rally feeling energized, ready to cast her vote for Affiliates all the way down the ballot.

For the first time in decades, the Affiliates had a legitimate chance of controlling Imperium's political agenda, of being the ones who dictated its path. If all went according to plan, in just two months' time, Liston would become the new Head of the Assembly. Banner's reign would finally end. And that was an occasion Raelynn couldn't wait to witness.

53

BANNER

Banner hadn't been this angry in a long time. The Expansionist rally, which was meant to rival the Affiliate one, hardly received any press coverage in the evening post. It was nauseating, knowing he'd also be seeing Liston's and Silver's faces on the front page of Beatum's newspaper. Even more nauseating were the blurbs about how the Affiliate Party understood the current state of Imperium and embraced change, while the Expansionist Party seemingly eschewed it.

Oh, Banner was fuming. And, to top it off, Kosabeus hadn't even gone to the rally. Apparently, something had come up at the Church, and he couldn't make it. Banner, Whitner, and Astrophel all spoke, of course, but Banner had been depending on Kosabeus. He was the best public speaker Banner knew; he was supposed to end the rally, to be the last one the attendees heard from.

Banner struggled to make sense of it all. He'd been so confident going into the rally, so sure the Expansionists would be able to knock the surging Affiliates down a few pegs. But no. If anything, the papers projected that the Affiliates' poll performances would improve. The reality of an Affiliate-dominated Cooperative was becoming more and more plausible.

After the rally, Banner barged into Kosabeus's office, and for the next hour or so, he'd berated Kosabeus, no doubt alarming more than one passerby. The sun had long since set. Grell was probably at home, wondering where her husband was. But Banner couldn't care less. Kosabeus wasn't going anywhere—not until Banner let him.

"You were supposed to be there!" Banner shouted for maybe the fifth time.

"Yes, I know. But the Church finally decided on our new Magista, and they wanted to set up a meeting between—"

"You think I give a shit about that?"

"It wasn't my choice, Cyno. It was all very last minute. The Church isn't exactly known for being—"

"You could've just told them you'd deal with it tomorrow."

"It doesn't work like that."

"What the hell are you talking about? You're the Head Prophate! You can make it work however you want!"

Kosabeus sighed. "Look. Cyno. I've already apologized. I don't know what else—"

"Save it." Banner turned toward the windows. "Maybe this is all a sign."

"A sign of what?"

Banner crossed his arms. "A sign that I should ask for a new Prophate."

Kosabeus smirked. "See how that works out for you."

"Is that a dare? Because I can end your career, you know. If I go down that hallway and talk to your new Magista, whoever the hell they are, they'll hear me out, and in a matter of seconds, you'll be out on the streets trying to make numa off your pathetic little jokes. Is that what you want?"

Kosabeus looked up at him from over his gray-rimmed glasses. He hardly ever wore them, but when he did, he appeared even shrewder than usual.

"You always get like this when things don't go your way. I believe you've threatened to get me fired ... oh, I don't know ... seven hundred times."

Despite himself, Banner chuckled. "And yet I just can't get rid of you."

"The feeling is mutual." Kosabeus flashed that characteristic grin. "But if you want to keep rolling with the threats, then please, don't let me stop you. I'm more than happy to be your punching bag."

Banner shook his head. He wasn't angry with Kosabeus. If anything, he was angry with himself—and, of course, Liston. He couldn't believe that in just a few weeks, he could lose everything he'd worked so hard for.

Kosabeus took a deep breath, his eyes carefully scanning Banner's. "I was wondering if you knew ... if Caine told you about Raelynn."

"What about her?"

Kosabeus adjusted his glasses with his forefinger. "Caine is under the impression that Raelynn is his daughter."

"I thought Caine's daughter was kidnapped, presumed dead."

"She was. But Caine believes that Nicolai Carbury abducted his daughter and gave her away to the Keeper system."

"What?" Banner's headache was worsening. This was too much to suffer in one day.

Banner had thought Caine was one of the sane ones. Caine was the very epitome of class and poise. He had never struck Banner as unhinged, which was impressive, given his tragic backstory. When Caine assumed the position of Head Justice, some dozen years ago, everyone knew him. The story of his daughter's abduction had been news for weeks, due to the characters involved. Caine's wife, Idri Carbury, was a former-Keeper-turned-Low-Justice, and Caine, at the time, was a local justice in Exora—a very prominent one too. And Carbury, Idri's brother, was the Lord Regent of Diplomacy, the leader of the Expansionist Party, and the Head of the Assembly. It was a story that had captivated the attention of Imperials everywhere. But once Caine was sworn in as the High Justice, he never uttered a word about the case. He was stone cold in his judgments, steady as a rock. But apparently, that steadiness was all a front.

Banner's headache was spreading, throbbing behind his eyes. "No. There's no way. Carbury ... why would he have abducted his own niece? And if Carbury did abduct his niece, then why would he have given her away to the Keeper system?"

"No idea. But if by some inconceivable chance—"

"No! We're not giving into this!" Banner pulled on his collar, to help himself breathe. "If we go along with Eliseo's delusions, he'll drag us down into madness too."

"To be fair, he's acting out of heartbreak. Caine was devastated by his daughter's abduction. And his wife … it absolutely shattered her. She was never the same. Can you imagine being in that situation, where your child is there one minute, and—?" Kosabeus cut himself off, suddenly remembering whom he was talking to. "I'm so sorry, Cyno. I didn't mean to—"

"Eliseo's daughter is dead," Banner snapped, mercifully choosing to ignore Kosabeus's insensitivity. "By pinning his hopes on this, by thinking that Raelynn might be his daughter, he's only setting himself up for more pain. Why can't he just accept the kid is dead?"

"Because he doesn't believe that," replied Kosabeus cautiously. "He's spent the last twenty years trying to find his daughter. He's convinced that if he can prove his daughter's alive and well, his wife will go back to normal."

Banner scoffed. "Maybe Eliseo's just as crazy as she is."

"That's not fair."

"Don't talk to me about what's 'fair.' Not after saying I wouldn't know what it's like to lose a child."

"I didn't—"

"Why did he tell you about this, anyway? Why didn't he tell me?"

"He didn't tell me. I figured it out."

"How?"

"At that dinner."

"How in the world could you have possibly—?"

"Does it matter? The point is, Caine's your friend, right? And as his friend, shouldn't you be a bit more … understanding? Whether Raelynn is his daughter or not, Caine will have closure. And won't it be better for him to know, one way or another?"

Though Banner still found the whole idea to be preposterous, he did appreciate Caine's friendship, and he knew all too well how painful it was losing a child. If there was even the slightest chance that Bayne had survived the attack, Banner would have spent the past decade trying to find him. He couldn't blame Caine for holding out hope, for believing that his daughter was still alive—and here in New Caelus.

Banner sighed. "No, you're right."

"Of course, I am." Kosabeus stood up. "But let's call it here for now, Cyno. Take the night off. And don't think too much about the Affiliates, okay?"

"Yeah, all right." Banner heaved a deep breath. "Sorry for keeping you here so late."

"It's fine. But please, heed my advice. Tomorrow is a new day. And you never know what might happen."

Afterward, Banner made his way to the Vice District. Expectedly, the area had quite the salacious reputation. Only adults were allowed to partake in the delights that the Vice District offered, such as casinos, bars, brothels, cigar lounges, and strip clubs. Banner had been coming here for years. He enjoyed its raw, uninhibited nature.

In Banner's view, Imperials were too sexually repressed. The Numentis theology preached about virtue, purity, and loyalty; promiscuity, it seemed, was viewed as sinful, as an affront to the very foundations of the Numentis faith. Banner disagreed. He'd always been open about his sexuality, and he'd never once felt ashamed to indulge in his curiosities. To him, monogamy was a way of forcing people into a box, of making them decide what sort of person they wanted to be with. He'd never felt a pressure or desire to spend the rest of his life with one person. He wanted to be free, untethered, unmoored.

Banner entered the first bar he saw. He scanned the room. Initially, he was underwhelmed by the patrons. But then, in the far corner, he saw someone he'd never expected to see in the Vice District: Nisha Corinth, Liston's Lord Dynast.

"Nisha," Banner said as he neared her. "Fancy seeing you here."

"Cyno." Nisha smiled, crossing her legs. He'd never noticed how long her legs were. They could probably do all sorts of things. "Why am I not surprised this is where you choose to spend your night?"

"Hey," chortled Banner, sitting next to her. "Before you judge me, you should remember ... you're here too."

"True. But I came here for one reason only. To hook up."

Banner had to admit, he was taken aback by her candor. Nisha had never struck him as the kind of woman who embraced the Vice District's hookup culture. Perhaps her one-sided infatuation with Kosabeus had turned her into a sex-crazed maniac.

"What a coincidence," said Banner, slinging his arm over the top of the booth, scooting closer to Nisha. "So am I."

Nisha laughed. "I'll need a few more drinks in me before I agree to do anything with you, Cyno. I know where you've been."

"But you're curious, aren't you?"

"Maybe." Nisha twirled her hair. "But I don't think it'd be a good idea."

"Because of Kosabeus?" Seeing her wide eyes, Banner added, "Yeah, I know about that."

Nisha's face reddened. "It's ancient history now," she said, far too hastily to be honest. She cleared her throat. "But I heard about your rally, Cyno. Not that great a showing, huh?"

"We did all right."

Nisha laughed. "You hardly filled your stadium. You call that 'all right'?"

Banner shrugged. "It could've been better, of course, but ... our voters always come through for us in the end."

"Face it." Nisha got very close to him. Her perfume was intoxicating. "Come Brumus, you'll just be a regular Lord Regent, and Lev will be Head of the Assembly."

Banner sniggered. "At least I'll be on the Assembly. Where will you be?"

"I'll get my due."

"When? Liston will be in his job for decades. He'll outlive us both. As Lord Dynast, you'll never get the acclaim you deserve. So, maybe you should start … planning your next moves."

Nisha furrowed her eyebrows. "What do you mean?"

"How do you want history to remember you—as a background character or a power player?"

"You know the answer to that."

"Then do something about it."

Nisha eyed him suspiciously. "You know I'm an Affiliate, right? That I support my Lord Regent?"

"Sure. But I also know you're more ambitious than you let on. No way you're happy being a Lord Dynast for the rest of your life. You want Liston's seat. I know you do."

"Doesn't mean I'll ever do anything about it."

"Doesn't mean you won't. Or shouldn't. We both know you're better suited for it, anyway."

"Lev's not a bad guy, you know."

"Doesn't mean he deserves all he's been handed. And let's be honest … it's been handed to him. He hasn't had to work like we have." Banner shrugged. "But I don't know. Maybe I just have a higher opinion of you than you have of yourself."

Nisha was silent as she polished off her drink. She then turned to Banner, a seductive spark in her eyes. "Shall we take this party back to your place, then?"

They made haste, retreating to Banner's apartment, which, coincidentally, was a ten-minute walk from the Vice District. The whole ride up the elevator, they couldn't keep their hands off each other. After their session in the elevator, they subsequently destroyed Banner's apartment. The night was even more delectable than Banner had thought it would be.

That was, after all, the magic of the Vice District.

54

ASTROPHEL

Astrophel was pacing back and forth, biting his thumbnail. He'd been reading the newspapers; he knew the Expansionists were losing steam. He'd spent the last few nights tossing and turning, worrying about what the Affiliates would do once they were in control. Their vision for the universe was so innately wrong, so grotesquely out of touch. They truly believed the Core would submit to economic and political pressures and renounce its heretical ways. Clearly, they thought Queen Quintella was a gracious, levelheaded ruler. Astrophel, however, knew the truth. The Core and Imperium could not coexist. For one party to rise, the other had to fall.

And Astrophel would be damned before he stood aside and watched the Affiliates give the Core exactly what they wanted: a weak leader. As Head of the Assembly, Liston would propose decreasing the military's budget and recalling most of Imperium's soldiers. That would be a disaster; it'd open the door for Coronian aggression and leave planets in Terraria, or Neutral Space, to fend for themselves. Imperium had to stand firm and keep the Core in check. It couldn't give up any ground; it had to push the Core into a corner from which it could never come out.

Why wasn't anyone else bothered by this? Avitus was allegedly an Expansionist, but he seemed wholly uninterested in the elections. Astrophel wasn't even sure if Avitus voted. But how could Avitus not be enraged? He was a veteran, for Mystis's sake; he'd seen firsthand just how brutal the Core could be. How could he support Liston and his naive policies?

"It isn't my place to question my Lord Regent," Avitus had told Astrophel once, which had bothered Astrophel to no end.

What were the Prophates supposed to do? Just parrot back whatever their Lord Regents wanted to hear? What was the point of that? Astrophel had opinions, and he had no intention of keeping them to himself. He'd shout them out from the tallest rooftop, if he could. More Expansionists needed to be like Banner; they needed to speak up for the party, remind the Imperial people of just how dangerous the Affiliates' policies would be.

Just the other night, on a popular Expansionist radio show, Banner had said, "The Affiliates are willing to compromise our security, to expose us to the Core's attacks. The Core has already tried to meddle in our elections before; this has been well documented. We all know they want the Affiliates in charge because the Affiliates are weak. Queen Quintella knows that Liston won't challenge her. As Head of the Assembly, I have always challenged her, and I will continue to do so. I will never let the Core forget the atrocities it's committed. Ten years ago, the Core shot down one of our Intelligence ships, unprovoked. My son was one of the victims. No other families should have to endure what I and so many others went through. That's why you should vote for the Expansionist Party. We will keep you safe."

Banner's performance on the show had been spectacular, and it'd made Astrophel wonder why Whitner wasn't doing the same. Sure, he'd heard Whitner give a few interviews, but he wasn't working nearly as hard as Banner was. That made Astrophel uneasy. Indeed, it was in Whitner's best interest to excite Expansionist voters, to encourage them to go to the polls and vote for Expansionists. Why was he seemingly taking a back seat, refusing to get involved?

"I think the tides have changed," Whitner replied simply. "The Affiliate rally blew the Expansionist one out of the water. People have made up their minds. They want a change."

"But you should be fighting for what you believe in."

"I've said what I needed to say. I'm not going to be begging people for their votes."

"That's not what I'm saying."

"Look. Astrophel." Whitner heaved a deep breath. "I know you're a diehard Expansionist, and I know you're upset by how things have shaped up. But we've done what we could. The rest is in the Imperial people's hands."

"But there's still time. We can ... er, you can ... reach out to them, remind them of all the great things the Expansionists have done for them. For five years in a row, rates of violent crime have been plummeting across Imperium, and—"

"And that's all well and good, but people are angry. They want change. They're tired of the status quo." Whitner shrugged. "Not much we can do about that."

"I don't agree."

"I know you don't. But that's the way I see it." Whitner stood up, his eyes on the clock. "But I should get going, Astrophel. I have a meeting with my Lord Dynast."

"Of course. I won't hold you up."

Astrophel remained where he was. He couldn't help but feel like he was in the wrong place. Though Whitner was an Expansionist, he wasn't the Expansionist he should have been. In many ways, Astrophel wished that Whitner could be more like Banner: a strong, decisive leader. Though Banner was, of course, deeply flawed, he was also an Expansionist loyalist. He believed in what the party stood for, and Astrophel knew that regardless of what happened on Election Day, Banner would not turn his back on the Expansionists. He would help them claw their way back, help the party reclaim some of the voters it'd lost.

The same couldn't be said for Whitner, who seemed mentally checked out or wildly unaware of just how damaging the Affiliates would be. They'd tarnish Imperium's reputation and undo decades of progress. Liston had, in Astrophel's eyes, proven himself to be an unfit leader. He wasn't at all pragmatic. He saw the universe as he wanted it to be, not as it was. He didn't seem to understand that the Core and Imperium were diametrically opposed. And as long as the Core existed, so, too, would tyranny and oppression. The Core had to be dealt with; Queen Quintella had to be deposed, once and for all.

But there was still time. Maybe Whitner would see the light and realize just how dangerous the Affiliates really were. Maybe he'd start doing more interviews and remind the Imperial people just how inexperienced the Affiliates were. It'd been decades since they'd had any sort of real political power; they didn't know what it took to keep Imperium safe. Now wasn't the time to give the Affiliates a try and see if they were any good. Now was the time to continue backing the party that had kept Imperium safe from the Core.

Astrophel took a deep breath. There was still time. They could turn this around. He couldn't panic now—not when there was so much work to be done.

55

KOSABEUS

T he morning commute always seemed the most pleasant on Spero. Kosabeus took off early, around five. He grabbed a quick breakfast on the platform before hailing the five fifty train. The trip was usually a little over an hour, but Kosabeus loved the scenery.

Grell, for her part, was always awake to give him a kiss goodbye, but she didn't leave home until a little later. This morning, however, she had been uncharacteristically quiet. There was a darkness in her eyes that Kosabeus hadn't seen before. It worried him. He hoped she was all right. He knew it was stressful for her, stepping in as Silver's temporary Prophate, but she was, by all accounts, doing a marvelous job. Kosabeus had always known she'd become a Prophate someday. He hoped this position would be permanent for her.

In an hour, Kosabeus was supposed to meet the new Magista. It'd been long overdue, but the Church was nothing if not sluggish. He still didn't know who it was—the higher-ups thought it was fun, for some reason, keeping it a secret from all the Prophates—but he was hopeful the new Magista, whoever they were, would be more progressive than the previous one.

"Kosabeus."

There was a knock on his door, and Kosabeus looked up and saw Weylon. It'd been a long time since they'd seen each other. Twenty years ago, they'd both been in the running to be Banner's Prophate. Kosabeus knew how angry Weylon had been when Kosabeus was offered the job; he'd exploded at the committee, demanding to know why they had chosen Kosabeus over him. They ran into each other a few times afterward, and Weylon was always frosty toward him. Last Kosabeus had heard, Weylon had moved to Doctro. So, what was he doing in New Caelus? More importantly, what was he doing in Kosabeus's office?

"Weylon." Kosabeus decided to be as polite as possible. "It's ... been a while."

Weylon sauntered in, looking around the office that could've been his. "It's smaller than I thought it'd be."

"Have you thought about it a lot?"

"Sometimes." Weylon forced a smile. "But it doesn't keep me up at night, if that's what you're really asking." Weylon stared at Kosabeus's most ornate white robe, which was hanging in the ajar closet, for a beat too long. Then he cleared his throat and continued, "I hope you don't mind, but ... I thought I'd come and see you early."

"Come and see me—?"

"I'm the new Magista," Weylon said, unable to hold it in any longer.

Now, that was surprising. Weylon wasn't a particularly ambitious person. Even though he'd applied to be a Prophate, Kosabeus hadn't felt like it was something Weylon was willing to fight for. Instead, it seemed like Weylon had simply ... expected to be handed the Prophateship, just like he'd been handed his positions on various committees. He wanted the prestige, apparently, but not the responsibility. Thus, it seemed strange that Weylon had been in the running to be the new Magista. Most Magistas left due to burnout or sheer exhaustion; a lot was expected of them, as they were one of the core pillars of the Church. If Weylon was under the impression that it would be an easy job, then he was woefully mistaken.

"Are you?" Kosabeus offered a smile. "Well. Congratulations."

"Yes, you sound thrilled."

"I'm just ... surprised, is all."

"Why?"

"Well." Kosabeus shrugged. "I know you wanted to be a Prophate, and ... applying to be the Magista is ... quite different."

"It's something I've wanted for a long time." Weylon's eyes fell on a photograph of Grell. "She's quite something, isn't she?"

Kosabeus eyed Weylon carefully. "Yes. She is."

"Way out of your league."

"I won't disagree with that."

Weylon scoffed, a hand on Kosabeus's desk. "I'm sure she's told you all about me."

"Grell has never mentioned you."

"Really? That's a shock. We go way back, you know."

"Fascinating."

In an instant, Weylon's demeanor changed. He stepped closer to Kosabeus, a cruel sneer on his lips. There was a strange flicker in his eyes, almost as though he were possessed.

"You'd do well to take me seriously," Weylon said, attempting to sound threatening. "Things are about to change around here, and if I were you, I'd watch what I say."

"I don't take kindly to threats."

"You think I'm threatening you?"

"I think you're trying to. But it isn't working."

"Clearly, you don't know how much pull I have as the Magista. I have the final say on who stays, who comes in, and who goes."

Kosabeus suppressed a laugh. "Look. Weylon. I know we have a past, but is this really the way you want to start off our relationship?"

"I just wanted to make sure you know your place, that's all. Let you know who's in charge here."

"And I've received your message, loud and clear."

Weylon's eyes narrowed. "You really think you're comfortable here, don't you? You think no one can ever touch you."

"I've served the Church for my entire life. They understand and appreciate all the sacrifices I've made."

"But maybe the Church needs a change. Have you ever thought about that?"

"I have." Kosabeus met his eyes. "I have some ideas, actually, that I thought we could discuss in our meeting today."

"Oh, we'll get to all of that. Someday. But for now, I just ... wanted to reintroduce myself, let you know where I stand."

"Yes, you've made that perfectly clear."

"Good." Weylon gestured toward the picture of Grell. "Tell your wife I said hello, will you? I'd love to properly catch up with her, now that I'm back in New Caelus."

56

VISCARDIA

Viscardia was in her office, killing time before her meeting with Liston, Silver, and Iaconetti. Iaconetti would be inaugurated as a Lord Regent after Aperysis—most likely alongside Liston's inauguration as the new Head of the Assembly—and Liston and Silver were eager to get to know Iaconetti better. And Iaconetti, for her part, was keen to get started. She'd told Viscardia numerous times how ready she was to have more of a say in how Logistics and Transportation operated.

Viscardia and the other Prophates—minus Grell, who still wasn't an official Prophate—had spent the morning meeting with Weylon, the new Magista. To say that Viscardia was disappointed in the Church's decision was an understatement. In Viscardia's estimation, Weylon would be just as unimpressive as all the other Magistas. He was far too aggressive in asserting his authority over the Prophates. She'd wanted the Church to hire someone more magnanimous, someone who didn't pit the Prophates against the rest of the Church hierarchy. Instead, they'd hired Weylon, who seemed to resent the Prophates for their positions in Imperial government.

"This is who they picked?" Viscardia had asked Kosabeus after the meeting.

"I know. It seems like more of the same, doesn't it?"

"He's no different from Riggs. In fact, he might even be worse. I mean, clearly, Weylon has no interest in creating a more open line of communication between the Prophates and the Erates. In fact, it seems he has some sort of vendetta against us and wants us to be kept in the dark about everything."

"He does." Kosabeus smirked. "He and I were in the finals, you know, to be Cyno's Prophate. I don't think he's ever gotten over it. Perhaps that has made him distrust all Prophates."

"So, we have you to blame for this?"

Kosabeus laughed good-naturedly. "I have to admit, I'm not optimistic that Weylon will be able to put our personal issues aside and work together, but ... I'm hoping he'll prove me wrong."

Viscardia didn't think Weylon would prove Kosabeus wrong. If there was one thing she knew for certain, it was that people didn't change. Indeed, Viscardia wouldn't be surprised if she found out that Weylon was planning some sort of coup against Kosabeus as a way to enact his revenge. It wouldn't be successful, obviously; Kosabeus was the face of the Church, and none of the members of the Prophate Committee would dare to make a move against him. But Viscardia couldn't concern herself with Weylon—not at the moment, anyway. She had to make her way to the Sphere to meet with Liston, Silver, and Iaconetti. Silver's spacious office was best suited for meetings with more than three people.

When Viscardia entered the Sphere, she ran into Grell, who'd just finished meeting with Silver. They didn't have much time to chat, but Viscardia assured Grell that she hadn't missed much in the meeting with Weylon. Strangely, though, when Viscardia mentioned Weylon's name, Grell seemed ... upset. Viscardia knew that Grell was under a lot of pressure, and she was anxious about whether she'd become a Prophate, but that didn't exactly explain her reaction. Viscardia couldn't quite put her finger on it, but it was almost as though Grell and Weylon had some sort of history ...

Viscardia was the first one to enter Silver's office. She quickly filled him in on

Weylon and told him she'd go into more detail later. Then, one after the other, Liston and Iaconetti came in. Viscardia hadn't felt this optimistic about the Affiliate Party's future in a long time. Looking at Liston, Silver, and Iaconetti, knowing that they'd do everything in their power to get Imperium back on the right track, Viscardia was filled with pride.

They started off talking about the polls. After the Affiliate rally, they'd experienced a surge in support, but that wasn't unique to the Affiliates. The Expansionists and Grounders had also received bumps in support after their respective rallies, and their voters expressed that they were more excited to vote than they were before. Indeed, it was clear that as Election Day neared, the three parties were doing all they could to motivate their base—and convince more moderate, unaffiliated voters to choose a side.

"I still think the numbers look good," Silver was saying, "but obviously, anything can happen. We've all seen this before. In fact, we saw a similar scenario only five years ago. Back then, it looked like the Affiliates had a chance of unseating a few Expansionists, but we didn't do enough to tell the Imperial people what our policies were. We spent too much time bashing the Expansionists and not enough time explaining how we'd solve Imperium's problems."

"And I think we've done a good job of improving our messaging," Liston agreed, nodding. "We've managed to flip the script, to force the Expansionists to make the mistake we made during the last election cycle. Instead of focusing on their core issues, the Expansionists are the ones lashing out, criticizing us for our supposed idealism."

Iaconetti added, "Obviously, we want to highlight our stances and let the Imperial people know what we'll be fighting for, but we also need to remind them that the Expansionists have had nothing but time to accomplish all their policy goals. They've controlled the Cooperative for decades. And so, we can point at their long, failed record and remind the Imperial people that the Expansionists don't have their backs, that they don't care, that their idea of 'safety' is a police state that robs us of our privacy and freedoms."

"No, that's right." Silver smiled at her. "But we want to make sure we don't, you know, give in to fearmongering."

"So, we'll be subtle about it. Maybe we won't mention the idea of a police state, but we can just plant these seeds, simply say that the Expansionists have had decades to improve Imperials' lives but haven't."

"Do you think it's a good idea to keep going after Banner?" asked Viscardia. "I know he's an easy target, being the leader of the Expansionist Party, and his approval ratings have been slipping, but I don't know. I've heard a lot of Affiliate candidates criticizing him, but I don't think it's landing too well with the Imperial people. To them, it's just more proof of how polarizing our politics have become."

"That's a good point." Silver leaned back, stroking his chin. "Maybe we should tell the Cooperative hopefuls to pivot and spend these last few weeks really driving home their policy goals. Keep Banner's name out of it as best they can."

"Because it's not like it's changing anyone's mind, you know? People either like Banner, or they don't. Hardly anyone is neutral on him."

"And we don't want to depress our turnout by going negative."

"Exactly."

They spent the next hour or so strategizing. Iaconetti proved herself to be just as capable as Viscardia had hoped she'd be. She hadn't been able to attend the Affiliate rally in New Caelus, as she was out at a conference, but she planned on stumping for the Affiliates in Vesper for the next few weeks. For hundreds of years, Vesper had been a Mystic Expansionist stronghold, but over the last few years, the Expansionist Party's aggressive rhetoric had started to erode that support. Thus, there were many undecided voters in that region, and the Affiliate Party and the Grounder Party were doing all they could to court those voters. As a soon-to-be Lord Regent, Iaconetti was a high-profile speaker, and she'd show the people of Vesper that the Affiliate Party hadn't forgotten about them.

"Here's to the Affiliates!" Iaconetti said as the meeting ended, and they all raised their cups in agreement.

57

WHITNER

Banner had always been stressed during election season, but this year, he was acting more erratically than usual. Clearly, he'd seen the warning signs, and he knew his days as Head of the Assembly were most likely numbered. He'd been doing more interviews, becoming more brash, doing all he could to turn the Imperial people against Liston and the Affiliate Party.

It didn't seem to be working.

But Banner just wouldn't relent.

"Cyno," Whitner told him as they returned from a campaign event for an Expansionist candidate, "all you've been doing is talking about Liston. You're giving him more attention than the Affiliates are."

"The Imperial people need to know that he'll fail them."

"They need to know why you won't. You need to tell them what you stand for, what—"

"They know what I stand for. But they've been deluded into thinking that the Affiliates are—"

"You really believe the people are that stupid? That they can't distinguish between—?"

"The Affiliates have managed to poison the well against me, against us, painting our party as some sort of out of touch, incompetent, war-hungry—"

"Then prove we're not."

"Dane." Banner stopped in his tracks, his eyes narrowed. "I'm tired of having this conversation. I've been hearing it from you, I've been hearing it from Kosabeus, and I'm sick of it. You two don't know what it's like being the face of the party. The one everyone attacks. Have you heard some of the things they say about me? What am I supposed to do? Just stand aside and take it?" He shook his head. "If Liston thinks he can one-up me by hiding in the shadows and letting all his cronies do his dirty work for him, then I'll do whatever I can to expose him for the fraud he is."

A frigid wind whipped up the street, sending a shiver down Whitner's spine. It was unusual for New Caelus to get this cold, especially before Brumus. Whitner hated the cold. And he hated watching Banner drift away from him, like a ship lost in the fog, with no desire to return home. Each time Whitner looked at Banner, he found it increasingly difficult to find his friend. Steadily, he was evaporating, vanishing into the air like smoke.

"Dane?" Banner's voice broke him out of his thoughts. "Did you hear me?"

"I heard you." Whitner heaved a deep breath. "But maybe I'm tired too."

"What?"

Whitner looked down at his feet. "I don't ... I don't think I ... I need some time."

"Time for what?"

"To think." Whitner ran his fingers through his hair. "I need some space."

"Really, Dane? You've chosen to do this now? When we're just weeks away from elections?"

"I've been feeling this way for a long time. I just ... I didn't know how to say it."

"No, you know what? It's fine. Because I've gotten sick of your judgments, anyway. If you want some space, you'll get it. Just don't come crawling to me when you find yourself all alone at night, wanting some company."

"You won't have to worry about that."

Afterward, Whitner practically stormed into Astrophel's office, no doubt alarming the poor man, who'd been filing some paperwork. Whitner wasn't really sure what Prophates did when they weren't meeting with their Lord Regent, but it seemed like they always had a lot of paperwork to do.

"Dane. I ... wasn't expecting you," Astrophel said, pushing his papers aside.

"I was hoping you'd be in. I just needed to ... vent."

Astrophel stood up. "Did the event not go well today?"

"The event was fine. But ... it'll be the last one I do."

"What?" Astrophel's eyes widened. "But ... this is the most crucial point of election season. We have to—"

"I've done enough. There's nothing more I can—or want to—do."

"You can't be serious!"

"Nothing we do in the last few weeks is going to change people's minds."

"But you have to try!"

Whitner shook his head. "You and Cyno are both so in your own worlds, so unaware of just how much the Imperial people don't want the Expansionists in charge anymore."

"But you can't give up, Dane! There's too much on the line. If the Affiliates win—"

"When the Affiliates win."

"If the Affiliates win, then it'll all ... nothing will be the same!"

Whitner shrugged. "Maybe that's a good thing."

Astrophel stared at him. "I can't believe you're turning your back on your own party."

"You know what, Astrophel? You and Cyno can keep doing whatever you want, try to make me do your bidding, but I've had enough. This election season has been going on for far too long already. As far as I'm concerned, the election's already been decided, and I'm not going to waste any more time or energy thinking about it. Whatever happens, happens. And I won't be losing sleep either way."

It was liberating, finally saying that aloud. It was even more liberating leaving Astrophel's office and walking home with his head held high. Banner and Astrophel could drive themselves crazy trying to save the Expansionists if they wanted to; Whitner didn't care.

The Imperial people would make their decision in a few weeks' time, and he wouldn't object to it. No matter what happened, he'd be just fine.

58

RAELYNN

Election Day was less than a week away. People were voting early all across Imperium, letting their voices be heard. Raelynn, of course, was one of them. She and Embry went to the polls together, then had lunch at a trendy bar in downtown New Caelus. Raelynn wondered if she'd ever be able to eat at every restaurant in New Caelus. There was so much variety here, so many places tucked away in alleys or side streets.

"You're in a really special position here, Raelynn," Embry was saying as they mindlessly strolled down the street, enjoying the fresh air. "Lev will be the next Head of the Assembly. And that'll give you all sorts of power."

Raelynn laughed. "If you'd told me this is where I'd be a few months ago, I would've thought you were joking."

"But here you are."

"But here I am." Raelynn smiled. "No, it's been great, really, but I don't think it'll change too much, to be honest. I mean, yes, the Affiliates taking control will make things a lot easier, but ... it's not like it'll be smooth sailing. Even with Liston as Head of the Assembly and the Affiliates in control of the Cooperative, it'll take some time to get the alliance with the Civitan through."

"You'll face some tough opposition to that," Embry acknowledged, nodding. "Not just with Expansionists, you know. A lot of Grounders don't like it."

"And even some Affiliates don't. And Liston knows that. But we'll cross that bridge when we get to it."

Afterward, Raelynn made her way to Liston's townhouse. They were going to discuss more of the details of Ambassador Barringer's trip to New Caelus. Apparently, she'd be arriving during Aperysis, as they'd expected, and she'd be staying for a week. She was bringing some envoys with her, and Liston had hinted it would be Raelynn's job to look after these envoys and make sure they were taken care of. Raelynn had never met a Civ before, so she was excited to get the chance to meet a whole group of them and show them around New Caelus.

When Raelynn entered Liston's townhouse, she heard voices coming from the library. She followed the sound, and she saw Liston and Avitus, standing in the center of the room, deeply engrossed in a conversation that Raelynn caught only the end of.

"... unstable, and you should do more to protect yourself," Avitus was saying.

"I'm not going to hire security guards to stand outside my home."

"You should. Becoming Head of the Assembly will make you an even bigger target, my Lord Regent. And there are people out there who—"

"I won't live my life in fear."

Raelynn cleared her throat and loudly knocked on the door. "I, um ... I hope you don't mind, but, uh ... your door was open."

"Of course, it was," muttered Avitus, his arms crossed. To Liston, he said, "This is what I'm talking about."

"It's Raelynn," Liston retorted.

"It could've been anyone."

Liston sighed, then turned to Raelynn. "Well, come on in, Raelynn. We have a lot to discuss."

Raelynn stepped into the library. She hadn't been expecting to see Avitus. A part of her was still recovering from her last interaction with him. She wondered if Avitus could tell just how scared Raelynn was of him. Or maybe Avitus just assumed everyone was scared of him. That would definitely be a good guess.

"Election Day's coming up," Liston started. "Have you already voted?"

"I just did today," Raelynn said proudly.

"Good. Yes, that's right. Embry mentioned you were going together." Liston smiled. "It seems the early voting numbers are up for all three parties, so we'll see how that plays out."

Avitus was silent. He was standing behind Liston, as immovable as a brick wall. Raelynn wasn't sure if she was just imagining it, but she could feel Avitus's eyes boring into her.

"But it looks like the Affiliates are doing remarkably well in Vesper," Liston went on. "We have Tinsley to thank for that. She did a marvelous job, stopping in various towns, talking to voters. She said she had quite the warm reception in Vitor."

"Did she?" Avitus's expression was unreadable.

"I know. I was rather surprised too, but ... she said people's excitement was tangible."

"That will certainly help you, my Lord Regent. If you can increase turnout in traditionally Expansionist areas, then you'll be on track."

Raelynn knew that Avitus was an Expansionist—or at least preferred their party platform—so it seemed odd for him to be hoping for an Affiliate victory. However, as Liston's Prophate, it was Avitus's job to support his Lord Regent, even when they disagreed. It was remarkable, really, how easy it ostensibly was for Avitus to put aside his own beliefs and throw his weight behind Liston and the Affiliates. But maybe it wasn't easy for Avitus. Maybe he was just an expert at appearing as unbothered as humanly possible.

"Yes, I'm optimistic," Liston admitted, unable to suppress his enthusiasm. "And if that happens, then Ambassador Barringer will come, and ... and everything will finally start to fall into place." Liston looked at Avitus. "And I want you to be there with us, to meet with the Civs."

A flash of something akin to rage crossed Avitus's face, but he quickly dismissed it. "If that is what you want, my Lord Regent," Avitus said, his head bowed.

"I know it won't be ... easy for you to sit across from Commander Heston and—"

"I can put aside my own feelings on the matter."

Liston smiled. "Thank you." He turned to Raelynn. "And Raelynn, Ambassador Barringer will be bringing a team with her. She has someone who is ... well, she's sort of like you, actually. She's been working for her for a few years—as an intern, I guess you'd call it—and she's apparently very excited about coming to Imperium. She's around your age, and I thought it'd be nice if you'd be the one to show her around, let her see just how special Imperium is."

"I'd love to," Raelynn said.

"Good." Liston heaved a deep breath. "It's just ... it's all so close now. For so long, this has all been hypothetical, but ..." He trailed off, shaking his head. "Anyway, I just ... I want to thank you both. Without you, we wouldn't be where we are right now."

"You're the one who let me in," Raelynn reminded him. "Without you, I'd be ... well, I don't know where I'd be."

Liston laughed. "I knew you were the right Audilla for the job. And you haven't proven me wrong." He gestured to the table. "Well, let's sit. We have a lot more to talk about."

59

GRELL

Grell was relieved that Election Day was almost here. She had to admit, she was getting sick of all the ads. It seemed like almost every radio show had turned into a news station. She couldn't escape it. She knew the elections were important, of course, and she'd already cast her vote, but she didn't think the coverage needed to be so expansive. She couldn't even go to the hair salon without being bombarded by billboards, for Mystis's sake.

"I don't know how you do it, Viscardia," Grell was saying as they entered the Church. They'd just gotten back from their lunch break. "I mean, I know you love this stuff, but even you must be reaching your limits."

Viscardia laughed. "I'm definitely looking forward to Aperysis. Let's put it that way. It'll be nice to just take a few weeks off and spend some time at the island house."

"Oh, it's beautiful out there."

"It is. Especially in alsius. You know, Raze and I would love to have you. Bring Eddard and Magdalena. We'll have a grand ole time."

"I just might take you up on that."

"You should. We're excellent hosts." Viscardia smiled. "But what's on your schedule for the afternoon?"

"Another meeting with the Prophate Committee, I'm afraid. I'm sure it'll be the same spiel, telling me they haven't made their mind up yet, that I just need to wait a little longer."

"They're really dragging their feet on this."

"I'd just like to know, one way or the other. If it's not going to be me, then they should just tell me. Stop keeping me in the dark."

"I agree." Viscardia heaved a deep breath. "Well, I'll let you get on with it. I have to get ready for my lecture at the New Caelus Numentis School."

"Good luck."

"Thanks. I'll need it."

Grell made her way to the Decio Room, which was where the Prophate Committee met. The committee included seven members, one of whom was the Magista. The Magista was the most powerful member of the committee, as his vote was worth three times as much as the other members' votes. Thus, he needed to convince only a handful of the other committee members to vote his way, and he'd get whatever he wanted.

Grell knew that her and Weylon's history would complicate matters. Weylon had told her in no uncertain terms that she would regret walking out on him. She fully expected him to destroy her dreams of ever becoming a Prophate. But even though a part of Grell wanted to be a Prophate—indeed, every Numite grew up with that aspiration—another part of her hoped they'd tell her she wasn't what they were looking for. Then she wouldn't be forced to deal with Weylon so often—and she wouldn't have to worry about him holding that over her head, telling her that the only reason she'd become a Prophate was because of him. She didn't want to give him that sort of power.

"Grell." Weylon was the first to speak. He smiled at her in that smug way. "We know you must be frustrated with how slowly this process has been going, but ... it's just, we have great candidates, and we want to make sure they're all given their due."

"No, I understand," Grell replied.

"Good. Because … it's not that we don't think you're great—and actually, Lord Regent Silver has spoken up in your defense—but, you see, Halliwell and Adelphi are also strong candidates. It's down to you three. And … well, only two of you will become Prophates. See, we have Lisbeth retiring, and we need to find Lord Regent Silver's permanent Prophate, so … that'll leave one of you out of luck."

Grell didn't know why he felt the need to explain all of this to her; she already knew all of this. Every meeting she'd had with the Prophate Committee for the past four or so months had been the same. She, Adelphi, and Halliwell were the top contenders, and the Prophate Committee was finding it torturous to choose from among them. The only difference this time was that Weylon was here, and he was the one delivering this speech.

Weylon went on, "But we can assure you we'll make our final decision a little after Election Day. So, not too much longer now. And we'll let you all know then."

"Is that all?"

"Yes. You may go."

Grell resisted the urge to roll her eyes. She exited the Decio Room as quickly as she could while also maintaining her civility. She smiled at each of the committee members and gave a little nod of her head, then headed toward her office. She couldn't believe the Prophate Committee had told her to clear her whole afternoon for that meeting. But on the bright side, it looked like she'd be able to go home early.

"Grell." Weylon knocked on her door. "I was hoping we could talk. Away from them."

"I'm not interested."

He ignored her and entered her office, closing the door behind him. "I shouldn't have pushed you like that. I know that you and Kosabeus … you've been through a lot." His eyes darkened. "And I'm sure it'd absolutely gut him if he ever found out that the only reason you stayed with him was because he was sick."

Seeing Grell's stunned reaction, Weylon went on, "You see, when I became the Magista, I got access to all sorts of confidential files. You know, I can't believe the Church managed to keep that a secret. Quite impressive, really. But when I saw the dates ... everything became clear. All at once, I understood why you broke it off, why you were suddenly so willing to give your marriage a chance."

"You don't know anything about my marriage."

"I know it didn't mean anything to you until that happened. Then you felt guilty, and—"

"I love Kosabeus," Grell snapped. "And if you just came in here to threaten me and try to get me to confess to something that—"

"You really think you're in a position to bargain here? Your future's in my hands. If you want to be a Prophate, you'll do what I ask."

"I'm never doing anything for you ever again."

"Don't give me that bullshit. You'll do whatever it takes to be a Prophate. It's what every Numite grows up dreaming about." Weylon sneered. "But you'll only get it if you—"

"Either make me a Prophate or don't. But I won't be forced into anything."

"Not even if I were to, say ... tell your husband—?"

"Don't you dare bring Kosabeus into this."

Weylon met her eyes. "You're never going to tell him about us, are you?"

"Get out."

"You say you love him, yet you refuse to—"

"I won't say it again."

"You know, if I was in his position, I'd want to know. So, maybe, being the good person I am, I should go tell him."

"If you were ever going to do that, you'd have done it years ago."

"But maybe I was waiting for the perfect moment. And maybe I've found it." Weylon grinned. "Just, you know, something to think about."

60

BANNER

He'd lost Whitner. That wasn't too much of a surprise, actually; Whitner had been acting distant for a while. Banner didn't take it too personally. He knew that Whitner wasn't as political as he was. Consequently, he was often more frustrated by election season than anything else. Once Whitner had some time to cool off, though, he'd come back, and he and Banner would go back to the way things were.

Besides, Banner had to admit, he'd been getting sick of Whitner's criticisms. For weeks, Whitner had been telling him he was too self-absorbed, that he wasn't approaching Election Day with a clear head. It was like Whitner was completely oblivious to the Affiliates' smear campaign against him. What, Banner was supposed to say nothing and just let the Affiliates spread their lies and brainwash people into voting for them?

Banner was Head of the Assembly, damnit. The position was his. And he wouldn't let Liston get it without a fight.

Banner stood up, a bit too quickly. His head started spinning, and he held onto his desk for balance. He was tired of going at Liston through other people, making vague comments to the press. He wanted to talk to Liston, face-to-face, and confront him about all of this.

The Spire was a couple of train stops away from the Hall, but Banner didn't mind. On the journey, he thought about what he'd say to Liston. There was so much he wanted to say, but he knew he'd have to keep it short and to the point. Banner was sick of people giving Liston the benefit of the doubt. Even after the Zenith fiasco, people had gone out of their way to defend Liston and claim that he was merely a victim of depression. That could have been true, of course, and it probably was, given Liston's history with alcoholism, but that still didn't excuse his ineptitude. How could people seriously think that Liston would be a good Head of the Assembly? What if the pressure was too much for him? Would he once again lock himself inside his office and drink himself into a stupor? Was that the kind of leader Imperium deserved?

Finally, Banner arrived at the Spire. Liston was on the ground floor, strangely enough, in the basement, tucked away like some unwanted child. Banner opened Liston's deceptively heavy door sans announcing his arrival with the customary knock. Liston didn't deserve a warning. He was wearing his glasses, sitting at his desk, and looking over paperwork. Automatically, Liston looked up after hearing the door open.

"Lord Regent Banner," Liston said, standing up. "What a welcome surprise."

Banner scoffed. "Save your pleasantries, Liston," he growled. Gazing around, Banner realized he'd never been in Liston's office before. "Some place you have here," he remarked. "While the rest of us are up in the clouds, here you are, underwater."

"Is that supposed to be metaphoric?"

"I don't know. *You're* the brilliant one." Banner stepped closer to Liston. "Figure. It. Out."

"So, what did you come here for? If not to speak in metaphors."

"To see you," said Banner, taking off his suit jacket, tossing it on Liston's couch. "And I figured since this is your office, this is where you'd be." He glanced at Liston's bar. "Care to join me for a glass of whiskey?"

"Why?"

Banner traced his finger along the bar's wooden counter. "I want to talk."

"And you need whiskey to do that?"

"It certainly helps."

"I'm afraid I'll have to turn you down."

"Why? Because you ... can't?"

"I don't know what—"

"Oh, please. Don't feed me that bullshit. I know."

"And what, pray tell, do you know?"

"That you're an alcoholic."

Liston's face betrayed no emotion. "And let me guess. You think that because that is what Darius Madden tells you?"

"No, I—"

"Because I hate to be the one to tell you this, Banner, but since you came to my office at three in the afternoon looking for a glass of whiskey, you might be the alcoholic here."

Banner furrowed his eyebrows. "I don't—"

"So, how about instead of whiskey, we have some water? Would that work for you?"

Banner put his hands on his hips. "And how do you plan on getting that? By breaking open your window?"

"Right there on the bar, there's a pitcher of ice water," said Liston, signaling with his hand. "See it?"

"Yes," said Banner distractedly, his eyes drifting to the pitcher.

"Feel free to take some."

Banner picked up the pitcher, then dropped it to the floor. It shattered, spraying water all over. "Pass."

Liston walked over to him, surveying the broken glass as if it were a crime scene. "Accidents happen," he offered.

"That wasn't an accident."

"You purposefully broke my pitcher?"

"You saw me do it."

"Then you owe me five hundred numa."

Banner raised an eyebrow. "You paid that much for a pitcher?"

"It was high-end." Liston reached for the broom beside the bar.

Banner grabbed him by the arm. "Leave it."

Liston looked down at Banner's hand. "You know," he said, pulling away, "you're lucky you didn't go into Diplomacy. Because your subtlety is ... lacking."

"Speaking of you Diplomacy Keepers, this should interest you." Banner leaned against the bar, his eyes on Liston, gauging his body language. Seeing the blank expression on Liston's face, Banner added, "Nisha and I had sex."

"And why would that interest me?"

"Because I got into your house," said Banner, peeling away from the bar. "Just like that, I can turn Nisha against you."

"Turn her against me?"

"I got her in my bed. I can get her anywhere else I want."

"Nisha's an Affiliate. She's loyal to the party, to the division."

"Are you sure about that?"

"Yes, I'm sure. Nisha would never—"

"—sleep with the enemy?" Banner scoffed. "I guess you don't know her as well as you think you do. Certainly not as well as *I* do now."

Liston shook his head. "Nisha would never do anything to hurt our division. Whatever happened between you two ... she would never go against our party."

"You really don't think she wants what you have?"

"I can't say I ever—"

"—thought about that? Yes, I know. You never had to. Because you had Avitus. And Carbury."

Liston's eyes darkened. "You don't know anything about Carbury."

"He was like a mentor to you. Or so I've heard."

"It wasn't my choice."

"But it gave you ... this." Banner gestured around the room. "You don't actually think you would've gotten this position without him, do you?"

"I don't owe him anything."

"I know you don't believe that."

"You don't know what I believe."

Banner neared Liston. "Do I revolt you?"

Liston threw Banner's suit jacket back at him. "Take this."

Banner caught his jacket with one hand. "Do I revolt you?" he repeated, never once looking away from Liston.

Liston crossed his arms. "What do you want, Banner? You didn't come here to tell me about Nisha or to talk about Carbury."

"Maybe I did." Banner looked Liston up and down. "Maybe I wanted a reaction."

"If you thought you'd get one, I'm sorry to disappoint you."

"Are you? Are you really?"

Liston furrowed his eyebrows. Banner could tell, he was starting to annoy him. Good. That was what he wanted. He wanted some sort of emotion from Liston, something to use against him.

"You know," Banner went on, "I've always been curious about you. You were the youngest Lord Regent in history. All that power at such a young age ... that has to do something to a man."

"I didn't let it."

"How?"

"I surrounded myself with the brightest people I could."

"How magnanimous. You know, if I recall correctly, you weren't a shoo-in. Your committee balked when they learned just how young you were."

"I proved them wrong."

"You mean Avitus spoke to them." Banner laughed. "Yes, I know all about the role he played in your rise to the top."

"I've earned my place here."

"So you say." Banner met his eyes. "But I don't buy it. I know there's a part of you that wonders where you'd be right now if it weren't for him."

Liston turned away from him. "You don't intimidate me, Banner."

"I should."

"And why's that?"

"Because I have power. *Real* power. What you have ... it's all an illusion. When people think of Imperium, they think of me."

"For now. But we both know those days are nearing their end—very soon, I reckon."

Banner gritted his teeth. "Even if you manage to win more seats, Liston ... even if you become Head of the Assembly ... you'll never have the pull I have. I worked for this. I didn't need anyone's help to become a Lord Regent. I did it all on my own. And Imperials respect that. They respect a man who's earned his place."

Liston laughed. "If you think people respect you, then you are more ignorant than I thought."

Banner narrowed his eyes. "The public's been duped. You Affiliates have been attacking me for months, making up all sorts of stories."

"Don't blame us for your missteps. You dug this grave all on your own. I didn't even have to hand you the shovel." Liston stepped closer to him, a spirited glint in his eyes. "You know, I thought I'd really have to work to turn the Imperial people against you, but I barely had to lift a finger. You imploded all on your own. Quite remarkable, really."

"Well, it's not over yet."

"Yes, it is." Liston gestured toward the door. "You may leave."

"I'll leave when I'm ready."

"No. You'll leave when I tell you to."

"I'll leave after I get what I want."

"Those threats may have a way with people in the Hall, but as you said, you're in my house now. And you don't scare me."

"Someday, you'll look back on this and regret it."

"I sincerely doubt that." Liston again pointed to the door. "Leave. Now."

As Banner left the Spire, a flurry of emotions coursed through him. Liston had been more self-assured than Banner had expected. He didn't flinch, and he didn't let Banner get under his skin. Maybe he'd learned from his mistakes, grown as a leader, evolved as a person. Maybe Liston was more confident now because he assumed—a bit too boldly, in Banner's opinion—that he would be the next Head of the Assembly.

And maybe he would be. But Banner wasn't going to give up or give in. If Liston was the next Head of the Assembly, then Banner would do everything he could to make his tenure as miserable and short as possible. He was going to make Liston pay for all he'd done.

One of these days, Liston would be at his feet begging for mercy.

And Banner, for one, couldn't wait to see it.

61

KOSABEUS

"Keep your Lord Regent in line!"

Those were the first words out of Avitus's mouth when he entered Kosabeus's office early on Fidem. Kosabeus was in a bit of a daze, as he'd just come from a rather taxing meeting with the Church higher-ups, who had all seemingly been won over by Weylon's vision for the Church. They didn't tell him what that vision was, of course; that would've been far too convenient. No, instead, they just kept insisting that the changes would be for the best and that the Church would be better than ever.

Kosabeus rubbed his temples. "What?"

Avitus stepped deeper into the office. "Banner came to see my Lord Regent yesterday. And he became ... heated. And aggressive."

Kosabeus had been worried that something like this would happen. Lately, Banner had been acting more unhinged than normal, doing interviews he shouldn't have been doing and saying things he most definitely shouldn't have been saying. More than a few times, Kosabeus had told him to reel it in, to keep his temper, to take the high road, but Banner, it seemed, was determined to whine about Liston all the way up until Election Day.

"I didn't ... I didn't know that," Kosabeus replied.

"Didn't you meet with Banner yesterday?"

"He didn't show up. He's been avoiding me."

"Well, when you do see him, tell him to stay away from my Lord Regent."

"I will." He stood up. "Avitus, while you're here ... what do you think of Weylon?"

"He's a blustering fool. Why?"

"It just ... it seems odd, doesn't it, for the Church to choose him? He's not really the Magista type, is he?"

"No." Avitus met Kosabeus's eyes. "But I assume that's not his end goal."

"How do you mean?"

"I think he's come back to New Caelus to get what he didn't get twenty years ago."

"You think he still wants to be a Prophate?"

"Well, don't you? He's always been bitter about it."

Kosabeus stroked his chin. "Lisbeth is retiring. Do you think Weylon will try and take her place?"

"No. They're clearly going to choose either Adelphi or Halliwell."

"Then what, he'll just ... wait around for another one to open up? That's his plan?"

Avitus shrugged. "Like I said, he's a fool. But it's obvious his ambitions exceed his current office."

Kosabeus nodded slowly. "Speaking of offices, I'll go to Cyno's, see if I can find him there. And I'll ask him about yesterday," he added, which Avitus thanked him for.

When he arrived at Banner's office, Milner tried to insist that Banner wasn't in. She wasn't a skilled liar, so Kosabeus walked past her and straight into Banner's office. And, lo and behold, there was Banner, conducting an over-the-phone interview with some Expansionist rag.

"... and yes, I ..." As soon as he saw Kosabeus, Banner's eyes narrowed. "Yes, these final days are the most important. Talk to everyone you know. And make sure they vote for Expansionists down the ballot. ... No, thank *you* for your time. ... Okay. ... Yes, bye." He hung up and glared at Kosabeus. "What the hell are you doing here?"

"You've been avoiding me."

"I've been busy."

"No, you've been unraveling. There's a difference."

Banner scoffed. "Not this bullshit again."

"Oh, so you're trying to tell me you haven't been going on tirades and—?"

"That's my job! That's what I have to do!"

"Do you even know how deranged you sound in your radio interviews?"

Banner stood up and pointed his index finger at Kosabeus. "I don't need to hear this right now."

"I think this is exactly what you—"

"I already had Dane on my back. I don't need you too." Banner's face was red.

Kosabeus neared him. "Did you go to Liston's office yesterday?"

"What?" Obviously, Banner hadn't expected Kosabeus to have heard about that already. "No. I mean ... yes ... but ..." He trailed off, shaking his head.

"And what did you think that'd accomplish?"

"I wanted to see him squirm! I wanted to look him in the eyes and let him know that I'm not going down without a fight."

"And do you think it worked?"

Banner scowled. "Look, I don't need you coming in here and—"

"Evidently, you do. All your recent actions have proven that I'm one of the only things keeping you from lashing out like this."

"You don't know what it's like to live under a microscope."

"Oh, come on, Cyno. Enough with the melodrama. You have no one to blame but yourself for this mess. And these ... interviews you're doing? They're not helping. They're actually making it worse. So, if you want my advice—"

"I don't. I don't want to hear anything from you. In fact ..." Banner looked toward the door. "Milner! Could you come in?"

Milner entered, but she stayed near the door. "Yes, my Lord Regent?"

"Could you escort Kosabeus out of here?"

"You can't be serious," Kosabeus said.

"Um ... yes, my Lord Regent," Milner replied, her eyes darting between the two.

"Cyno." Kosabeus tried to make eye contact, but Banner was pretending to be fascinated by something on his desk. "Don't shut me out. Not like this. Not before Election Day."

Awkwardly, Milner walked up to Kosabeus, and she cleared her throat. "Kosabeus, my Lord Regent has asked you to—"

"I want him to say it himself."

"I believe he already—"

"No, I want to hear him say that he wants me to go, that he thinks he can do this all on his own." Kosabeus crossed his arms. "Well?"

Banner slowly looked up. "I want you to go. And I'll do this all on my own."

Kosabeus scoffed. "Fine." He brushed past Milner. "I know my way out."

He took the first train he could home. The day certainly hadn't gone as he'd expected. It'd been filled with one strange encounter after another. But now that he was home, he could put it all behind him and unwind.

Grell was out in the sunroom, tending to her plants. This room was the primary reason they'd bought the house. The sunroom boasted stunning views of the old-growth forest, and a brook passed through the property, adding wonderful ambience. Grell heard Kosabeus, and she turned around, a smile on her lips.

"You're home!" she said, walking over to give him a hug and a kiss.

"Yes. Finally." Kosabeus glanced around the sunroom, smiling. "I see why you love it out here so much."

"It's the perfect place to decompress."

"Hard day?" he asked as they sat down in opposite wicker chairs.

"Not hard, per se. Just … apparently, the Prophate Committee will be meeting after Election Day to determine whether or not I'll get the Prophateship. And then, who knows how long it'll be until I hear? I just … the waiting is killing me."

"I know. But I have a feeling it'll be good news. At the very least, you have one friendly face on the committee."

"What do you mean?"

"Weylon. He said you two knew each other." Grell bit her lip but said nothing. "And he has sway in the committee, so … I don't think you should worry about it, my darling." Kosabeus leaned back and sighed. "Cyno's practically banished me as his Prophate."

"What? Why?"

"Apparently, he doesn't like that I talk to him. I'm sure after Election Day, he'll come to his senses, but … I have to say, it'll be quite nice to get a bit of a respite from him."

Grell laughed. "How do you think he'll take the loss?"

"Poorly. But he'll take it."

Grell stood up and ambled over to him. She took his hand in hers. "Do you want to go for a stroll before dinner? It's still light out. We should have enough time to go to Paradise Pond and back."

Kosabeus grinned. "I'd love that."

62

ASTROPHEL

Astrophel wasn't naive. He knew the Expansionists' prospects were worsening by the day. But he also knew that forces had been shifting within the Church—forces that could, if properly exploited, help him gain the power and prestige he so desired.

It was clear that Weylon, their new Magista, didn't like Kosabeus. And it was also clear that Banner and Kosabeus had had some sort of falling-out—a rather serious one, from the sounds of it. Astrophel didn't want to get his hopes up, but he was optimistic he would be able to take these two facts and use them to his advantage.

He'd asked Weylon if he was interested in a meeting, and Weylon said he was. Astrophel thus made his way to Weylon's office, which was located on the top floor of the Church. Weylon had stunning, unobstructed views of the gardens. His office was much airier than the Prophates' offices, with vaulted ceilings and plenty of windows. Astrophel, however, knew this office had only the illusion of power; in his eyes, true power in the Church belonged to the Prophates—and, more specifically, the Head Prophate.

"Astrophel." Weylon smiled warmly at him. "You're the first Prophate who's gone out of their way to schedule a meeting with me."

"I apologize for my colleagues' obtuseness."

Weylon waved a glib hand. "They're quite stuck in their ways."

"They can be." Astrophel heaved a deep breath. "And I think that's one of the main issues with the Church."

"Oh?" Weylon leaned back in his chair, biting the tip of his pen. "How do you mean?"

Astrophel shifted in his chair. "Since I became a Prophate, I've noticed ... well, I don't think our leadership is as competent as it could be."

"And by that, you mean—?"

"Kosabeus." Astrophel cleared his throat. "I'm talking about Kosabeus."

Weylon grinned. "I appreciate your candor, Astrophel, and I ... listen, I have my own reasons for ... doubting whether Kosabeus is truly capable of giving the Church what it needs, but ... the Prophate Committee won't be persuaded to investigate the matter unless we're provided with sufficient evidence."

"What would count as 'sufficient evidence'?"

"Well." Weylon sighed. "The most damning piece of evidence would come from Lord Regent Banner himself. If Lord Regent Banner expresses any issues or concerns with Kosabeus, then the Prophate Committee would have no choice but to open an investigation."

"I see." Astrophel's mind was racing. "So, if Lord Regent Banner were to speak out against him, do you think ...?" He paused for a moment, then went on, "Do you think the committee would actually remove him?"

"It's hard to say. Kosabeus seems to be quite popular within the Church, but he, like every leader, has his critics." Weylon leaned forward. "All I know is that without Lord Regent Banner's input, Kosabeus won't be going anywhere. Do you understand what I'm saying?"

"I do." Astrophel nodded absently. "I'll reach out to him."

"Please do." Weylon rested his elbows on his desk. "Believe me, nothing would make me happier than seeing Kosabeus kicked out of the Church. But this sort of move has to come from the outside. It has to start with Lord Regent Banner."

That was all Astrophel needed to hear. Over the past few months, Astrophel had concluded that it wasn't enough for him, being Whitner's Prophate. He wanted more; he wanted to work for a Lord Regent who not only had power but also used said power to enact meaningful change. Even if the Expansionists lost the Cooperative, Banner would still be the most powerful Expansionist in government. He was the one Astrophel wanted to work with; he was the Lord Regent who would help the Expansionists rebuild. Whitner, on the other hand, wouldn't lift a damn finger. Astrophel couldn't advise a man like that, a man who refused to do the bare minimum to help his party save Imperium.

Though Astrophel didn't dislike Kosabeus, per se, he was in the way. With Kosabeus out of the picture, Astrophel would be able to step in as Banner's Prophate. It'd be a seismic shift, ousting Kosabeus from the Church, but it would pave the way for Astrophel's ascension to the Head Prophateship. This was why he had reached out to Weylon in the first place. Indeed, he knew Weylon would view him more favorably than the other Prophates, and this would all but guarantee that Astrophel would be inaugurated as the new Head Prophate. He couldn't wait for that day, for that gorgeous white robe to be his.

In order to see that dream become a reality, he had to first take care of Kosabeus.

63

RAELYNN

Raelynn made her way to Liston's townhouse to listen to the election results as they rolled in. Liston had invited only a handful of people over, such as Silver, Viscardia, Iaconetti, and a few high-profile Affiliate Cooperative candidates. Taymor and Embry, as Grounder loyalists, had politely opted not to attend, as they knew the Affiliates would want to celebrate their victories. Strangely enough, though, Avitus had decided to come to Liston's townhouse, but he seemed to be keeping to himself. This was most assuredly not where he wanted to be; however, it seemed that supporting Liston was more important to him than remaining in his comfort zone.

For the first few hours, the results were unsurprising. Races were called that had been predicted months ago, and there hadn't been too many upsets. After a while, however, the tide started to turn, and some Affiliate candidates were winning seats that Expansionists had been holding on to for decades. As the night went on, and the Affiliates continued to pick up seats, the mood became more and more exuberant. As each race was called, the idea of an Affiliate-dominated Cooperative became less of a dream and more of a reality.

"We just need four more seats," Silver was saying to Liston. "Four more seats, and the Cooperative is ours!"

From Raelynn's point of view, Liston didn't seem as excited as Silver was. There was a sense of foreboding on his face, as though it were finally dawning on him what was about to transpire. His life would never be the same again. He'd be the new face of Imperial government, and all of Imperium's successes and failures would reflect on him. It must have been a daunting feeling, one that Raelynn would never truly be able to understand.

At last, a little before midnight, the final race was called, though the results had been clear long before then. The Affiliates now controlled thirty-two of the seats in the Cooperative, the Expansionists controlled twenty-two, and the Grounders controlled sixteen. In all, the Affiliates had gained eight seats, the Expansionists had lost twelve seats, and the Grounders had gained four seats. No doubt, this was a devastating blow for the Expansionist Party; they hadn't lost more than just a handful of contests in years. For the next few months—and even years—they'd be forced to reassess their messaging and canvassing strategies. Though Raelynn was disappointed that the Affiliates hadn't won a majority—they had only a plurality—she still knew this was a tremendous victory.

"Congratulations, my Lord Regent." Avitus stepped out of the shadows and placed his hand on Liston's shoulder. "You won."

Liston looked up at him. "It really happened."

"You'll have to make your speech later on this morning. Do you know what you'll say?"

"Yes, I ... have a good idea." Liston cleared his throat. "I can't believe we actually did it."

"I told you we would," Viscardia said.

"I know you did." Liston smiled at her, but his smile seemed forced, and there was a hint of apprehension in his eyes. "It's just a lot to take in."

"Everything will be different," Silver piped up, unable to suppress his grin. "We finally have a chance to make things right."

"And we will. We have to."

64

BANNER

It was over. He'd said it many times, that the Expansionists were done, but he hadn't meant it. But now Banner was confronted with the frightening reality. He was no longer Head of the Assembly.

In one night, Liston had stolen his title, just like he'd stolen so much else. Banner could hardly breathe. He hadn't expected Election Day to be so disastrous. It would take years for the Expansionists to rebuild their image and mollify their angry constituents. The party wouldn't blame Banner; they would do everything in their power to protect him. And in time, he'd be able to prove to them all once again why they'd chosen him as their leader.

Caine had come over to Banner's apartment for drinks. They listened to the election news at first but decided to turn it off once the outlook became irreparably grim. They sat in silence for a while, lost in their own thoughts.

"Cyno." Caine's face was contorted in a weird expression of empathy. "I know tonight didn't go the way either of us wanted."

"No," Banner mumbled, rolling his shoulders. "Not at all."

"But we can't give up. We'll regain our lost seats. Maybe pick up a few more. This is the Affiliates' brief moment in the sun, but it will pass."

"I doubt that."

"You never know. Maybe the Affiliates won't be as productive as people think. Maybe they'll fail."

"And maybe they won't. Maybe they'll do everything they've said they'd do. Maybe Liston will be Head of the Assembly for the rest of his damned life."

"We can't let that happen." It was almost adorable, how optimistic Caine sounded. Their world was crashing around them, but he still held out hope. "Liston's taken too much from me."

"Right," said Banner, nodding. "Raelynn. Your ... daughter." He met Caine's eyes. "When will you hear back about that?"

"I already have."

"What?" Banner stared at him. "Why didn't you say anything earlier?"

"Because ... I guess I'm still ... processing it. But ... she's my daughter." Caine heaved a deep breath. "She's my Seryph."

"So, what does this ... what will you do?"

A smile formed on Caine's lips. "I'm going to get my daughter back."

65

GRELL

She'd been dreading this moment for years. A part of her had hoped it would never come to this—that she could just continue acting like it hadn't happened and move on. But Weylon's reappearance in New Caelus had changed everything. She had to make sure she told Kosabeus before he heard it from Weylon. That was the only chance she had at some sort of redemption.

She was in the living room, pacing the floor, waiting for Kosabeus to return. Election Day hadn't gone in the Expansionists' favor, and though Kosabeus considered himself to be an Expansionist, he'd told Grell numerous times that the Expansionist Party was lost. Maybe this loss would force them to look inward and make some drastic changes, he'd said. He'd spent the day at the Church, holding sermons, trying to comfort Imperials of all political persuasions and let them know that regardless of the electoral results, Imperium's best days were still in front of them.

Grell bit her nail. This was going to be brutal. She had no idea how he'd react. Kosabeus had never been a volatile person, but this was unprecedented territory. He had every right to be angry. More than that, he had every right to hate her. She had done so many hurtful things. The affair with Weylon was one of them, but even worse, she'd—

She heard the front door open. She froze on the spot. This was it. The time of reckoning was finally upon her. She'd have to confess to everything, every horrible thing she'd ever done to him.

"Grell?"

"I'm in here." Her voice was surprisingly steady.

Kosabeus came in, somehow looking handsomer than ever. She hated that. She hated that she'd spent the early part of their marriage completely taking him for granted. He didn't deserve that. He had never given her a reason to stray, had never once made her feel as small as Bayne had, yet she had betrayed his trust. If she lost him because of all of this, then she deserved it. She wouldn't blame him if he never wanted to speak to her again.

He smiled at her—for maybe the last time. "Oh, my darling," he said, shrugging out of his jacket, "you have no idea how glad I am to finally get some time off. Well, until Aperysis, that is."

"You've been working so hard."

Grell tried to maintain some semblance of normality. After all, she wanted to treasure these precious moments with Kosabeus as long as she could. In just a few minutes, everything would be different. Was it so wrong for her to want to relish this while she still could?

"All for nothing, apparently. The Expansionist Party has veered so far from its original path I don't even recognize it anymore." He sighed. "I guess we'll have to wait and see how the transition goes. Hopefully, Cyno steps aside gracefully."

"Don't count on that."

"Oh, I know. Wishful thinking." Kosabeus chuckled, bending down to kiss her. "But we don't need to talk about—"

"Kosabeus." Grell couldn't take it anymore. Shakily, she reached for his hand and pulled him over to the couch. "We ... there's something I ... we need to talk."

"What is it?"

He looked into her eyes, and for a second, she wondered if it'd be better to just keep this all to herself. But she knew she couldn't. He had a right to know everything.

Grell could feel her pulse quickening. "I ... this isn't easy for me to say."

"Is something wrong?"

He sounded so concerned. The way he was looking at her nearly broke her heart. She had no one to blame for this but herself.

Grell gripped his hands more tightly. "I just ... I want you to know ... I love you so, so much." She choked up, shaking her head.

Kosabeus squeezed her hands, offering her his support. "I love you too, Grell. You can tell me anything. You know that."

Grell nodded silently. "I know. But, um ... what I'm going to tell you ... it might change things for you, but ... I'll still love you. And I'll do whatever I can to prove that to you."

"Grell, you're scaring me. What's wrong?"

She heaved a deep breath, tears in her eyes. "There's something you should know."

66

ASTROPHEL

Astrophel couldn't believe it. All his worst nightmares had come true. Liston would be the new Head of the Assembly, and everything the Expansionists had fought so hard to preserve was now at risk. It was nauseating thinking about that future, fearing what the Affiliates would do with their newfound power and relevance.

It was clear to Astrophel he was in the wrong position. He knew he couldn't achieve all he wanted to as Whitner's Prophate. If he stayed where he was, he'd never be more than a footnote in history, a forgotten Prophate. He needed to be close to someone with real influence, someone who could effect change and regrow the Expansionist Party.

Imperium needed to be liberated, to be saved from the Affiliates, and if Whitner wasn't willing to stand up and speak out against the Affiliates, then Astrophel needed to find someone on the Assembly who would. Only then could Imperium's future be secured.

He thus found himself at Banner's apartment, early in the morning. Astrophel wasn't sure if Banner was awake—or alone—but he assumed he would be, given how horribly the elections had gone. No doubt, Banner was pacing the floor, stewing, unable to get the awful taste of defeat out of his mouth.

"Astrophel." Banner furrowed his eyebrows. "I didn't ... what brings you here?"

"Dane will never do what it takes to save our party," Astrophel blurted. "He's content to just ... stand aside and let us crumble into oblivion. But I won't let that happen."

"I'm happy to hear that, but I don't understand how—"

"You're the leader of the Expansionist Party, and you're the only one who can resuscitate it."

"Some would say that I'm the reason we lost."

"I don't believe that. You were fighting alone, with no help from your fellow Expansionist on the Assembly."

Banner crossed his arms. "I thought you and Dane were close."

"He'll never get me what I want."

"And what is it that you want?"

"A seat at the table." Astrophel swallowed hard. "Power."

"And you think I can give that to you?"

"I know you can." Astrophel stepped closer to him. "I want what you want: the Affiliates out of power."

"It'll take a while for us to accomplish that, you know."

"I'm willing to do whatever it takes."

Banner raised an eyebrow. "Are you?"

"I'll never turn my back on the Expansionists." Astrophel shifted on his feet. "Things are changing in the Church, you know. Our new Magista ... he wants a change. And he and I, we think that change should come from the top."

"What are you trying to say?"

Astrophel was now very close to Banner. "With Kosabeus gone, I can ... I'd ask to be transferred, to become your Prophate instead. And together, we could rebuild the Expansionist Party."

Banner stared at him. "You'd really ... make a push to get rid of Kosabeus?"

"I deserve his position. And his title. He's had his time. Now it's my turn."

Banner laughed. "I must say, I admire your confidence, but ... I don't see the Church taking the bait. Kosabeus is their golden child."

"That's why I need your help. If you go to Weylon, our Magista, and issue your grievances against Kosabeus, then the Church will have no choice but to open an investigation. And, more often than not, when a Prophate is criticized by their own Lord Regent, the Church sides with the Lord Regent."

"And you really think I'd do that, that I'd ... go against Kosabeus?"

"He can't offer you what I can. He's not one of us. He doesn't have the Expansionists' best interests at heart."

"You do know he's an Expansionist, don't you?"

"A Mystic Expansionist." Astrophel practically spat the words, shaking his head. "They might as well be Affiliates, the way they view the universe."

Banner crossed his arms. "So, what are you, then? A Hawk?"

"A Fundamentalist." Seeing Banner's scrunched nose, Astrophel hastily added, "We're not all deranged zealots, you know."

"Forgive me for being ... skeptical, given everything you're saying. I mean, you came to my home to tell me that you're planning a coup against Kosabeus. That's hardly the act of a—"

"The Church needs to be cleansed," Astrophel insisted. "We need to reassess, to look to the future. I know what must be done, and if I'm given the chance to see it through, I know I can make things right, put everything back where it's supposed to be." Astrophel stiffened. "Are you with me?"

"I don't know." Banner made a face. "I may have my issues with Kosabeus, but ... I rather like him. I don't know if I—"

"He isn't willing to do whatever it takes to get you back where you belong. He won't fight to save the Expansionists. In fact, I wouldn't be surprised if after this election cycle, he suddenly comes out as an Affiliate. Is that who you want as your Prophate? Someone who doesn't believe in you, who doesn't think you're the leader Imperium needs?"

Banner studied Astrophel. "You really think that highly of me?"

"I do. I always have." Astrophel subtly brushed his hand against Banner's leg. "We could do incredible things together."

A coy smirk formed on Banner's lips. "And if I do that ... if I speak up against Kosabeus ... what will you do for me?"

Astrophel moved his hand up Banner's leg, stopping at his thigh. "I think that's obvious, don't you?"

"I'd still like you to say it."

"I'd prefer to show you. In there."

Banner held the door open. "Then come on in."

67

AVITUS

Liston would soon become the new Head of the Assembly. Avitus would have been lying if he said he wasn't concerned. It infuriated him, how casual Liston was about his own security. His townhouse was almost always unlocked. Avitus had lectured Liston about this dozens of times over the years, trying to remind him of the prestigious position he had in Imperial government, but Liston refused to change his ways.

Indeed, Liston didn't seem to understand that, as a political power player, he was a target. There'd been numerous stories over the years about Lord Regents receiving strange parcels and threatening letters, about stalkers and would-be assassins. But Liston was unmoved. He continued to leave himself exposed, apparently content with the idea of being murdered in his bed.

"After Aperysis, you'll be inaugurated as the new Head of the Assembly," Avitus was reminding Liston. "I think it'd be prudent if you hired a few more guards and—"

"We're not going through this again."

"But my Lord Regent—"

"This is a safe, gated neighborhood. No one can walk in unannounced."

345

Liston heaved a deep breath, running his fingers through his hair. "I can't have you worrying about me too."

"'Too'?" Avitus cocked his head to the side. "Who else have you been talking to?"

Liston sighed. "Embry has expressed her concerns about my safety, but ... I told her what I'm telling you. I'm fine. I mean, Banner is able to go to all sorts of bars and—"

"Banner isn't my concern—or my Lord Regent. You are."

"And I appreciate your vigilance. But really, Avitus, there's nothing to be worried about." Liston smiled wryly. "If someone did wish to harm me, they'd be foolish to try and do so with you around."

"But I can't be around all the time."

"And I'm not asking you to be. But ... I'll be safe here. I promise."

Avitus nodded mutely, deep in thought. He'd been here before, acting as the Prophate of the Head of the Assembly. Last time, it'd been Carbury—the most infamous Head of the Assembly in living memory. Though Banner had been a disaster in his own right, his stupidity had, thankfully, prevented him from being as dangerous as Carbury. Carbury had known the ins and outs of the system better than anyone else, and he took great joy in exploiting them to his advantage.

Avitus knew that Carbury's position as Head of the Assembly had warped him, turned him into an extremist, but he also knew the same would not happen to Liston. No, Liston, on the contrary, would be the greatest Head of the Assembly Imperium had ever known. He would carve a name for himself in history, and he'd no doubt surpass Carbury in terms of influence and prestige.

"I believe in you, my Lord Regent," Avitus said.

"I just hope I'm up to the task."

"You are." Avitus placed his hand on Liston's shoulder. "You have time to prepare, my son. It will be months before your inauguration. You should enjoy this time while you can, relish the taste of your victory, and allow yourself time to just ... step away from it all. These will be the last few weeks of peace you'll ever have."

Liston nodded knowingly. "It was different when we were just talking about it hypothetically, but now that it's real—"

"—you're scared. Every Head of the Assembly has felt that way. But you must remember that the Imperial people made their choice. By voting for your party, they were voting for you. You're the leader they want. And you're the leader they deserve. I know it's a tough burden, my son, but you won't be bearing it alone."

"I know." Liston turned to him, a shadow flashing across his eyes. "Everything will be better, won't it?" he asked quietly.

"Imperium's best days are still before her. I've always believed that, and I always will."

68

RAELYNN

Raelynn had asked Embry to come over to her place to give her some advice. She had a couple of weeks before she had to be back in New Caelus to meet Ambassador Barringer and her team, and she wanted to make the most of them. Embry was far more worldly than she was, and she knew all of Imperium's best-kept secrets.

"What kind of place do you want to go?" asked Embry as they leafed through a few different travel brochures.

"Somewhere quiet. Not a major city. And preferably somewhere more … northern."

"Okay." Embry pushed aside the brochures that were no longer contenders. "So, you're looking to go somewhere … scenic? Lots of trees, water, that sort of thing?"

"That sounds perfect."

Embry nodded absently, skimming through the brochures. After a few moments, her eyes widened, and she excitedly hit Raelynn's shoulder.

"Hey, what about this place?" She picked up a travel brochure on Bridger's Lake. "It's a small town in Exora, renowned for its beauty. It has a small population ... looks right up your alley."

Raelynn took the brochure from her and studied it carefully. She'd never heard of Bridger's Lake before, but somehow, the picture seemed ... familiar. Curious, she read the description below: *A beautiful, serene landscape tucked away in a grove of mature, majestic trees. A perfect place to escape the pressures of life and become one with nature.*

"What?" asked Embry. "What is it?"

"Nothing." Raelynn cleared her throat. "I just ... I think this is the place."

As she stared at the brochure, Raelynn had the strangest feeling that she was, finally, after all these years, coming home.

APPENDIX 1: THE LORD REGENTS

CYNO (SIGH-no) **BANNER**: the Lord Regent of War and Defense; the Head of the Assembly; the leader of the Expansionist Party; 57 years old

DANE WHITNER: the Lord Regent of Intelligence and Espionage; 57 years old

LEVIN LISTON: the Lord Regent of Diplomacy; the leader of the Affiliate Party; 35 years old (Also called **LEV**)

PINN BRYSON: the Lord Regent of Finance and Business; the leader of the Grounder Party; 72 years old

FARZAH (FAR-zuh) **TAYMOR**: the Lord Regent of Science and Medicine; Embry's mother; 49 years old (Also called **FAR**)

RAZE SILVER: the Lord Regent of Media and Technology; Viscardia's husband; 39–40 years old

NIX ABNER: the Lord Regent of Logistics and Transportation; 54 years old

APPENDIX 2: THE PROPHATES

KOSABEUS (Kuh-SAY-bee-us): the Prophate of War and Defense; the Head Prophate; Grell's husband; 44 years old

ASTROPHEL (ASS-tro-fell): the Prophate of Intelligence and Espionage; 32 years old

AVITUS (Uh-VEE-tus): the Prophate of Diplomacy; 68 years old

LISBETH: the Prophate of Finance and Business; 74 years old

PUCK: the Prophate of Science and Medicine; 37 years old

GRELL: the temporary Prophate of Media and Technology; Kosabeus's wife; 39 years old

VISCARDIA (Vih-SCAR-DEE-uh): the Prophate of Logistics and Transportation; Silver's wife; 38 years old (Also called **VIZ**)

APPENDIX 3: OTHER PLAYERS

BAYNE BANNER: Banner's son; died at 27 years old

BASILIA (Buh-SILL-EE-UH) **BARRINGER** (BEAR-in-jer): the Civ ambassador to Imperium; 57 years old

ARIES BRARE: Justice; 75 years old

ELISEO (Ell-EE-SEE-o) **CAINE**: the High Justice; 60 years old

IDRI (EYE-dree) **CAINE**: Caine's wife; Carbury's sister; 56 years old

NICOLAI (NICK-o-LIE) **CARBURY** (CAR-BURR-ee): the former Lord Regent of Diplomacy; the former Head of the Assembly; Liston's patron; Idri's brother; died at 44 years old

NISHA (KNEE-shuh) **CORINTH** (CORE-inth): the Lord Dynast of Diplomacy; 45 years old

CORLANDER (CORE-land-er): Liston's secretary; 45 years old

EDDARD: Kosabeus and Grell's son; 9 years old

FALEY: Silver's secretary; 47 years old

FERBER: Justice; 54 years old

GARIN: the former Prophate of Intelligence and Espionage; died at 73 years old

HARLYN HARRIES: the Lord Dynast of War and Defense; 38 years old

HESTON: the leader of the Civitan; 75 years old

TINSLEY IACONETTI: the Lord Dynast of Logistics and Transportation; the upcoming Lord Regent of Logistics and Transportation; 40 years old

BENTON (BEN-tin) **KERRELS** (CARE-ulls): Intelligence officer; Taymor's husband; Embry's father; died at 41 years old

LUBIANCO (Lou-bee-AHN-co): Justice; 61 years old

RAELYNN (Ray-lin) **MABRY** (MAY-bree): 23 years old

DARIUS MADDEN: Expansionist radio host; 53 years old

MAGDALENA (MAG-duh-LEAN-uh): Kosabeus and Grell's daughter; 6 years old

MILNER: Banner's secretary; 41 years old

MORN: Justice; 48 years old

NIGHTINGALE: Justice; 55 years old

RIGGS: the former Magista of the New Caelus Church; 66 years old

ABRAXOS (Uh-BRAX-is) **SILVER:** Silver and Viscardia's son; 6 years old

GRAY SILVER: Silver and Viscardia's son; 12–13 years old

SARIELLE (SARE-EE-elle) **SILVER:** Silver and Viscardia's daughter; 8 years old

STRAFE (STRAY-f): Justice; 53 years old

LEDGER SURRETT: waiter; Banner's fling; 19 years old

EMBRY TAYMOR: reporter; Taymor and Benton's daughter; 24–25 years old

DESMOND VALE: reporter; 45 years old

WEYLON (Way-lin): the new Magista of the New Caelus Church; 49 years old

APPENDIX 4: WORLD INFORMATION

Days of the Week

OTIUM (OH-SHE-um): equivalent to Sunday

SPERO (SPARE-oh): equivalent to Monday

FIDEM (FIGH-dum): equivalent to Tuesday

PERITIA (Per-EE-SHE-uh): equivalent to Wednesday

BEATUM (BEE-chum): equivalent to Thursday

ORTUS (OR-tiss): equivalent to Friday

DOMUS (DOUGH-miss): equivalent to Saturday

Seasons

ALSIUS (ALL-see-us): equivalent to winter

ROBUS (ROW-bus): equivalent to spring

SOLIS (SOUL-is): equivalent to summer

FOLIUM (FOAL-EE-um): equivalent to autumn

Months of the Year

BRUMUS (BROO-mus): equivalent to January

ALGUM (AL-gum): equivalent to February

TREMO (TREM-oh): equivalent to March

IGRIS (EYE-griss): equivalent to April

PARTURA (PAR-TOO-RAH): equivalent to May

ASTRUM (ASS-trum): equivalent to June

SIDUM (SIGH-dum): equivalent to July

AESTUS (AY-stis): equivalent to August

BRAYTIS (BRAY-tiss): equivalent to September

FLAGEO (FLAG-ee-oh): equivalent to October

MESSIO (MESS-ee-oh): equivalent to November

CIEMO (SEE-EM-oh): equivalent to December

Regions

BOREAL (BOAR-EE-ul): The Snow Capital (north)

MARELLUS (MARE-uh-LISS): The Political Capital (south)

EXORA (Ex-ORE-uh): The Food Capital (east)

VESPER (VESS-purr): The Art Capital (west)

UMBIUM (OOM-BEE-um): The Trade Capital (central)

Cities

ANIMORIA (An-ih-MORE-ee-uh)

BATILLUS (BAT-uh-liss)

BELIA (BEEL-EE-uh)

CARITO (Car-EE-tow)

DOCTRO (DOCK-tro)

LIGVA (Lihg-VUH)

NEW CAELUS (NU CAY-liss)

PACALIS (PACK-uh-liss)

SATIAS (SAY-she-US)

VITOR (VEE-tore)

Division Headquarters

THE HALL: the headquarters for War and Defense

THE CENTER: the headquarters for Intelligence and Espionage

THE SPIRE: the headquarters for Diplomacy

THE COFFER: the headquarters for Finance and Business

THE LAB: the headquarters for Science and Medicine

THE SPHERE: the headquarters for Media and Technology

THE AXLE: the headquarters for Logistics and Transportation

ABOUT THE AUTHOR

Brianna MacMahon is a thirteen-time-award-winning author who hails from Corning, New York. A lifelong writer, she honed her skills at Hartwick College. Even though she was a history and political science major, Brianna wrote as a creative outlet. In the momentous year of 2020, she attained her master's degree in political science from Syracuse University. During the pandemic, she focused more on writing as a legitimate career. When she isn't writing, she enjoys hanging out with her family, reading, going for long walks, and watching her favorite comfort shows on repeat.

Follow her on Instagram and TikTok, @authorbriannamacmahon, for book updates, and check out her website, https://authorbriannamacmahon.com, to join her mailing list, learn more about her books, and purchase directly from her! If you love the book, please leave a review on whichever platform you used to purchase it, as this helps out a ton!

www.ingramcontent.com/pod-product-compliance
Lightning Source LLC
Chambersburg PA
CBHW051318190726
48290CB00001B/216